HIS TO LOVE

Nothing sparked his interest until the frame suddenly filled with Abby. Her brown hair was pulled loosely back and tied at her nape with a narrow white ribbon. She wore faded denims and a pale green shirt, tails out, short sleeves cuffed midway down her arms. It was the casual kind of outfit she'd always favored. No frills. No fuss. Strictly comfort. She looked like the girl of his youth, his first true taste of yearning.

Unaware of his filtered observance, she stooped beside Denny, her arm settling around his thin shoulders, as together they watched the blurring, flashing lights of the Himalaya ride sweep up and around and down again, carrying its passengers on a fast, dizzying trip to nowhere. Abby's expression mirrored her son's—a mix of awe, excitement, and trepidation. He held the camera steady on her and for a moment—no longer than it took for the shutter to fall a second time with a soft *ka-thunk*—memories twisted through him of other nights, other carnivals, of other sweet-smelling, tender summers when she had been his to love.

SUPER ROMANCE

<u>BOOK YOUR PLACE ON OUR WEBSITE</u>
<u>AND MAKE THE</u>
READING CONNECTION!

We've created a customized website just for our very special readers, where you can get the inside scoop on everything that's going on with Zebra, Pinnacle and Kensington books.

When you come online, you'll have the exciting opportunity to:

- View covers of upcoming books
- Read sample chapters
- Learn about our future publishing schedule (listed by publication month *and author*)
- Find out when your favorite authors will be visiting a city near you
- Search for and order backlist books from our online catalog
- Check out author bios and background information
- Send e-mail to your favorite authors
- Meet the Kensington staff online
- Join us in weekly chats with authors, readers and other guests
- Get writing guidelines
- AND MUCH MORE!

Visit our website at
http://www.kensingtonbooks.com

I Remember You

Karen Crane

ZEBRA BOOKS
Kensington Publishing Corp.
http://www.kensingtonbooks.com

ZEBRA BOOKS are published by

Kensington Publishing Corp.
850 Third Avenue
New York, NY 10022

All Kensington titles, imprints and distributed lines are available at special quantity discounts for bulk purchases for sales promotion, premiums, fund-raising, educational or institutional use.

Special book excerpts or customized printings can also be created to fit specific needs. For details, write or phone the office of the Kensington Special Sales Manager: Kensington Publishing Corp., 850 Third Avenue, New York, NY 10022. Attn. Special Sales Department. Phone: 1-800-221-2647.

Zebra and the Z logo Reg. U.S. Pat. & TM Off.

First Printing: December 2004
10 9 8 7 6 5 4 3 2 1

Printed in the United States of America

*For Paula and Genell,
my tribe of brave friends.
Thank you.*

Author's Note

I remember the small town in which I grew up. Sweetwater is not that town. I've relied loosely on my memory to construct this fictional place beside the Arkansas River and used the actual Flood of 1993 as a springboard for pure invention. Although anyone who knows the area may recognize a familiar name here and there, this is a work of fiction, and all characters, places, and incidents are products of my imagination or are used fictitiously and should not be construed as real. Any resemblance to actual events, locales, organizations, or persons, living or dead, is entirely coincidental.

Chapter 1

After the accident, county crews worked overtime setting up barricades along the river road. It was, as a few grumbling souls pointed out at the time, shutting the barn door after the pony had run, and most folks thought—though not many said so aloud—that there wasn't ten cents worth of difference between hitting a concrete barrier at ninety miles an hour and sailing like a misfired missile into the muddy Arkansas River. But once the new four-lane opened up on the other side of Sweetwater, and the town's center shifted slowly but surely south, nobody much ever traveled the old road anyway.

There were, of course, a few long-time residents who preferred a leisurely drive along the narrow, twisting two-lane that cut frighteningly close to the river in some places and clung close to the limestone bluffs in others. And it was true the old road was the quickest route home for the handful of folks who still lived out near Shellcreek Lake. Evenings and weekends, bicyclists favored the winding, shaded road, their sleek wheels skimming the pavement, their yellow, orange, and red helmets flashing like tanager wings as they rode the curve of the big brown river.

In summer, the old road was a haven for teenagers as well. Undeterred by the posted warnings, the youth of Sweetwater sought out the shadows along the riverbank, bypassing the barricades to find a secluded spot to be alone or to gather as a group. Among the sheltering anonymity of the river birches, sycamores, and stately oaks, they used the road as a rite of passage, displaying the careless bravado of souls too young to believe death could ever come for them. With only the rush of the water to contradict them, they speculated on the accident, pointing out the probable spot where the souped-up red Firebird left the pavement and sailed into local history. The story and its moral were as ingrained in their adolescent psyches as any historic event, shaded by time and infallible youth into folklore, into a scary tale that turned girls wide-eyed with horror and boys into sagacious drivers who knew just how they would have conquered that fatal twist in the road.

Every few years, local authorities cracked down on the teen offenders, posting new warnings and running articles in the *Sweetwater Tribune* advising parents of the dangers. Patrolling the barricades never lasted long, though, because the police force was skimpy at best and, even at its peak, was made up mainly of adults who, at one time or another, had been young and restless and knew the pleasures of gathering in innocent rebellion along the river. Even at the height of any Let's Keep Our Children Safe! campaign, the teenagers of Sweetwater simply found new ways to get where they wanted to go.

For the most part, the old road was abandoned to the whims of the river and was simply the road less traveled.

Jeff Garrett avoided the river road as a matter of principle. He had lectured his daughter all of her life, threatened her with every punishment he could think of, up to and including life imprisonment, if she ever even thought about going near the river and, as a good father and an upstanding citizen of Sweetwater, he felt it was his duty to practice what he preached. Of course, for a man who'd lost just about everything he'd ever cared about on that old river road, it wasn't much of a sacrifice to stay away from it. But he never said that to Lexie. Or to anyone else. And after sixteen years, he hardly even glanced at the turnoff when he passed by on the highway.

But on the day he forced Gideon to return home from his self-imposed exile, the road beckoned to Jeff like an old friend. The memories pulled at him, coaxing him toward the river where once he had been innocent and invincible, a young man with a bright, brave future. As the highway sloped gently toward the valley of the Arkansas River, a strong Oklahoma wind skidded across the hood of his SUV, urged him with a brisk, persistent nudge to make the turn, to take his father back with him to the place and the moment when everything had changed . . . and, somehow, make it right again.

He gripped the steering wheel tighter, held the SUV steady, and pretended he didn't even notice the turnoff as they shot past at an accelerated clip on State Highway 64.

"Just 'cause I haven't been back in sixteen years doesn't mean I forgot the way to get there." Gideon Garrett stared out the windshield, his body language as irritable as his voice. "You afraid to drive the old road?"

"No, I'm not afraid," Jeff answered, although he was. "I didn't think you'd want to go near the river."

"I didn't *want* to leave a perfectly good house in a perfectly fine town to move back to this hellhole, but that didn't stop you from selling my home right out from under me, now did it?"

"Dad, we've gone over this a million times. You can't stay by yourself any longer, and I can't keep driving back and forth to Heavener to take care of things for you."

"I never asked you to do one damn thing but leave me alone."

Which was true enough. Gideon hadn't asked for Jeff's help since the accident. And Jeff had never once asked for his father's forgiveness. But there were some things no one ought to have to ask for. "You need help whether you want it or not. Dr. Bowen made that very clear to both of us."

"Bowen's a quack. Besides, I had plenty of friends in Heavener who were looking after me just fine until you decided I wasn't competent to make my own decisions."

Jeff knew from experience there was no point in mentioning that Gideon's *friends* existed largely in his imagination. He'd closed himself off from meaningful interaction with other people the day Alex died, and to Jeff's knowledge, his father had stayed pretty much to himself ever since. Which was why, a few months ago, when Gideon had fallen on his back steps, he'd stayed there most all of one day, unable to move, until Jeff had shown up, quite by fortunate chance, and taken him to the hospital in Ft. Smith. Luckily, no bones were broken that time and all Gideon had gotten out of the accident was a mottled set of angry bruises, a cracked rib, and the convoluted idea that his son believed he was incompetent. He'd argued over every step of the process to sell the house and transfer his belongings to Sweetwater. He'd fought Jeff to a standstill on details so unimportant they'd have been laughable under different circumstances. He'd protested loudly and long, despite knowing from the start there could be only one reasonable conclusion. Inevitably, Jeff had won the battle, although he was fully aware he'd lost the war with his father before the first shot was fired, on the day his mother had died and his brother, Alex, had been born.

Sarah Talbot had been a blossoming fourteen when she stepped out of a phone booth in Gruene, Texas, and walked right into Fate, which had placed Gideon Garrett, tall, handsome, and nearly twice her age, right smack dab in her path. He'd caught her in mid-stumble, bought her an ice cream, and that, according to his account of the meeting, had been all it took for love to strike him squarely in the heart. He'd waited four long years for her to grow up and, as he put it, experience what the world had to offer, before he wooed her, wed her, and moved her—bag, baggage, and a polished cedar hope chest—to the Gulf, because Sarah had said she'd like to look out of her window and see nothing but endless waves of water.

So Gideon had found a house with a view and a job teaching English to the graceless seventh graders of Galveston so that Sarah could have her wish. He'd encouraged her to get more education, which should have mollified her parents but didn't. They hadn't wanted her to marry a man so much older, a man who, in their eyes, had stolen her heart and her youth before she had a chance to discover her potential. He had taken Sarah away from them and they couldn't forgive him for falling in love with their daughter. And they never stopped reminding her that if she left him, she could come back to live with them.

Over the years of his marriage, Gideon had exacted a subtle revenge for their lack of faith in him and his love for Sarah, and after she died, he'd moved himself, his sons, and the remnants of their daughter's life to Oklahoma, just far enough to be beyond the reach of the, by then, elderly Talbots. He decided he would be enough for his sons, that they didn't need to know their grandparents, that he would teach the boys all they ever needed to know about their mother. In the solitary arrogance of his grief, he nurtured the belief that if only the Talbots had accepted him and made him welcome, he and Sarah could have stayed in Gruene and raised their family there. If only the Talbots hadn't interfered,

Gideon would never have moved Sarah to the house with the ocean view and the damp, salty air, which should have been healthy, but instead brought in the bacteria that eventually settled in her lungs and, under the stress of her second pregnancy, robbed her of the ability to breathe. By the time the doctor had performed a clumsy cesarean in a futile attempt to save both mother and baby, Sarah had lost the strength to recover, and all that Gideon had left of her was a four-pound infant no one expected to live, three-year-old Jeff, and a dusty hope chest in the closet at home.

But if Gideon had lost his beloved Sarah, he determined he would not lose this baby she'd wanted so desperately. This second son, Alex, would live, no matter what it took to save him.

The cost, as it turned out, was Jeff's claim to his daddy's heart.

And now there was no one else to take responsibility for Gideon in these last years of his life. No one else to bring him home. No favorite son to persuade him that living out his remaining years, surrounded by the little bit of family he still had and in the company of people who'd known him before the accident, was a good thing. There was only Jeff, who wished he could just say to hell with it and be done, once and for all, with trying to please his father.

"I told you I wouldn't stay." Gideon sat, stiff as a shot of old Scotch, seat restraint dangling unused, a clear indication rebellion wasn't limited to adolescence. "Just 'cause you've gone to all this trouble to move me, don't think you can keep me here once I decide to go."

"The bus station is right where it was when you left," Jeff said, half hoping Gideon would decide to go. "Buses going in one direction or another come through town every day. Any time you've got the cash for a ticket and the determination to go, you get on one."

Gideon huffed, acknowledging without grace that he barely had the determination to get himself up and dressed in the mornings. "Mae Wade still run the old folks' place?"

"It's a residential care home, Dad. People your own age. Three good meals a day, somebody to talk to any time you feel like making the effort, people you'll remember, like Joe Malone and Lowell Robbins. Miz Violet and Miz Rose. And the house is as neat and tidy as ever. The whole place has practically been rebuilt since the last time you saw it. It's more like an apartment complex than a house. Private rooms and baths and that big porch for when you feel like sitting outside. There are flower beds around the house and a good-sized vegetable garden, if you want to work with your hands. I think you're really going to like it there. Lexie helped me put up some pictures and I bought you a thirty-two inch television for your room. Already wired for cable. Has a remote and everything."

"She won't want me there," Gideon said matter-of-factly, ignoring all benefits and enticements. "Mae never had a good thing to say about me. She thought I egged Charlie on to drink, blamed me 'cause she married the wrong man."

"That was a long time ago, Dad, and I don't think Mae ever blamed you."

"Well, you'd know who was to blame, wouldn't ya?" Gideon's tone was gruff and accusing, ready to quarrel with the devil over which corner of hell was the hottest.

Jeff's jaw clenched, but he was tired of fighting with his father. He'd taken the blame for a lot of things that weren't his fault—and a lot of things that were. At this point, one more either way didn't make a whole hell of a lot of difference. Slowing the SUV, he edged toward the right lane as they approached the first of three Sweetwater exits. On the left, the new Best Western

sported a jaunty red banner that proclaimed the hotel
was Now Open! Ahead, the fast food signs of a growing
community sprouted like colorful weeds on the outskirts of town, and the Kmart parking lot was filled with
various makes and models of cars. A housing addition
was going up on the other side of the old Lakeside
Amusement Park. The wooden trusses of the new
Methodist Church could be seen rising just over the
crest of the hill. All of this growth was new since Gideon
had left. All of it was bringing new life to a town that
had been courting disaster sixteen years ago. All of it
made Jeff proud that he lived in this place at this time.

But Gideon stared straight ahead, looking neither
left nor right, determined to see nothing but the gray
highway that stretched on past the town to places he
would never go.

"We're building a new library," Jeff said, hoping to
spark some interest. "The bond issue passed just last fall
and it's scheduled to open next year. You'll never believe who's bought the old Potter Library building,
either." He paused, but only long enough to work up a
soft laugh to go with the disclosure. "Rayburn Swann.
He's a lawyer now and says he's going to turn the library into office space. You remember Rayburn? He
used to come around every summer, going door to
door, selling whatever crop he could pile into the rear
end of his dad's old Ford pickup. Remember that time
Alex jumped up on the tailgate and popped it loose?
There was watermelon and cantaloupe rind in the gut-
ters for days until we finally got some rain. Nearly
everybody in the neighborhood came out and picked
up the best of the busted fruit and we had ourselves a
fine picnic right there in our front yard, despite the
heat. Rayburn was awfully good-natured about the
whole thing, too." Jeff glanced at his dad. "I saw you
give him money. He told me later it was more than he'd
made that entire summer."

Not a glimmer of recollection or interest altered Gideon's set features. He was a stubborn man, for sure. But Jeff wasn't his son for nothing. He'd get his father to talk about something other than the great injustice of growing old. Sooner or later, one way or another, he'd get the old man to talk. "I have to stop by the newspaper office," he said, knowing that would get a rise if anything would. "It'll take a few minutes, so you may as well come in and see where I write all those scathing editorials."

"I'll wait in the car," Gideon said and then sat in silence as they drove past the old cotton mill at the edge of town, past the gray concrete walls that hadn't seen meaningful occupation for fifty years until just a few months ago when a new manufacturing firm had bought it and begun refurbishing the building to make fishing tackle. The glass plant, too, was long gone, its furnaces still standing like a benevolent beacon behind Wayne's Auto Repair shop, Country Store Hardware, and Lee's Lawn & Garden, all small businesses that now flourished along Morrow Road in the shadow of old enterprise.

As Jeff made the turn onto Main Street, he glanced at Gideon to see if he noticed the colorful banner strung across the top of the Sweetwater Historical Society building. *SUMMER DAZE BEGINS MEMORIAL DAY WEEKEND*, it proclaimed, marking the traditional kickoff of the summer season. But Gideon didn't indicate by so much as a blink that he noticed the sign . . . or any of the shops that now lined Main Street. The bright canvas awnings, the hand-lettered signs, the store fronts decorated with enticing colors for the Summer Daze Best Window Design Award contest, the familiar sight of old Mr. Humphries dragging his ancient Radio Flyer red wagon along the sidewalk on his daily walk to the post office, or Leah Johnson heading through the front door of Gina's Cute Curl salon . . . none of it brought a spark of remembrance to Gideon's set and frozen expression. None of it aroused a visible flicker of interest. None of it seemed to register with him as the familiar place he'd once proudly called home.

Gideon had handpicked this town because of its proximity to the river, which made the area green and gave a dark, fertile richness to the soil. He chose Sweetwater because of the cotton mill, the glass plant, and the other industries that nurtured dozens of little businesses and promoted a solid, middle-American pride in the community. He'd deemed the town and its surroundings as a good place for a single father to raise his sons. For nearly twenty years he'd taught English at Thomas Potter High School, plodding through a sea of eager and not so eager learners. And every summer, often on a double shift, he worked at the box factory, earning money for the boys' college education. It had been a matter of pride for Gideon, an example he wanted to set so that both Jeff and Alex would understand how important their education was to him, how much he was willing to sacrifice for their future. For his part, Jeff would have preferred more time than sacrifice from his dad, and Alex, the wild child, definitely would have benefitted from stricter supervision in the long days of summer. But Gideon had always been oblivious to the needs of his firstborn and blind to the faults of his second, and when Alex died, nothing and no one mattered to him anyway.

Jeff slowed as he made the turn onto Second Street and the Trib office came into view. Not because he thought Gideon had any interest in seeing the newspaper office. But when you owned a place, as Jeff owned the Trib, you slowed down just to feel the thrill of seeing a thing you'd made yourself and that still, somehow, brought you so much pleasure. He was a good newspaperman, an asset to the community, a mover and a shaker, a neighbor, a contributor to the local economy, a co-owner of industry. He was proud of his success, proud of this one single thing he managed to do absolutely right.

"Never did put up those awnings, did ya?" Gideon eyed the sturdy brick building with pursed lips and a singularly unimpressed gaze. "I told you there'd never be much profit in reporting who said what at the school board meetings."

"The paper does all right," Jeff said, defending his choices in the best way he could.

"You should've sold out five years ago when you got that offer from Gaylord."

"How did you know about that?"

"Melanie told me," Gideon said succinctly, and the sweet smugness of the words all but dripped from his tongue. *Melanie told me.* Jeff felt the sting of her treason, even though the revelation didn't go deep enough to wound him. It wasn't the atom bombs of crises that blew a marriage to Kingdom Come. It was the little betrayals, the sins of broken faith, the careless words that picked it apart, seam by seam, from the inside out. "She wanted you to sell, thought you were an idiot for not getting out when you had the chance."

Jeff clamped his jaw shut to keep from stating flat-out that Melanie had no right to discuss the newspaper—*his* newspaper—with anyone. Least of all, Gideon. But in sixteen years, Jeff had kept his counsel and never allowed either Melanie or his father to goad him into an admission that his marriage had been a failure from the start. He certainly wasn't going to do so now. He pulled into his parking space in front of the *Sweetwater Tribune* and killed the engine. "This may take a while. You want to come in with me?"

"I've been in there before."

"Not since I've owned it." His hands still on the steering wheel, Jeff looked over at Gideon, wondering if some day Lexie would be as frustrated with him as he was now with his father. "I've made a lot of changes. I think you'll be surprised."

Gideon sniffed. "I'll be surprised if you ever stop yakking at me and get on with your business. I don't want to have to wait all day."

Jeff swiped the key from the ignition and pocketed it as he got out of the car, careful not to slam the door, careful to keep the aggravation out of his voice when he said hello to D.J. Owens who was sweeping the sidewalk in front of his jewelry store two doors down.

"Who ya got there with ya?" D.J. asked, leaning on his broom while eyeing the tinted windows of Jeff's SUV.

"My dad," Jeff said and walked right on inside the *Tribune*'s front door, waylaying the need to answer further questions, at least for the moment. The cool hustle of the newspaper office enfolded him immediately, and he paused for a second, as he always did, to inhale the mingled scents of old coffee, old smoke, old newsprint, and ink. The smells lingered from times past, before computers and laser disks, before off-site printing presses and online Web sites, when a newspaper office had been the hub of a whole community's incoming information. The history of Sweetwater was encompassed in this square, squatty old building; it had been lived and breathed, witnessed and written in these rooms. For ten, going on eleven, years now Jeff had had the best seat in the house to see tomorrow's history filter through this newsroom. That, somehow, more than anything else, gave him the deepest satisfaction.

"Jeff! Man, am I glad to see you." Mark Williams gestured for attention clear across the bustle of the room. "Okay this ad, will you? Scott left early to get out to the high school to cover Channel 8's *Wicked Weather* show and G.W. just dropped this off. I don't know why the man can't make up his mind. It's not like he hasn't been alternating the same five dry cleaning specials for the past umpteen years."

"What are you doing here?" Millie Simpson asked in between answering one call and pressing the multiline phone bank to catch another. "I thought you were going to be out all day. *Sweetwater Tribune*," she said into her headpiece, her voice switching from personal to professional in a polished second. "News, sales, or classifieds?"

"Didn't take as long as I expected," Jeff answered, making his way past the old-fashioned wooden spindle gate that separated the front office from the back. Not that it served more than a strictly decorative purpose, since every desk but two was out in clear view of anyone walking in through the front door. But Jeff liked the open feel of the newsroom. He liked to hear the ringing of the phone and the chatter among the staff. He liked the busyness of the newspaper business, and most of the time he left his office door open, inviting in anyone who wanted to take the chair across from him and chat for a while.

"Hey, Jeff!" Sam Caldwell was in his usual position, feet propped on his desk, phone to his ear, one hand covering the mouthpiece—Sam didn't believe in using the mute button—pencil ready, as if the next big story was going to pass him by if he didn't have a writing instrument in his hand. The wall beside his desk was a regular Rolodex of phone numbers and scribbled notes, some so smudged as to be almost unreadable. But Sam knew every one by heart and its connection to whatever story he was working on. "Check out my feature on the water district's noncompliance with EPA standards," Sam said to Jeff. "That's gonna get you some letters to the editor, I guarantee. You probably shouldn't expect them to be too friendly, either."

Jeff grinned, sure that Sam's column would generate some spirited debate. Sam loved any topic he could turn controversial and when one fell into his lap—like the water district compliance report—well, he didn't believe in keeping the public in the dark. It was what Sam loved more than fly-fishing and since controversy never hurt sales, Jeff was all for it.

He okayed the dry cleaning ad before walking into his office and leafing through the phone messages Millie had left for him. He shuffled a few papers around the top of the desk, checked his e-mail, returned a couple of phone calls, and glanced through Sam's article, purposely stalling for no better reason than to keep Gideon waiting and aggravate him a bit. It had taken a considerable effort these past few months to maintain his own civility in the face of his father's hostility. It wouldn't hurt Gideon to wait in the car for a quarter of an hour.

Jeff was just grabbing up a couple of computer disks to work on at home and some reference material for this week's editorial when he heard Millie's personal voice rise with pleasure. "Hi, Mr. Garrett! It's so great to see you back in Sweetwater. You remember me, don't you? Millie Rydell . . . well, it's Simpson now, but I was a Rydell when I was in your English Lit class my senior year. You were the best teacher I had."

Jeff headed for the door, uncertain if his father would be reasonably polite or crush Millie's enthusiasm with sarcasm. But Gideon's voice, while gruff, was not unkind. "You were smaller then," he said, which made Millie laugh.

"Well, that was twenty years and four kids ago," she said with her usual good nature. "I've plumped up some since high school. You look just like I remember you, though. Very distinguished."

Gideon looked around, distracted perhaps by the noise, taking in the office with a narrowed gaze. "Thank you," he said almost too softly for Jeff to hear.

"My class is having a reunion over the Fourth of July weekend." Millie said, ignoring the persistent ringing of the phones. "Now that you're back home, maybe you'll come. It would be great if you would."

Jeff loved Millie for trying, but he didn't trust Gideon not to make a scene, so he walked quickly across the newsroom. "Hey, Dad," he said, casually. "Did you get tired of waiting?"

"D.J. Owens came right up to the car and just opened the door to talk to me," Gideon said, the aggravation back in his voice. "I decided the only way he'd leave me alone was if I came inside. So I did."

"Well, now that you're here, what do you think of the place?" Jeff hated that he'd let the question come out like that—so hopeful, so needy. He hated that he'd allowed the question to come out at all, but some vengeful demon from his childhood compelled him to ask. "It looks good, doesn't it?"

"The newspaper in Heavener is twice this size," Gideon said succinctly.

And that, Jeff knew, was what he got for asking. "Let's go," he said, moving toward the door. "I'll see you tomorrow, Millie."

"Bye, Mr. Garrett, 'night, boss," Millie called before she went back to answering the phones.

Jeff didn't make any attempt at conversation after that. He drove in silence down Second Street to Garfield Avenue, past the office, the bank, and Debolt's Pharmacy on the corner. Once upon a time, Gideon had spent lazy Saturday afternoons in the drugstore, shooting the breeze with Ed Debolt, the two men ironing out the town's problems while Jeff and Alex slurped root beer floats at the soda fountain. Ed had taken out the counter several years ago, making room for the knickknacks and perfumes that kept the doors of the pharmacy open. If he hadn't owned the building, hadn't pulled in some decent rent from the tenants in the lady's clothing boutique next door, he'd have been out of business two weeks after the Big City Discounts complex held its grand opening. The boutique was doing good business, though, enabling Ed to go to work every day, sell a bottle of perfume here, a little Maybelline and Cover Girl cosmetics there, and fill a few cold remedies and prescriptions for a dwindling customer base.

"Ed Debolt is still in business," Jeff said forgetting he'd meant to let Gideon stew on his future in silence. "You ought to stop in and say hi one of these days. You two used to have a lot to talk about."

"He was always a blowhard and a braggart. Don't know why you'd think I want to waste my time talking to him."

"You're going to have to talk to someone, Dad." A mistake to put it that way, like an ultimatum, a challenge. "There are still a lot of people in town you'll remember."

"Just 'cause I remember who they are doesn't mean I have a solitary thing to say to them."

Gideon was determined to make himself and everyone else miserable. So, let him sit in grumpy solitude in his room at the Wade House for a week or so. Maybe then he'd be a little more congenial, more willing to put out a bit of effort. "Here we are." Jeff turned the SUV into the drive of a sprawling, white house with a wrap-around veranda, on which wooden rockers sat empty in the late afternoon heat, awaiting the cool shade of the evening and company. "The Wade House. Home, sweet home."

Gideon peered through the windshield, no sign of recognition or acceptance in his set and angry expression. "I suppose," he said. "This is as good a place to die as any."

Chapter 2

Home. That mysterious, magnetic point of beginning hovered just down the highway like the shadow of a storm and it took all of Abby Wade Ryan's considerable determination not to make a U-turn and drive like hell in the opposite direction. She had never planned on returning to Sweetwater like the prodigal child who was all used up and had no place else to go, but in the last few months, she had exhausted every other option. Home, as it turned out, was the only resource she hadn't depleted, the only choice she had left.

Selling the house in Lisle had been the worst of it. The house hadn't been much, but she'd always thought of it as her ace in the hole, the one thing she could count on to be there, no matter what stupid stunt Mitch pulled. But knowing how he loved to surprise her, she should have realized he'd pull one stunt too many and die young, leaving her with a fistful of debt and no credit. The insurance settlement had vanished in a blink, but not the bills. So the house had gone, too, and with it all the security she'd tried so hard to hang on to, along with the foundation of the life she'd pretended she had. And now, here she was on Oklahoma Highway 64, driving a Chevy Blazer with too many miles on the odometer, too little tread left on the tires, hauling a Go West rental trailer packed to the air vents with her life's leftovers, and dreading every inch of blacktop that brought her closer to the place she'd never stopped referring to as home.

Beside her, her eight-year-old son tied knot after meticulous knot in the two-foot-long, frayed piece of rope he never went anywhere without. From Lisle, the small suburb just west of Chicago where she and the boys had lived until yesterday, all the way to Oklahoma, Denny had tied knots. When the length of rope couldn't hold another one, he untied them all and started over again. He wasn't noisy or demanding or restless. He didn't pester her with questions or requests to stop. He didn't squabble with fourteen-year-old Kyle in the backseat, who'd been spoiling for a fight every day since he hit puberty and was in an especially vile temper over this move. Denny, her shy, sweet, troubled child, just tied one knot after another after another.

Behind her, Kyle's furious stare heated the very air she breathed, scorched it with his impotent anger, making her tense and jumpy just by virtue of not knowing when or how he'd mount the next challenge. No wonder Denny concentrated so deliberately on his knotted rope. No wonder she kept changing the radio station, tuning out the instant a voice intruded, tuning in anything remotely resembling music. Country-western, rock, pop, classical, religious. She didn't care as long as there was the faintest chance that music soothed the savage breast and kept the peace just a little while longer, just—*please God*— until she reached her mother's house.

Mae would be waiting, Abby knew, worried that they weren't already there, watching the street as if she could will them safely home. For all of her childhood, Abby had seen her mother stand at one or another of the front windows, pulling back the curtains to look out at the street, waiting for Charlie,

Abby's father, to come home. And he always had. Sometimes not until the next day. Sometimes in the wee hours of the morning. Sometimes right on time. But always on a random schedule that kept Mae anxiously at the window and Abby, always, in a state of anticipation, eager for the moment when her big, exuberant father would walk through the door and call for his little princess.

Now, of course, she understood Mae's vigil, the daily stress of marriage with a man who was addicted to alcohol and gambling and whatever other temptations crooked an alluring finger. She knew firsthand the tension in never knowing if her husband would come home drunk or sober, on time or late . . . or not at all. She was well acquainted with the worry, the anger, and the fear that gradually faded into an oppressive indifference because it was impossible to live indefinitely with the knowledge that sooner or later there would be a moment when all was lost, when the family was finally, irrevocably shattered. Mitch's death had been startling, sudden, accidental, and Abby had seen it coming for years. She just hadn't wanted to admit the truth . . . that they were all—Mitch, her two boys, herself—drowning in the troubled waters of an unhappy marriage.

The silence from the backseat broke suddenly with a fierce drumming of fingertips against the car window, a rhythm both intentionally annoying and persistent. With a sigh, Abby prepared for another round in her son's ongoing war with her, his next attempt to engage her in battle. The impatient drumming stopped as abruptly as it began and was immediately replaced by a strategic series of impatient sighs and shuffling sounds, oversized feet in even bigger athletic shoes itching to kick the back of her seat. Glancing in the rearview mirror, she met the glittering gaze of her lanky firstborn and wished she'd kept her eyes on the road.

"I could have stayed with Cameron." Kyle's petulance had grown strident during the trip, his desire to escape this move increasing with every mile. "His mother said it was okay."

"I'm your mother," Abby said as patiently as she could. "And I said it was not okay."

"You want me to be miserable, don't you?" Kyle leaned sideways to catch her eye again in the mirror and pin her with the accusation only a rebellious adolescent could make so absolute. "You never liked my friends. You'd rather have me chew tobacco and say, 'gosh, darn it' like those hick country kids in Grandma's hick country town than be with the people I really care about. You probably think I'll make new friends, but I won't. I'm going back to Chicago and you can't stop me."

Beside her in the front seat, Denny hunched his shoulders, concentrating hard on the rope in his hands, but Abby saw the tears welling in his eyes, the way he blinked furiously to hold them in, and her anger with the self-centered teenager in the backseat increased tenfold. How she had conceived and nurtured two children so much alike in appearance and yet so very different from each other and from her was a mystery. Their birth certificates stated she was their mother, but some days—a lot of days, lately—she wondered if somewhere, adrift in the world, might be two children whose eyes and hair were dark like hers, if somewhere there might be a boy who didn't fret and a teenager who wasn't so angry. Surely somewhere in the wide world were two sons who would have loved having her as their mother.

"I mean it, Mom." Kyle nudged her further with his push-it-to-the-wall attitude. "You'll be sorry you didn't listen to me once I'm gone."

She saw the turnoff and slowed the Blazer, careful to adjust for the movement of the trailer behind as she made the turn, only realizing as she left the highway that this road had significance. If she hadn't been angry, exhausted, and anxious about the summer ahead, she would never have pulled off onto the old river road. It seemed, at best, a bad omen. But the situation with Kyle couldn't wait, so she drove only a short distance around the first curve, until the shoulder of the road widened and gave her room to pull over.

On either side of the narrow two lane, rich bottom land yielded a lake of spring grasses, dotted with islands of tall oak and pecan trees. Ahead, the road cut close to the river for about a mile before it zigzagged back to hug the limestone bluffs. The road alternated like that, between the river and the bluffs, for a good five miles before the terrain opened up again at the outskirts of Sweetwater.

Growing up in this small town beside the river had given her a certain ownership in the land, a sense of place she couldn't dislodge, a knowledge of where she belonged and why. She had navigated the river road in daylight and dark, walked the banks of the river at midnight, and climbed the bluffs in the heat of a lazy summer afternoon. She'd been kissed for the first time in the shadow of a huge river birch about two more miles down the road, and she'd come close, so close, to giving up her virginity not far from where she was right now. But Jeff had been stronger than she and determined they would wait until she'd graduated high school. So she'd waited and loved him all the more for his self-discipline, for the old-fashioned way he honored her.

And he'd betrayed her innocence anyway.

The moment she killed the engine, the familiar, throaty murmur of the river flowed over her like a lullaby. The touch of the breeze on her skin was like the feel of a favorite old shirt. The musky green scent of the grasses held the memories of her youth. And just being here again brought it all back. *Home. The accident. The aftermath.* All the possibilities that had been her life before and the regrets it had held since. Once upon a time, she had loved this old river road, but Jeff had spoiled that for her, and when she left Sweetwater after the accident, she vowed she would never look back.

Yet here she was, returning like an arsonist to the fire that had burned her, coming back in search of the only place she knew where she could begin to heal herself and her sons.

She leaned across and opened Denny's door. "Let's stretch our legs," she suggested with a smile.

He looked at her through eyes as blue as the first spring periwinkles and nodded, but he unfastened his seatbelt without enthusiasm and cast several hesitant looks at her face before he slid off the seat and stood in the angle of the open door, twisting the length of rope in his little boy hands. "Aren't you coming with me?" he asked, his small whispery voice exactly opposite in tone and attitude from his older brother's. "I don't wanna be out here by myself."

"You're such a whiner, Den. I'm ashamed to say you're my brother."

Abby turned in the seat, met another set of eyes, also periwinkle blue, but frosted in an icy, self-righteous angst. "Get out, Kyle," she said. "Now."

He did so, slamming the door and scuffling after her to the back of the Blazer with the hunched-shoulder walk and sullen face he'd developed overnight at the age of eleven. She realized now she should never have let his rebellion get this far out of hand, but in the months since Mitch had died, she hadn't found the will to do anything but fight with Kyle. He'd worn her down with his bottomless resentment, tested her a thousand times with his defiance, and she was bone weary with trying to love him. Straddling the tow bar, she opened the back of the Blazer, got a Coke out of the ice chest, popped the tab, and took a long, cooling swallow. Then she pulled Kyle's soccer bag from the center of the loosely stacked suitcases and tossed it to the ground at his feet.

"Get your soccer ball out and take it over there." She pointed to a gathering of trees a safe distance from the road and the river. "Kick it until you can't kick it anymore. Then kick it a few more times for me. When you're through, put it back in your satchel, put the bag in the truck, and get yourself buckled into your seat. We are going to Sweetwater and we are going as a family. I know you don't like it. I'm not crazy about the idea myself. But frankly, whether or not you hate the idea of living here is not my concern at the moment. I'm your mother, Denny is your brother, Grandma is the only other relative you have, and you will live with us until you are old enough to live on your own. You will be respectful, and you will learn to keep your mouth shut, because I swear to you, Kyle, if you make this any harder for Denny, I will personally and gladly make certain you are miserable. Do you understand me?"

He glared at her until the tension vibrated like a rubber band stretched taut between them, threatening and resilient. Then with a shrug more aggravating than his silence, he got out the black-and-white checkered soccer ball and bounced it on his knees as he strolled away from her. As always lately, her heart was torn between the ache of loving this awkward, skinny, angry manchild and wishing she could send him to a strict military school somewhere far, far away from her.

"Mom?" Denny's whimper turned her thoughts from one problem to another. If Kyle hid his fear in anger, Denny's oozed like a chronic nasal drip. There was no soccer ball for him to kick around, only the knots he tied as an outlet for his anxiety. He took no comfort in her oft-repeated assurances that the move would be good for all of them. Somehow, Abby knew that her younger son was worried mostly about her . . . and that was perhaps the hardest thing to deal with in the escalating turn of events that had brought them here.

"Want to take a nature walk?" she asked, as if it were what she wanted more than anything.

"I guess." Denny hadn't smiled since he was five and found out his mom wouldn't be staying with him during kindergarten. From that point on, he worried. When he awakened in the morning, he worried he would be late, that his clothes wouldn't fit, that he'd lose a tooth during the day and get blood on his shirt, that he'd use the wrong color crayon or color outside the lines. He worried she would get mad if he didn't eat all his oatmeal or he'd be sick if he did. He worried that Kyle wouldn't be there when he got home in the afternoon. He worried that he wouldn't be as smart as the other kids, that he'd never be as big as his brother, that he would forget to get off the school bus, or that he'd get off at the wrong stop.

Abby had tried counseling, bribes, reassurance, and flat out ignoring the problem in the hope it would disappear. She'd talked to teachers, school psychologists, and church pastors. She'd been to four different family therapists and taken a class on child development. She'd even tried to persuade Mitch that Denny needed some paternal interaction that wasn't centered around the game of football . . . an idea as foreign to Mitch as doing anything in moderation.

Mitchell Ryan had been her great experiment . . . nothing like Jeff, a little like her father, a whole lot different from her, and therefore, initially, she'd found him completely fascinating. He was from Chicago, rough around all the edges, a bit dangerous, more than a little overconfident, and with enough savvy to know he needed someone to help him smooth out the coarseness. He'd earned a football scholarship to Kansas University and was already in his senior year when she arrived on campus. Mitch had been bold and blond, highly handsome, with a corduroy charm that was both graceless and disarming. He was the quarterback, a revered athlete, everybody's hero, a Big Man on Campus . . . and at eighteen, she'd been wounded, vulnerable, lonely, and oh so very flattered by his attention. It had seemed a match made in heaven. At the time that had been as far as she could—or cared—to see, and their impetuous, hasty coupling only led to an unintended pregnancy and a marriage that never stood a chance in hell.

"Want the rest of my Coke?" Abby held the can out to Denny.

"They put formaldehyde in there."

She looked at the can, then at him. "How do you know that?"

"I read it in a magazine." He read voraciously, far ahead of his grade level, finding new worries with every news article, learning forbidding words faster than she could locate the antonyms.

"Maybe you should try some lighter reading this summer. You could even take a vacation from books for a couple of months."

"Mom!" He looked completely appalled by the idea. "I like to read and . . . and what else would I do?"

"Play baseball? Climb trees? Go fishing?"

He bit his lip, pondering the possibility she might be serious. "I like reading. And you still shouldn't drink that stuff."

"I'll make you a deal. I'll stop drinking colas if you'll run out there and take that ball away from your brother."

He looked at the soccer ball as Kyle sent it slamming against a tree trunk, chased it down, and sent it crashing into the tree again. "He'll just get mad."

"He's already mad," she answered with a shrug. "So what have we got to lose, huh, Champ? I say we run out there and take him . . . together. What do you think?"

Denny's hand slipped into hers, his eyes sought the nuances of her face to see if she was teasing. His little fingers entwined with her bigger ones, squeezing hard, seeking reassurance and comfort and maybe courage, too. She hoped with all of her heart this move would prove to be the turning point for Denny. He needed to play and run, fight and argue, make friends and skin his knees. And laugh. If he learned how to laugh again, then she might, at least, be able to consider this move as a good decision instead of the only hope she had. "Your call," she said, smiling, trying to will him into carefree childhood.

"Okay, Mom. Let's take him."

It was only what he knew she wanted to hear, but still, it was a start. So Abby gave him a wink and pulled him, with both hand and heart, across the grass toward Kyle. Somehow, someway she would make this all come right for her boys, she would prove to them she was worthy of their love and respect. But first, she was going to snare that soccer ball and kick it as hard and as far as she could. Then she was going to chase it down and kick it again.

Mae Wade stood by the window in the upstairs guest suite, straightening the lace panels with strict swipes of her fingers along the creases, telling herself she was simply waiting for Jeff to bring up the last box of Gideon's things, and not watching the street, waiting for Abby and the boys to pull into the drive. They might not be here for hours yet, but still she couldn't stay away from the windows, couldn't stop watching for them, like a bad habit, like an old woman with nothing to do but wait and worry.

"We sit down to dinner at five-thirty and clear the sideboard at seven," she was saying, by rote, to Gideon. "Breakfast is anytime between seven and eight-thirty. Lunch is come and go, eleven to one. If it's too hot or too cold in your room or something isn't working properly, you'll have to tell me, because I'm not a mind reader. Other than that, you can do pretty much as you please so long as it's not botherin' somebody else."

Gideon sat like an angry lump in the room's only chair. "I'm surprised Jeff didn't have bars installed on the window to make sure I don't crawl out when you're not looking."

Mae could remember a time when Gideon was a good man, a kind man, one of the best men she knew, but as she turned from the window to look at him now, all she saw was a pair of old eyes so full of bitterness and betrayal he couldn't see anything clearly. "Any time you feel like leaving, Gideon, you just walk right on out the front door. Nobody will lift a finger to stop you."

Jeff nudged the door open with the edge of a cardboard box, carried it in with a slight *huff* of exertion, and placed it with the other two. "That's it, Dad. Everything except the box of books. It's heavy and I'm flat too tired to carry it up the stairs tonight, so I'll bring it by sometime tomorrow."

"Throw it in the river for all I care. And don't be coming back tomorrow. You've got what you wanted now, so just go on and leave me alone."

Jeff flushed with anger, and his jaw set in a line as stubborn and proud as his father's. "I'll see you tomorrow, Dad. Miz Mae." With a bare nod in her direction, he turned on his heel and was gone, the strike of his footsteps on the stairs echoing his annoyance.

Mae stood there a moment too long, wiping her

hands on her gingham checked apron as if she could wipe the unpleasantness from the air around her.

"You think I owe that boy an apology, don't you?" Gideon snapped, turning his frustration on her. "Well, he's not getting one in this lifetime. Not that it's any of your business, no matter what you're standing there thinking."

Mae smoothed her apron. "I was thinking I'd best get out to the kitchen and help Lora with makin' dinner."

"Don't be cooking anything on my account," he said gruffly.

"I've got six boarders, seven now, counting you, and only Lora to help with the cooking and cleaning. We'll be sittin' down to dinner tonight and every other night at five-thirty, with or without you." She moved crisply to the doorway, annoyed that he'd managed to upset her. "And just so we understand each other, Gideon, you are the only person in this household who cares if you go to bed hungry."

His voice, all rough and angry and stubborn, followed her through the doorway, shutting her out before she could shut him in. "I won't be staying."

"You suit yourself," she said and pulled the door closed behind her.

Standing there in the upstairs hallway, she wished she'd never let Jeff talk her into this. She hadn't liked the idea of having Gideon at Wade House even before she'd gotten the call from Abby, and now the anxious churning in her stomach twisted into a double knot of worry. Maybe she should have sent money to help Abby pay off the debts. Or maybe she should have offered to keep the boys for the whole summer instead of just the couple of weeks they usually spent with her during their summer break. Abby could have stayed in Chicago and looked for a place to rent, found herself another job. She had a college degree, for Pete's sake, and nurses were always in demand somewhere or another. Mae could see where Abby would need to work days instead of an alternating schedule because of the boys, but she couldn't believe it was as difficult as Abby claimed to find a straight day position in at least one of Chicago's hospitals. Mae wouldn't have accepted defeat. She would have found the job she wanted and stood her ground until she got it. And she'd never have sold her home. Ever.

But Abby wasn't strong like Mae, didn't have her determination to keep on keeping on. She was Charlie's daughter all through. As a little girl, she'd dawdled and daydreamed her way through the years, never looking at life like it was, seeing people how she wanted them to be and not how they were. Look how she'd loved Charlie, who did nothing to deserve even one tenth of all the devotion Abby heaped on him. It had been enough to drive a mother mad, except that Mae had never had extra time to go a little bit crazy.

With a sigh, she headed on down the stairs, knowing the next few days would tell the tale. Abby would either be aggravated at Mae for trying to help or aggrieved because she didn't think Mae was doing enough. Mae had done her best, tried for years, but there was just no understanding between her and her daughter, and that was the truth. Which didn't mean she wasn't willing to help. Why, she'd barely even hesitated when Abby called with news the house in Lisle had sold. She'd done what any mother would have done under the circumstances . . . she'd told Abby to bring the boys and come live with her until the worst was over.

It hadn't occurred to her then that the worst just might be the two of them, mother and daughter, living once again under the same roof.

As if arriving home toting a sullen teenager, a neurotic eight-year-old, and a whole trailer full of failure wasn't bad enough, the first person Abby laid eyes on had to be the last person she ever wanted to see again. Jeff Garrett stood with one foot on the porch steps and one on the ground, turned toward the house, talking to the three men who boarded at Wade House: Lowell Robbins, Archie Johnson, and Joe Malone. Jeff stood much the same way he'd stood a thousand times before on those same steps, looking up at her, talking to her, drawing out an achingly sweet good night. Abby couldn't imagine what he was doing here now. Had Mae told him she and the boys were moving back? Outlined the series of events that had cost her a job, a home, and the illusion of her own independence? Invited him over to join some perverse welcome back party?

Abby turned off the ignition, unable to take her eyes off him. She'd lived all of her life since the accident intent on forgetting Jeff even existed. Yet the very minute she returned and saw him, she knew that she hadn't forgotten and that a part of her still hated him for the pain he'd caused, blamed him, however unfairly, because she'd made such a mess of her life.

"Look, Kyle, it's Archie and Joe . . . and Mr. Robbins." Denny perked up at the sight of his grandmother's rambling old house and the familiar faces on the front porch. "And Lexie's dad. Maybe Lexie's here, too."

"Nah, I doubt it." Kyle leaned toward the window with an eagerness that belied his indifferent tone, and Abby realized her son hadn't recovered from last summer's adolescent infatuation with Lexie Garrett. Jeff's daughter. Melanie's daughter. It figured somehow that Kyle, her rebel child, would choose Lexie, the one girl in town whose mother would have an apoplectic fit if he so much as darkened her doorstep.

The boys hopped out of the car and slammed their doors, moving up the front walk with the careful gait of children who don't wish to appear eager. Denny looked anxiously over his shoulder, making certain Abby wasn't about to drive off and leave them behind. Taking a deep breath, she got out of the Blazer and walked slowly around the hood to follow her boys.

The men on the porch called to them in an overlapping greeting.

"Hey there, Kyle. Denny."

"What took you so long?"

"We've been waiting supper for you."

Then Jeff turned around, his foot leaving the porch to find support on the ground, his face registering shock, surprise, and an instant's guilty pleasure. "Abby," he said as if he were happy to see her, as if he hadn't sacrificed her love as carelessly as he'd forfeited his brother's life.

"Jeff," she responded with a studied and cool indifference. Then she sent a wide smile sweeping toward Joe and Archie and then on to Lowell, who couldn't see her but whose thin face was wreathed in welcome. "Why aren't you three handsome men out saving the world?"

"Now, Abby, you know we don't go anywhere afore we've had our dinner," Archie said gruffly.

Lowell stepped forward, his white cane tapping. "We've been too busy twiddling our thumbs, waiting for summer to get here so these boys would come and entertain us."

"You're looking good, Abby," Joe said. "Haven't I always said Oklahoma air agreed with you?"

The screen door swung open, and with a whoop of welcome Lora swooped both boys into her arms like a mother wren. A very large mother wren. "It's 'bout time the three of you got here. Mae was near drivin' me nuts with her frettin'."

"Supper's ready." Mae stepped onto the porch, her mouth lifting at the sight of her grandsons, her gaze warm, but not entirely welcoming as it shifted to Abby. "You look worn out," she said. "I wish you'd listen to me when I tell you that's too long of a drive to make in one day."

Which was, Abby supposed, the closest her mother could come to *I'm glad you're here*. "We made it just fine," she replied, which was as close as she was willing to get to *you're right*. She started to walk past Jeff as if he wasn't there, but instead, she stopped and turned toward him. Better to look him square in the face right here and now and prove to herself that the only feeling she would ever allow him to stir in her again was a sweet and pure indifference. "Isn't Wade House a little out of your way?"

"I could say the same to you."

"Not anymore." She gestured vaguely at the rental. "The boys and I have moved back . . . so I have a good reason to be here."

"As of this afternoon, Dad is one of your mom's boarders, so as it turns out, I have a good reason to be here, too. Is that going to be a problem?"

"Not for me," she said, moving past him, wanting merely to reach the solid foundation of the only home she had, too tired to feel more than a fleeting concern over his presence on her mother's porch.

"You want to join us for supper, Jefferson?" Lora asked, unaware of the tension and the history, a come-one, come-all graciousness in her invitation.

"Not tonight." Jeff stepped away from the porch, away from the group gathered there. "But thanks for askin', Lora. Maybe I can take you up on that invitation some other time."

"Bring Lexie," Denny called with little boy enthusiasm, and the men burst out in smiles.

"Yep," Joe agreed. "Next time, bring Lexie with ya."

Abby made her way up the stairs to give Lora, then her mother, a cursory and hurried hug. She saw the wariness in her mother's eyes and tried to answer with a reassuring gaze. *It's all right, Mom. You don't have to worry about me staying forever. It's just for awhile, I swear. Just until I can patch up two small, broken hearts.*

Mae's smile revealed only a mother's concern for her daughter, and perhaps the regret that life had turned out the way it had . . . for her and her child. Or maybe it was simply the way she always looked at Abby. Strong, solid, resigned, the only person left to turn to, the only one who would, however reluctantly, take her in. Abby sighed and motioned the boys inside. Coming home was bad enough. Coming home a failure in Mae's eyes was worse.

For as long as she could remember, Abby had borne the burden of being her daddy's girl. How often had she heard her mother say that Charlie Wade had never had a thing except dreams and his daughter's adoration? It was always Mae who managed the money, Mae who worked the business, Mae who kept food on the table and a dry roof over their heads at night. And now Abby could no longer provide those basic necessities for her own children, so Mae would have to take up the slack once again. It was enough to make Abby wish she had had any choice but this one, any place to go other than here. But she was trying her best to see things true, and she knew home was exactly where she needed to be.

Let her mother play the role of martyr. Let her chastise Abby's failures with her silence. Abby would bear those indignities and more for her boys, and somehow in the process, she'd show Mae and this whole town that although in many ways she was still her daddy's girl, she was also very much her mother's daughter.

Chapter 3

The kitchen was quiet, as it always was, when he walked in. Jeff tossed his keys on the counter, then picked them up again and hung them on the appropriate hook of the decorative copper doghouse on the wall. *Jeff. Melanie. Lexie.* They each had a designated hook, a place to keep their keys. The other two hooks were empty . . . as they always were. The key holder was for his use because Melanie disliked having to pick up after him. Keys, clothes, an empty glass—the item was unimportant. Only the fact that he'd left something where it shouldn't be. Years of living with her had taught him it was easier to hang up his keys than suffer the consequences of leaving them on the counter. Keeping the peace was the name of the game in the Garrett household. So he looped the key ring on the hook, thereby making one less disappointment for Melanie, one less crime he had to answer for. He opened the refrigerator and looked inside, hopeful that someone else would have thought to stock it, knowing beforehand that it would be as bare as it had been this morning.

He'd have to go to the store later, but with a bit of luck, there'd be enough of something in there so he could throw together a decent supper. Eggs, maybe. Lexie wasn't crazy about breakfast foods at any time of day, but she wouldn't say anything. To his regret, she'd learned it was easier to eat whatever was put in front of her than to risk her mother's displeasure with a protest. Letting the refrigerator door swing shut, Jeff moved to the sink and looked out at the backyard. Grass needed cutting, and he should have pruned the butterfly bush last fall. It had grown leggy and wild this spring.

Abby had been leggy and wild once.

The thought was just there, complete with images of the way she once had been, the way she had looked today. Okay, so he'd tried not thinking about her and that didn't seem to work. Maybe if he let his memory run its course, turned it loose with all the thoughts he'd been trying to avoid, he'd forget she was even in town.

Home.

She'd moved home. She'd sworn she was never coming back, yet she was here. Time could change a person's mind. He knew that for a fact. But somehow he never thought Abby would eat her words. She'd said them so forcefully for one thing. And with such conviction. She'd hated him desperately then. He suspected she still did. There hadn't been a glimmer of forgiveness when she'd looked at him today, not a speck of regret for the friendship he'd squandered, the love he'd sacrificed so readily. But then time had taught him nothing if not that regret was the property of the one who'd made the choice.

A car rumbled to a stop in front of the house. He could hear the shoddy muffler and the high-pitched chatter of a vehicle filled with teenage girls. He should get started on supper. But he was still standing at the sink when the back door banged open and his daughter walked in. She was lean and self-consciously supple, in the way of a child who has only lately become a woman. Jeff thought she was unspeakably beautiful. That scared him a little. It also made him prouder than any man had a right to be. It all came down to that, to Lexie. He could weigh all his regrets, all he had given up, against the one benefit of being her father and know he'd make the same choice all over again.

"Hi, Dad," she said, tossing her bag on the table and heading straight for the refrigerator. "Have you been to the store?"

He hated to disappoint her, although it wasn't exactly a rare occurrence. "Sorry. I just got here myself. Today was the day I brought your grampa back to Sweetwater, remember?"

"Oh, yeah." She stood in the vee of the open refrigerator for another hopeful minute before she stepped back and let it close. "How did that go?" She wrinkled her nose, knowing as well as he did that there'd never been a chance in hell it would go well.

"He's delighted with his new place. Couldn't thank me enough for helping him get moved in."

She laughed . . . and that alone made the day better. "Right, Dad. He probably cussed you out all the way from Heavener to Sweetwater. Poor Grampa."

"Poor Grampa?" Jeff repeated. "What about poor Dad? I think I'm the one who deserves any sympathy you're doling out over there."

"I don't believe in giving you too much sympathy," she said airily. "One parent feeling sorry for themself is plenty." She stopped, an anxious crease appearing on her brow. "Sorry. I know Mom can't help it that she has so many headaches, it's just . . . well, my friends don't even want to come over here anymore because she's such a . . ." *Bitch.* The word hovered in the air, but Lexie replaced it with a less costly, "grump."

"She doesn't mean to cause you problems, Lexie." But even as the automatic words left his mouth, he wasn't sure they were true. For years, he'd thought Melanie couldn't help it, that the headaches were simply more than she could handle. But lately he'd begun to wonder if they weren't merely her means of escape . . . from him, from Lexie, from the discontentment that dominated her every waking moment. "Tell you what. When you get back from camp, I'll cook burgers for the whole cheerleading squad. I'll work on Mom while you're gone and have her all excited about it by the time you get home."

Her smile was weary with effort and wiser than his offer. "Thanks, Dad," she said. "That'll be great."

She knew it wouldn't happen. The knowledge was in the set of her shoulders, the sad curve of her smile. She'd known too much disappointment already in her short life, and Jeff decided he'd make sure the cookout came to pass, even if he had to promise Melanie the moon to get her to agree to it. "I'm hungry for an egg and"—he checked the refrigerator, pulling out drawers and moving aside jars to check the contents—"cottage cheese omelet." He peeled back the lid of the cottage cheese container and grimaced before setting it in the sink. "On second thought, I prefer plain omelets, nothing but eggs and eggs. How does that sound to you?"

"Super," she said without enthusiasm.

He sighed. "What the hell, let's order pizza."

But before he could pull out the phone book and look up the number, he heard Melanie's footsteps on the stairs and tensed. "Hi, there," she said pleasantly as she came into the kitchen. "Looks like the two of you are up to something." She glanced at the countertop—clear—then at the set of keys dangling from the rack, and smiled. "I hope you're plotting what we're having for dinner. I'm so hungry I'd eat anything that doesn't eat me first." She looked in the sink, smile fading, nose wrinkling with displeasure. "Ooh, who left that in the sink?"

Jeff moved to empty it, but Melanie already had the tap on, steaming with heat, to rinse the rancid food down the disposal. "I'll do it," she said, her voice cool but not unpleasant as she thoroughly cleaned a plastic tub, which she then put in the dishwasher, where it would be thoroughly washed again before it was wrapped in a plastic bag, and only then placed in the trash container. The outside trash container. No dirty garbage left the Garrett household, no sir.

"You must be feeling better," Lexie said, tentatively testing the mood. "Headache gone?"

"It's never gone, Sweetness." Melanie smiled a patient, long-suffering smile. "But it does seem better this evening." She shifted the smile to Jeff. "Did you get Gideon moved?"

"Fighting every inch of the way."

"You uprooted him, Jeff. You can hardly expect him to be happy about it."

"It's a question of need, Melanie."

"And convenience. Your convenience." She was the devil's advocate and Jeff's emotions were too raw from the day to take her on.

"Yes," he said tightly. "I moved him strictly for my convenience."

The victory was too easily won, but Melanie continued to smile as she turned to her daughter. "Homework tonight?"

"School's been out for a week, Mom. It's summer break." She looked at Jeff. "Forget the pizza, Dad. I'm not very hungry." And grabbing up her bag, she was gone like a wisp of smoke, her feet tapping out a quick two-step up the stairs.

"Pizza?" Melanie asked, the smile replaced with criticism. "You were going to give her pizza for dinner? You know that's about as nutritious as cardboard. Plus it's just dripping with fat, and she has to watch her weight. You know that, Jeff."

"She hardly eats at all. If anything, she could stand to gain a few pounds."

"I'm sure you'd be happy if she got fat as a pig so no decent boy would ever ask her out and she could be daddy's little girl forever."

"How can you say something like that, Mel? How can you even think it? I only want Lexie to be happy."

Melanie shrugged. "You have a funny way of showing it, feeding her pizza and junk food when I'm not looking."

"You're never looking, Melanie. That's the problem."

"Oh, so once again, it's my fault. You're priceless, Jeff. Just priceless."

But her tone said he was of no value at all. To her. To Lexie. To anyone. Turning his back to her, he braced his hands on the lip of the sink and looked again at the overgrown backyard. "Abby's home."

Just that quickly—two words, *Abby's home*—and the already cool air turned frigid, the silence thick as an iceberg. "Abby?"

"Abby Wade," he supplied because he wanted to feel the weight of her name on his tongue again, not because either one of them had any doubt as to whom he referred.

"Abby Ryan," Melanie corrected. "I imagine she's only dropping off those rowdy boys of hers at Miz Mae's, like she does every summer. Someone told me her husband got killed in some kind of barroom brawl a few months ago, but I didn't see anything about it in the Trib."

Jeff wouldn't have printed the story even if someone had sent it in, but Melanie knew that, of course. She just wanted to remind him that she had her sources, too. "Abby is moving back, Melanie. I saw her this evening as I was leaving and she told me."

The chill deepened in the kitchen. "So . . . you've spoken with her?"

There was no reason to deny it. "Yes."

"At the Wade House." It was confirmation and condemnation and Jeff turned around to acknowledge it. "Yes."

"Well, what a coincidence, the two of you running into each other there. And so convenient, too, with you moving Gideon in there today. How long have you and your lover been planning this little reunion?"

"That's not fair, Melanie. I've had no contact with Abby for sixteen years. You know that. You've watched me like a hawk and there's never been anything. Not once. Nothing."

"I suppose that would depend on whether we choose your definition of *nothing* . . . or mine."

It was a fight he'd lost a long time ago, but somehow he kept going into the ring, slugging it out for a prize neither of them cared about anymore. "I doubt she'll have two words to say to me now that she's back." He leaned against the sink, knowing he was damned, no matter how many olive branches he extended. "I'm sure you'll be happy to know she still hates me."

"Then that makes it unanimous, doesn't it?" Whirling on her heel, Melanie was out of the kitchen and gone, only the slam of her bedroom door marking the fury of her departure.

Funny. A teenager in the house, and the only person who could get away with slamming a door was her thirty-four-year-old mother. But it wasn't funny at all. The viciousness of Melanie's words lingered in the kitchen, the venom in her voice left a sludge of unhappiness in his gut. They'd married for Lexie, made a family because the baby was already on the way. But Jeff had hoped affection would come. In time, perhaps, even something akin to love. He'd thought they could build a relationship out of disaster. Instead, their marriage was as empty as the promises he'd made. Except, of course, for Lexie. Beautiful Lexie.

Straightening, Jeff jerked away from the counter, opened the refrigerator, and pulled out the carton of eggs. Someone had to fix dinner. And he was the only someone left. The only someone who cared.

Throwing open a cabinet, he grabbed a skillet and tossed it onto the gas burner with a metallic *clank!* The pan rocked and rattled against the grate, then fell, clattering to the floor . . . and with the noise, a hot, molten anger surged inside him. Anger because Melanie hated him. Anger because Abby had come home. Anger because Lexie would have to eat eggs for supper.

He picked up the carton of Homeland's Large Grade AAs and pitched it overhand into the sink, taking a vengeful satisfaction in watching the eggs shatter, splattering bits of shell and gooey yolk all over the pristine white porcelain. Then yanking his keys from the hook, he walked to the foot of the stairs and yelled, "Lexie, come on. I'm taking you out for pizza."

Chapter 4

For the first time since she'd decided to move back to Sweetwater, Abby finally accepted that home was, in fact, where she'd wanted to be all along. Seated now around the huge old oak dining table, surrounded by the mismatched family of boarders and the genuine camaraderie of their welcome, she felt a budding confidence that, finally, the worst was behind her. She wasn't alone anymore. She was with people who liked her, people who loved her boys, people who accepted this homecoming not as failure, but as a welcome surprise.

"And then, what did you do?" Lowell leaned in, his eyes alight despite their inability to see, his whole body intent on hearing Kyle's story. "Did you kick him in the keister?"

"Lowell Robbins!" Effie Jackson reached across Archie and gave Lowell's hand a prim, schoolteacher spat. "Now don't be putting words in the boy's mouth. 'Course, he didn't get violent over a sandwich. Kyle's too smart for that."

"Violence is no way to handle trouble," Rose Delaney agreed, her gray head bobbing with eagerness to hear that Kyle had indeed kicked some butt.

Rose's sister, Violet McAfee, pointed her fork at the boy. "So? What'd you do?"

Joe thumped his fist on the table. "Would you women be quiet and let the boy have his say?"

All eyes turned to Kyle again, and Abby was pleased that here, at least, he could be the center of attention in a positive way, even if she wasn't particularly happy with him over the incident under discussion.

"I got up from the table and picked up my lunch." Kyle held his audience for a dramatic beat, before he continued with a carefully crafted, offhand shrug. "Then I dumped it in the trash and said, *'Dig it out, Godzilla, and it's all yours.'*"

Effie and Rose applauded as gleefully as they did everything else. The men all nodded a consensus of approval.

"Stood up to him." Archie helped himself to another yeast roll. "That's the only way to deal with a bully. If you'd given him the sandwich, he'd never have let you have a minute's peace."

"Yep," Joe agreed. "Can't ever let a fellow like that think you're afraid of him. You did the right thing, son."

Kyle beamed with pride, and Abby caught his *see-there* glance, interpreting it correctly as the scorecard he kept with razor sharp precision. *See, Mom. They think I did the right thing by standing up to that asshole.* The bottom line, of course, being that she had been wrong. Right and wrong were so starkly black and white for him, so many shades of gray for his mother. Abby knew her own mother must have thought her equally obnoxious once, but that didn't make Kyle's attitude any easier to bear. He'd received a bloody nose and a three-day suspension from school for the fight that followed the incident in the cafeteria, and apparently all he'd learned was to take his fights off of school property. But she wasn't going to rain on his parade. She was flat out of steam, for one thing. And for another, her mother's heart wanted him to feel good about something today, even if it wasn't entirely the truth.

Violet shifted the gaily wrapped package in her lap so

she could lean forward and address Kyle sternly. "But you threw away your lunch," she said. "That wasn't so smart."

This time Kyle's shrug showed more embarrassment than cockiness. "I wasn't hungry."

"His nose bled all over everything." Denny announced proudly. He'd spent two months worrying about the loss of all that blood, but suddenly, his big brother was a wounded hero. "He coulda died."

Kyle thumped Denny with his elbow. "Don't talk about stuff like that at the table."

"I can if I want to," Denny said, although he hunched down in his chair, worried now that he'd made his big brother mad.

"You just take some more strawberries, honey." Lora leaned right across Denny to scoop more berries onto the remains of Kyle's angel food cake, as if overfeeding him now would make up for his having missed a meal two months ago.

"Me, too?" Denny extended his plate for more dessert, tilting it carelessly in his eagerness and sending the syrupy remains of cake and berries in a sliding rush toward disaster. Abby started up out of her chair, but Mae's hand touched his arm, bringing the plate back into alignment with Denny hardly the wiser. Abby sighed and settled back. After so many years of doing everything herself, of trying to head off every disaster, it was nice to have a helping hand.

"I hear a car," Lowell said.

"Now, who'd be comin' out here right at supper time?" Rose wondered aloud.

Joe speared a third helping of fatty roast beef. "Probably Jeff, coming back to check on Gideon."

"Comin' back to get a home-cooked meal, more likely." Effie sniffed her displeasure. "That wife of his doesn't lift a finger without claimin' it brings on one of her headaches."

Abby busied herself with the food still on her plate. Jeff and his wife were none of her concern, and she had no inclination to feel even a grain of sympathy for him. He'd chosen Melanie. For better, for worse. Headaches, home-cooked meals or not.

"He's comin' to make sure that stubborn old man ate his supper," was Rose's conclusion.

"Well, then, he's wasted a trip," Effie pronounced. "Gideon'll eat when he gets hungry enough. And Lora, don't you go taking that ornery old man any angel food cake, either. He could've come down to supper and not spent the evening sulking in his room by himself."

"It was his own choice." Violet pushed her plate and glass back, then lifted the colorful package from her lap and set it on the table in front of her, where she fussed with the red satin bow. "Besides, I don't believe it is Jeff coming to check on his father. I think it's somebody come to visit Mr. McAfee. He hasn't had company in a month of Sundays."

"He's been dead for twenty years." Joe nodded at the oblong box in which Mr. McAfee had resided since his death. Violet McAfee was an odd little woman, sternly literal except when it came to her late husband's cremated remains, which were with her at all times. She talked about him as if he were alive, consulted him on matters she perceived to be of interest to herself and others, and always kept his box wrapped and ready for any and all occasions. As it was June, he was decorated for Father's Day in a cool green print with colorful red, blue, and yellow ties winding across the paper. The red bow topped off the package, giving the whole theme a natty touch. It was, according to Lora, one of his better outfits.

Archie snatched another yeast roll from the bread basket and tucked it inside his shirt for a late night snack. "Well, if someone has come to visit old Mac, it'll

likely be a ghost. Which would be the best entertainment we've had around here in forty years."

"You haven't lived here forty years." Violet liked
being the eccentric widow, and while she could make
light of her late husband, she didn't like anyone else to
do so. "And you wouldn't know real company if they
walked up and tweaked off your nose."

"That's what you think," Archie said. "Why, I . . ."

The knock at the front door didn't put a stop to the
conversation at the table, rather merely fit into the yam-
mering beat of the boarders as they fussed with one
another like fractious children. Mae looked toward the
door, a certain weariness etched into the lines of her
face as she moved to get up. Abby pushed to her feet
first. "I'll get it," she said. "Sit, Mom," she insisted when
Mae started to protest. "I'm closer. You should finish
your dinner. It's probably just some kid selling magazine subscriptions or something."

On the way to the front door though, it occurred to
Abby that it could be—probably was, in fact—Jeff returning to check on Gideon, and she lifted her chin,
savoring a quicksilver flowering of animosity. Little
more than a wink of emotion, a flutter of something
that wasn't exhaustion. And that, in itself, felt good.
The silhouette on the other side of the frosted glass
panel resembled Jeff's in size and shape, and she was
prepared to see him when she opened the door, prepared to be cordial but cool. *Jeff.* She had his name
ready on her tongue, indifferently polite. And for an instant after she saw him on the other side of the screen,
she couldn't wrap her mind around the realization that
it wasn't Jeff at all, but a stranger. No one she recognized at all.

"Hi," she said, falling easily into the rhythms of a
small Midwestern town where strangers were suspect,
but not initially unwelcome. "Can I help you?"

"From the smells coming from inside there, I sure hope so," he replied in a casual, unassuming way.

"You're looking for a meal." Abby well remembered a time when strangers had shown up regularly at the Wade House, as if it were a restaurant. Some of them had paid. Some of them hadn't offered anything more than gratitude. Mae had fed them all alike.

"Yes, ma'am." His voice had a hint of drawl. Not deep South, but somewhere nestled between here and there. "And a room for the night, if you have one."

"This is a boarding house. Not a hotel. You'd have a much more comfortable night down at the Comfort Lodge. It's right off the highway. You can't miss it."

He looked hopeful. "I have it on good authority from Amy who's working the evening shift at the Tank 'n' Tummy convenience store that the Wade House is the best place in town to eat. I've got photo IDs, good credit, a sterling character, and a healthy appetite."

Abby frowned, reluctant to allow a stranger entry no matter what credentials he offered.

"I'm sick of carryout pizzas and microwave popcorn overcooked in a hotel lobby," he pressed, looking forlornly hopeful.

"You're in luck," she said with a smile. "The Comfort Lodge doesn't even have a microwave."

His shoulders sagged, and she noted the signs of weariness around his eyes and the perfectly nice way he accepted her refusal to take him in. But for all she knew he could be a serial killer. "I'm sorry," she said, lowering her voice. "It's just that Wade House is really more for elderly people, and I honestly don't think you'd be very comfortable here."

"You don't look elderly," he pointed out. "You can't be more than . . . what? Twenty-one?"

Obvious, but cute. So she gave him half of a smile. "I'm the daughter of the house," she said. "And old enough to know better than to be bribed by blatant flattery."

"I can be more subtle."

She allowed him more smile for that one. "It won't help. Sorry."

"Abby?" Mae called from the dining room.

"I've got it under control, Mom," she called back, knowing her mother would have this stranger in the house and at the table before she could offer even a token protest. "If you'd like," she said to him, "I'll give you directions to the hotel. The Dairy Queen is right across the street and they used to flip a mean hamburger. I haven't been there in a long time, but I'm sure it's still the best burger in town."

His smile was quick, with a kind of boy-next-door charm that was somehow both deeply familiar and oddly reassuring. "So, you're turning me away from the inn?"

She opened her mouth to say yes, but Mae was suddenly beside her, opening the door wider, ready to welcome in a stranger before she even knew what he wanted. "Are you looking for a place to stay?" she asked, usurping Abby's role and undermining her refusal with a smile. "Something to eat?"

"Yes," he said eagerly, his glance apologizing to Abby for taking what was offered. "I'm Noah Walker. I'm an environmental field researcher for Burdick Labs in Memphis. I'll be in Sweetwater a couple of weeks, maybe longer, to study samples of the river water and the surrounding soil. If you have a room to rent, I'd be more than happy to pay extra for meals. I was just telling . . . Abby . . ." His gaze came back to her with a *don't-hold-this-against-me* look in his earthy brown eyes. ". . . how tired I am of eating in greasy spoon diners and getting carry-out from the local pizza places."

"There's always room for one more at the Wade House," Mae announced with the easy hospitality she swapped for a living wage. "I can give you room and board for a hundred and sixty dollars per day, plus tax, or the room alone for a hundred and a quarter. If that's agreeable with you, come on in. We were just finishing our supper and there's plenty left over." Mae pushed open the door, heedless of security or a simple check of identity or Abby's insistent frown. "You just go right on in there to the table and Lora will get you a plate. Lora," she called into the dining room, "we've got a straggler for supper. Everybody, this is Noah Walker. Y'all introduce yourselves around the table."

Abby crossed her arms at her waist as she watched the stranger hesitate, then move through the entry to the dining room. Mae smiled approvingly, in her element as proprietress of Wade House. "There," she said, wiping her hands on her apron. "He seems like a nice young man."

"He's a stranger," Abby said softly. "You should not have invited him in without knowing something about him. You could be putting us all in danger."

Mae used the corner of her apron to rub a smudge off the frosted glass. "I've been taking in folks for a lot of years, Abby. I'm careful when I need to be careful."

"You didn't even ask to see his driver's license."

"Don't start out telling me what I should be doing, Abby. You've been gone a long time, and you've forgotten how we do things in Sweetwater."

"Bad things can happen even in Sweetwater."

Mae acknowledged that with a crisp nod. "Bad things can happen anywhere. It's just my way to believe nothin' bad is going to happen here tonight because I offered a bed and some vittles to a stranger. It might be a good thing if you let yourself believe that, too." She turned and followed the new boarder into the dining room, leaving Abby with no recourse but to close the door and wonder if she understood anything at all about her mother.

Chapter 5

Abby shoved another packing box toward the back of the trailer, scooted it to the edge, then jumped flat-footed onto the pavement. She paused just long enough to press her fists into the ache in her lower back before she hefted the box into her arms and headed for the house. Two steps into her trek, the screen door slammed back on its hinges, and Kyle was across the porch and breezing past her on the front walk even before the door banged shut in his wake. She heard his *huff* of exertion as he scraped another box off the lip of the Go West trailer, and as she started up the front porch steps, he was close on her heels. "I'm fifteen, Mom," he said, his voice aggrieved and unaccommodating. "You can't expect me to share a room with an eight-year-old."

"Fourteen," Abby corrected. "You're fourteen."

He discounted her math in a scoffing breath. "Only for a few more days."

"Closer to a month, Kyle. Don't be in such a hurry to grow up."

"You just want me to stay fourteen forever so you can boss me around for the rest of my life."

"Believe me, Kyle, I do not want you to stay fourteen one second longer than absolutely necessary."

He'd been in a hurry to be born, arriving nearly two months before he was due, convinced he was a grown-up from the start . . . and he'd never taken kindly to her opinion that he wasn't. She maneuvered through the doorway, smiling her thanks at Joe, who held the screen door open until she and Kyle were through. "Thanks, Joe. You're a lifesaver." She hoped her son would mutter his own stilted thank you, but Kyle was intent on his purpose and didn't seem to realize any gratitude was in order.

"Where you goin' with the boxes?" Joe asked. "I thought y'all were staying out in the old garage apartment."

Abby headed up to the second floor, her thighs protesting the climb, her arms aching with the weight of the box. "These are just linens and household things," she said. "Mom has the apartment all fixed for us, so we won't be needing this stuff until we get a house of our own. For now, everything's going up to the attic."

"I'll grab a box and help you."

"Thanks, Joe, but Kyle and I can do it. There're only a few more boxes and I don't want you straining your back or anything trying to carry them. Mom will have both our hides if you hurt yourself."

"I'm not scared of Miz Mae." And with that, Joe stepped out and let the screen door close with a *whap* behind him.

Abby took the stairs at a measured pace while Kyle prodded her with his own agenda one step behind her. "You could put Denny in your room," he suggested with casual deliberation. "He'd rather be with you, anyway."

"You're sharing the room with your brother, Kyle, and that's final."

"I could stay in the big house," he persisted. "Grandma said I could use that storage room next to Lora. I'll clean it out myself. And I'll paint it and everything. You won't have to lift a finger to help me."

Abby paused at the top of the stairs, resting the edge

of the box on the bannister rail while she caught her
breath and gave her arms a brief respite. "You're staying in the apartment with me and Denny," she said. "I
know it's crowded. I know you don't want to share a
bedroom. But we are still a family and I am doing the
best I can."

"Well, your best *sucks!*"

"Kyle!"

"Everything about this sucks and you know it, Mom.
You just won't do a fucking thing to change it."

She rounded on him. "Don't ever use that kind of
language when you're speaking to me, and never
again here in your grandmother's house."

"Yeah, fine," he said, defiant in his frustration. "You
let me have my own room and we won't have this
problem."

"We won't have this problem, period. Do you understand?"

"Sure. You want me to be miserable."

"Drop the attitude, Kyle, before I decide the attic
is the best place for you."

His icy stare held hers, and then he shrugged. "At
least I wouldn't have to share it with that little freak you
call my brother." Brushing past her, he allowed the box
he carried to jostle her elbow. A deliberate nudge. A
gotcha last from him to her. Abby ignored it for the moment. This wasn't easy for him, she knew that. She
understood his desire for privacy, his need for independence, the anger of feeling powerless. But for now,
she had to think about what was best for the three of
them as a family. She had to get a job and pay off the
last of the debts before she could even begin to look for
a place to rent. The summer. That was all she needed
to pull the threads of their life back together.

Not that Kyle was likely to have any faith in her ability to do that. During the downward spiral of Mitch's
alcoholism, she'd blindly turned her attention from

mothering her boys to surviving her marriage. A mistake she could see clearly from the perspective of months down the road. But one that now had to be redressed, even if it could never be completely forgiven. Abby understood she had a lot to answer for . . . both to her sons and to herself. That's why they were here. So she could stop worrying on all fronts and concentrate on one—giving her boys back a mother they could count on.

But that didn't mean she was going to allow her rebellious teenager to walk all over her. She'd count to ten. Maybe twenty. Then she'd go after him. She was the parent. He was fourteen for twenty-one more days and the rest of this one. And someday—*some day*—he'd have a teenager of his own, which was all the revenge a parent ever really wanted anyway.

As she reached eight on her *one one-thousand, two one-thousand* count, she heard the intentionally heavy, slightly muffled sound of his feet on the attic steps. By the time she reached twelve, the attic door banged on its hinges, followed by smaller, faster footsteps and a loud *thud* as something heavy—probably, hopefully, only the packing box—made elaborate contact with the floor. Then came a strident, "Get out of the way, Denny! Didn't you hear me coming up the stairs? What are you doing running up and grabbing the box like that, anyway?"

"Mom told me to help," Denny wailed in response, an unwitting scapegoat in Kyle's struggle for independence.

"Well, that wasn't any help, was it? Now, look what you've done."

Abby closed her eyes for a second, wishing that could drown out the muffled argument. When it didn't, she stretched the stiff muscles along her neck, settled the box more fully into her arms, and moved on down the hall. Overhead, the yelling escalated. Their fighting

echoed in the walls and down the stairs, the angry
thumps and bumps of their inept wrestling, the indis-
tinct threats of violence that bounced between them
like a plastic ball in a ping pong match.

"You better get that stuff back in the box before
Mom gets up here!" Kyle threatened.

"You'd better help me!" Denny fired back, managing to hold his own despite his insecurities. He stewed
over the arguments afterward, worried endlessly over
what he'd said, what he wished he'd said, if his
brother would ever like him. But in the heat of battle,
he gave back verbal tit for tat.

This scene only reinforced Abby's decision to stay out
in the old apartment, regardless of Mae's objections. It
was the right place for her rowdy boys and as near to a
real home as she could make for them at the moment.
They would eat meals in the main house, share in the
sense of community the boarders provided, but they'd
have privacy, too. That was important, Abby believed.
Otherwise, they'd become Mae's charges, dependent
on her strength and stamina, but resentful, too, of her
heavy-handed love. They would become something
more than boarders but less than family, and Abby had
no intention of allowing that to happen.

The attic argument grew louder, and she walked
faster, was almost to the turn in the hall when a door
jerked open on her right, startling her even before a
gruffly familiar voice demanded, "Who the hell is
doing all that yelling?"

She recognized the voice even though she hadn't
heard it in years. Gideon Garrett. The father of Jeff and
Alex. The most feared—and revered—teacher at
Thomas Potter High School during all of her growing
up. A big, burly man who thundered out Shakespeare
in class, forced the love of literature down the throats
of both scholars and slackers, assigned essays in equal
measure as reward and punishment, and was, by the

sheer power of intimidation, the one teacher whose class every student was proud to boast of having survived. Away from the classroom, he'd been a ferocious coach, a no-nonsense fan, a proud and self-disciplined man who expected more of himself and his sons than he demanded of anyone else. Abby had been afraid of him from the first, and she was chagrined to feel, still, a touch of panic at the sound of his voice.

"Hello, Mr. Garrett," she forced herself to say, hoping she sounded like the mature woman she was and not the gangly student she suddenly felt like. "Sorry for the noise. My sons are having a little . . . disagreement." She moved the packing box to her left, giving it balance with her hip, as she faced Gideon Garrett and looked him squarely in the eyes. The last time she'd seen him had been at the memorial service for Alex. There had been three funerals in three days in Sweetwater, and by the time the bells droned out the summons to the fourth and last one, Abby had thought her tears were spent. But one look at Jeff's father, broken with grief, stunned by betrayal, had wrenched the sobs straight from her heart. She had never cried so hard before or since and, even at the time, she had understood she was mourning not only Alex's death and her own shattered dreams, but the knowledge that Jeff's treason had made her Gideon's ally.

He frowned at her now, older, grayer, with eyes grown bitter beneath the weight of a fierce sorrow. "Abby? Abby Wade? What the hell are you doing here?"

She glanced at the box in her arms and gave the barest of shrugs. "Moving in."

"I thought you escaped this hellhole of a town."

Not knowing how to reply, she simply said, "Well, I'm moving back."

"Why would you do a damn fool thing like that?"

She was inclined to bow her head, as if she deserved

detention for her misjudgment. It was none of his business, but he'd once been an authority figure in her life, and she heard herself answering, "Sometimes home is the best place to be."

"That's a load of crap."

What did he know? This wasn't a class in English Lit. This was life. Her life . . . and she didn't owe anyone an explanation. "I heard you had moved in," she said. "I imagine we'll be seeing each other around the house."

"Does Jeff know you're back in Sweetwater? Does he know you're here, at your mom's place?"

"He was leaving last night just as I was arriving and we said hello."

Gideon came close to smiling. "That ought to complicate things."

She couldn't imagine why her being in Sweetwater should make one iota of difference to Jeff or anybody else. Not that she cared if it did. Jeff had chosen his life, just as she'd chosen hers and, overhead, her sons were screaming at each other, their voices raining down like the rumble of a bad storm.

"I'm telling Mom!"

"Go ahead, you little creep. See if I care!"

Gideon's face creased with displeasure. "Your sons, I presume?"

She lifted her chin, disliking him as suddenly now as she had been instantly wary of him all those years ago. "They're a little out of sorts," she said, offering not a hint of apology. "Boys tend to get that way when they have to spend part of their summer working instead of playing."

Memory touched a nerve and his expression softened with an unexpected reminiscence. "Alex was like that," he said, the gruffness dying away in his voice. "He thought summers were meant to be spent in the pursuit of pleasure. You remember how he was, don't you?"

She wanted to deny him the solace, to say she could

barely remember Alex at all. But why should she allow Gideon the power of coercing her into a lie? In the years since the accident, she'd forgotten most of what she'd ever known about Alex Garrett, except that he'd believed every moment of every day was his gift to squander. He'd been the proverbial grasshopper, spinning grandiose dreams while the rest of the world toiled. Jeff had been the one who worked to buy a car, who planned ahead, who juggled school, sports, a job, a social life . . . and time with one special girl. Alex had done exactly what he wanted, when he wanted, and with any girl he chose. He'd done nothing to justify Gideon's pride in him, while Jeff had tied himself in knots trying to gain one pure moment of his father's approval. "Alex knew how to enjoy himself," she said, committing to nothing more than that shared remembrance.

"He did, didn't he?" For whatever reason, Gideon seemed to take pride in that fact as he closed the door, shutting her out as brusquely as he had let her in.

Abby stood looking at his door until the pounding of feet on the attic stairs snapped her back to reality and she braced herself to referee another pointless feud.

"I'm not sharing a room with that little turd," Kyle said as he tore past her in a blazing hurry. "I don't care what you do to me." He stormed down the stairs to the floor below and was out of the house with another bang of the screen door.

Upstairs, Denny was crying. She couldn't hear his tears, but her mother's heart felt his hurt and confusion, and she decided it was better to offer comfort to the son who wanted it than to give counsel to the one who didn't.

"Abby?" Mae called from downstairs before Abby could take one step toward the attic door. "What's going on up there?"

With a sigh, she set the packing box on the floor and moved to the stair rail, leaning over until she could see her mother in the foyer below. "Nothing, Mom. The boys had a disagreement. That's all."

"We can't have that kind of noise in the house. You remind the boys about how some of the boarders take naps after lunch. You tell them Grandma said to mind their manners."

"I'll take care of it, Mom."

"See that you do." Mae's voice diminished as she walked away. "You're just gonna have to take a firmer hand with your boys, Abby."

And so the failure began. She couldn't control her children. She couldn't control her life. She couldn't find a job . . . or keep one. She couldn't in a million years be the daughter Mae wanted her to be. A door opened and closed behind her, and she bent to pick up the box with a certain urgency, not eager to have to apologize to whichever boarder had been awakened by all the commotion.

"Here, let me help." The box was lifted from her hands, its burden settling away from her and into the arms of another. "Where are you going with this, anyway?"

It was last night's stranger. Noah. Something. If he'd told her his surname—and he probably had—she'd forgotten it in her exhaustion. "Upstairs," she said, gesturing vaguely upward with her chin. "To the attic. I'll show you."

"I'll find my way. Why don't you take a minute or two? It sounded like you could use a break."

His smile was nice, yet vaguely unsettling somehow, as was the rush of her apology. "I'm sorry the boys disturbed you."

He shrugged off her concern. "They're just being boys and they're not bothering me. I was just in my room getting some aspirin. You wait here. I'll be back in a sec."

Abby watched him head down the hall with the box marked "odds and ends," knowing she ought to go with him, show him the way. But she was tired of all the *ought tos,* weary of all the *shoulds.* What she'd really love was a long soak in a hot bath, followed by a long nap. But a minute or two by herself was better than nothing.

Already she could hear the deep, unintelligible rumble of Noah's greeting to Denny and her son's hesitant, muted reply. Leaning her shoulder against the wall, she forced herself to concentrate on breathing in and out and nothing more until she heard the tread of footsteps—one set heavy, one set lighter—descending the attic stairs.

"I can tie a running figure-of-eight knot, too," Denny was saying, all trace of tears gone from his little boy voice. "I had to study a long time to figure it out, but I finally got it."

"Maybe you could teach me," Noah answered. "I can't remember that one, but I think it cost me a badge in Cub Scouts."

"I can show you." Denny wasn't smiling as he came around the corner, but he wasn't crying either. "I'm really good at tying knots."

Noah smiled at Abby over Denny's blond head. "Let's get the rest of the boxes upstairs for your mom. I have some work that has to be done this afternoon, but maybe you could show me how to tie one of those running figure-of-eight knots after dinner tonight."

"Hi, Mom." Denny passed Abby, sparing her a brief glance as he walked by, his attention eagerly focused on the man beside him, his little shoulders squared with grown-up purpose. "I can show you the butterfly loop, too, if you want. It's pretty simple. I don't think you'd have any trouble learning it."

"Great," Noah said, and Abby silently blessed him

for shifting her son's focus from negative to positive. "We'll be back with another load," he called over his shoulder to Abby. "You can wait right there."

That was a nice thing to say. And she did take her time in following her would-be helpers down the stairs and out onto the sun-bathed porch. On the lawn, there was a gathering at the open back of the rented trailer . . . and laughter all around. Joe was there, Denny and Noah, too. Mae had come outside, and Lora, still in her apron and sunbonnet, had wandered over from the garden at the side of the house. Kyle stood, one hand thrust into the back pocket of his baggy jeans, the other dangling long and loosely at his side. He was smiling, transformed from the sullen youth of a few minutes ago into a handsome, gregarious young man who was so obviously—at least in his mother's eyes—in love and exquisitely self-conscious in front of the girl of his dreams.

Lexie Garrett was her mother's daughter, with hair like spun gold and a body already blossoming with womanhood. All she seemed to have inherited from Jeff was the earthy brown of her eyes, a feminine version of his throaty laughter, and, perhaps, a certain determined set to her chin. She was already fifteen, older than Kyle by three months, almost to the day. Abby remembered getting the *Sweetwater Tribune* in a plain manila envelope and seeing the announcement her mother had circled in green marker. *Jeff's daughter,* Mae had printed below the grainy picture of the baby, as if Abby might not know. The birth announcement had begun with a boldface line, "Mr. and Mrs. Jefferson Garrett," and then continued in regular type, ". . . proudly announce the birth of their daughter, Alexis Sarah Garrett." There had been more, a listing of grandparents—all deceased, save one—and the information that Jeff was currently working toward a degree in Journalism from the University of Tulsa and was presently the Assistant Sports Editor for the *Sweetwater Tribune*.

Abby, far from home, newly married, pregnant and weepy, had read the announcement through a dozen times. Then she'd carefully torn the entire newspaper into strips, front page to back, and flushed it down the toilet a handful at a time. It had been a stupid thing to do because she'd clogged the plumbing and had no explanation to offer Mitch, who'd been understandably upset when they'd had to pay to have the pipes cleared. But she couldn't very well tell him that the birth of Jeff's daughter had extinguished her last tiny hope, had forced her to face the fact that the accident and its aftermath were real and not just a huge misunderstanding. Somehow the birth announcement had brought home to her the bitter reality of not only Jeff's choices, but her own.

None of this was Lexie's fault. She was purely innocent of her father's deceit and her mother's duplicity. Which didn't stop Abby from wishing Kyle had chosen someone else—almost anyone else—as the object of his first grand passion.

Denny glanced back and saw her, then sidled away from the group to call to her, motioning her down to join them. "Hey, Mom. Lexie's here."

He said it as if she'd be thrilled, as if Lexie's presence was a gift to be savored. Sweetwater was a small town in every way that counted, and it had been inevitable her sons and Jeff's daughter would come into contact. The boys had been spending a part of their summer vacation with Mae for years, returning to Abby every August with news of who they'd played with and what they'd done. But last August, the events most talked about centered around one girl and one name. Lexie.

Denny openly adored her, repeating often and fervently that she was fun, beautiful, smart, that everybody loved her, that he loved her, too. The more he said about Lexie, the less Kyle had to say. But Abby couldn't fail to note the way her teenaged son ducked his head whenever the name came up. As his mother, she caught the glimmer of secret passions in his eyes, the soft, reticent curve of his smile and knew he was smitten. She had seen that same awestruck expression before—on the September day when Melanie Martin had joined the Senior class at Potter High.

"My name is Melanie Joy Martin," she'd said, her blond curls catching the light, her dimples flashing, her California style an intriguing novelty in the conservative Midwest. "I'm from San Diego and I just moved to Sweetwater. I love music and I love to dance and I just know I'm going to love all of you!"

She'd meant the boys because it was quickly clear Melanie wasn't interested in friendship, despite her efforts to ingratiate herself with those, like Abby, who dared to doubt her sincerity. But in the end, few could resist Melanie's pretty smile and her eagerness to embrace her new life in this small town. Even the teachers fell in love with her, accepting her excuses for barely passing grades, not at all reluctant to blame her lack of academic progress on family misfortune coupled with another state's inefficient educational system. To Abby, though, it had been clear Melanie did only what she had to do to win acceptance from the adults and everything in her power to become the most sought after girl in school. She viewed every male as a potential conquest and every other female as a competitor to be annihilated by fair means or foul. Not many saw her that way and, in truth, even Abby envied Melanie her moonstruck hair, the melting vulnerability in her soft blue eyes, the seductive lure of her woman's body. Every boy at Potter High was struck dumb with teenage lust, and her skill at bewitching the opposite sex spilled over to faculty and alumni, as well. There wasn't a single male in town she couldn't have had for the crooking of a finger.

Except one . . . and he, of course, was the one she wanted.

"Come on, Mom." Denny slipped up beside Abby and took hold of her hand, tugging her down the steps and toward the circle at the back of the Go West trailer.

"Hello, Mrs. Ryan," Lexie said, Jeff's smile flashing like a precious memory across her face. "It's so nice to see you again."

"Hello, Lexie. It's good to see you, too." In the past, on the brief occasions when Abby was in Sweetwater, she'd managed to avoid more than a nodding acknowledgment of Jeff's daughter. Now that would be impossible. Lexie was a presence in Kyle's life and, vicariously, in Denny's. Her grandfather was a resident at Wade House. Jeff had already given Abby fair warning he would be visiting Gideon on a regular basis. Abby knew she had to get past her own prejudices, understood it wasn't fair to punish the child for her parents' sins. Lexie had her mother's beauty and her father's charm, but she also possessed a sweet innocence of spirit completely her own. She deserved a chance.

"Do you have a busy summer planned, Lexie?" Abby asked.

"A couple of weeks at cheerleading camp. Other than that it'll probably be another boring summer."

Joe guffawed. "Now, Lexie, quit trying to make it sound as if you're not the most popular girl in town with somethin' or other goin' on every minute."

"You know that's not true, Mr. Malone." Lexie flashed a modest smile. "My parents hardly let me do anything, and Dad says I can't date until I'm thirty."

"But that doesn't stop the boys from hangin' around, does it?" Joe winked broadly at Kyle. "I remember when Abby was your age. Mae didn't want her dating either, but that didn't stop the boys from comin' around. Your daddy, especially. And your uncle. And a whole passel of others. No, ma'am. There was never a dull minute around Wade House in those days, was there, Mae?"

Mae sniffed. "Not enough for my taste, that's for sure."

"Pshaw!" Lora set her fists on either side of her ample waist, daring anyone to dispute her. "You're always sayin' how you had a horde of young 'uns underfoot back when Abby and Jeff were dating. You loved ever' minute of it, too, and don't you be lettin' these children think otherwise."

Kyle's gaze flicked to Abby, questioning and accusing. She'd never told him about Jeff, never considered it anything her sons needed to know. Until now, when the omission felt, somehow, like a crime.

"The boys know I don't mind if they invite their friends by." Mae nodded brusquely at her grandsons, as if anyone would know she hadn't meant what she'd said. "The boarders like a bit of bustle now and again."

"Truth is, it does us all a world of good to have you young people around," Joe said. "Ya don't have to worry about being quiet, either, cause most of us can't hear worth a hoot anyway."

"Not to rush anyone, but we'd better get these boxes moved out of the trailer before this afternoon gets away from us." Noah moved forward and Lexie jumped from her seat on the trailer's edge, tossing a smile at Kyle, who caught it and returned it with heartbreaking enthusiasm.

A black SUV pulled alongside the curb to park behind the trailer and Lexie's smile brightened. "Hi, Dad," she said and, as Jeff stepped out of the Mercedes, she stepped forward to greet him. "I was hoping I'd see you here."

He closed the car door and draped an arm across her slender shoulders. "This is a pleasant surprise. I thought you were still at practice."

"We finished early and I had Melissa drop me off." She snuggled briefly against his side, becoming for an instant just a little girl who adored her daddy. "I figured you'd come by to see Grampa sometime this afternoon and I could catch a ride home."

"So you came to see your Grampa, huh? I'm sure Kyle being back in town had nothing to do with it." Jeff smiled at Kyle, easily claiming a familiarity Abby hadn't known existed between him and her sons. "I see you and Denny have been helping your mom get moved in."

"We've been emptying this trailer all morning." Kyle stated it as if the whole thing had been his idea, as if he were speaking man to man, as if he and Jeff had an understanding. "We're almost done."

"Wait'll you see my rope, Mr. Garrett." Denny stepped right up to Jeff, eager for his fifteen seconds of attention. "I've been practicing the knots just like you showed me and . . ." He pointed back at Noah. "I'm gonna teach him how to tie some of the hard ones."

Jeff's interest expanded to the group of adults, settling on the newcomer with a certain hesitancy.

"This here's Noah Walker. He's in town to check out the river," Joe said, leaning in promptly to make the introduction. "Noah, this is Jefferson Garrett. He spends his days pretending to be a journalist and way too many evenings trying to convince me and Archie he actually knows what he's doing down there at the *Tribune*."

"Welcome to Sweetwater." Jeff stepped forward to offer a hand and Noah stepped forward to shake it.

The blare of a car horn, loud and long, tore through the moment, drawing the two men apart. A sleek, white Cadillac sped past the trailer and came to an abrupt halt, half-in, half-out of the driveway. And just that quickly the camaraderie on Mae's front lawn turned edgy. Melanie had that affect. Always had. From the start, she'd displayed a special talent in pitting friend against friend, parent against child, brother against brother. Now, as the Mercedes sat cooling in the driveway, the whole group on the lawn, young and old, held a collective breath . . . waiting for Melanie to get out of the car.

The door opened and a melodic tone chimed into the sunny afternoon. She stepped out slowly and turned to face her observers. *Camera on one.* Every move she made seemed choreographed and deliberate, every action—from the positioning of her fingertips on the car roof to the way she pushed her sunglasses up to the top of her head—had a studied perfection. Melanie Martin Garrett was a beautiful woman. Her hair glistened with the silver-gold of her youth. Her skin still retained a fragile, almost translucent, luster. Age showed, though, in the tiny wrinkles of discontent at the corners of her mouth, and there was an icy stillness in her face that only long unhappiness could have etched. But there was a piercing fire in her eyes as they met Abby's across the top of the Cadillac.

"Hello there, Abby," she said, her voice soft and eerily pleasant. "Jeff told me you were back in town." She turned her head as she acknowledged the others, her lips parted in a dead ringer of a smile. "Hello, Miz Mae. Miz Lora. Joe." Her gaze skimmed past Jeff to settle on Noah, studying him with the air of a courtesan, the interest of a lioness. "Hello," she said. "You must be the stranger everyone's talking about."

Noah responded with a cautious tone, "This town must have some grapevine if *everyone* is talking about me."

"I suppose I do have an inside track, since my husband is the editor of our only newspaper." She turned the flirty sunshine of her smile toward Jeff, never quite catching him in its light. "You tell me everything, don't you, darling?"

Lexie angled a shoulder into Jeff's broad chest. His arm slipped around her, but whether it was him trying to protect her or the other way around, Abby couldn't tell. "What are you doing here, Mom?" she asked. "You almost never go out in the afternoons."

"I'd like to know the answer to that, myself," Jeff said.

Melanie's engaging laughter blended for a moment with the tone still pulsing rhythmically from the Cadillac's interior. "Anyone would think you two weren't expecting to see me, that you're not pleased I feel almost like my old self today. I don't know why you're surprised. I'm sure I mentioned this morning at breakfast that I'd be visiting my father-in-law this afternoon. Isn't that the only reason any member of our family would be here? Why else would we bother Miz Mae and her family if not to take care of Grampa?"

The implicit threat wasn't lost on Abby, but damned if she'd let this woman intimidate her or her sons. She turned her smile, purposely, on Lexie. "I hope you never feel you have to have a special reason to drop by, Lexie," she said. "You're welcome at Wade House anytime."

"That's right, Lexie." Mae offered swift and unexpected support. "You come anytime you want."

Melanie slammed the car door, abruptly shutting off the automated chime, and the ensuing quiet felt thick and dangerous. "Let's go up and see Gideon." She came around the front of the Cadillac and onto the front walk. "Lexie? Let's go." It wasn't a question. Command was threaded through the words, giving them a steely *or else* hardness. "Jeff?"

"You go ahead, Mel," he said. "Lexie and I will be up in a minute."

"Lexie? Sweetness?" Melanie extended a hand to her

daughter, her voice sliding into a persuasive cadence. "Come and go with Mommy. You know you want to."

Lexie hesitated, then pulled away from her father and moved, like a soldier deserting the battlefield, to Melanie's side.

Abby felt rather than saw Kyle move to follow the girl and reflexively, she put out a hand to stop him. This was not his war and she intended to keep him out of it.

Melanie threaded her fingers with her daughter's and swung their hands as they walked up the path to the steps. On the second step, she stopped and turned to call over her shoulder. "Come on, Jeff. Gideon's waiting for us."

"I'm going to help bring the rest of these boxes inside," he said and then tacked on an unnecessary and deliberate, "Abby's boxes."

Melanie's smile curved with beautiful precision. "Of course, you are," she said. "You're always such a hero."

Then she led her daughter up onto the porch and into the house, abruptly releasing the group on the lawn from whatever hypnotic spell she had so skillfully woven among them. Noah sprang forward to grab a box from the trailer and offer it to Joe, who was waiting to carry it inside. Kyle snagged two small boxes marked "bath stuff" and moved to catch up with Joe. Lora chattered to herself as she went back to work in the garden. Mae sent Denny to seek out the last of the strawberries for supper before she bustled around to the side of the house and out of sight.

"How long are you going to be in town?" Jeff posed the question to Noah as he grabbed a box marked "kitchen appliances." "I know someone who'd love to pick your brain about water quality."

And a moment later, only Abby was left standing outside on the lawn, alone except for the company of an old, unwelcome resentment and a new and reluctant feeling of sympathy for Jeff.

Chapter 6

"Don't walk away when I'm talking to you," Melanie said.

Jeff yanked a denim shirt off its hanger with enough force to create an agitated twanging of wire hanger against metal rod. "I was getting a shirt." He stepped out of the closet as he jabbed an arm through one stiff cotton sleeve. The dry cleaners had over-starched the shirt again. An occurrence that only seemed to happen when Melanie took it upon herself to gather up and drop off his dirty laundry.

"I realize you don't want to discuss this with me, Jeff. I'm not stupid. But don't think for a second I'll turn a blind eye while you embarrass me in front of our daughter and everyone else in this town. If you're going to show such disrespect for me, then you can at least confine it to the privacy of our bedroom." She stood, perfectly calm, perfectly composed, in the center of the room, hands clasped, breathing normally, while he was already so angry he had to concentrate just to button his shirt.

"*We* don't have a bedroom, Mel. But if you're so concerned about privacy, you should have closed *my* bedroom door when you came in. Or do you want Lexie to hear this?"

"That's just like you, Jeff. Blaming me, as if I want

to argue with you like this. As if I don't want what's best for Lexie."

He walked over and closed the door. Because he knew she wouldn't. "I'm taking her to the goddamned carnival, Melanie. You didn't want her to go unsupervised, so I said I'd take her and whoever else she wanted to invite. How the hell was I to know she'd invite Abby's son? Or that you would care if she did?"

"You knew exactly who she meant to invite and how I'd feel about it. I wouldn't be surprised if you planned the whole thing just so you'd have an excuse to spend time with your precious Abby."

"I'm spending time with my daughter," he said tightly. "This isn't some secret rendezvous. Hell, half the town will be there. Even if I wanted to conduct some kind of illicit affair, believe me, I wouldn't do it at the Summer Daze Festival."

"Of course you would, Jeff. You do whatever you want, whenever you want, and the people in this town stand in line to applaud you for it. They all feel sorry for you because you've told them I'm a horrible wife and a terrible mother. I know what they say about me. I've always known. But that doesn't mean I'll stand back and wring my hands while you carry on with your high school girlfriend."

"This isn't about Abby," he said, although Melanie's quarrel with him always had been, at one level or another, about Abby. "This is about Lexie inviting a friend to go with her to the carnival."

"After I expressly told her to stay away from that boy."

"She's fifteen, Melanie. Telling her to stay away from someone is like waving a red flag."

"Especially when you encourage her to defy me. Honestly, Jeff, sometimes I wonder if you care anything about her at all. Kyle Ryan is bad news. He's nothing but trouble waiting to happen. His father was an alcoholic who died in a barroom brawl, for God's sake. His mother can't even hold down a decent job. Now that she's a widow, I'm sure she'll expect her mother to take care of her and her kids while she sits over there thinking of ways to get you away from me."

He almost took the bait, almost opened his mouth to defend Abby, to declare once and for all that he was nothing to her. And that she was nothing to him. But he wasn't stupid, either. "You believe what you want, Melanie. I'm taking Lexie to the carnival."

"And that boy?"

His jaw clamped in frustration. "Yes, Mel. Lexie invited Kyle and I'm taking him, too."

"Against my wishes."

"If that's the way you want to look at it, yes."

She nodded, indicting him in one simple motion. "So, none of this can possibly be your fault."

There was no way to win this, but he made one last attempt to reason with her. "Look, Melanie. Lexie likes Kyle. If anything, she probably feels a little sorry for him. Inviting him to the carnival was a thoughtful thing for her to do, the kind of thing she does because she's a great kid. Don't turn this into something it isn't just because you've never liked Abby."

"And you've never stopped loving her. Your feelings for Abby are at issue here, Jeff. Not mine."

Down the hall, Lexie's stereo, and the throbbing rhythms of *Lady Marmalade,* kicked up a decibel, pulsing a new thread of tension into the room. Jeff knew the walls of this house could never be thick enough to protect her. "Go with us, Melanie," he said, forcing himself to make the concession. "Then you'll know that this year's carnival will be no different from any other. Lexie and her friends will ride the rides and spend their money on cotton candy and Pepsi. I'll take a few pictures for next week's paper and talk to people I haven't seen for a while. If you go, I'll even treat you to a ride on the Ferris wheel."

"I'm not going anywhere near that river," Melanie said, attacking him from a different angle. "And I can't believe you'd take our daughter there, either."

"The park is more than a mile from the river. That's no reason for Lexie to have to miss out on the carnival."

"What about this reason? I'm terrified something will happen to her if she goes anywhere near that place."

"You're terrified of not getting your way, Melanie. Let's not pretend this has anything to do with the river or what happened there."

Her eyes misted with sudden tears. "You act as if I don't love my own daughter, as if I want to punish her for your mistake."

Somehow, she always brought it around to that—his mistake. He faced the mirror and carelessly ran a comb through his thick, dark hair, noticing—not for the first time—that the silver at his temples was no longer blending in with much subtlety. He was going gray. Which could be considered a sign of maturity. Or just a marker of how fast a lifetime passed, whether spent in honor or remorse. "I'm taking our daughter to the carnival tonight," he repeated for the last time as he turned again to Melanie. "Don't bother to wait up for us."

The tears evaporated. "If anything happens to my daughter, Jeff, I will hold you personally responsible."

My daughter. It was her ultimate threat, the bottom line of their relationship. *"I'll take her away from you, Jeff,"* she'd said often enough for him to believe her. *"I'll make sure she never looks at you the same way again. You know I can. You know I will."* He did know, which was why he stood here now, bound by that first mistake, entangled in all the mistakes that had come after. "Nothing is going to happen to Lexie," he said and walked out of the room.

"I guess I shouldn't have invited Kyle to go with us to the carnival." Lexie, her learner's permit barely a week old, kept her eyes on the road, her hands in the proper ten and two positions on the steering wheel. She kept her voice offhand, her expression carefully neutral. "I didn't think she'd get so upset."

"This isn't about you, Lexie. Or Kyle. You know that."

She signaled her turn, far in advance of the intersection. "Sure," she said. "I know." They'd had this same conversation in one form or another her whole life. It was choreographed right down to the smile she flashed at him now, reassuring him she was okay, that she understood what they never said aloud.

Melanie's erratic moods were their secret, the private truth they skirted around, but never openly acknowledged. Tonight Jeff hated the charade even more than usual, but he played his part, too, and changed the subject. "Do you remember that time you brought Joey Horton home with you and announced you were going to adopt him?"

She winkled her nose either in disbelief or disgust, it was hard to tell which, as she eased the SUV to a careful stop well back from the stop sign. "Joey Horton?"

He nodded. "I think you were five. Maybe six. One of your more precocious stages."

"I can't believe I ever wanted Joey Horton for a brother, no matter what stage I was in."

"Oh, you didn't want us to adopt him. You'd decided he needed a mother and you were going to be it."

"You're making that up." She looked carefully in both directions before moving forward into the intersection. "I never even liked Joey. He had this really annoying habit of sticking his finger in other people's ears."

"That must have come later, because you were all set to get a lawyer and go to court to adopt him. Maybe you thought you could break him of his bad habits, I don't know. I do remember you told him to call me Gramps."

Lexie slid him a skeptical glance. "If you say I told him to call Mom, Grandma, I'll know you're lying."

He smiled and settled more comfortably in the passenger seat. "I may not be the dad you deserve, Lexie, but I've never lied to you." Even as he said it, the lie clutched in his gut. The sin of omission. The half-truth of silence. Those were lies, too, and he was guilty. But not in her eyes, and that, perhaps, was the only thing that saved him. "You're the most important person in my life, Lexie. No matter what anyone ever tells you about me, I want you to remember that."

"No one's going to say anything bad about you, Dad. Especially not to me." She braked as a dark blue pickup drew alongside them, slowing the SUV, and then checking her left mirror nervously until the truck had passed. She was overly cautious. Or overly conscious of his presence and wanting so much to show him she was a good driver. "And besides," she said firmly as the pickup's taillights disappeared into the early evening haze. "What makes you think I'd believe them if they did?"

Her smile was pure sunshine, her faith in him still rooted in a little girl's unshakable ideal of her daddy. In her eyes, he was protector, buddy, coach, pal, teacher, and manic fan. He was stronger, smarter, better than any of her friends' fathers and wise enough to allow her a healthy measure of independence while never letting her forget she wasn't alone. He made her laugh when no one else could, and he always kept his promises. He was the one man who would never find a single flaw in her. To him she would forever be the most beautiful, the brightest, the best at whatever she tried, and she loved him now as she'd loved him from the start . . . with a fierce, untested loyalty.

"I want you to know how proud I am to be your dad," he said, emotion thickening helplessly in his throat. "No matter what happens, Lexie, I want you to know how much I love you, how much I'll always love you."

She glanced at him curiously before she signaled the turn onto the cracked and narrow two-lane which would take them to the Wade House. "I love you, too, Dad."

It was enough, but he felt compelled to add, "I've made a lot of mistakes in my life, Lexie. I want you to understand I'm not perfect."

"Believe it or not," she said. "I do know that."

Her sudden giggle engulfed him in gratitude. Despite Melanie, and yet because of her, too, he had more than any man had a right to expect. "You always were too smart for your old pa," he said, grinning back.

"Dad?"

"Yes?"

"You don't mind about Kyle, do you?"

"No, why would I?"

"Because you used to date his mom?"

Jeff barely hesitated. "That was so many years ago I can hardly remember."

"Mom remembers. She thinks you still love Mrs. Ryan."

"I wish you hadn't heard that, Lexie, because it's not true. Nothing about Abby Ryan is the way your mother made it sound."

"Why does she do that, Dad? Why does she make everything into a big deal when it doesn't have to be?"

Because she could. Because misery loved company. Because she hated him more than she loved their daughter. "I don't know, Lexie. That's just the way she is."

The lie came full circle as a glint of late afternoon

sun hit the windshield, striking gold through Lexie's hair. She raised a hand to shield her eyes, and Jeff flipped down the visor on her side, then on his. "Should be a good night for the carnival," he said. "There's going to be a full moon . . . and you know what that means."

"Sheriff Ray is going to have his hands full?"

Jeff laughed. "It means this will be the best Summer Daze Festival we've ever had."

"You say that every year, even if it's not a full moon."

He looked over at her and smiled. His daughter. His. "I'm always right about it, too," he said, settling more comfortably in the passenger seat. "And just for the record, I think you're a very good driver."

Her cheeks flushed with pleasure. "Thanks, Gramps."

Chapter 7

Jeff aimed the camera—a Nikon F5—adjusted the telephoto lens, and snapped off a shot of Barbara Ann Wertz, gray hair fuzzed around her flushed face, as she lifted another batch of her famous Danish cheese puffs out of the deep fat fryer. The smell of hot grease and powdered cinnamon-sugar curled out of her booth and meandered through the park grounds with a *come hither* aroma, drawing carnival-goers of every age, size, and shape. Barbara Ann only made the melt-in-your-mouth pastries once a year now that her husband, Harold, had developed high cholesterol. Despite annual campaigns by Mary Jo and Ginger down at the Sweetwater Café to get the recipe, Barbara Ann kept her cheese puff secrets. And since carnival time was the only time they could be had, there was always a line in front of the silver concession trailer with its red-striped awning.

Jeff clipped off a half-dozen shots of people waiting in line, caught beefy and bald Beau Hartshaw as he stepped away from the booth, his mouth open, ready to bite into his much anticipated cheese puff, and captured Lisamarie Goodnight batting her pretty eyelashes at young Jimmy Truladoe. Jeff knew he'd have to keep Sam from running that picture in the Trib and stirring up the ancient feud between Harlan Goodnight and Jimmy's Granny Trudy. Why those two old people hated each other so much was anybody's guess, but Jeff didn't want his newspaper held responsible for striking the spark that set hostilities in motion again. Sam, on the other hand, lived for opportunities to stir up trouble, and Jeff had to remind him on a weekly basis to exercise some discretion.

"Way to go, Austin!"

"Whoo-ee, that was sweet!"

Jeff swung around, already adjusting the focus on the cheering group of teenagers grouped around the basketball toss. He clicked off a series of shots as Austin Lingo, Sweetwater's six-foot-seven hope of someday making it to the NBA, sank a winning basket and walked off with a huge purple alligator as his prize. Turning in an unhurried circle, Jeff snapped pictures of whoever came into frame. He nabbed a shot of Brad Lawrence, the vice principal at the high school, kissing his bride of three months as their cage swung gently at the top of the Ferris wheel. As he directed the camera lens back toward the midway, Jeff captured a shot of Terri and Larry Vincent at the merry-go-round, each with an arm around the thick, diapered waist of their toddler, grinning like lunatics as Little Larry jumped and wiggled, awaiting his first ride on a carousel. The camera passed over, then swung back to the Howard twins, matching eight-year-olds in flowered coveralls and ponytails, plotting mischief on their unsuspecting brother, Justin, who was tearing off a cottony plume of spun sugar candy as he approached their hiding place.

Jeff moved on without recording the twins' larceny, figuring the Howard kids had plenty of practice in outsmarting each other and an equal number of un-avenged crimes between them. No reason to document one more. He and Alex had fussed and wrangled their way through many a summer themselves. Many a winter, too, for that matter. They'd even had one serious altercation at the carnival that involved flying fists, some kicking, a fair measure of pushing and pounding, a bit of mediocre wrestling, and a final, near-concussion-level collision of heads. The incident had left Alex with a chipped incisor and Jeff with a tooth-sized scar above his left eye. They'd been too boastful of their separate injuries to stay mad at each other for long, though. What fun was having stitches in your head if you couldn't one-up a measly chipped tooth? And vice versa.

The excited squeals of the Howard twins escalated as they raced past Jeff, having snatched their prize right out of Justin's hands. "I'm telling Mom!" he screamed as he came pounding after them.

Jeff stepped out of the way and had to pick his way over the obstacle course of power lines that snaked from the generator at the back side of the midway to the various concessions. He clicked off a couple of shots of a torn poster tacked onto the back of the ticket booth. Summer Daze! How Sweet It Is! it proclaimed in a colorful calligraphy.

He and Alex had survived plenty of carnivals, a childhood's worth of sweet summers, an edgy level of sibling rivalry, and they'd still managed to grow up with some brotherly affection intact. Until that last summer. Until the rivalry bled over into real conflict. Until they each wanted the same girl.

For the longest time, Jeff hadn't been able to remember his brother with anything but regret. Guilt had been the only emotion he allowed himself to feel, the only emotion he felt he had any right to feel.

But then Lexie was born and gradually the good memories came back. Slowly at first, but they came back. And he'd learned to appreciate times like now when a memory flicked through his consciousness, bringing a fleeting peace, an instant's pleasure, allowing him to set aside the ending for a moment and remember some of the good that had come before.

With a mechanical jolt, the carousel revved into motion. The calliope slurred and then launched its jaunty, brassy music into the cacophonic noises that were part and parcel of the carnival. Jeff moved back into the flow of human traffic and swung the camera in a slow circle, adjusting the focus as he went, looking for that one shot that would best capture the spirit of this year's carnival for the Trib's front page.

Opportunities were everywhere he looked, but nothing sparked his interest until the frame suddenly filled with Abby. Her brown hair was pulled loosely back and tied at her nape with a narrow white ribbon. She wore faded denims and a pale green shirt, tails out, short sleeves cuffed midway down her arms. It was the casual kind of outfit she'd always favored. No frills. No fuss. Strictly comfort. She looked like the girl of his youth, his first true taste of yearning.

Unaware of his filtered observance, she stooped beside Denny, her arm settling around his thin shoulders, as together they watched the blurring, flashing lights of the Himalaya ride sweep up and around and down again, carrying its passengers on a fast, dizzying trip to nowhere. Abby's expression mirrored her son's—a mix of awe, excitement, and trepidation. Jeff snapped the picture before he realized he meant to do so and, though she couldn't have heard, she must have sensed the intrusion because she turned her head and saw him. He held the camera steady on her and for a moment—no longer than it took for the shutter to fall a second time with a soft *ka-thunk*—memories twisted through him of other nights, other carnivals, of other sweet-smelling, tender summers when she had been his to love.

Rising now, she took Denny's hand and walked toward the carousel as if neither the moment nor the memories meant anything to her at all.

"Hey, Dad! Dad! Up here!"

Lexie's voice, floating on laughter, drifted down to

him, and he looked up to see her poised atop the shifting floor of the Spook House, illuminated by the flashing lights behind her and protected from a fall by a section of safety fencing that was made to look broken and brittle for effect.

He lowered the camera and waved. "You've gone through there a dozen times already. Aren't you scared yet?"

She laughed and shook her head. "But it's scarier than last year's."

Screams erupted from inside the fun house, magnified by the interior microphones into hollow, echoing shrieks of laughter. Lexie laughed, too, tossing her head and sending strands of her moonstruck hair brushing across the face of the boy who stood close beside her. She turned to say something to Kyle there on the narrow passageway and he leaned into her, ducking his head and putting his ear near her lips in order to hear her over the noise. Jeff watched the tilt of her head as she leaned back to listen to Kyle's response and recognized the protective, claiming slant of his shoulder as Kyle bent forward to speak into her ear.

From the moment the boy had hopped into the backseat of the SUV tonight, Jeff had told himself Lexie was just being nice to the new kid in town, that there was nothing even vaguely romantic stirring between his daughter and Abby's son. He'd told himself there was nothing there for a father to worry about. Except, of course, that as a father, Jeff worried about *nothing* on a regular basis. And now his heart thudded painfully at the sight of them together, at the sparkle of excitement he could see in his daughter, at the yearning written so clearly on Kyle's young face. It was there . . . those first almost unconscious steps into awareness. And Jeff wanted to grab Lexie back and keep her as his little girl for another year or two or ten. Yet at the same time, he felt a conflicting pride that she was growing up and into her own life.

As he'd always known she would.

As he wouldn't want to stop her from doing.

Which didn't mean he wasn't sorely tempted to climb the facade of the Spook House and tear that boy's hands off of his daughter. Before he knew it, he'd raised the camera and fired off several shots, recording what exactly he wasn't sure, but feeling somehow vindicated nonetheless.

"If you get a good one, could I have a copy?"

It was Abby's voice, her request rerouted his attention, and he lowered the camera as he turned to find her beside him. "What?"

"A picture," she said. "Kyle never lets me take his picture and I thought if you got one, maybe you'd let me have a copy."

"Sure." He felt awkward suddenly and eager. "I operate on the theory that if I shoot enough rolls of film, a few frames are bound to turn out. We'll hope there's at least one good shot of the kids."

The kids. How odd to be saying that to the woman he'd once believed would be the mother of his children. "Where's Denny?" he asked, looking past her for the little boy. "Don't tell me you let him ride the Himalaya without you? That used to be your favorite ride."

"He opted for the merry-go-round." She turned to look toward the carousel. "For the fifteenth time." She waved and Jeff followed her gaze to where Denny straddled a golden-maned lion that was frozen forever in a silent mighty roar. "He's not a particularly daring little boy."

"Maybe he's just afraid you'll get sick riding the Himalaya."

She looked at him. Frowned.

"It's happened before," he defended his remark. "And you know how much kids hate to be embarrassed by their parents. I'll ask him if he wants to ride it with me."

"I'd rather you didn't," she said, her eyes turning again toward the Spook House, worrying over the same bit of *nothing* that was bothering him. But Lexie and Kyle were no longer on the parapet, and another set of teens had taken over the platform. Abby brought her chin down slowly and met his eyes, sharing one unguarded instant of concern before she looked away, withdrew again into herself. She rocked slightly on her heels and stuck her hands, unself-consciously, into the back pockets of her jeans. It was a pose as familiar to him as the carnival itself. He'd seen her stand like that a million times. He used to like to trap her hands there with his own, liked the way her body had curved into his in response, loved the smile she offered as a teasing ransom. "Well, okay," she said now, her voice dismissing their past as if it had never been. "I just wanted to ask you about the picture."

"Sure." He wanted to say more, to keep her talking, to keep her from going away, from leaving him. He wanted to ask her why she'd rather he didn't ride any of the rides with Denny. But, of course, he knew. "I'll let you know how the shots come out."

She nodded, turned, and strolled over to the metal fencing that encircled the merry-go-round, her hands coming free to swing gently at her sides as she walked, the corners of her mouth lifting as she watched for her son to circle around on the upbeat of the music.

Jeff thought about framing the shot—capturing Abby's expressive silhouette while the carousel blurred with movement behind her. She lifted one hand in a wave as the lion whirled past, but Denny kept both hands wrapped around the pole, holding on with all his might, and he looked neither right nor left to see her. It would have made an interesting picture—the little boy on the lion, his face set and unsmiling, determined to finish the ride he'd begun, the mother wanting him to know she'd be there when it was over—but Jeff didn't raise the camera.

He just stood in the middle of the fairway, jostled by the crowd, isolated amidst the noisy clutter, watching Abby, who stood only a few feet away, closer than she'd been to him in years . . . and he felt more alone than he had in sixteen summers.

Chapter 8

ryank432: grounded? what for?

lexiegarr: she says it's because I left the bathroom in a mess but it's really because of the picture in yesterday's paper . . . the one of us at the spook house.

ryank432: your dad was the one with the camera.

lexiegarr: she can't ground him so i'm the one who's stuck in my room for a week . . . for leaving a bottle of hairspray out! i hate her!

ryank432: parents suck. they should go away and not come back until we're eighteen.

lexiegarr: or like ever.

ryank432: yeah. we don't need them telling us what to do all the time. my mom's always on me about something.

lexiegarr: at least your mom doesn't ground you for no reason.

ryank432: no, she makes me share a room with my twerpy little brother.

lexiegarr: i think denny's sweet.

ryank432: that's cuz you're a pushover.

lexiegarr: i'm not either. i'm tough!

ryank432: yeah, sure, whatever you say.

lexiegarr: i am tough. i have to be to live with her. I HATE BEING GROUNDED! I HATE HER!!

ryank432:   want me to come over and do the rescue thing?

lexiegarr: you'd do that?

ryank432:   give me five minutes to find a ladder.

lexiegarr: that's sweet, but not tonight. too risky.

ryank432:   tomorrow night?

lexiegarr: maybe. yes, okay.

ryank432:   you mean it? i can see you tomorrow night?

lexiegarr: if you want to.

ryank432:   i want to.

lexiegarr: you'll have to sneak out.

ryank432:   not a problem. you?

lexiegarr: i do it all the time.

ryank432:   where do you go?

lexiegarr: a place by the river. i'll take you there . . . unless you're scared of the dark.

ryank432:   i'm from chicago. nothing here in hicksville can scare me.

lexiegarr: you might be surprised.

ryank432:   i won't be scared. i can't wait to see you.

lexiegarr: you won't see me for almost two whole weeks once I leave for cheerleading camp. i've never not wanted to go before.

ryank432:   maybe you'll still be grounded.

lexiegarr: no, she wants me to go.

ryank432:   i wish you didn't have to. will you miss me?

lexiegarr: maybe. will you miss me?

ryank432:   every second. can't you sneak out tonight?

lexiegarr: no, you'll have to wait. be tough . . . like me.
ryank432:   what time tomorrow?
lexiegarr: midnight. not sooner.
ryank432:   are you taking me to a dark and scary place by the river?
lexiegarr: if you're brave.
ryank432:   i'm the bravest.
lexiegarr: bring a flashlight anyway.
ryank432:   will do.
lexiegarr: then i'll see you tomorrow @ midnight.
ryank432:   tomorrow @ midnight.

Chapter 9

The air was filthy rich with morning, dense with dew and a shadowy coolness, thickened by a noisy chorus of birdsong. A blue jay squawked loudly from the low-hanging branch of a river birch as Abby trotted down the steps of the garage apartment and walked around to the side porch of the house. Squirrels scattered from their breakfast hunt at her approach and a newt scurried across the sidewalk and darted under Mae's leafy rhododendron. At the base of the concrete steps that led up to the wide veranda, Abby stopped to yawn. Linking her fingers, she extended her arms over her head, palms out, pushing up into a long, luxurious stretch.

A hint of breeze held the promise of heat, and she knew without having to think about it that the day would soon turn gloriously hot, that the air would swelter by noon, and the sun would be relentless and unforgiving until long after supper. Only midnight would bring relief again, sheeting the air with this same sweet softness until dawn banded the horizon tomorrow morning and the summer heat gathered for another assault. It seemed like a very long time since she'd felt certain of anything, not deep in her gut where it counted, and if simply knowing the day ahead would be a scorcher made her feel confident and calm, then Abby would accept that as the gift it was.

Allowing herself one more cleansing yawn, she planted one foot firmly on the ground, propped the other Nike-clad heel on the middle step, and eased into a pleasantly painful stretch. She hadn't had a real run since before the For Sale sign went up at the house in Lisle. But today she was turning over a new leaf, getting back into shape.

Whatever that meant.

At the lowest point in her marriage, she'd been in the best physical shape of her life. She'd pushed her speed until she could run a mile in eight minutes, three miles in twenty-one. She'd pushed herself until she could outrun Mitch . . . to his consternation and her own secret delight. But as soon as she outpaced him, he stopped. Stopped running. Stopped trying. Stopped pretending they had anything in common except a dying marriage and two sad little boys.

Her mother hadn't raised a quitter, though, so Abby kept running, kept trying, kept pretending. But the faster she ran, the harder she tried, the more she pretended that disaster wasn't nipping at her heels, the closer it came. Until finally, with Mitch's death, it had caught her.

Clasping her ankle with both hands, she extended the stretch across her hips and down through her right leg. Across her shoulders and back, along her hips, her thighs and calves, she recognized the protest of muscles ignored into complacency. A month ago that would have been enough to make her reconsider. But not today. Today, she would run as far and as fast as she could. She would run until she convinced herself to take the job she'd been offered in Tulsa. She'd run until driving over an hour one way to the hospital seemed like a fair exchange for a paycheck. She'd run until she could justify the shift work and the time she'd have to spend away from the boys as a necessary evil. She'd run until she could no longer hear her mother's voice circling in her thoughts like a fussy, fretful crow. *You need to work, Abby. You need to start building up some kind of nest egg. You need to think about how you're going to manage when Kyle is ready for college. You can't afford to wait, Abby. You can't afford to be so picky. You need to get a job.*

Abby knew all those things. She was, after all, her mother's child. She understood that Mae nagged out of fear, that her intention wasn't to be critical, but concerned, that the core of her complaints was rooted in her sense of responsibility and her own perception of love. Abby remembered the fights, the tears, the tension, and eventually the silence that had existed between her parents. A down-to-earth pragmatist and a pie-in-the-sky dreamer, Mae and Charlie had probably never had any real shot at creating a happy home. Their relationship wound its way through Abby's memories, their unhappiness scarring her childhood and her young psyche, and she realized now that she had repeated its pattern in her own marriage. Except she'd gone sooner to the silence with Mitch, not giving up the fight as her father had done, but taking it underground. And here she was, doing the same with her mother. Allowing Mae to fret and peck, allowing herself to be motivated by guilt and the childish desire to please her mother . . . and resenting both Mae's lack of trust and her own lack of courage.

Okay, so maybe she had dawdled and dragged her feet about looking for work. It wasn't as if she hadn't sent out a dozen résumés even before she loaded the Blazer and left Chicago. It wasn't like she'd been lolling around the house, refusing to fill out applications or go on interviews. There hadn't been any calls to answer, and she couldn't just manufacture an opening somewhere. But the more Mae had fussed about her being without a job, the less enthusiasm she'd had for finding one, the harder Mae pushed her toward hospital work, the more Abby wished she could do something else, anything else. How was it that she had come this far in her life, faced up to so many untenable truths about herself, only to arrive under Mae's roof and rebel like the child her mother still seemed to believe she was? Had she always cut off her nose just to spite her mother?

Oh, yes, Abby thought, this morning she would run. She wanted to run.

Up on the veranda, the screen door opened outward with a low screak and Noah stepped out. He was dressed as she was, in dark running shorts and a white tank, white running shoes sleekly expensive and top of the line. Except hers weren't that new. Or expensive. It could be that his just looked better because of the contrast of his tanned ankles emerging from the snowy white band of his sport socks, but somehow she didn't think that totally accounted for the difference. The truth was Noah looked like a serious runner, a dedicated runner, tanned and fit, with no sign of neglect showing in any of his impressive muscles.

He caught sight of her and grinned. "Wow, a running partner. This place has the Comfort Lodge beat all to pieces."

She smiled in return. "You should know by now that at Wade House we pride ourselves on going the extra mile."

He trotted down the steps to stand beside her at the base of the stairs, hands loose at his sides, head up, looking as if he owned the morning and a piece of the sky. "Great morning for a run," he said. "There's nothing like fresh air to clear a headache. How far do you usually go?"

"It's two miles to the doughnut shop. Whether or not I run back depends on how many doughnuts I eat." She changed legs and settled into another long stretch, turning her head to look at him, gauging how quickly he'd register the joke.

He considered it before giving a solemn nod. "If

you drink eight ounces of water in between bites, it shouldn't slow you down. Theoretically."

She smiled.

He smiled back . . . and then he widened his stance, leaned over and put both hands flat on the sidewalk, his knees barely even flexing under the strain. He did the single stretch with the sort of athletic grace that seemed both effortless and arrogant. Abby had seen Mitch do the same exercise a thousand times. With the same cocksure ease. Before they were married and for a long time afterward, Mitch had maintained his physical edge with hardly any effort, taking a fierce pride in what Mother Nature had granted him without prejudice or personal sacrifice. But then, one day, Abby had run faster, and after that his belly bulged, his ego shrank, and he gave up any effort at challenging his body to be something it no longer was. She admired Noah's agility, the powerful sinewy flow of his body and, somehow, she resented him for reminding her of the husband she'd chosen.

"You don't mind if I run with you?" he asked, although it wasn't really a question. Something in his tone, too, reminded her of Mitch. Something about the way his voice conveyed a granting of pleasure, rather than a request it never occurred to him might be rejected.

"I don't mind," she said. Because he wasn't Mitch. Because she was tired of running alone. "As long you'll buy the doughnuts."

"If Miz Mae heard you say that, her homemade buttermilk biscuits would burst right into flames."

"We all have our problems." Moving away from the stairs, Abby did a couple more stretches, pulling left heel to left hip, then right heel to right hip. "For instance, I need a job."

"So I've heard." He came up beside her, waiting for her to finish stretching and set the first pace of their run. "The talk at the breakfast table is running six to zero against taking the Tulsa job. The men—Joe, especially—don't want you driving that far everyday. Too much wear and tear on your vehicle, not to mention your nerves. The women—Miz Violet, mainly—believe hospitals are too demanding and would prefer that you oust someone named Holly the Hussy and take over her position with the elementary school."

"And do you have an opinion?"

"Well, I'm very interested in meeting Holly the Hussy, whether you take the job or not."

Abby laughed and began a leisurely jog across the summer lawn. "Let me hazard a guess that all of this discussion took place when my mother was out of earshot."

"Not all of it," Noah said, falling easily into step beside her as they reached the pavement. "Day before yesterday, she told everyone at the table they needed to get busy mindin' their own business. Which they did, until she left the room again."

The automatic play of her mother's voice whirred into gear in Abby's head. *You need to work, Abby. You can't afford to wait, Abby. You can't have everything you want, Abby.* But she didn't want everything. She wanted a job that left her enough time and energy to raise her sons. More now than right after Mitch died, she felt they needed the security of her presence. The harder Kyle tried to push her away, the tighter Denny clung, the more she sensed that they were afraid she, too, wouldn't be there when they needed her. But she had to work to support them, too, and she had yet to find an acceptable compromise between the two. "I imagine I'll take the hospital position," she said, unable to see another choice. Unless she wanted to clerk for minimum wage at the Piggly Wiggly . . . and she didn't even want to imagine what Mae would have to say about that.

"Sweetwater isn't exactly a hotbed of employment opportunities."

"Oh, come on," he said, nudging up the pace before Abby had even settled into it. "I'm sure I've seen a Help Wanted sign in the window of Baxter's Barber Shop. I bet you'd be great with a razor and some hot lather."

She laughed again, surprised at how easy it was. Mitch had been able to do that, too, catching her with some silly, nonsensical remark. He'd been charming and funny and exciting. In the beginning. She couldn't figure out why he was so much on her mind this morning. Noah didn't really look like him, even if there was some intangible resemblance. "I would be great at haircuts," she said. "I used to cut the boys' hair when they were little."

"There you go. Problem solved."

"If only it were that simple."

He made the turn at the corner a half-step ahead of her. "Sometimes it helps to think outside the box. Just because you have a nursing degree doesn't mean the only thing you can do is nursing."

"I suppose there's always the Piggly Wiggly, but I didn't struggle through school with a toddler on my hip so I could earn minimum wage." Abby heard her voice, but the words coming out of her mouth belonged to Mae, spinning sourly out of the litany inside her head. It was her mother who believed being out of work was shameful. It was Mae's idea that not using the college degree that had cost so much money was unthinkable. Driving to Tulsa wasn't so bad, Mae had said. Why, people did it every day.

But then it wasn't Mae who had to make the sacrifice.

It was Abby and her boys.

"I didn't say anything about minimum wage," Noah continued, still a step ahead and gaining ground. "If you don't want to drive to Tulsa—and I sure wouldn't blame you if you didn't—then you should look for a job here in Sweetwater."

"And where—other than Baxter's Barber Shop—do you suggest I should look?"

"I don't know. There must be a doctor or two in a town this size. Maybe you could start there."

"Dr. Grayson gets an endless pool of medical tech students from the Community College and the clinic just filled their nursing position with a PA." She heard the gruff edge in her voice and made an effort to soften it. After all, Noah was only trying to help. "I checked with both places already."

They ran in silence for a moment, only the slap of their shoes on the concrete for conversation. "And Holly the Hussy?" he asked, making it not quite a question.

"Holly Crandell," Abby supplied. "School nurse. The one and only. She's probably ten years from retirement. Maybe more."

"What about a nursing home? Is there one of those somewhere around here? I've heard they're always hiring."

"That's because the pay is substandard, and the workload is heavy and emotionally draining." She nudged her pace up to come even with Noah. "I don't think I could do it . . . not at this point in my life."

"Okay. So there aren't any nursing jobs . . . what else can you do?"

"Well, I can tap dance a little."

"Mmm, I can see it now—'Abby, the tap-dancing barber.'"

"Tempting," she said. "But I don't think this town is ready for anything that . . . upscale."

He grinned back at her. "I guess we need to scale back your job search to less dramatic talents then. What else do you enjoy doing?"

There had been a time when she would have reeled

off an answer as long as her arm, but now nothing came to mind. Which felt odd. And a little frightening. "I don't know. It's been a long time since I actually thought about that. I'm not even sure I would say I enjoy working as a nurse."

"You need a change, Abby. Something to challenge you. Just look at me. Happy as a crawdad because I love what I do. Every day's different. Rivers change almost moment to moment. I never know what I'm going to discover next. Maybe you should get a job like mine."

"Hanging out with the gnats and mosquitos while you test for nasty germs and who-knows-what-kind of awful pollutants in the water?" She wrinkled her nose at the thought of it. "Not my cup of tea, believe me. No pun intended."

His grin was quick and ready. "The old Arkansas is a little heavy on the bugs," he said. "But that just means it'll keep me busy and in the area for a month or so, and that makes me happy."

"I'm glad you like it here."

"I do. There's something about it that . . . I don't know. It feels familiar to me, I guess." He shrugged. "But then I've been in a lot of river towns and, in one way or another, they all seem familiar. It's like the past and the present coexist in them, overlapping somehow, until it's almost impossible to tell the difference. I like thinking about that, imagining how this town would have looked twenty years ago." Having drawn a full step ahead again, he had to glance back to look at her. "What can I say? Put me anywhere near a river and I'm in my element."

"I hate the river."

"Then I guess I won't worry about you trying to take over my job." His skin glistened with the sheen of exertion, and Abby felt the prickle of sweat wicking up through her pores as she forced her body to move faster, to draw even with him yet again. They were running now, faster than she would have preferred, their shoes striking the pavement in rhythm, their breathing soft, but audible. "Let's see now," he said. "We've eliminated tap-dancing barber and my line of work. I think we're making progress. Now all we have to do is come up with a career field that interests you. It doesn't even have to be a career. Just one of those ideas that appealed to you as a child. What did you want to be when you grew up?"

"A princess." She said the first thing that came to mind. "My daddy used to tease that he'd stolen me from the royal family of Persimmon Hollow."

"A grave loss to Persimmon Hollow."

"Then for one whole summer—I think I was eight—I wanted to become one of Charlie's Angels." She smiled, remembering. "I'm afraid none of my little girl ambitions had much basis in reality."

"Before you went to college then. You must have considered doing something other than nursing."

She had. The memory sobered her in a heartbeat. She and Jeff had planned out a whole future together. He'd go to the local junior college while she finished high school. They'd go to KU together. He'd major in Journalism, she'd major in Marketing, and afterward, they'd take the money his grandparents had left in trust for him and buy their own newspaper. Not here. Somewhere else. Some other small town, as yet undecided. They'd spent hours talking about it, planning for it, dreaming of how it would be. She wasn't sure now that she hadn't simply shaped her dreams to match his, but what did that matter? She had planned her life around him and seen it all shatter over the course of one horrible night. From then on, she'd made her own plans. Badly, as it turned out, but her own nevertheless. She'd chosen nursing,

Mitch, motherhood, and a life in a big city far away from home.

And with the irony life so often supplied, Jeff was doing without her what they'd dreamed of doing together.

"I once thought I'd work at a newspaper." The words flowed from her thoughts and onto the air with barely a break.

"Newspaper," he said. "That's perfect. The other day I overheard Joe asking Jeff if he'd hired somebody or other's replacement down at the Trib yet. And then yesterday, when I was down there talking to Sam about the water district, he mentioned it, too. I can't remember what the position is, though. Sales, maybe, but it'd only take a phone call to find out."

"I couldn't work at the Trib."

"Sure you could. Might not be exactly what you were hoping for, but it's close. And at least you'd be working while you look for another nursing position."

"I can't work at the Trib," she repeated, watching him steadily pull ahead of her again. "It's . . . complicated."

"So is driving back and forth to a job in Tulsa. We all choose our poison, Abby. It's just a matter of which way you want to go."

She hadn't thought of it that way, didn't want to think of it that way. "I can't explain," she said. "It's . . . well, complicated. That's all."

"If you say so. But it seems to me that's just cutting off your nose to spite your face."

She nearly stumbled, but caught herself before the misstep. Was *that* what she was doing? Again? Giving up what she wanted, what she had to have, to keep from dealing with what she didn't want to face? But how could she work at the Trib with Jeff? "Jeff and I have a . . . a history, for lack of a better word. I don't think he'd hire me, even if I asked."

"I've heard the history. Some of it, anyway." Noah

seemed unimpressed with her excuses. "The talk at the breakfast table isn't all about your job search, you know."

That was the other thing about small towns—no topic was taboo, no history unconnected. But whatever he'd heard wasn't the whole of what had happened. Not by a long shot. "It was a long time ago."

"We all have a past, Abby. The trick is not to let it dictate the present. You need a job. There's one at the newspaper. Seems to me you'd at least want to check into it."

He outpaced her then, and she was two full strides behind when they reached the intersection of Sixth and Main, where yellow lights flashed a warning above an oblong sign. "It's summer." Noah jogged impatiently in place as two cars crept, one after the other, through the school zone. "Why doesn't someone turn off the flashing lights?"

"Someone will, in another month or so."

"Just before school starts?"

"That's the way things are done in a small town. Inefficiency is part of the charm." She stepped off the curb and into a fast run, determined he wouldn't pull ahead of her again. Or maybe it was her own tumbling thoughts she wanted to outrun.

"How much farther to the doughnut shop?" He was breathing hard when he caught up with her and his tank top was streaked with sweat, but he continued to match her pace for pace.

Abby was sweating, too, and her breath didn't come as easily as it had when she'd been running regularly. Still, she could see she was in better shape than Noah. "A little less than a mile," she said. "Are you sure the fresh air is clearing your head?"

"I have a dull headache," he admitted. "It's nothing, really. I always push myself too hard when I run. I know better, but I do it anyway."

Mitch had done the same thing, despite her unsolicited advice to start slow and stay slow for a longer length of time. It was the steadiness that built endurance, not the pace. But then Mitch had never had what it took to endure. Not in running. Not in life. If only she'd seen that from the beginning. Except *if onlys* led to the inevitable *but thens*. *If only* she hadn't married Mitch . . . *but then* she wouldn't have Kyle and Denny. *If only* Jeff hadn't betrayed her . . . *but then* there would be no Lexie. *If only* was a wisp of nothing. *But then* was two boys with Mitch's blue eyes and wide smile. *But then* was a dark-eyed girl who, for better or worse, held the key to Kyle's heart.

If only was regret. *But then* was the reality Abby, herself, had created, the truth she had to face.

"We can make a turn here, if you want," she said now, offering Noah the choice. "We've come about a mile already and two miles up and back isn't bad for a start. Especially since you're not feeling well."

"There you go, thinking like a nurse again." He kept running, pushing the pace and himself. "It's just a dull headache. It'll be a memory by the time we reach the dime store. Get outside your box, Abby, because I am not going back to Wade House without some doughnuts."

"Then you have to set a slower pace. Otherwise, we'll be hitching a ride home because we're too exhausted to take another step."

Noah frowned, but he slowed down. "Maybe you should consider becoming a personal trainer. I have a feeling you'd be good at that."

"I don't doubt it for a second." She smiled at him.

He smiled back and by the time they made the turn in front of the Sunrise Grocery, which had once been the dime store, they'd settled into an easier, more agreeable pace. It crossed Abby's mind to wonder how he'd known the old store had been there, but then, as he'd said, small towns were alike, past and present, and no one ever forgot, or hesitated to say, where something once had been. It was, as she'd said, part of the charm.

Chapter 10

Noah pulled over onto the shoulder of the road and stopped the Jeep. He waited for the Ford pickup that had ridden his bumper for a dozen blocks to pass, then killed the engine and got out. The Cherokee belonged to Burdon Environmental Labs and had been Noah's traveling companion for nearly three years. His only companion, unless he counted the crates, boxes, tubes, and chemicals he toted from point to point. Burdon Labs provided the tools of his research, too. The notebooks he filled with dates, times, geographical notations, meteorological conditions, water temperature and flow rate, flora, fauna, and entomology stats, and various other analytical data. All of the things he needed came with the vehicle. He'd be getting a new car in the fall. Perhaps another Jeep. Perhaps not. Administration made those decisions, rarely asking the field agents for recommendations or an opinion. Many of his counterparts groused about the system, feeling they ought to be consulted since they were the ones doing the driving.

Noah didn't care. He liked the anonymity of driving a car that someone else had chosen, enjoyed the possibility that the next one would feel right, would be a model he'd driven before and particularly favored. He never had to worry about paying for insurance, maintenance, or repairs—things he often had difficulty remembering to do—and he was encouraged, even expected, to put 50,000 to 70,000 miles a year on the odometer of whatever car he drove. His personal goal was 80,000 per annum and already the Jeep had rolled over the 200,000-mile mark. And he still had a good five months left to clock in that extra 40,000.

Of course, if he continued to dawdle the days away in Sweetwater, he'd fall short again.

Noah walked around the front of the Cherokee, reaching into his pocket for the prescription bottle he always carried. He tapped two tablets into his hand and tossed them back dry. Dr. Gossman had advised him that the drug would work faster and more efficiently if taken with water. But Noah couldn't remember to take bottled water with him in the car, and when he needed relief from a headache, he couldn't wait. So as often as not, he took the pills dry.

Gravel slipped beneath his foot and he felt the jerk of his shoelace as it pulled loose. Propping his foot on the front bumper, he bent to tie it and felt an achy soreness in his muscles, the hangover of a hard run. For five days straight, he'd run on the cusp of morning. Twice Abby had run with him, holding him to a more moderate pace, warming up and cooling down; but on the other three days, this morning included, he'd run full out and hard, start to finish, pushing his body to the limit, and then pushing that extra bit harder. Doc Gossman wouldn't like to hear that, either. But Noah did very few things in moderation; he couldn't seem to grasp the concept without someone to coach him. He loved running, even though he still hadn't figured out if he was running furiously toward something or hell-bent away from it.

Straightening, he looked down a sloping incline at the football stadium below. Next to it was a field house and a parking area, then further down was a larger parking lot and a long, low building he knew was the high school. On a whim, Noah left the Jeep and jogged down the hill. The stadium was deserted, the score board unlighted, the bandstand abandoned for the summer, but the moment he stepped onto the field, it all came alive for him—the crowds, the lights, the huddle break, the slam of body blocks all around him, the moment when the football left the quarterback's hands and sailed end over end into his ready arms. And then the run. The beautiful exhilaration of the race to the end zone. Noah had loved it all. He remembered the thrill of it, the rumble of the announcer's voice blaring into the autumn night, the electrifying pleasure of listening for his name. . . .

The memory flirted with him, teased him with the belief he was that cocky youth, the runner no one could catch, the receiver who scored the most touchdowns. But he was merely a man with muscles still aching from his morning exercise jaunt, standing on a deserted football field that was just like the football field in hundreds of other small towns all across the country. This one was no different. Games had been won and lost here, heroes made and hearts broken. One team grew up, moved on, and another took its place. And in the way of childhood, memories of those days could hold as much make-believe as truth.

As he walked up the ramp, he let his hand slide over the metal banister. The pole was hot from baking in the sun, so he released it and climbed the concrete steps. Halfway up, he chose a seat and sat alone in the stone bleachers, soaking up the warmth, half hoping something else would jog his memory and allow him to relive those moments when he'd been sure of who he was and what life had in store for him. A girl had broken his heart back then. He remembered the terrible pain of that, even though her face and name were forgotten. Maybe that was why the divorce from

Stacy had caused him mostly inconvenience. He'd like to blame someone he couldn't even remember for the hard edge surrounding his heart, point to his past for the problems that had ultimately doomed his marriage. He could have rebuffed Stacy's accusation that he was a cold, heartless bastard with the information that he had once loved a girl with purity and passion. But, of course, he hadn't thought of it at the time and Stacy would never have believed him anyway.

A car backfired and then chugged into view. It stopped in front of the field house and its cargo of leggy teenage girls piled out of the two-door jalopy and proceeded to unload a vast amount of backpacks and bags from the trunk. Noah observed the collection of girls with interest, noted the high-pitched excitement of their chatter, the way they laughed together like it was a team effort. They all wore beige shorts, black sleeveless tees, and Keds so white they had to be brand new. Their bodies were slim, athletic, and tan, their hair streaked various shades of summer blond. He counted five girls, judged their average age as sixteen, considering one, at least, had a driver's license, and blatantly admired their youthful beauty from his unobserved seat in the stands.

Another car pulled into the parking lot and dropped off three more girls, two brunettes and a redhead. A van came next, followed by a blue SUV, a green pickup, and a silver-gray event bus with Sweetwater Public Schools printed in sweeping black lettering on the side.

The girls, fourteen of them now, swarmed the bus like a gaggle of curious geese, their excitement and voices rising in unison, their giggles a sweet song in the open air. Noah knew it was time to go. He'd spent too long already enjoying their lovely allure, feeling a little like a voyeur, a little like an uncle watching his favorite niece play at being a grown-up. Either way, it was time to go.

As he stood to leave, a white Cadillac whirled into the parking lot and screeched to an angled stop behind the event bus. The passenger door was thrown open and another long-legged blonde got out. She bent to say something to the driver, pulling the door in until the window glass caught the sunlight and reflected it directly into Noah's eyes. He brought up a hand to block the glare, and for several moments all he could see was that glimpse of silver-blond hair, which had become so familiar in his mind he could almost feel its silky texture on his skin. But that was just another illusion, a mix-up in his brain created by the brightness striking his eyes, the headache, and the medication. The sensation would pass. It always did. Eventually.

The annoying dark spots in his vision faded and he saw Lexie Garrett, dressed like the others, walking toward the bus with another girl, toting a backpack, a piece of rolling luggage, and a pair of black and silver pom-poms. About the time Lexie hefted her bag and tossed it into the baggage compartment under the bus, the driver's side of the Cadillac opened and Melanie Garrett stepped out and said something to her daughter.

Noah watched as the girl stopped and shook her head, firmly denying whatever request her mother had made. But another few words from Melanie and Lexie returned to the car and allowed a maternal hug that appeared unwelcome on one side and unnecessarily fussy on the other. Once released, Lexie bounded away to be with her friends and, in a matter of minutes, all the girls were on the bus and out of view, although their exuberant squeals could still be heard.

Melanie continued to stand beside her car, looking

as gorgeous as the first time Noah had seen her at Wade House. He figured she was the kind of woman who'd look beautiful in sackcloth, the kind who liked knowing a man could hardly take his eyes off of her, the kind who understood the power she could yield with a smile. And when she looked toward the bleachers, he felt somehow she'd known he was there all along.

She didn't wave or acknowledge his presence in any way, but he had a sense that she was taking his measure, testing him. And relief filtered through him in an uneven trickle when she finally got back into her car and drove away.

So, logically, he should have felt a jolt of alarm when he crested the hill and saw her white Cadillac idling beside his Jeep.

But instead, he felt merely a curious, rather careless, anticipation.

Chapter 11

"I thought you were going to call the hospital." Mae dusted her hands on her apron as she shadowed Abby through the foyer and out onto the porch. "You better call them before you leave."

"I'll do it when I get back."

"You're going to fool around and lose this job, Abby, and then what are you gonna do?"

Abby bit off the sharp reply she wanted to make and kept her voice calm, pleasant even. "I'm not going to lose the job, Mother. I told the hospital recruiter I'd let her know today and I will. This really isn't anything you need to worry about."

"Somebody needs to worry about it, 'cause it's getting to be clear as rainwater that you don't care if you get a job or not."

"I care, okay? I know I need a job. I'm going right now to see about one. And I *will* call the hospital as soon as I get back."

"I don't know what's got into you, Abby. And I sure don't know why you keep putting this off. The hospital's steady work. It's what you trained to do. What kind of job are you hoping to find by shilly-shallying around like this?"

The day was a scorcher and between heat and humidity, the air was almost too thick and heavy to breathe. Abby's nerves were already coiled into anxious knots over what she was about to do, what it had taken several days to talk herself into doing. Then, as if summer heat and sheer apprehension weren't enough, here was Mae with a conversation Abby did not want to have.

"The kind of job where I don't have to be seventy-five miles down the highway if one of my sons needs me. The kind of job where I don't have to work weekends and holidays. The kind of job that will allow me to raise my children with a minimum of help from anyone else. That's the kind of job I'm looking for. That's the kind of job I'm still hoping I can find."

Mae's lips thinned with ready censure as she turned back toward the house. "You're a dreamer like your daddy. He thought if he just waited around, somebody'd walk up and fork over a wad of money for somethin' he was gonna invent. But he never invented anything except pipe dreams. And he never could hold a job. I'd hate to think you're gonna turn out like him, Abby."

"That's not fair." Abby's voice was low, but Mae must have heard the emotion in it because her hand went instantly still on the door handle. "I am not a failure, Mother, and I want you to please stop treating me like one."

Mae looked at her long and steady. "Life is hard, Abby. You always thought you'd be the exception to that. I wish you coulda been. I wish you didn't need a job, but you do, and it's time to get on with getting one."

There was no sympathy in her mother's eyes. Abby didn't know why she kept looking for it there or why she felt she needed it. "I'll be back in an hour," she said and turned to go.

"Where are you going?"

She could have held it back, but she was tired of

running away from unpleasantness. "The newspaper. I'm going to ask Jeff to give me a job."

"What?"

"You heard me."

"Don't be daft, Abby. He's not crazy enough to hire you, even if you're crazy enough to ask him."

"You're probably right."

Mae took two steps across the porch and reached the top of the stairs as Abby reached the bottom. "You stay away from that newspaper office," she called after her. "You're just lookin' for trouble if you go in there. You know it'll be trouble, Abby."

She did. She knew there would be a price to pay. She knew the cost would not be all hers. But if she was choosing poison, then she owed her boys the one less toxic for them. They needed her now. She'd come home thinking the solidity Mae and the boarding house could offer would be enough. But the knots in Denny's rope were getting tighter, and he'd started wetting the bed. Kyle was increasingly secretive and withdrawn, openly hostile or sullenly silent, spending most of his time at the computer or staring fixedly at the ceiling. Abby knew the pressure inside them was building and she knew she had to be close by when it broke. Her history with Jeff had happened a long time ago. A lifetime ago. It should have no bearing on either one of them now. She'd never planned to live anywhere near him, but here she was. She'd thought she could simply pretend he didn't exist, but his father lived in her mother's house and her son was starry-eyed over his daughter. Everywhere she looked, the past looked back at her. She couldn't escape it.

She could, however, choose to make peace with it.

And if that caused trouble, well, so be it.

"Don't go there, Abby. Don't borrow that kind of trouble."

That kind of trouble. Melanie. That was the trouble

Mae was talking about. The name that hovered on the edge of her voice.

Melanie, the spoiler.

Melanie, who had played brother against brother, friend against friend.

Melanie. Jeff's wife.

But to name the demon was to claim it for her own, and Abby was not giving Melanie that kind of power over her. It was Jeff who'd made the choices. He'd promised his love to Abby and then turned to Melanie for sex. He'd counseled Alex to be cautious, while he played fast and loose behind his brother's back with his brother's girl. Melanie had created the deadly triangle, but it was Jeff who'd claimed the demon.

Jeff who owned it still.

Abby could take the job in Tulsa and never even ask about the job at the *Tribune*. But that would be letting the past decide the present, and she was through doing that. She needed a job. If Jeff would give her one, she'd take it and be glad of the opportunity. Because that's all it was. That was all she wanted.

"You worry too much, Mom," she said as she opened the Blazer door and tossed her purse inside. "There's not a snowball's chance Jeff is going to hire me."

But she thought he ought to have to tell her so. Face to face.

"What do you *mean* you thought of a better story?" Jeff was angrier than he'd been in a coon's age, furious with himself for hiring this arrogant kid who seemed to believe he had a good shot at the Pulitzer after only two months on the job and a dozen botched assignments. "Are you saying *this*"—he tapped the pages in front of him on the desk—"isn't the story I told you to do?"

"Would you just listen to me?" The kid—Rob Maynard—got red-faced and blustery when on the defensive, which was most of the time. "I know you sent me over there to do the interview with old man Keener, but that's not news. Nobody wants to read another rambling D-day account from that old geezer just because he lived to tell it . . . over and over and over again. World War II happened like a million years ago, and just because it's coming up on the Fourth of July we shouldn't have to plaster the town's one ancient war hero on the front page of our newspaper and call it patriotic. I wrote something fresh. If you'd read it, you'd know that, and we wouldn't have to have this conversation."

The phone on his desk buzzed, which probably kept Jeff from going over the top of his desk and punching the kid in front of it. He jerked up the receiver and snapped a curt "Yes?" into it. Three seconds later, he slammed it down. "There are so many holes in what you just said to me, Maynard, I hardly know where to start. But let me give it a shot." He shoved back his chair and rose to his feet. "First of all, he's *Mr.* Keener and. . . . No, on second thought, just get the hell out of my office."

"Okay." Rob took a step toward the door, gesturing widely toward the papers. "I'll come back when you've had a chance to read that. We can talk about it then."

"I have a better idea. You're fired. Now, I don't ever have to talk to you again."

Rob laughed, compounding his mistake. "You can't fire me. I'm the best reporter you've got and you know it."

"Out." Jeff came around the desk and backed the kid to the doorway.

"I'm going," Rob said, hands out, palms up, idiot grin on his ruddy face. "But you're going to want to talk to me once you've read my story. It's the best thing I've done to date. Trust me, it's primo."

"Here's a scoop for you. You're unemployed."

Rob's smile started to fade. "You don't mean that."

"If you're not out the front door in five minutes, I'll put you out. Take whatever is yours with you because I don't ever want you to come into this building again."

"You'll be sorry," Rob threatened. "You're not going to find anyone else with even half my talent who's willing to work as hard as I do for this sorry excuse of a newspaper."

"Call me crazy, but I'm willing to risk it." Jeff stepped into the doorway and Rob stepped out, turning on his heel and bumping hard into someone behind him.

"Don't go in there, lady." Rob put his hands on her arms and moved her out of his way. "He's a freaking lunatic."

Jeff reached for him, intending to escort him out, but he saw Abby and stopped. Millie's message on the phone registered. *Abby's on her way back.* And now she was here. Outside his office. Standing there, looking after the hulking reporter who had barreled into her.

Abby.

In the one place he'd never expected to see her.

"Let me guess," she said, her eyes coming to him, stunning him with the curve of her smile. "You're the big, bad editor who's making him rewrite his masterpiece."

"I'm the big, bad editor who just fired him for not doing what he was told."

Her eyebrows arched as she turned her head to look at Rob's retreating back, then at Jeff again. "Wow," she said softly. "You don't even look angry. Do you fire a lot of people?"

"Only the stupid ones."

"Hmm." She adjusted the strap of her shoulder bag, smoothing the leather with her thumb. "I'll try to remember that."

He couldn't imagine why she was here, but he had a sudden vision of Gideon at his surly best, wearing out his welcome, and Mae sending Abby to say he'd have to find some other place to live. "Is everything all right? At the house? Dad's okay?"

"Huh? Oh. Yes. Fine. Well, he was fine last time I saw him. He stays in his room a lot, doesn't socialize much." She seemed uncomfortable, but then Gideon made everyone uncomfortable one way or another. "I'm sure someone would have told you if he wasn't fine."

Jeff nodded, dumbfounded by her presence and the relative normalcy of her conversation, astounded that she was looking at him without hate and bitter disappointment in her eyes. He didn't want to question this unexpected gift . . . but he didn't want to trust it, either. His stomach felt queasy. The residue of anger, maybe. Or hope. "You, uh, want to come in?" He gestured behind him at his office and then stepped back so she could walk past. If she wanted. Or not.

"Oh," she said as if it hadn't occurred to her he might invite her inside. "Sure." But she made no move to go in.

"Jeff!" Sam yelled from across the room. "What d'ya wanna do about the Brookwood Development?"

"We're running the editorial on Sunday," Jeff called out over the newsroom clatter.

Sam waved an acknowledgment and went back to talking on the phone. Rob slammed a desk drawer, tossed Jeff an ugly glance, then kicked a chair on his way out the door. Phones rang. Computers hummed. The fax machine buzzed. Millie answered a call and greeted Becky Starks, who'd come through the door as Rob went out. She wanted to place an ad, she told Millie, who held up a finger asking her to wait. Millie then pointed at Jeff, indicating the call was for him. He shook his head, his signal that she take a message. She nodded, then turned back to Becky. Scott Wyatt pushed away from his desk, rolled his chair to the credenza behind him, stuck a stubby No. 2 yellow into the pencil sharpener, pulled it out pinprick sharp, and rolled back to his desk. Everything in the office was normal . . . the hubbub, the clamor, and the chatter. Everything was the same as it always was.

Except that Abby was in it.

He experienced a small but prideful thrill that she was seeing it now, up and running at its hectic clip, him at its helm. "It gets a little noisy this time of day," he explained.

"I haven't been in here since I was a kid."

"It hasn't really changed much."

"I guess not." Her glance swept the room, came to him again, and slid away before she walked past him and into his office.

"You want some coffee?" he asked. "Or a Coke? There may even be some doughnuts left, but I wouldn't count on it."

"No, thank you. This isn't really a social call."

He should have expected that, but it caught him off guard and he hesitated halfway to his chair. Of course it wasn't social. Or friendly. What it was, though, still carried a big question mark.

The phone rang and he reached over to answer it, barely aware of Millie's voice in his ear, of the information she was relating. "I'll call him back," he said and hung up, not even sure his answer made sense.

Abby had dropped her purse by one of the two chairs in front of the desk and wandered over to his photo wall, a cliché he'd always hankered to have. He wondered if she'd notice the picture of him with

Ozzie Smith, wondered if she even remembered how much he liked baseball, how he'd often told her he'd consider himself a success when he could hang a photo like that on his wall.

"Ozzie Smith. Shortstop. St. Louis Cardinals." She turned and came back, settling into the chair in one fluid move. "Kyle would kill to have a picture like that," she said. "He's a sports fanatic."

"I know. We've talked about it. I guess I ought to invite him down to see my photo wall sometime."

She nodded . . . and he was suddenly aware of her tension, of the way she ran the pad of her thumb across the pads of her fingers, and he knew she was nervous. It struck him as pathetic that he still remembered her habits, that he'd felt an instant impulse to reassure her, and he wished suddenly, forcefully, that she'd never come back to Sweetwater. "Is there something I can do for you, Abby?" he asked, seeing no reason to wait her out.

She lifted her chin, moistened her lips. "Yes. I heard there was a job opening and I wondered if you'd let me apply for it."

"A job?" he repeated, sure he'd misheard her.

The moment stretched out and she said nothing to correct him, didn't make even a token attempt to laugh away the sheer absurdity of being in his office asking him for a job, didn't do anything except watch him grapple with the question. "You want a job." He said it again, fixing it in his mind. "Here. At the newspaper."

"Yes."

She sounded serious, and he decided she must be. "I thought you were an R.N."

"I am. I haven't been able to find a position, though, and I need a job. I don't have any experience in this line of work, but I once thought I'd be good at it." She held his gaze for a beat. "You once thought I'd be good at it, too."

"That was a long time ago, Abby. And it's not that I think you couldn't do the work now. . . ." Hell, she knew this was impossible. He shouldn't have to offer any explanation. "We just don't have any openings at the moment. Otherwise . . ."

Silence met his lie. He'd just fired a reporter. Practically in front of her. And there was Mark's position in sales. He was leaving at the end of the month. Jeff hadn't advertised to fill the slot, figuring someone would hear about it and come in.

And someone had.

"That's not true," he admitted. "There are openings. Which one did you want to apply for?"

"Sales," she said. "I talked to Joe about it. He said I'd be a natural, since I'm familiar with the town and know quite a few of the people who advertise in the Trib."

So she'd done some homework, hadn't just popped in on a whim. "But you've never done any sales? No advertising experience?"

Her thumb made another pass across her fingertips. "No. What I do have to offer is a willingness to learn and a positive attitude. I'll give you a hundred percent effort." She paused, offered a small smile. "And I'm not stupid."

"It's hard work, Abby. You may be a hometown girl, but there are no easy sales."

"I'm not asking for easy, Jeff. I'm asking for an opportunity. That's all."

That's all. As if he might think she wanted something more. He settled back in his chair, lulling himself with its familiar creaks into thinking this was just another interview. One of hundreds he'd done. He turned a pencil in his hand, letting the monotony of the movement give him time to think. "Are you looking for an opportunity to get out of nursing altogether, or would this be just a stopgap job until something in that field comes along?" *Truth, Abby,* he thought. *Tell me what you're really doing here.*

She struggled with it for a moment, hesitant maybe to give him anything personal. "I've been offered a position in Tulsa at one of the hospitals, but I hate to spend that much time on the road. This has been a . . . a tough year for my boys. I think it's important I'm with them as much as possible. Working here would allow me to maintain a better schedule and be close by when they need me. I've thought about this, Jeff. I wouldn't ask you to consider me for the position if I didn't think I could do it."

Again, she tossed the ball back to his court. As if she wanted him to tell her all the reasons this wouldn't work. As if he could just say he didn't know how he would feel about seeing her every day, talking to her the way he talked to his other employees, being reminded every which way he turned that he could have made other choices in his life, taken a path that would have included her in it.

But there she was, waiting for an answer.

"I don't think it's a good idea, Abby."

A look came into her eyes then. A look he'd seen before. A flash of anger. Resignation. Disappointment. And he realized she'd expected him to refuse her. She'd come here anticipating that he would deny her a job for no better reason than his own regrets. He'd hired other people with fewer qualifications than she'd already presented. Mark, in fact, had been a science teacher before he'd come to the paper. Scott, too, had been a happy accident. Jeff had made mistakes—he'd hired Rob Maynard on the basis of a sharp résumé and a slick presentation—but he'd always prided himself on giving every applicant the benefit of the doubt, the courtesy of thorough consideration, and, if possible, the opportunity to prove his or her worth.

Could Abby do the work? Probably. If she had walked in off the street, an old acquaintance who gave the same explanation for wanting the job, would he hire her? Probably. He'd ask more questions, try to gain a feel for the type of employee she would be, but he wouldn't automatically rule out the possibility. If she had been only the mother of two young boys who were having a tough time—he'd heard the boarders talking and knew Kyle and Denny weren't adjusting well to the recent changes in their lives—would he have hesitated to give her a chance? No. If she had been anyone else, he would have told her to fill out an application and they'd have gone forward from there. It was that simple.

"If you want to fill out an application, Abby, I'll consider it."

"You will?"

He nodded and got to his feet, wanting her out of his office, needing this uncomfortable interview to end. "Ask Millie for the form. Fill it out and leave it with her. I'll let you know my decision tomorrow."

"Thank you," she said . . . and just those two words made him feel as if he'd done the right thing. "I know it would be a . . . *challenge* . . . for you to work with me." She stood, too, and picked up her purse. "But I need the job. I wouldn't ask you to do this if I didn't. I know Melanie won't like it."

"Melanie?" *Melanie.* Amazing that she hadn't even crossed his mind until just now. She should have popped up like a furious red flag the very second Abby had stated her reason for coming to see him. But it hadn't occurred to him that Melanie had any part in this. What he did at the newspaper was his decision. What he did, how he did it, who he hired or didn't hire was none of her business. He'd made that clear to her from the start. "Melanie has nothing to do with this, Abby," he said, wanting to be sure she understood. "This is strictly business. My business."

She seemed a little startled at the fierceness of the words, but all she said was, "Okay."

"Okay." He followed her to the doorway. "I'll talk to you tomorrow then."

She drew a deep breath, looked out at the bustle of the newsroom. "I think I'd like it here," she said and then she walked away.

The reality of it hit him as he watched her weave past desks and chairs. Abby had asked if she could work for him. He'd agreed to consider it. She was going to fill out an application, and he was going to look at it. And tomorrow he would call her and tell her—no. Because how could he say yes?

She stopped at Millie's desk, leaned against it, and exchanged a smile and a laugh with Millie. Across the room, Sam waved to Abby and she waved back. Smiling. Friendly. A part of the very rhythm of this town. He knew if she had been anyone else he would have hired her on the spot. She would fit into the ebb and flow of the newsroom. She would like working here. Sam, Millie, Scott, and the rest of them would like working with her. Jeff knew that the same way he'd known he shouldn't hire Rob Maynard. But he'd hired Rob, anyway, against his better judgment. And now he'd fired Rob and needed a reporter and a sales manager.

He turned on his heel and went back to his creaky old chair behind his scuffed and cluttered oak desk. He picked up the pages Rob had left behind and dropped them into the wastebasket. Then he pulled them out again and read the story, beginning to end. It was good. There was no doubt the kid had talent.

Jeff tossed the story back into the trash with no regrets, answered a call and then another. He retrieved his messages from Millie, talked to Scott about the assignments Rob had left undone, dialed Lexie's cell phone to see if the cheerleading squad had settled safely in at camp yet, but the call went straight to voice mail so he left a message to call him back when she had a chance. He worked on next week's editorial, had a brief meeting with Mark about the advertising accounts, and listened to Sam's gleeful summary of his latest run-in with a county commissioner. It was late in the day when he pulled Abby's application from the corner of his desk where Millie had laid it. He saw Millie's broad checkmark in the upper right-hand corner, signifying that she'd checked the references, although he doubted she'd done any more than phone the hospital in Chicago to verify Abby's last place of employment. In the margin next to the hospital name, Millie had written in the former employer's comment: *Good, dependable worker.*

This brought Jeff right back to a moral dilemma, what one of his professors had referred to as the Blink Factor. When faced with truth, there were two choices: Stare it down or blink.

And this was one time Jeff wanted badly to blink.

Hiring Abby, having her in his personal territory on a daily basis, would be, as she'd put it, a challenge. He didn't doubt that he could treat her the same way he treated the other employees. He didn't doubt that she'd maintain a purely professional, even overly professional, distance. He knew the past didn't haunt her as it did him. He knew he could pretend it never crossed his mind either.

But that would be a blink.

He could simply say no, offer no explanation or make up one, and thereby preserve his comfort zone.

And that would also be a blink.

He wished again that Abby had never come back to Sweetwater. But then he wished he had never let her go in the first place. He'd given her no choice. He'd stolen something precious and irreplaceable when he'd told her he was going to marry Melanie, that the baby she carried was his. His hand clenched on the application and he wadded it into a tight ball and tossed it into the trash with Rob's potentially prize-winning story.

Jeff walked out of his office, saw the empty desks, the dimmed lighting, and found Millie rinsing out the coffee pot in the kitchen. She looked up as he stopped in the doorway. "I saved you a cup," she said. "It's in the microwave. Just punch warm-up."

He did. Not because he wanted coffee, but because he wanted company. "Thanks, Mil. You're my favorite brunette."

"You're lying, but I like you anyway." She squirted liquid soap into the pot, searched through the drawer for a round brush, then scrubbed at the coffee stains the same way she did everything—with enthusiasm. "I was kinda surprised Abby came in about the job, her being a nurse and all. But I think she'll be good here. She's personable, you know. Easy to talk to. What I hear, she's had a rough time the last couple o' years. When's she gonna start?"

"Start?"

Millie sent a frown over her shoulder. "You're mighty distracted today. When's Abby going to start work? It'd be good if Mark could show her the ropes before he leaves."

"I haven't hired her." The microwave dinged and Jeff took out his cup, knowing the coffee would be hot and bitter enough to wake the dead. But it gave him something to hold on to, and he seemed to need that at the moment. "I haven't decided if I'm going to hire her."

"Oh. Hmm." Millie finished rinsing the pot and set

it upside down on a towel to dry. "Well, that's it then. I'm going home. See you tomorrow."

"Good night, Mil." Jeff carried the coffee back to his office, knowing Millie had presented him with another truth he needed to stare down. There were only a handful of people who'd consider it odd for him to hire Abby. Nobody much remembered that the two of them had dated through high school, and their breakup had been merely a side note in the aftermath of the accident. Their lives weren't the only ones changed by the tragedy—four families had been caught in the headlights of the town's collective grief. Few knew the role he had played in causing the accident, fewer still blamed him even half as much as he blamed himself.

Reaching down, he pulled out the discarded application and smoothed it with his hands. *The truth,* he thought. If he blinked, life would go on as it had for the last sixteen years. Some good stuff. Some bad stuff. But pretty much the same stuff.

If he stared it down, everything would change.

He drank the bitter coffee and stared out the window until the summer light began to fade.

Then he picked up the phone and called Abby.

Chapter 12

The trouble with motherhood, in Mae's opinion, was the off switch.

The first time she held that squalling, newborn, blanket-bundled baby in her arms, she'd been whopped with a bumper crop of protective, maternal instincts. They'd come over her like gangbusters, switched on like a floodlight down an abandoned mine shaft. Feelings she hadn't even known she could feel exploded in a fierce passion that forever changed the way she viewed the world and everything in it. This child, this tiny girl she'd carried beneath her heart, gave new meaning to life, turned her in a new direction, and breathed into her a consuming compulsion to safeguard this new little person at any cost. Thirty-four years later, Mae still hadn't figured out how to switch off the desperate yearning to stand between her daughter and danger.

Because, once again, Abby was looking the wrong way and couldn't see the trouble coming at her. *Asking Jeff for a job at the newspaper.* Why, she might as well stand in the middle of Main Street with a paper sack over her head and dare the past to smack her down one more time.

Mae glanced the length of the supper table, hoping to catch her daughter's eye, talk sense into her without having to say a word. But Abby wouldn't look her way. She didn't want to hear sense. She thought Mae was too bossy, worrying about things Abby was certain she could handle. So she avoided even casual eye contact by talking—a little too animatedly—with Noah. Their conversation bordered on flirting, their smiles—his, especially—bespoke the prospect of a deeper attraction. Mae didn't like the idea of that, either. The last thing Abby needed to do was get herself involved with another man. Not with Mitch—bad as he'd been—only months in the grave he'd dug for himself. Not with the boys so freshly wounded by his death.

Yet that was the way of women. Always wanting to believe a man was the answer. Always thinking they couldn't face the future alone. Mae had never wanted another man after Charlie. He'd been handsome and charming when he'd set out to woo her, and she couldn't believe he'd chosen her out of all the young women in the county. He could have had any one of them, that's how beguiling he'd been. She'd never been pretty or had much in the way of social graces, but Charlie had pursued her recklessly, said she was the only woman with good sense who'd put up with his monkeyshines. Fool that she was, she'd fallen for him. Hook, line, and sinker. They had married in haste, too anxious to get under the sheets together to think twice about what the future held for two such disparate souls. He was a dreamer. She was practical all the way to the soles of her feet. He brought nothing but pixie dust to the marriage, while she had the house and a willingness to do whatever she must to keep it. Maybe she would have thrown him out on his ear within months of the wedding if she hadn't gotten pregnant right off the bat. Or maybe she wouldn't have. There hadn't been an off switch for how she felt about Charlie, either. The initial electricity between them had fizzled out under a deluge of alcohol and anger, leaving her distrustful of men in general and charming men in particular, but somehow she'd never really gotten over being in love with the man she'd married.

Truth was, Noah Walker reminded her of Charlie Wade. It was nothing she could set her finger on and say *this . . . this is what bothers me*. Noah hadn't been a bit of extra trouble. He was likable enough and quick with a compliment. He didn't talk about himself much, which was odd in a man, but not a bad thing. Still yet, when she looked for substance in him, all she came up with was another handful of pixie dust.

She stabbed a bite of new potato, fresh from Lora's garden, and let her glance wander down the table to linger on her grandsons. Kyle, who ate like a machine, sucking in calories he'd burn off before bedtime. Denny, who hardly ate at all, picking at his food only when he thought somebody was watching. Kyle was always in a hurry to escape back to his computer and whatever—or whoever—he found so interesting in it. Denny was almost always the last to leave the table, sitting there tying knot after knot into that length of dirty, old rope until everyone else had wandered off to their room or out to the porch.

Mae's heart ached for them both. Lost boys, they were. Each, in his own way, courting trouble. And when she thought about them, her heart hurt for Abby, too. Mitch hadn't left his family much to work with . . . too few memories worthy of remembrance, too many best forgotten. Mae wanted to help, wondered if she ought to try and talk to Abby again. But whenever had talking done either one of them, daughter or mother, a lick of good? They were two sides of a coin, destined to forever see a different view of the pocket they were in. Mae knew she'd given good advice when she'd told her daughter to stay away from that newspaper office. But Abby didn't want advice. She wanted the help she'd asked for and nothing more. She was a dreamer, Charlie's daughter was, wanting to believe she was doing the best thing for her sons, unable to see how she was courting trouble, too. And there wasn't one blessed thing Mae could do about it. Not one.

"Somebody's here," Lowell announced. "I heard a car pull up outside."

"Jeff, probably," Joe said, unconcerned. "He must've got through at the paper early tonight."

"I don't know why he bothers comin' here." Rose daintily salted her green beans for the third time, and then Mae moved the shaker out of sight as soon as it was set back down on the table. Rose had a bad habit of overusing salt, which was not good for her blood pressure. For that matter, none of them needed extra salt. But Lora insisted on having condiments on the supper table. And no one could be more mule-brained than Lora.

"Jeff's a good son. He visits his father nearly every day." Violet adjusted Mr. McAfee's box, which rested on the table next to her plate, and her fingers restlessly stroked the wrapping paper. "I don't know why Mr. McAfee's son never comes to visit him."

Rose leaned toward her sister, patted the fidgety hands. "You don't have a son, Vi. You have daughters. Joanie and Jane. Remember?"

Violet frowned. "Do they visit their father?"

"Sundays and holidays," Rose assured her, straightening as she returned attention to her dinner. "They brought him that red-and-white-striped wrap and the fancy blue bow he's wearing for the Fourth of July, remember?"

"I'm not sure it's right for a man to dress like the American flag," Violet said. "Maybe Mr. McAfee would rather wear his dress blues. He was in the Air Force, you know."

"He looks great in what he's wrapped in." Lora paid the compliment promptly. Mr. McAfee's renowned service to his country was a tale often told at the dinner table, and Violet would happily repeat it now unless someone changed the course of the conversation, which was Lora's aim in adding, "Now, Rose, what were you saying about Jefferson?"

"I was saying," Rose repeated, "that I don't know why he bothers to visit his father because half the time Gideon locks him out in the hall, and the other half he lets him in just so he can gripe at him."

"You should stop lettin' the old geezer eat in his room, Mae," Archie advised between bites of meatloaf—his second helping. "He gets hungry enough, he'll get past some of that meanness."

"It's not Jeff's car," Lowell said to no one in particular. "Motor sounds different."

Joe swiveled in his chair at the far end of the table and drew aside the lace curtain. "Cadillac," he said. "Looks like Gideon will have to take out his meanness on Melanie tonight."

A pause . . . no more than a heartbeat of a moment . . . noted the intrusion of tension in the room, a splinter of uneasiness. Mae couldn't keep from looking at Abby but, except for a slight tautness around the mouth, could see no sign of concern. Foolish girl. Melanie was like a bottle rocket, just waiting for the spark to set her off. She was a wildfire ready to burn down anything that got in her way.

And Mae knew, if Abby didn't, that asking Jeff for a job at the newspaper this very afternoon meant the match was struck and the fuse lit.

"What would *she* be doing here?" Violet asked, her myopic eyes showing more confusion tonight than usual.

Joe released the curtain and turned back to his dinner. "Looks to me like she's bringing a plate of food."

"We've got more'n we can eat now," Effie said.

"Probably bringing somethin' for that old grouch upstairs." Lora, who was justifiably proud of her cooking, set her tea glass on the table with a brusque *thud*. Bringing food to Wade House was, in her mind, akin to insulting the Pope. "That old man wouldn't know good eatin' from green grass."

"I'll bet she's baked us something special." Archie, ever on the lookout for sweets, nodded sagely.

"Melanie doesn't cook." Rose glanced over the tabletop. "Where's the salt?"

"All women cook. It's their God-given talent," Archie said. "I've got five bucks says she's bringing in an apple pie."

"Five bucks says it's half of the hamburger she had for lunch." Rose took the bet and upped the ante. "Ten bucks says it's cold and greasy."

"Why would she bring half a hamburger?" Joe asked.

"Because she doesn't cook," repeated Rose, as if it ought to be obvious.

"Mr. McAfee cooked." Violet fussed with his bow— a vivid blue with miniature American flags tucked in to show his continuing patriotism, despite his being nothing more than a box of ash. "He made plum jelly every summer and beef stew in the winter. He could have been a chef, you know."

"Hello?" Melanie jostled the screen door with her hip and stepped inside, holding a foil-covered plate gingerly between the hot mitts covering her hands. The free fall of conversation stopped abruptly, and heads—that is, every head but Abby's—turned to watch her walk from the entryway to the edge of the dining room. For somebody who'd made poor health her religion, Melanie seemed in fine fettle. In fact, Mae had rarely seen anybody look better. Silver-blond hair swept back with a crafted carelessness. Lips freshly shaded a lush peach. Make-up lightly, skillfully applied to appear natural and flawless. Linen slacks bearing the rich wrinkles of quality, her blouse a cool, elegant cotton. And yet, as striking as Melanie undeniably was, Mae preferred Abby's artless beauty. Purely maternal prejudice, perhaps, but the way she saw it nonetheless.

"I'm so sorry to barge in on your dinner like this, Miz Mae." Melanie's smile couldn't have been sweeter or looked more sincere, but her lovely eyes were, as always, cool and calculating, layering every word with hidden meaning. "I'd planned to be here before y'all ever sat down at the table, but this silly casserole took forever to bake. It's Jeff's and Dad's favorite and it takes me nearly all day to make, but I do believe the Garrett men are worth the extra trouble."

"Is that a hot apple pie?" Archie kept an eye on the foil-wrapped plate. "That'd be worth some extra trouble, for sure."

Effie frowned at him across the table. "She just said it was a casserole."

Archie frowned back. "Rose said it was a hamburger."

"*Half* a hamburger." Rose, a spry, sassy eighty-four and long past the age of worrying about social blunders, offered Melanie a blunt explanation. "I bet Archie you brought Gideon your leftover lunch."

"Why on earth would I bring my father-in-law a hamburger from the Burger Barn when I can make his favorite meal, instead?" Melanie seemed pleasantly puzzled, as if this must be a joke among the old people.

"Because you don't cook." Violet delivered the punch line . . . and the hot mitts tightened on the foil, crimping the edges a little as annoyance flash-danced and fled, barely altering Melanie's sweet-as-honey smile with its passing.

"Did Jeff say that?" Irritation coiled within the soft, cajoling tones of her voice. "As if anyone else would tell such a fib about me. That husband of mine . . . sometimes I don't know what to do about his teasing, but you all surely know better than to take him seriously."

"Well," Rose observed in the stern schoolteacher voice she'd honed to uncomfortable perfection over the course of forty years in a classroom. "What I do know is that your husband looks seriously unhappy for a well-fed man."

"He is *not* unhappy." Melanie caught herself, smiled to demonstrate her willingness to be teased. "Looks are deceiving, Miz Rose, and I certainly hope you don't believe everything my husband says about me. Like all men, he does tend to exaggerate."

"I don't exaggerate," Joe said.

"What a whisker, Joe Malone!" Lora couldn't let that pass. "You lie like a rug."

"A rug lays." Effie, also a former schoolteacher, intervened with a prim correction. "A man lies."

"That's what I said." Lora nodded, her point confirmed.

Discomfort hung like a cloud over the dinner table while Melanie hovered there in the doorway, behaving as if her presence was an unappreciated gift. Pushing back her chair, Mae started up from the table.

"Oh, now, don't get up." Melanie nodded at Mae's chair, everything about her sweetness and light again. Except for those chilling eyes. "I know my way around your home, Miz Mae. Why, I must have been here dozens of times with Alex back when we were all in high school. As I remember, there was always a crowd of kids here. I can't think of a single person in our senior class who wasn't invited at least once. Can you think of anyone you might have left out, Abby?"

Directly addressed, Abby turned slowly in her chair, chin up, eyes steady, but over-bright. For an instant, Mae caught a glimpse of the old Abby, the scrappy, unapologetic Abby, who hadn't liked Melanie from the start and had seen no reason to pretend otherwise. *That* Abby would have squared off like a boxer and declared she had never invited Melanie to Wade House. *That* Abby would have thought it ludicrous for someone, who had manipulated and wheedled her way into popularity the way Melanie had, to remember so many years later the one house to which she hadn't been invited. But even in that brief glimpse, Mae realized what she'd seen was only a shadow of the girl who had flown through these rooms in a flurry of plans and idealistic dreams, merely a wisp of a future that had never materialized and yet was held forever within the memory of these walls.

Abby's lips curved up at the corners, although she didn't smile. "I don't believe I ever invited Alex," she said. "Although that never stopped him from showing up anyway."

"Nothing ever stopped Alex." Melanie made it sound as if she and Abby were old friends sharing the memory of someone they'd both known and lost, as if she'd played no part in the losing. "He never listened to anyone except Jeff. And I do believe he would have done anything for *you*."

Noah's fork spiraled to the floor with a *pling* and that was all the interruption Mae needed. She was out of her chair and beside Melanie in a heartbeat, stepping in to protect her daughter from things best left in the past where they belonged. "Let's take this on up to Gideon," she said to Melanie as she reached for the foil-covered plate. "He's probably wondering where you are with his supper."

"He ate already." Effie made the statement with uninhibited satisfaction. "Came down, piled up a plate, and went back to his room."

"Guess he didn't expect you'd spend all day cooking his *favorite* casserole for him," Rose said.

Mae ignored them, but the foil plate crimped further under the tension in Melanie's hands, showing that she was not immune to the sarcasm. Or that she accepted it with any grace. "Thank you, Miz Mae, but I can manage just fine by myself." She jerked the plate out of Mae's grasp and smoothed the crumpled edges with the mitts. "He'll want to eat this while it's still hot."

The plate wasn't hot. Or even tepid with warmth. But Mae wasn't about to challenge Melanie's claim. There had been whispers around town for years about her temper, about the storms she'd whipped up with neighbors, about her sudden outbursts in the grocery store, at the dry cleaners, anywhere she felt slighted or inconvenienced. Mae didn't cotton much to gossip, but she had seen the hatred in Melanie's eyes just now, heard it in the crooning, baiting tone of her voice when she spoke to Abby. So Mae stood her ground, squarely between her daughter and the wildfire that was Melanie Garrett. She stood there until Melanie was up the stairs and out of sight. She stood there until she heard Gideon's door open, heard the deep vibrations of his voice welcoming Melanie in. Mae stood there until she heard Noah say something to Abby, heard Abby's shaky reply, heard Rose ask again for the salt, heard Archie say, "What's for dessert, Lora?"

Only then did she return to her place at the table.

A smoky sunset ushered in scattered clouds and a cool front from the east, which in turn lured the older people out to sit on the porch. Summer had relaxed its death grip on the heat, allowing the remnants of a spring breeze to stir the echoes of long ago Junes when whole neighborhoods sat outside and conversed across thick, grassy yards while their children played Olly, Olly, Oxen Free until well after dark.

Abby sat on the top porch step, arms draped across her thighs, hands loose, fingers restless, and did her best to think about something other than how badly she needed a job. A last gasp of sunlight parted the clouds, struck the hood of Melanie's white Cadillac, and reflected across the lawn in a wide golden stripe. What she knew about cars—especially newer models—wouldn't fill a tri-fold pamphlet, but Abby could tell by looking that this one hadn't seen a lot of use. The tires gleamed black with that new car shine, and the tread showed no wear. The Garretts were doing well, if the autos they drove were any indication. She wondered if Melanie had run through the trust fund Jeff's grandparents had left him or if the newspaper was really doing a booming business. If he hired her to work there, she'd probably have a fair idea of the *Tribune's* income in a few weeks.

Not that it mattered one way or another. She was simply curious, that's all.

And, of course, he wasn't going to hire her. She'd been an idiot to ask.

Beside her on the step, Denny turned a page in his book and read as he absently untied the knots in his rope. She read a couple of lines over his shoulder. *The Adventures of Huckleberry Finn*. He'd read it before. This must be his third or fourth time. She was proud of his reading skill, glad he'd found the world of stories, even if she did wish he could experience just one of the adventures Twain had imagined for his characters. Just one. But Denny kept his nose in a book and his fingers busy with knots, and he felt safe from the frighteningly real world outside the pages of print.

She let her leg drop over to nudge his, once, then again. He reached down and scratched his shin, unaware of her move to snag his attention. She nudged him again, more firmly. "You're missing the sunset," she said.

He blinked, his thick bristle of sandy-brown eyelashes brushing against his cheek as he struggled to come out of nineteenth century America and into the present. "What?"

Abby pointed. "The sunset. You're missing the sunset."

He looked. "Pretty," he said and once again lost himself in the book.

The *plunk, plunk, plunk* sound of a bouncing ball came from the side of the house, down the driveway, and a moment later, a big orange basketball bounded up off the pavement and rolled across the front lawn. Noah followed and scooped it up on the run. "Hey, Denny," he called, tossing the ball into the air and catching it. "Wanna throw some hoops?"

"No, thank you," Denny answered, never even glancing up from the page. Abby butted him with her knee and he looked at her, puzzled. "What? I said no thank you."

So much for subtlety. "Go and play a little ball. It'll be good for you."

"Reading is good for me," he countered.

"Everything is good for you in moderation."

He bent his head to the book. "Not everything. Sunburns are bad for you. And cigarettes are bad for you. And poison ivy is bad for you. And . . ."

"Okay, okay, not everything is good for you. But even the things that are good for you aren't good for you if you do them to the exclusion of everything else."

"I don't." Denny turned a page and kept reading. "I help Lora in the garden and I help Grandma sometimes. I'd use the computer if Kyle wasn't always on it. You never tell him to go outside and play."

There was a good reason for that. She wanted her eight-year-old to broaden his horizons; she had to fight her fourteen-year-old rebel child to keep him within even the most lenient of boundaries. Two different boys. Two different problems. "Fine," she said to Denny. "Read. I'll shoot hoops with Noah." Pushing up from the porch, she trotted down the steps.

"You show him how it's done, Abby girl." Joe's voice boomed out from the shaded porch.

"Yeah," Archie seconded. "You show him how we do it in Sweetwater."

Noah grinned, backed onto the pavement and teased her with a slow dribble of the ball. "What's this, Denny?" he called. "Sending in the B team to wear down my edge before you take the court?"

"B team?" Abby feinted right, lunged forward, and stole the ball in mid-bounce. She moved closer to the goal and took a shot that sliced neatly through the net. "Captain of the 1987 3A State Champions Girls' Basketball team, thank you very much."

Noah chased down the ball and bounced it back. "You could have warned me you were sending in a ringer, Denny."

Denny looked up, interested. "What's a ringer?"

A new word. Possibly the only thing he liked more than re-reading a favorite story. "Ringer is someone who's very good at basketball—or any sport—and is substituted in to win the game," Abby explained.

"A ringer," Noah corrected, dribbling slowly toward Abby, who positioned herself to defend the goal. ". . . is *supposed* to surprise the opponent with superior skill, but sometimes the strategy backfires." He gauged his shot and took it. "Member of the 2002 YMCA Men's Amateur Tournament Champion Team, thank *you* very much."

The net barely moved as the ball swished through. Abby jumped for the rebound but only managed to tip the ball, which sent it bouncing down the drive, where it struck the hood of Melanie's Cadillac and set off the car alarm. The *bleat, bleat, bleat* pierced the evening calm, ripped a hole in every activity from basketball to rocking chairs to reading and filled the vacuum with its irritating blat. Noah retrieved the ball, tossed it to Abby, then trotted over to try the car door. "Locked," he called to her. "We'll need the key to turn it off."

"I'll send Denny to get Melanie's key." Abby clutched the basketball and raised her voice above the noise, but Noah wasn't listening. His whole attention had diverted to the upstairs dormer, the gabled window in what had once been Abby's room and which now belonged to Gideon Garrett. She followed his gaze to see Melanie framed in the sepia reflections of the setting sun, unmoving and unmotivated by the fact that her car alarm squalled like an injured beast.

With her hair gilded bronze by the dying light, Melanie stared down at Noah and he stared up at her and, in that moment of exchange, Abby had a fleeting sense of having seen this before, of having felt the same faint chill of premonition she experienced now. It was gone in an instant, but it left behind an unsettling association. The night of the accident, Alex had been here, on this front lawn, looking up at Abby's window. And she'd been looking down at him. It had been the last time she saw him alive and the only time he'd allowed her to see his unhappiness. The memory was vivid and vulnerable in her mind, sharpened by regret, etched with the knowledge that she had hurt him.

"Hey!" Noah cupped his hands to his mouth to yell, then gestured pointedly at the car. Melanie vanished from the window, the screen door opened and Mae stepped out onto the porch saying something that was lost in the noise. Archie reached up to adjust his hearing aid, Violet draped her sagging bosom over the red, white, and blue box as if she were protecting Mr. McAfee's dusty ears, and Rose and Effie leaned forward in their rockers, each explaining at the top of her voice to Mae how the basketball had come to hit the car and set off the alarm. The moment for remembering was gone and Abby bounced the ball once on the pavement, and then again.

By the fifth bounce, Melanie stepped through the doorway, moved unhurriedly past Mae, and walked to the edge of the porch, where she aimed her remote key at the Cadillac. The alarm stopped as abruptly as it had started, but the noise echoed in the dusk, lingering in the air like gasoline fumes that burned the nostrils long after the polluting vehicle had passed by.

She then descended the stairs like a beauty queen, conscious and confident that all eyes were on her, certain of her grace and exquisite beauty. Her smile, as she approached, was serene and vaguely intriguing. In high school, Abby and her friends had dubbed the look: *Melanie as Madonna.* The virginal expression owed more to Madonna, the singer, than the Blessed Virgin, but its effect on men—and a lot of women— couldn't be disputed. They had lined up in droves to worship her. Even now, as Melanie turned toward her, Abby felt the pull of her seductive charisma, recognized its allure, the nameless danger lurking beneath that cunning innocence.

"You may be outclassed, Noah." Melanie bent the faint smile his way. "Abby probably didn't tell you she was the star player of our girls' basketball team in high school."

"As a matter a fact, she did warn me she was the team captain."

"Count yourself fortunate then. She's always been such a shy, modest little thing. We couldn't get her to brag about her accomplishments, no matter how hard we tried."

The comment implied that theirs had been a close, personal friendship, that they knew each other well, remembered their time together fondly. Which couldn't be further from the truth, yet the lie sounded sincere, real. If Abby hadn't known better, she might have believed it herself. "Don't let Melanie fool you, Noah. I'm quite susceptible to vanity when it comes to my hook shot." Turning, she poised to demonstrate and arched the ball cleanly through the net. "Now that," she said, "was a beautiful basket."

"It was, for a fact." Noah scooped up the ball and thumped it against the pavement in a rapid dribble before making a run at the goal and dunking the ball. He rebounded in one fluid move and came down grinning, showing off for the queen. "But not as pretty as that."

Melanie's smile opened like a flower, admiring and overtly sexual. "And here I thought Abby was out here beating your socks off. I didn't know you were so talented, Noah. You must have been a basketball star in high school, too."

Tucking the ball beneath his arm, he lifted his shoulder in a careless shrug, even as his expression conveyed a prideful acceptance of the compliment. "Just a few club leagues the last couple of years."

It was exactly the sort of response most men made to women like Melanie. Taking her comments at face value and preening under the attention. Letting her loveliness and coy admiration seduce and flatter him. Believing—as she meant for him to do—that he alone would be man enough to satisfy her. Abby felt a twinge of disappointment that Noah fell for it like a duck for a decoy.

"Abby was one of Potter High's best athletes, you know," Melanie said. "She and Alex received the most valuable player awards all three years of high school. Of course, he played football, even won a partial scholarship to play at OU, but he died tragically that summer. Drowned in the river." Her eyes cut back to Abby. "I don't remember, Abby. Did they give you a scholarship, too?"

Abby suspected Melanie recalled every award presentation—and each recipient—with unambiguous clarity and resentment. "Yes," she answered. "As a matter of fact, I did earn a scholarship. In academics."

"Oh, that's right. I remember now. You were always smart. I remember the whole town drooped with disappointment when you got pregnant and had to drop out of college. Jeff took it especially hard but, like everyone else, he was thrilled to hear about your marriage and the baby." She turned to Noah. "Life is funny, you know. While Abby went off to college somewhere in Kansas, I stayed here and married her sweetheart. And by the end of the first semester, she'd gone and married a football player none of us had ever heard of and tossed aside her scholarship for true love." Her laugh was designed to dazzle and, by the look on Noah's face, it worked just as beautifully now as it had in high school.

Never mind that her words belittled Abby's choices, that her throaty laughter hit its intended target and injected its poison.

"So what about you, Noah Walker?" Melanie poured more seductive power into her voice, enchanting her prey, drawing him in. "Are you ever going to tell what mysterious twist of fate brought you to this yawn of a town?"

"It's hardly a mystery," he said. "I'm doing an environmental study of your river."

Melanie moved closer, stepping inside his personal space, her lips slightly parted, her face lifted and tempting, invitation in every move she made. "How very fascinating."

He leaned toward her, signaling a willingness to go along with whatever she had in mind. "I seem to have an unsatiable fascination with the unpredictable."

"What a coincidence. So do I."

Abby had seen Melanie weave her spell before, so she wasn't surprised to see Noah caught in her web. Stronger men than he had buckled under the sheer sexuality Melanie exuded like the scent of an exotic flower. Still Abby had a sense that this flirtatious play had happened before. There was an easiness to the co-quetry, a teasing subtext to their conversation, a very real sense that this was role-playing and not the real deal. Inside the house, the phone rang. Noah and Melanie stepped apart, but Abby thought she could still see the connection, the gossamer threads of an alliance that wavered but held fast. She moved forward and took the ball from Noah, then turned and sank a basket, catching the ball on an easy rebound, wondering why, after all this time, Melanie felt she still had to prove she could have any man she wanted . . . especially if she thought Abby wanted him, too.

The phone rang again.

"Denny? Will you go in and get that?" Mae asked, her voice sounding loud against the soft screak of the rocking chairs and the slow, unhurried dribble of the basketball on the pavement.

Denny marked his place in the book, stood, and scuffed inside, the screen door whacking the door frame behind him. The phone rang again and then went quiet.

Melanie strolled to her car and ran her hand across the hood. "I'm assuming one of you all-stars hit my car with your basketball. Did either one of you check for damage?" Her fingers covered the slick white surface in narrowing circles. "I think there may be a dent. Right here."

"Really?" Noah joined her at the car. "I didn't think the ball hit hard enough for that." His hand went to where hers rested. She didn't move, letting his fingertips brush hers in a moment's caress. Their eyes met, sharing the knowledge of a mutual attraction, and Abby looked away.

Embarrassed. Disgusted. And maybe a tiny bit envious, too. Because Melanie was still beautiful and able to steal a man's attention away from Abby so easily it was laughable.

Eyeing the basket, Abby concentrated, focusing only on the exact spot she wanted the ball to go.

"Mom! Telephone!" Denny yelled, hinges squeaking as he batted the screen door back and forth between his palms. "It's Lexie's dad. He wants to talk to you."

Abby felt the instant cut of Melanie's eyes, the instant fury that boiled over and came at her in a scalding flood of hatred and unfounded jealousy. Releasing the ball, she watched it spin, end over end, toward the basket, and she knew, even before it hit the rim, that it was a miss. The ball shied off the goal and made a hollow sound as it escaped down the driveway. Noah moved to catch it, but Melanie stepped in front of him and picked up the ball.

"Be careful, Abby," she warned, and tossed it back. Hard.

Abby caught the throw, felt the sting of it in her palms, felt old animosities return with the suddenness of a bad case of heartburn. A thousand words sizzled on her tongue, acrid and unadvised, but she couldn't stop herself from tossing the ball back. Not as hard, but just as pointed. "Perhaps, Melanie, it's you who should be careful."

"Mom," Denny yelled again. "Telephone! Didn't you hear me?"

She held Melanie's gaze for a long moment, then turned on her heel and headed for the house.

Chapter 13

Melanie had the scissors in her hand when Jeff found her in the formal dining room. The room that had been so important to her when they built the house. The room she insisted they had to have for company. The room *company* had never seen because there was never any *company* to see it. The room even the three of them never ate in. Lexie had once tried to use it as a place to do homework, but Melanie didn't like the thought of a spiral-ring binder scratching the surface of the table or a pencil nib pressing too hard into the beautiful wood. She didn't want fingerprints or smudges marring the shine of the rich walnut. The table and its matching buffet had belonged to Jeff's grandmother, his mother's mother, and were the only genuine heirlooms he owned. They were the only pieces of old furniture Melanie had deemed good enough for the new house, the only part of Garrett history welcomed into the marriage. His Grandmother Talbot had obviously taken loving care of the pieces, and now they sat, unused and unappreciated, in a room no one ever saw.

Jeff could go weeks at a time without even remembering the house had a dining room, but tonight as he came out of the kitchen and headed for the stairs, he saw the light and heard the slide of scissors across paper, the metallic slice of the hinged blades. "Melanie?" He called her name before he reached the doorway, thinking it was odd that she'd be in the dining room, odder still that she wasn't already in bed, dosed into sleep by her migraine medication. But there she was, sitting at the table, her hair hanging forward in a sleek fall of fairy gold, her head bent over the picture she was cutting from an open magazine. Other magazines were scattered across much of the tabletop—*Town & Country, Texas Monthly, House Beautiful, Southern Living, Architectural Digest*—and scraps, lots of slivered scraps of slick paper littered the floor around her chair.

"Melanie?" he repeated, aware that the mess meant she was either upset or angry. Probably both.

She didn't look up. Not right away. Just kept cutting around the outline of a chair or a sofa. Jeff couldn't tell which it was. Already there were dozens of cutouts stacked on the table in front of her. The magazines had been mutilated into meticulous bits of paper . . . a fireplace, a sofa, chairs, an ottoman, a miniature vase of vivid flowers, each outer petal cut precisely, perfectly in detail. He didn't need to ask what she was doing. She subscribed to home decorating magazines by the dozens. It was an ill-concealed joke at the post office that anything with a picture of a house on it or the word *house* in it must be for the Garretts. It wasn't unusual for Bernie Hayes, their postman, to park his mail truck in front of their house and start his neighborhood round from there, rather than tote the weight of Melanie's magazines any farther than absolutely necessary.

And she read them all, page by glossy page, imagining her house, herself, her life in a different setting. She stripped pages she favored from the binding and filed them neatly away to look at again later. She cut out detailed objects, as she was doing now, and kept files of those, too. All labeled by room, by style, by color. When her headaches allowed, she could spend hours arranging her paper playhouse, moving the pretend furniture here or there, imagining different color schemes, changing out accessories, thinking of ways to improve the house she'd never been, never would be, happy with.

At first, Jeff had thought building a new house would bring her out of the depression that had plagued her after Lexie's birth. He'd believed the details of planning their home would distract her, that its completion would satisfy her, that living in it would bring contentment for them all. For a couple of months, Melanie had gone around humming under her breath, smiling easily and often, happy with the plans for *her* house. But then the architect had phoned Jeff with a concern: Melanie had made changes that more than doubled the expense and radically altered their original plans. One look at the new rendering had sent a chill down Jeff's spine. The house Melanie had planned was a larger, lavish version of the Wade House.

He'd understood then that she meant to punish him for having loved Abby instead of her.

"You're late," she said, laying the finished cutout in one of the neat piles. "You're very late."

He saw no reason to acknowledge the obvious. "Did Lexie call from camp?"

"No, Lexie didn't call, but then neither did you. Are you going to tell me where you've been or do I have to guess?"

Any guess she made would be wrong. Any answer he gave would be unacceptable. She was spoiling for a fight, here in her sacred dining room, backed up by the pristine cutouts of what she thought her life ought to be, cheered on by the slivers of paper she'd allowed to drop on the floor at her feet as a warning for him to tread carefully.

"I was at the newspaper." He set his soft-sided leather briefcase down beside the door, giving up any hope that he could postpone this confrontation. "Then I stopped at Beckett's and had a couple of beers."

Her eyes narrowed on him, a clear, cold sapphire blue. "You must think I'm so stupid. I know what you did . . . and it was nothing as innocent as having a couple of beers at the local bar."

He didn't know what she thought he'd done and cared even less. He was untouched by her accusations, indifferent to her anger. Tonight in his office, while he'd thought about Abby, about the past and the present, he'd squared his heart with his head. He was through subjecting himself and his daughter to Melanie's tyrannical moods. He was through worrying about the hurt she could—almost certainly *would*—inflict on them both. He was through demonstrating to Lexie that marriage was merely a staging ground for war games. He was through with the lie. He was through.

Looking at Melanie now, he was alert to the wild gleam in her eyes, aware that she was in a rage worthy of angels and born in hell. And he felt nothing. Not guilt. Not remorse. Nothing. Except perhaps an odd sort of pity. She was sad, really. All that anger. And not an ounce of truth in it all.

"I know you were with her." Melanie pointed the scissors at him. "I know you called her tonight. You *called* her, Jeff. At Wade House. You made a date to meet your lover while I was there, visiting your father."

He supposed he should have expected that. Even before he'd known her well, back when she was nothing more to him than his kid brother's girl, he'd noticed Melanie had a remarkable talent for being in the right place at the right time. Or wrong place, wrong time, depending on which side of the situation you stood. Over the years, he'd come to recognize it as calculated cunning. She was like a panther, blending into the darkness, every sense alert to change, waiting for any movement, however slight, perceiving all avenues of escape before the target even came into view. He'd watched her cultivate her sources—men, mainly, but women, as well. He'd seen her draw them in with pretty smiles and mock flattery, capture them with false interest, use them to find out whatever she wanted to know, and leave them none the wiser. He himself had been caught in her traps. Snared into one too many arguments, over something she had no way of knowing, to believe it could be coincidence. Melanie spied on him. Her sources reported on his comings and goings. She probably knew to the minute what time Abby had walked into his office this afternoon . . . and what time she'd walked out. It shouldn't surprise him that Melanie had beaten a path to Wade House on one pretext or another. Or that she'd been lying in wait for him tonight.

"I don't have a lover," he said.

"You're not even a good liar, Jeff. I was there when you called. I saw her face. She *is* your lover. Don't insult me again by denying it."

"There's nothing to deny. I have never been unfaithful to you, Melanie. Not once. Yet from the moment we married, you've accused me and condemned me for affairs that never happened except in your imagination. If I deny it, you call me a liar. If I offer no response, you claim my silence is proof. Tonight—*now*—is the end of it. I'm not playing this game ever again. You can believe whatever the hell you want."

"Oh, please, spare me the melodrama. You'll do anything, say anything to protect the poor Widow Ryan. You know it and I know it. I'm sure the whole town knows it."

"What bothers you more, Melanie. That I phoned Abby tonight? Or that the whole town might know about it?"

The rage in her eyes was fire and ice, a flame that rose blue-hot out of the frozen winter inside her. "What bothers me is how little consideration you have for my feelings. You humiliated me in front of everyone with your clandestine phone call. They all know what's going on, Jeff. Lexie won't be back in town for ten minutes before she knows it, too. How do you think she's going to feel when she finds out you're carrying on with that . . . that *boy's* mother? What are you going to say to your precious daughter then?"

"I'll probably say that boy's mother applied for a job at the Trib and I hired her."

"You *hired* her? Oh, now, isn't that just too convenient?"

He wouldn't give her the satisfaction of a response. Not again. Not ever again. Leaving Melanie was an option he'd kept in reserve for years, bringing it out for examination every so often, turning it in his mind like a multifaceted diamond, occasionally trying it on for the pleasure of how it fit, endlessly fascinated by the possibilities it presented. But always, always, he'd weighed the price of his freedom and known the cost would be Lexie. Which was more than he could afford. Much more than he was willing to pay. She would take Lexie away from him. Without compunction. Without compassion. Glad for the misery it would cause him. Uncaring of the pain it would cause their daughter.

However naively, he'd believed when at last the time came to leave, the past wouldn't matter. Lexie loved him. She wouldn't believe her mother's lies about him. But then it had never been Melanie's lies that stopped him from going. Truth hidden, concealed, protected like a precious pearl became the uncertain danger, a secret grown dark and ugly and menacingly large in its omission. But for good or ill, the time had come to ransom himself and his daughter.

Turning abruptly, he heard the scissors *snap*, recognized it as a warning. But he walked away from the anger and anguish of his bankrupt marriage, each step firmer than the last, feeling almost light on his feet as he took the stairs two at a time and walked down the hall to his bedroom.

Dragging a suitcase out from under the bedstead, he laid it open on top of the mattress. He pulled out the top drawer of the bureau, expecting to find clean underwear, socks, t-shirts. This morning, when he'd dressed for work, there had been neat stacks of each. Laundry he'd washed, dried, folded, and placed in the drawer, as he did every weekend. But now, the drawer contained Melanie's winter sweaters, layered four deep, two across, folded for minimum wrinkling, separated by a square of tissue paper, and nestled on scented drawer liner with a small cedar sachet tucked in each corner to discourage the summer moths. He closed that drawer and opened the second. More sweaters. The third held her flannel sheets and the wool throw she kept on her bed during winter. He didn't look any further, knowing nothing of his would be found in any drawer in his bedroom. Probably not in his closet, either.

She'd moved his clothes.

For someone as incapacitated by migraines as Melanie claimed to be, she could accomplish an amazing amount of work in a few hours. When it suited her. And generally, when it suited her was the time she deemed would inconvenience him the most. She couldn't have guessed what he hadn't even known himself until just a few minutes ago. But here again was another example of her uncanny sense of timing, the way in which she tried to cut off an avenue of escape before he was even aware he meant to take it.

Lifting the suitcase off the bed, he carried it into her room. The bedroom they'd shared for less than five of the sixteen years they'd been married. Before he'd understood that her idea of marriage didn't mesh with his. Before he'd realized her greatest joy came from undermining his.

So he'd moved to the extra room, clothes and all. Only to discover the next day or the next week or six months later that Melanie had moved everything back into her room. Sometimes she left the hanging clothes. Sometimes she left the items in the bureau. Sometimes she took a little of both, but usually, like today, she moved it all. Moved it without comment. Switched his personal belongings to a different closet, a different drawer. A reminder that she could rearrange the order of his life without his knowledge or consent. She never asked. He never caught her in the act, and if he questioned her, she simply answered that they were married and the last time she'd checked, husbands and wives shared a bedroom.

It wasn't that simple, of course. Nothing with Melanie ever was. He'd tried leaving the clothes where she'd put them, which meant sleeping in one room and going back and forth to get his clothes out of the other. He'd put a lock on his door and received a bill from the locksmith she'd called to open it. He'd insisted they go to marriage counseling, and quickly realized his truths were no match for her ability to win sympathy with fabrications. That had been the first time he tried to leave her. That had been the time she'd put Lexie, sobbing and hysterical, on the phone to beg him over and over again to *please, please, please* come home, wailing in her heartbroken, little-girl distress that if he didn't come home she would never get to see him again.

Maybe he could have won custody in court. Maybe. But even if he had, Melanie would have disappeared with Lexie and he'd never have found them. He knew that as surely as he knew the phone calls would never have stopped. Always unexpectedly and at random intervals, there would have been his daughter on the line, crying for him, wanting him, believing he didn't want her, breaking his heart a thousand times over. Melanie would have made certain he suffered, just as she would have raised Lexie in an atmosphere of blame and disappointment, nurturing hatred and distrust in her innocent heart. He could have settled for joint custody or visitation only, but Melanie would have found some clever way to get around that, too. She would have used Lexie against him, accused him of God knows what to get her way, made certain his daughter blamed him for every drop of rain that fell, every bad thing that happened.

Tossing the suitcase onto Melanie's bed, Jeff went to the dresser and—as he'd expected—found his jockeys next to her panties, his socks mingled with her hosiery, his T-shirts cohabiting with her nightgowns. He separated them, pitching his things into the suitcase, leaving her things in disarray. Then he went to the closet, pulled shirts from hangers, folded slacks in hurried thirds, and laid them end to end on top of the rest. Shoes he stuck into an old duffle, leaving just enough room on one side for his toiletry bag. And when he was done, he had one suitcase, one duffle bag, and a new sense of self-respect.

The only other thing he meant to take from this house was his daughter.

He looked up, startled to see Melanie in the doorway, her expression cool, her stance relaxed. Only her knuckles showed white where she gripped the scissors, flexing the blades open, then closed. Open. Closed. If her hand moved a quarter inch closer to her body, she'd have nicked the fabric of her slacks.

Slinging the duffle's strap across his shoulder, he grabbed the handle of the suitcase. "I'll pick Lexie up at the high school when she comes home from camp. The bus usually gets in around noon. I'll take her to lunch, tell her I've moved out and then bring her here, so you can talk to her." He paused. "I assume you'll want to talk to her."

Melanie's smile was lethal. "Yes, Jeff. I will definitely want to talk to her."

He heard the threat in the words, felt the fury in her stillness, registered the silence of the scissor blades at her side. "All right, then," he said and took a step toward the door.

She didn't move, so he stopped. "Are you sure you've thought this through?" she asked. "You can't be unaware of what the scandal will do to Lexie."

The statement was so exactly like her, so manipulative and full of censure, as if she were helpless to prevent a disaster he was determined to cause. "It has finally dawned on me what this marriage has already done to her, Melanie, what it *will* do to her if it continues. And our divorce doesn't have to be a scandal. I'm willing to end this amicably."

"Oh, I'll just bet you are. Unfortunately, it's always a scandal when a man leaves his wife for another woman. Even your adoring public won't be so sympathetic this time. And I can promise you, Jeff, you will lose your daughter over this." She smiled then, taking pleasure in the thought of his pain. "You really should reconsider your choices here."

"It doesn't need to be like this, Melanie. You're miserable. I'm miserable. Together, we've made Lexie miserable. We should have reconsidered our choices a long time ago."

"But you waited until Abby Wade came home, didn't you, Jeff?"

And around they came to the same damn argument. He locked his gaze on hers and walked purposefully toward her. She held her ground long enough to bait him into altering his stride, then stepped back out of the doorway. He brushed past her, in a sudden and suffocating need to get out, to be somewhere, anywhere, she wasn't. All the way down the stairs, she stayed two steps behind him. Her rage breathed like a living thing, hot on his heels, and when he hit the last rung, he kept moving, swinging left and going straight through the kitchen to the back door. The second his hand touched the latch, though, he thought of Lexie and stopped, bracing himself as he turned to make one last stab at reason.

"I'm not leaving because of Abby," he said. "I want you to know that."

Melanie, her beauty enhanced by the heat of anger, halted in the center of the pristine kitchen and stood there, seething with a strangely serene wrath. "Abby ruins everything, Jeff. You've never been able to see that. You could never admit it was your precious Abby who ruined your life, that it was her fault Alex was so drunk that night. She's as guilty as you are for sending him on that wild ride down the river road. But did you ever hate her for what she did? Oh, no, not Abby. You hated me instead, blamed me for everything that went wrong. And you went right on loving her, didn't you, Jeff? From that night to this one, you never stopped loving her. So don't expect me to believe your leaving has nothing to do with Abby. Unlike you, I am no one's fool."

"For the last time, Melanie, this is between you and me. Leave Abby out of it."

"The only time you ever left Abby out of anything, Jeff, was the first time you fucked me."

The word slapped him with its ugliness, slandered him with the uglier truth of his act and his utter stupidity in committing it. In one mindless, drunken moment, he'd betrayed his brother, Abby, and every principle worth having, trading it all away for a pleasure that evaporated the instant he reached for it. In one senseless act, he'd destroyed everything.

"There isn't a day that goes by, Melanie, I wouldn't sell my soul to change what I did."

A low, rich laughter began in her throat and bubbled over into melodic glee. "Silly me. After you killed your brother, it never occurred to me you might have a soul left to sell."

His hand clenched hard on the cool brass knob, and then the door was open and he sprinted out into the summer night. The duffle slid from his shoulder, the suitcase dropped to his side, and he bent over, clutching his knees, letting the blood rush to his head. A familiar sickness rose inside him, thrashed in his stomach, pummeled his gut. *Alex.* Jeff knew if he closed his eyes he'd see the accident, hear the abrasive scrape of metal against metal, feel the pull of the steering wheel in his hands, and watch his brother's car spin out on the rain-slicked pavement, hit the air, and flip end over end into the flooded river. He'd relive it all, as he'd done hundreds of times before, and the last awful image to linger would be Alex's face, distorted by rain splatters on the glass, staring at him through the car window, as they raced side by side around that final curve.

And then would come the memory of Abby's face when he'd told her what he'd done and what he now had to do.

Jeff's head throbbed with the intensity of his regret. Ever and always the regret.

Straightening, he rubbed his hands hard against his face, pulling himself away from the edge one more time, forcing images from the past into the darkest corners of his mind. The air was heavy with heat and humidity, thick with a coming storm, but he breathed it in thankfully and filled his lungs to bursting, then released it all in a long, slow exhale. He repeated the exercise until he felt calm again, in control. Behind him, no sound came from the house. No laughter. No threats. No accusations either just or unjust. Nothing. There was only the sound of the cicadas and the midnight whispers of a sleeping town.

It wasn't until he reached down for the suitcase and duffle that he realized he'd forgotten his briefcase. Left it in the dining room. *The hell with it.* He wasn't giving Melanie another shot at him tonight. But then he remembered the steely slice of the scissor blades in her hand, imagined the contents of his briefcase shredded. In the mood she was in, she might cut up the whole thing, leather and all. He'd have to go back for it.

The door was ajar, just as he'd left it, but she was no longer in the kitchen. He listened, hoping she'd gone upstairs, praying he could get in and out without seeing her. Or being seen.

If he hadn't been trying so hard to be quiet, he never would have heard it. A soft *scritch* of a sound. Like the scratching of mice in a cupboard. Irritating and alarming in its repetition. Impossible to name.

Impossible, that is, until he reached the doorway of the dining room and looked in to see Melanie with the scissors, blades yawning open as she carefully, meticulously carved a large, malicious *X* into the polished surface of his grandmother's prized table.

"What are you *doing*?" He strode forward, grabbing her wrist with one hand and the scissors in the other. The blade was razor sharp and sliced across his palm, but he hardly felt the sting as the scissors fell to the floor. His hand would heal, but what she'd done to the table would remain forever. He reached out tentatively, sick at heart, to touch the scars, and it was then he saw the gouge marks. Obviously, she'd begun the destruction much earlier, long before he got home, inflicting her anger in pointed stabs into the thick walnut.

Abby, she'd spelled out.

And now she'd cut an *X* through the name. A deep, spiteful *X*.

He could hardly bear to look at her and hated her in that moment more than he would ever have believed possible. With her wrist clenched in his grip, violence flirted with his reason, seeming for an instant like a rational, reasonable response to her venomous act. He could snap her wrist in one move, punish her with physical pain, as she had punished him with her willful destruction. But one look into her eyes brought him to sanity and disgust, and he flung her hand away from him. It hit the table with a sharp *whack!* and she immediately cradled it in her other palm and drew it close to her body.

She smiled at him with an unapologetic elation. "Ouch," she said, and then lifted her shoulder in a careless shrug. "I warned you, Jeff. Abby ruins everything."

Repulsed, he stepped backward, fumbling for the briefcase behind his back, unwilling to turn his back on this woman he'd too long called his wife. Keeping his eyes on her, he walked backward from the room.

Swiftly out of the house.

Into the night and away.

Going anywhere—*anywhere*—but where she was.

Chapter 14

•

Winter, spring, summer, or fall, football fever burned bright at the Sweetwater Café. Co-owners, Mary Jo Jenkins and Ginger Mahoney, shared a not always friendly rivalry—Mary Jo being a fanatic about OU and Ginger being equally manic about Oklahoma State. College football was the meat and potatoes of their contention, but it had been known to carry over to professional leagues as well. On any given day, the women might be feuding about the Broncos versus the Raiders or the college rankings or who should win the Heisman Trophy. The two had bought the café, sight unseen, in 1982, from Dorothy and Tom Dempsey, who'd taken over when Dorothy's dad died right after World War II. Tom had lost an arm in the war, but he cooked one-handed for nearly forty years and got so good at it that he proudly demonstrated his skill to anyone who wanted to watch. Dorothy told everyone who came in the café they wouldn't find better eatin' and entertainment even at the State Fair.

Times change, though, and when Mary Jo and Ginger arrived from California, the Sweetwater Café got religion. The gospel of football. No one in town—not even Alice Bearpaw, who worked the window at the post office and generally knew something about everyone—had any explanation for why two thirty-something females from the West Coast would take up residence, much less want to operate a business, in a small Oklahoma town. From the moment they arrived, the women stood out from the mostly conservative crowd. They wore woven sandals and long flowery skirts, embroidered cotton tops, and no make-up, and if either one of them had had a decent haircut in the previous ten years, it certainly didn't show. As Alice finally summed it up, they were nothin' but two old hippies and therefore suspect from the get-go.

But they were smart enough to get their finger on the pulse of the town within a few weeks. Smarter still to turn sports—the one activity practically everyone in town had a passionate opinion about—into a cash cow. The women hadn't owned the café six months before word of their rivalry filtered through the community and set the grapevine of gossip aquiver. Had they really divided the Sweetwater Café down the middle with the black and orange colors of the OSU Cowboys on one side and the crimson and cream colors of the OU Sooners on the other? Was it possible two women from California understood the importance of football in the "Sooner" state?

People who hadn't frequented the Sweetwater Café much in the past found excuses to check out the rumors. Regular customers during the week began showing up for Saturday morning breakfast or lunch on Sunday after church to get Mary Jo's or Ginger's top pick for the day's games. Not everyone was thrilled with this obsession, of course, but there was no stopping those who believed in the pigskin, and before anyone quite realized what had happened, Mary Jo was on the School Board, Ginger was Treasurer of the Garden Club, and the two women were accepted as members in good standing of the community.

Abby, Jeff, and Alex had spent many an hour sitting in one of the crimson and cream booths, drinking Cokes and discussing how strange it was that no one in their straight-as-an-arrow hometown questioned the fact that Mary Jo and Ginger also shared a house, a car, two dogs, and a yearly vacation. Alex's theory was that the two women shared a whole lot more than that. The idea of a gay couple living right in the middle of Sweetwater had seemed hilarious and exciting and highly intriguing to the teens back then. What if the two women really were *lesbians*? What if someone saw them *holding hands*? Or *kissing*! Alex was chock full of mischief and scandalous ideas on how he and Abby could sneak into the house and obtain incriminating evidence. He teasingly pleaded with her to be adventurous, to accompany him, to share with him the fame and attention they were bound to receive when they exposed the "big secret."

Even as she laughed at his preposterous plans, Abby had felt a twist of shame in finding humor at the expense of two women who'd never been anything but pleasant to her. But she'd gone along with the joke because Alex was funny and she knew Jeff didn't like the flirtatious nature of his brother's overtures. Idiot child that she'd been, she had enjoyed the power of knowing these two brothers were vying for her attention, that she could provoke or placate their rivalry on a whim. As far back as two years before the accident, Abby had been playing with fire.

Then Melanie arrived to set them all ablaze.

Small wonder then that entering the Sweetwater Café for the first time in sixteen years had Abby a bit on edge.

But when she pushed open the door and a cheery, tinny chime played out the first few bars of "Boomer Sooner," she felt right at home. The fight song meant Mary Jo's team had beaten Ginger's in the last football game between the state universities. That was the deal the women had struck. Whichever team won that bedlam match-up had bragging rights—in the form of the door chime—for the whole year. In all the times she'd been in the café, Abby had heard the Cowboy's tune only a few times, even though she was a sucker for the underdog and secretly rooted for them every year. Still in all, the place looked much as she remembered, with its clashing colors and the competing stripe of black and crimson that ran straight through the room, from the kitchen, over the counter, and across the floor to the front window. Even the signage on the glass was divided, with *Sweetwa* in orange and black and *ter Café* in crimson and cream.

Since the last time Abby had been inside, the television had grown from a nineteen-inch RCA, wedged between the big Bunn coffeemaker and the eight-slice toaster, to a larger Sony on a suspension shelf high up on the wall. The diner was clean as a whistle and as ugly as the fans when their team lost. Good smells of good food and the noisy clatter of a busy eatery at the end of the breakfast rush brought on an instant and affectionate nostalgia for a time in her life when she'd been happy. She had laughed with innocence in this café and, somehow, the memory of that laughter welcomed her back.

"Abby Wade!" Ginger called out through the rectangular opening between the kitchen and the front. "Where have you been? M.J. and I have been expecting you to come in here ever since we heard you were back in town."

Mary Jo turned around so that the view of her ample rear changed to a view of her ample bosom. "Abby," she said with pleasure. "You're as beautiful as ever and don't look a day older than the last time you were here. Not a single day older, does she, Gin?"

"She looks older, M.J. Put your glasses on." Ginger shook her head, her long gray-streaked, reddish hair braided, knotted, and netted on top. "I'm not saying she looks *old,* mind you, but she doesn't look like a kid anymore, either."

"Oh, she does, too." M.J. flipped her hand, motioning Ginger to butt out of the conversation. "You'll always look like a kid to me, Abby. And to Gin, too. She just hates to admit she's a day older, but anybody with one good eye can see she's aging without much grace."

"And a blind man could tell you eat garlic for breakfast." Ginger banged her hand down on the bell and hollered, "Order up!"

Mary Jo made a face and turned to pick up the platter of food.

Abby stood inside the doorway, her own greeting still unvoiced and apparently unnecessary. A glance covered the room, quickly discerning that Jeff wasn't there. She had a bad feeling about this, had known when he called back this morning and asked if she'd meet him here at the café that he'd changed his mind about hiring her. His voice had been different. Strained. Abrupt. A hundred and eighty degree shift from the way he'd sounded last night when he'd told her the job was hers if she wanted it.

And she did want it. For her boys. For convenience. For the challenge. She wanted it because she wanted to show her mother that playing it safe wasn't always the smart thing to do. She wanted it because she needed to believe some part of her still belonged in this homey old town. She wanted it because she felt her sons needed roots that stretched deep into the rich, river soil. She wanted to work at the newspaper because it represented a dream denied, and she needed to discover how much of that dream, if indeed any of it, still resided within her.

She wished now she'd insisted Jeff say whatever he had to say on the telephone. Coming here wasn't exactly a smart idea. For one thing, they'd be seen, and no matter how professional and businesslike their conversation and behavior, this was a small town and gossip was its lifeblood. And for another, the Sweetwater Café wasn't exactly neutral territory. After so many years, it should have been, but how could she have guessed the memories would still be here, lying in wait for her return, ready to remind her of the optimistic girl she'd once been, the true believer.

Abby took her emotional pulse, felt the beat of an eighteen-year-old's rosy expectations, and inhaled a deep breath of reality.

"Hey, Abby." A bald, broad-shouldered, brawny man waved at her from a table on the demarcation line.

She didn't have a clue who he was until the pale, dark-haired woman sitting across from him turned around. "Hi, Abby. Remember me?"

"Melinda," she replied. "Of course I remember you. And . . . Beau? Beau Hartshaw, is that really you?" Abby walked over to their table, wondering how it was possible for anyone to change so much. But if he hadn't been sitting with Melinda, his girlfriend since the fifth grade and now, presumably, his wife, Abby wouldn't have had any idea who he was. In school, he'd been a rotund boy, with a ruddy complexion and chipmunk cheeks beneath a shock of sandy brown hair. Now, he was . . . well, nothing like that.

"I've changed some." He offered up a self-conscious grin as he ran a hand over his shiny head.

Abby laid her hand on the back of Melinda's chair. "You've changed a lot. I didn't even recognize you."

"People say that to him all the time." Melinda sat back as Mary Jo slid two hot breakfast platters onto the table. "It's mostly the hair, although he looked a lot different even before he shaved it off. He always wanted to be a fireman, you know, and he had to get in good physical shape before the department would even talk to him."

Beau grinned at Abby. "I grew a bit, too, after high school. Up, instead of out for a change. I'm a firefighter over'n Tulsa, now. We live there, too. No kids. Just me and Melinda. But we come to Sweetwater for breakfast every once in a while to grease up the old arteries."

Abby nodded at the platters. "That ought to do it."

He leaned toward her, pointing his fork at the mound of scrambled eggs. "Egg substitute," he whispered. "But we never say that too loudly in here."

"I understand," she whispered back.

Melinda cocked her head. "You by yourself, Abby? 'Cause we'd be happy for you to sit with us. We could catch up on where you've been and what you've been doing since high school."

"Oh, thanks, but I'm meeting someone."

"Anyone we know?" Beau asked with a wink.

There was no getting that small town nosiness out of a person, Abby supposed. No matter how changed they might be in appearance. "Jeff Garrett," she stated matter of factly. "I'm going to be working for him at the *Tribune*. Starting Monday." She said it firmly, as if confidence alone could make it true.

"Really?" Melinda's smile was quick and pleasing. "That's great. I always did hope you and Jeff would get back together somehow."

The comment struck Abby as odd, but not really surprising. Small towns exist within a paradox: change is constant, and nothing ever changes. Beau had changed in appearance, but he was still with his longtime girlfriend and, therefore, recognizable. The last time Abby had seen this couple she'd been with Jeff, and it was still within that context that they viewed her. Melinda's remark was nothing more than a connection, and it was connections to the past that formed Sweetwater's close community, not necessarily the truth of the present. "I'd better scoot," she said. "But it's great to see you guys."

"You, too. Good luck at the newspaper." Melinda's smile shifted from Abby to the pancakes on her plate.

"Yeah, we'll be watching for your byline." Beau peppered his eggs with enthusiasm, and Abby headed for a booth on the far back wall.

Tossing her purse in ahead of her, she slid across the black vinyl. Before she could straighten in the seat, a heavy mug thunked onto the tabletop and Mary Jo filled it to the brim. "Coffee?" she asked when she was through.

Abby grinned. "What would you do if I said no?"

"Drink it myself. You ready to order?"

"Just the coffee, thanks."

"You sure? I can whip you up a heart-stopper of an omelet, or Ginger will make you a plate of French toast that will melt in your mouth."

"Tempting, but I'll just have the coffee for now."

"Okay, then." Mary Jo started away, then doubled back, leaning in as if what she had to say was a great secret. "It's good to have you home, Abby." She bustled off, making the rounds, refilling coffee mugs, chatting with customers wherever she stopped.

Abby lifted the cup, breathed in the steam and, with it, the aroma. *Ahhh.* She blew against the cup's rim, then sipped, rolling the heat to the back of her throat, feeling the warmth spread downward when she swallowed.

I always did hope you and Jeff would get back together somehow.

Much as she hated to, Abby admitted her mother had been right about at least one thing. Mae had tackled Abby again just this morning, said she ought not take the newspaper job, that there'd be talk, that people remembered more than Abby thought they did, that some would view her working with Jeff as more than it was, that there'd be consequences, trouble. Vague, but dire, predictions flowed from Mae's mouth with the predictability of the sunrise and sunset. She had always been able to find the negative in anything Abby wanted to do. There'd been a time, some long ago, indefinite moment in Abby's memory, when her daddy could tease Mae about being a Gloomy Gus until he'd coaxed her into laughing at her own prognostications. But he hadn't lived long enough to teach his daughter the art of deflecting her mother's criticism. If it was, in fact, a thing that could be taught. After his death, Mae had seemed to lose her sense of humor altogether, and Abby had lost her balance. Leaving daughter and mother forever at odds, each trying to make sense of the other.

"More coffee?" Mary Jo was back, offering a refill. "There's enough left to top off your cup."

Abby shook her head. "I'm fine, thanks."

"You positive I can't get you something to eat?"

"No, really. This is great."

"Sing out if you change your mind." Mary Jo leaned in close again, the fine tip of her long, still-dark braid swinging forward across her shoulder to brush the edge of the table. "You know, as I recall, you never used to sit in the losers' section."

Abby became fully aware that she was on the OSU side of the room, surrounded by pictures and memorabilia in orange and black. Alex had insisted they sit on the other side, even if they had to wait for a table to open up, because he intended to play football for OU. He'd been too small. Everyone told him so, but Alex ignored them and sprinted for the goal. Again and again and again. It was the only thing Abby had ever known him to do with unswerving purpose, the only thing he'd ever wanted badly enough to earn.

"I didn't really think about it," Abby answered now. "I'll be more choosy where I sit next time."

"See that you are." Mary Jo darted off again, slipping behind the counter to pour out the last of the coffee and start a new pot brewing.

"Order up!" Ginger banged her hand down on the bell.

"Boomer Sooner" chimed out as the door opened and a young couple entered. He was lanky. She was young. They held hands all the way to their table. Ginger greeted them with familiarity and a reminder that she didn't cook hamburgers for anyone before eleven o'clock.

The door opened again almost immediately, admitting Harold Wertz, who took the booth opposite Abby's. He ordered an iced tea and the blue plate breakfast. Mary Jo said she had strict orders from Barbara Ann not to serve him anything but the low cholesterol breakfast—fruit, Egg Beaters, and wheat toast—and he didn't need the tea either, because it gave him heartburn, so he'd be getting a glass of skim milk instead.

Abby sipped her coffee and eavesdropped until the door opened for the third time and Jeff walked in. He waved hello to Mary Jo, answered Ginger's, "Hey, Jeff!" with a cheerful, "Hey, yourself." He stopped to talk to Beau and Melinda, grinned at Harold's lament about worrisome old women who ought to mind their own business, was questioned about the previous night's town council meeting by two different men in two different booths, and paused to pat the lanky youth on the shoulder and say hello to the girl. All before he glanced toward the back and saw Abby.

He skirted the tables to come to her, sidestepping other distractions with a smile or a nod, and slid onto the vinyl seat. "Mary Jo?" he called. "Could I get a cup of—"

"If you'll get your elbows off the table." She was beside him, a mug in one hand, a pot of fresh brew in the other. "When's the last time I didn't put coffee in front of you the next minute after you sat down?"

He pulled back and held up his hands in surrender. "I can't remember."

"You bet your bippy you can't, because it never happened." Mary Jo poured the coffee and topped off Abby's cup. "Anything else I can get for you two?"

"Abby?" He addressed her easily, as if they'd been here, like this, a hundred times before.

"Just the coffee." She smiled her thanks to Mary Jo and took a sip of her warmed-up caffeine.

Jeff lifted his mug in a salute. "I'm fine, too, thanks."

"Order up!" Ginger called and dinged the bell.

"I'll be around if you change your mind." Mary Jo, her braid swinging like a pendulum, was off to pick up the order.

And it was just the two of them, both aware that they'd never been here, like this, before.

"Hello," he said.

"Good morning," she answered.

Jeff looked twenty-four hours past weary, and the fine lines around his eyes and at the corners of his mouth mocked the carefree way he'd entered the café and greeted his friends and neighbors. Abby bit back a stupid impulse to ask what was wrong. None of her business. Not her concern. He'd married Melanie. It was actually a wonder he didn't look a lot worse.

She sipped her coffee and waited, certain he meant to withdraw the job offer. That's why he'd wanted to meet her here instead of in his office. That's why he sat there rotating his coffee cup in place. Once. Twice. Three times before he lifted it and took a drink. Then he set it on the table again, studied her for a moment, and offered a half-hearted smile. "You're probably wondering why I called this meeting."

"I'm hoping you've decided to triple my salary," she

said, matching his attempt at a lighter tone. "Just to show how confident you are in my as yet unproven talent in sales."

His laugh had low energy, but it was a laugh all the same. "I'm confident you'll be equally talented at the salary I offered you last night."

"Darn. I guess it was a bit optimistic to expect a raise before I actually start working."

"You're considered a temporary hire for three months," he explained. "After that, we'll talk about a raise and employee benefits."

"In three months, we'll talk," she repeated. "Does that mean you're still going to hire me for the job?"

"Didn't I tell you that on the phone last night?"

"Well, yes . . . but I thought . . ." She lifted her coffee cup and replaced it again in its saucer without bringing it anywhere near her mouth. "I thought you'd changed your mind."

"My decision's made, Abby. I'm not going to change my mind." He contemplated the steam rising from the surface of his coffee. "You, on the other hand, may want to reconsider. Something happened last night after I spoke to you on the phone. Something I think you need to know."

"That doesn't sound much like a conversation anyone should have on an empty stomach."

"Who's got an empty stomach?" Mary Jo was back, a chubby zephyr of efficiency. "Can't have that," she said as she refilled their cups again. "What you two need is a cinnamon bun. And you're in luck because Ginger's taking a pan out of the oven this very minute."

Jeff turned the full power of his disarming smile on Mary Jo, even though his fingertips thrummed restively on the tabletop. "That sounds great," he said. "We'll have one."

"One and two forks?" M.J. asked, her attention diverting toward the door as it opened and "Boomer

Sooner" chimed. "Morning, sheriff," she said with a toothy grin. "I swear you've got a nose for Gin's cinnamon buns." She turned back to Jeff and Abby, checking to make sure she'd topped off their cups. "It's the darnedest thing I've ever seen," she informed them in a rambling commentary. "He walks through that door almost the minute she opens the oven. It's downright uncanny." Shaking her head at the mysteries of life and Sheriff Ray's keen sense of timing, Mary Jo bobbed behind the counter to grab a clean coffee mug and still managed to get the cup on the table in front of the sheriff before he could set his hat down. "Gin!" she yelled over her shoulder. "The sheriff's here to see you!"

"Hey, sheriff!" Ginger's voice came muffled from far back in the kitchen. "I'm icing your buns right now."

Melinda and Beau laughed aloud. The young couple tittered together. Harold Wertz glanced up from slicking peach preserves on his wheat toast. Mary Jo hustled through the swinging door into the kitchen. Jeff took a drink of coffee and leaned slightly forward to confide, "Ginger hangs a white dishrag out back whenever she puts a pan of rolls in the oven. Sheriff Ray has a window in his office with a good view of the alley. Once he comes in, Ginger retrieves the dishrag. You'd think Mary Jo would have figured out their system by this time, but she continues to believe it's a big mystery."

"Or pretends to believe. Even a little mystery can be good for business."

"You're sounding like a salesman already."

"You bet your bippy I am," she said with a smile. "And you haven't seen me in action, yet. Just wait until I actually start working."

"That's good to hear." He hesitated, then looked squarely and soberly into her eyes. "I left Melanie last night," he said. "And I've just come from meeting with Rayburn Swann. I'm filing for divorce today."

For a minute she couldn't breathe, startled by the admission and the anger so tightly held in his voice. She could see it in his eyes, too. Feel it in the tension that kept him still and unmoving. Like an early morning fog, it seeped into her, where it turned into aggravation that he had so abruptly involved her in the private details of his life, in his personal agenda. She reached for her purse. "Unless you're meeting individually with every one of your employees to share this same information, I believe this particular meeting is over."

"Abby, wait."

"More coffee?" Mary Jo zipped by, blocking Abby's exit for a moment. "Did I ask if you needed cream or sugar?"

"We're doing great, Mary Jo," Jeff said. "Thanks."

M.J. crossed to Harold Wertz, told him to finish his glass of milk, and called across the room to Sheriff Ray, asking him for the details on his new black and white cruiser.

"Hear me out, Abby. Please."

She leaned forward. "I'm not interested in having a private discussion about your personal problems, Jeff. And if you hired me because you thought—"

"Melanie believes you and I are having an affair," he interrupted, speaking low, but forcefully. "Which I believe makes this a little more than just my personal problem."

Caught by surprise, Abby slumped back in her seat. "An affair? I haven't been back in Sweetwater long enough to have had an affair, even if I'd been remotely inclined to have one."

"Oh, we've been carrying on a long-distance affair ever since you left. And she's decided that you have now moved back to Sweetwater to steal me away from her." The clefts in his cheeks—mature versions of the dimples he'd flashed often and effectively as a boy— deepened without a hint of humor. "Believe me, I

Zebra Contemporary

To start your membership, simply complete and return the Free Book Certificate. You'll receive your Introductory Shipment of 3 FREE Zebra Contemporary Romances, you only pay $1.99 for shipping and handling. Then, each month you will receive the 4 newest Zebra Contemporary Romances. Each shipment will be yours to examine FREE for 10 days. If you decide to keep the books, you'll pay the preferred subscriber price (a savings of up to 30% off the cover price), plus shipping and handling. If you want us to stop sending books, just say the word… it's that simple.

FREE BOOK CERTIFICATE

Yes!

Please send me 3 FREE Zebra Contemporary romance novels. I only pay $1.99 for shipping and handling. I understand that each month thereafter I will be able to preview 4 brand-new Contemporary Romances FREE for 10 days. Then, if I should decide to keep them, I will pay the money-saving preferred subscriber's price (that's a savings of up to 30% off the retail price), plus shipping and handling. I understand I am under no obligation to purchase any books, as explained on this card.

Name _____

Address _____ Apt._____

City_____ State_____ Zip _____

Telephone (____) _____

Signature _____

(If under 18, parent or guardian must sign)

Thank You!

Offer limited to one per household and not to current subscribers. Terms, offer and prices subject to change. Orders subject to acceptance by Zebra Contemporary Book Club. Offer Valid in the U.S. only.

CN124A

lll.....l.lll......ll.ll.l.l.l..l..l.l.ll..l.l.l.l.l..ll..l.l.ll...l

Zebra Contemporary Romance Book Club

Zebra Home Subscription Service, Inc.

P.O. Box 5214

Clifton , NJ 07015-5214

PLACE
STAMP
HERE

know how ridiculous that sounds. How ridiculous it is. But Melanie is a fierce opponent, Abby. She proved that to me again last night and now, I fear, she intends to prove it to you."

Melanie had long since proven to Abby her prowess as an opponent. She'd stolen Jeff right out from under Abby's nose, won the spoils of victory before Abby realized there'd been a war. "And just what do you think she can do to me, Jeff? Take away my birthday?"

"It isn't that simple."

He was right in that respect. There had never been anything simple about living in a place like Sweetwater, where an innocent conversation could percolate through the town in a matter of hours, arriving back on your own doorstep as something not innocent at all. The fact that she and Jeff were together at the café this morning could easily filter from Melinda to Beau's mom, Peggy, who might mention it to her sister, Jean, who could pass it along to her daughter, Liz, who would certainly tell her husband, Danny, who worked with Rick Malone, whose wife, Debbie, wouldn't waste any time in calling her father-in-law, Joe, to report that Abby and Jeff were back together. Sometimes, the degrees of separation in your hometown didn't stretch any farther than two tables away. And at any point in that dissemination, Melanie could intercept the gossip and inject her own venomous interpretation.

But then, Melanie could walk through the door and see them together herself. She'd already manufactured an affair out of whole cloth, so it wasn't as if she relied on real evidence to support her claims. Melanie had never been concerned about the truth, and Sweetwater would never be large enough to provide anonymity to a homegrown girl like Abby. And that wasn't what she wanted, anyway. She wanted to work and take care of her sons. Period. Let Melanie make what she could of that. Let Melanie discover, if push came to shove, that Abby could be a fierce opponent, too.

"Make it simple, Jeff," she said calmly. "Keep me out of it."

"She'll never let that happen." The anger vibrated in his voice, a flinty resentment crimped the corners of his mouth. "Melanie will haul you into court as the other woman even though she can't provide a shred of evidence. She'll lie. She'll twist the truth. She'll do whatever she must to win. And she won't give a damn who gets hurt in the process."

"And this is the woman you married." Abby would have recalled the words instantly if she could have. Instead, they hung there between them, spiteful, ugly, dangling the *what-might-have-beens* before him like wilted flowers on broken stems.

"Yes," he said, because there was no defense he could offer.

Abby hated this whole conversation. Mae had tried to warn her, yet here she sat, facing Jeff, about to be embroiled in his battle, already tangled up in Melanie's web.

"One hot cinnamon bun, two forks," Mary Jo announced as she slid the plate onto the table and slapped down two napkins and two forks. "I'll be back with more coffee in a few minutes." She was off again, delivering more rolls, promising more refills.

The scent of sweet cinnamon wafted like a heavy perfume all across the restaurant, making Abby's mouth water despite the sick feeling in her stomach. She'd recognized Melanie as a spoiler within two weeks of meeting her. She'd tried to warn Alex. It had never occurred to her Jeff might need a warning as well. But that wasn't her concern now. He'd offered her a job. She'd accepted. And she'd be damned if she'd let Melanie take it away from her without a fight. "If she tries to name me as correspondent in your divorce, I'll sue her for slander so fast every head in town will spin. And you can tell her I said so."

"I'll do everything in my power to keep you out of it, Abby. I just thought it was important for you to know I'm filing divorce papers today and that you're directly in her line of fire."

"I'm taking the job," she said, chin up, ready to fight him for it if necessary. "Even if you'd rather I didn't. And just so it's crystal clear between us, I don't owe you anything except a good day's work for a good day's pay."

"Understood." He reached for her hand. A reflex, probably. Maybe a holdover from the past. Maybe he meant to shake hands on the deal. But in the instant before he touched her, she pulled back, dropping her hand into her lap, finding her dignity in denying him even such an impersonal touch.

"Be careful, Abby. Please . . . just be careful."

"I have a lot to do," she said. "Thanks for the coffee."

"Boomer Sooner" played out its annoying announcement again, but Abby was too busy untwisting the purse strap in her hands to pay attention. As she scooted toward the end of the bench seat, though, the pause registered. That split second when the clatter and conversations stopped, then hastily resumed, as if the diner itself had taken a startled breath. She glanced up, but by then Melanie was already at their booth.

"Well, isn't this just like old times?" Her smile floated effortlessly on the perfect bow of her lips, excitement glinted gold in her azure eyes. "Scoot over, Abby, and I'll slide in here next to you."

Abby scooted back the way she'd come because, as so often inexplicably happened with Melanie, the first impulse was to please her, the realization of what one should have done instead came a second too late to be of any use. And so, Melanie slid into the booth, her smile shifting from Jeff to the man standing uncertainly in her wake. "Sit, Noah," she said. "Jeff will make room for you, won't you, sweetness?"

Noah scrunched in next to Jeff, the two men exchanging awkward hellos.

"Ooh, yum. Ginger's cinnamon buns. I haven't had one of these in ages." Picking up one of the forks, Melanie speared a layer of the roll and twisted until it tore, then popped the yeasty curl into her mouth.

Her eyes went wide like a little girl's and her fingers flew to fan her lips. "Hot," she mumbled around the food, then with a couple of broad chews, she swallowed and blew out the leftover heat. "But worth it. God, those are good. Have some, Noah."

"You just said it was hot," he replied, smiling in that lamb-to-the-slaughter way men had when under the asphyxiating attention of a beautiful woman.

"Men are such babies." She twisted off another curl with the fork, put it against her lips and blew, softly, sensually, then extended it across the table like a holy offering. "Now, try it."

There was a moment, not exactly a hesitation, but more of a contest between the two of them, in which she dared him to be seduced, in which he held back his response. Then, as if it were an orchestrated move, he opened his mouth and took the bite, sliding his lips over the tines of the fork in a way that turned the dare back to her . . . and embarrassed Abby by its sheer sexuality. It was almost like watching an old video of the four of them. Melanie and Alex playing with innuendo, toying with each other and with Abby and Jeff, delighted when their actions produced embarrassment or discomfort.

"There, now," Melanie said, satisfied. For the moment. "Isn't that the best thing you've ever tasted?"

Noah chewed, swallowed, and agreed with a noncommittal tilt of his head. "Maybe. Maybe not."

He reminded her of Alex just then, the way he used to tease Melanie by never quite submitting to her coquettish demands—at least, not in Abby's presence, anyway. Noah favored Alex a little, she thought. Around the eyes, perhaps. Or maybe it was the slide of his smile. Or maybe it was Mitch she was reminded of and the discomfort of having to sit across the table from him while he flirted with the cute, blond waitress. Either way, Abby had already exceeded her limit on nostalgia.

"Don't you guys want some?" Noah asked, pushing the plate toward Abby, behaving as if it were nothing to flirt with another man's wife. Even when that man was sitting right next to him. "Melanie's right. It's pretty spectacular."

Abby shook her head. "I really need to get going."

Noah shifted the plate again. "Jeff?"

"No, thanks." Jeff's voice held no inflection, but his jaw contracted with anger. "I don't have much of an appetite this morning."

"Bad night?" Melanie asked. "What a shame. Especially since someone at this table obviously ordered one roll and two forks." She raised her voice, projected it out across the room. "Mary Jo? Bring another cinnamon bun over here, please. And two more forks. Oh, and an ice water, too."

Mary Jo took her time clearing off Harold's empty dishes.

"Freaking lesbo," Melanie muttered under her breath, but her good humor remained unscathed. "You'll never guess where I ran into Noah this morning. At the clinic. I thought I ought to have a doctor look at my wrist." She held up her right arm and let the long, loose sleeve of her blouse fall back to show the Ace bandage wrapped delicately around the wrist. "It's only bruised, but you know how doctors are. They have to do X-rays and ask all kinds of questions."

She smiled sweetly at Jeff. "They like everything explained and on record." Spearing the roll again, she pulled off a section and nibbled at it. "Did I ask you what you were doing there, Noah?"

"Prescription refill."

"Oh, that's right. I remember. Headaches, wasn't it? Lingering effects from a car accident, I believe you said."

"I got sideswiped by a pickup truck outside of Memphis several years ago," he explained to Abby. "And I do have some lingering effects, but the headaches are mostly allergy related. So don't put on your nurse's hat, okay?"

She smiled, deciding he didn't really remind her of Alex or Mitch at all. "Okay. I've put the white cap away and on Monday I start my training at the newspaper."

"Oh, my goodness, that's right." Melanie, who never liked being upstaged, reclaimed the spotlight. "I'd forgotten. We talked about that just last night, didn't we, Jeff? About how convenient it would be to have Abby at the newspaper." Leaning an elbow on the table, Melanie cupped her chin in her palm and managed a devoutly sincere expression. "So much better than having to train someone who isn't familiar with the town and the bass-ackward way people do things around here. Plus, as Jeff said last night, giving you Mark's sales position is simply the Christian thing to do."

Abby's fist clenched beneath the table. "I see you're still as kind and considerate as you always were, Melanie."

"I've found people don't really change all that much," Melanie said, nibbling on another layer of the cinnamon roll. "And I do still pride myself on being kind to those less fortunate. As you well know."

"Melanie." Jeff's voice grated, reprimand and warning all bound up in three sharp syllables.

"Yes, sweetheart?" She offered him the space of a breath to challenge her again, then turned her dazzle back to Noah. "You see, Noah, why Jeff runs the business. Have you ever met a more forceful man?"

Noah fell under her spell again, if, indeed, he'd ever fallen out of it. His smile seemed attached to hers as if when her lips curved upward, he couldn't keep his from doing the same. Melanie had that effect on men, but Abby felt again that extra sense of connection she'd noticed last night between Melanie and Noah. There seemed to be a certain familiarity between them, a definite ease that was unusual for such a short acquaintance. But Abby knew she hadn't imagined it. She could tell from the stiff set of Jeff's shoulders that he recognized it, too, and she wondered if it bothered him, wondered if Melanie's actions had the power to hurt him. Because there was no doubt she intended to hurt him if she could.

"Which is why he chose a forceful woman to be his wife." The caress in Noah's voice held the reassurance of a kiss.

Abby had to get out. Now. Not a moment later.

"Coffee." Mary Jo thumped two clean mugs on the tabletop and tipped the pot to fill them.

"I don't drink coffee," Melanie informed her. "I'll have a large glass of cold water. From a bottle. Not out of the tap."

Mary Jo didn't dignify that with a response. "You want more coffee, Abby?"

"I'm leaving, Mary Jo, but thank you. Everything was as delicious as I remember."

"But you didn't eat anything."

"I'll make up for it next time."

"See that you do." Mary Jo drifted off, coffee pot in hand, and Abby felt a twist of pleasure in knowing Melanie wouldn't be getting a glass of water anytime soon.

But then, Melanie didn't seem in any hurry.

"Do you plan to force me to crawl out under the table?" Abby asked pointedly.

Melanie laughed. "Are you that desperate to leave me alone with these two gorgeous men? You used to, at least, put up a fight, Abigail." Her pretty gaze shifted from Noah to Jeff and stopped. "Oh, do quit glaring at me, Jeff. I'll let your precious new employee out. There's no need to get ugly about it. All she has to do is say please."

"Get up, Melanie." Jeff's furious tone brooked no argument, and with the prettiest of pouts, Melanie slid to her feet and stepped aside so Abby could scoot out.

Abby managed to say good-bye to Jeff and Noah, called out a falsely cheerful, "See you later," to Mary Jo and Ginger, waved to Beau and Melinda, and popped out into the heat of the mid-morning sun, feeling like she'd run a marathon and knowing Jeff had been right about one thing.

She did need to be careful.

Chapter 15

With a sudden loud clanking, the transmission went out on the Blazer. Abby tried to shift, hoping she was wrong, but the stick slipped from point to point without engaging a gear. And she was coasting on the busy state highway. Slower and slower and slower. She thumped the steering wheel with the flat of her hand, frustrated with the car, her wasted morning, and the huge, shiny-new Hummer that took up all the space in her rearview mirror. Horn blaring, the yellow ATV pulled out into the other lane and gunned past her, the female driver yelling and gesturing behind the tinted windows of her tank. Abby mouthed a few pithy words in reply but her heart wasn't in it.

The Blazer continued to slow, and she steered it off the pavement, onto the gravelly shoulder of the road and killed the engine. Too bad she abhorred guns, since shooting the vehicle right now could only be considered a mercy killing. Instead, she'd have to have it towed and resuscitated, if that were possible, which she knew from past experience would be expensive—catastrophically expensive—and considering her dwindling capital, it'd be quicker to shoot a hole through her checkbook and be done with it.

Resting her forehead on the steering wheel, Abby waited for the dismal frustration to subside and remembered how Kyle had pleaded with her to buy a cell phone. *You shouldn't be driving that old car without one, Mom. What if you get stranded someplace? What if you need help?* She knew him too well to believe his concern for her safety was entirely selfless. He wanted a cell phone, was—according to his laments—the only teenage boy in the whole world who didn't own one, and he would share with her if that's what it took. He'd made a thousand promises he'd never keep, vowing he wouldn't use it for long distance, wouldn't go over the allotted minutes, would keep it with him at all times, and would never allow a conversation with his friends to prevent him from taking her call or from calling home at any time she appointed. He'd made some pretty persuasive arguments, even before he'd hit on his latest strategy of convincing her that he and Denny—Abby gave him extra points for adding guilt to the mix by cleverly mentioning his little brother's penchant for worry—were concerned about her driving an old junk heap of a car.

Well, he'd have more ammunition for that argument now, even if it was next to impossible to be stranded in Sweetwater. Someone would stop to lend a hand or offer her a ride. At least she hoped the residents of her hometown hadn't grown distrustful and suspicious in the years she'd been gone. She'd been welcomed warmly by the business owners she'd visited in the last couple of days. Of course, making a sales call with Mark along to supervise wasn't exactly a litmus test for being accepted back into the community with open arms. Neither was it a gauge of whether anyone would stop to help a stranded traveler in a black Blazer with Illinois license plates.

Abby sighed. She'd wasted the morning trying to persuade Brian, the prissy, twenty-something manager of Sports World that she could handle his ad for the Fourth of July supplement and that he didn't need to go over the layout and pricing again with Mark. Her first call on her own and she hadn't been able to sway the customer, hadn't convinced him she knew what she was talking about. Maybe this job was a bad idea.

The midday sun beat down on the Blazer and the interior temperature rose like a sauna. Grabbing her purse, she rummaged inside, came up with a clip, and anchored her hair up off her neck. She debated locking her purse inside the car, but decided that would be a dumb move in any town. So, with the straps slung across her shoulder, the bag flopping against her side, she set out to walk across the overgrown field on her right, heading for Rawson Road, where she'd be less apt to get run over by another Hummer and more apt to find a ride with someone she knew.

Mosquitoes, stirred out of their daytime lairs, whined past her ears as she plodded through the knee-high grass and swatted futilely to discourage them, flattening one little bloodsucker on her bare arm and flicking another off her cheek. A bumblebee buzzed by, paying her less attention than she paid it. She stepped too close to a killdeer nest, frightening the little plover into performing its injured act in order to lure her away from its nest. As she circled away from the killdeer's territory, the heat and humidity hovered like scavengers, and Abby felt the first drops of perspiration bead up between her breasts. A few more steps and the sweat gathering at her hairline trickled down the side of her face. Her blouse began to feel moist and tacky, her bra damp and uncomfortable. Stickweeds slapped against her legs and left their tenacious seeds clinging to her slacks, where they clustered in random fuzzy dots on the dark fabric. By the time she was out of the overgrown field, she was practically on tiptoe, trying to keep from stepping down too hard on any one of the multiple goatshead sticker burs that covered her sandals and pricked her feet with their nasty thorns.

She stopped on the pavement and gingerly removed the sandals, slinging her hand quickly back and forth when a sticker transferred its barb to her index finger. Sucking the sting it left behind, she tasted the salty blend of sweat and hand cream. She rubbed her finger with the pad of her thumb, and then holding the sandals carefully by the back straps, she slapped the soles together, trying to knock off some of the cantankerous burs. The rumble of bass, pulsing its rhythm into the summer air came at her, its source unseen, but already so loud she felt the vibration skimming the surface of her skin. Boys and their stereos. They were all going to grow up to be deaf old men, who would loudly deny the noise of their youth had made them hard of hearing. In the next instant, a flashy black truck roared into view, painted flames licking across the hood and down the sides, tires the size of tractors, chrome pipes adding flash and an extra blast of pizzazz, the engine and stereo throbbing with enough energy to stop a heart. Abby glimpsed a cab full of laughing teens as the truck flew past in a blaze of speed and adolescent extravagance, the *boom, boom, boom* fading fast into the distance.

She blinked, thinking for half a second she'd seen a familiar blonde in the mix. Which she knew was impossible. Kyle didn't know many kids in Sweetwater yet, and the idea that he'd roll out of bed before noon of his own free will was unlikely, to say the least. No need to borrow trouble before its time, as her mother often said. Good advice this morning as she had plenty of trouble right here and right now without adding in extra concern about her teenager. Abby scratched the mosquito bite on her arm, then swiped at the sweat dripping off her chin and started walking.

When the next vehicle appeared, coming at her from the direction of town, she was miserable and would have gone anywhere with practically anyone just to get out of the sun. Fortunately, her rescuer was Noah, and inside his Jeep Cherokee the radio played soft rock at a reasonable volume and the air conditioner spilled out beautifully cool air. "Ah," she said as she slid the seat belt around her and leaned back with a sigh. "This may be as close to Heaven as I can get today."

"That doesn't make me an angel, but it's a good pickup line."

She was too hot to smile. "Technically, you get credit for the pickup."

"Good deal. I need all the credit I can get." He reached over and pulled a bur off the front of her blouse.

It was a harmless move, his fingers barely brushed the fabric, but she pulled away, not really understanding why. Except that she didn't like the familiarity, the penetration of her personal space without invitation. She'd barely seen Noah since that morning he'd come into the diner with Melanie. Job training and acclimating her internal clock to the new work schedule took up much of Abby's energy. What was left over belonged to the boys. She had no idea what had kept Noah busy, although she had wondered once or twice if Melanie had anything to do with his frequent absence from the dinner table of late.

"Let me guess," he said. "You're out here on your lunch hour selling ads to passing motorists."

"The transmission went out in my Blazer."

"Bummer." He sounded like Kyle. When Kyle spoke, that is.

"Yes," she said in return. "Bummer."

"Do you want to use my cell phone to call a wrecker?"

She let her head drop back against the headrest and closed her eyes, still feeling flushed and overheated. "I'd rather call a travel agent. Plan a trip to someplace tropical. With lots of ocean. Cool breezes. Cabana boys bringing me frosty drinks and frozen grapes. Do you think I could swing a trip like that with the trade-in value of the Blazer?"

"Mmm," he pondered. "You might want to set your sights a little lower. Say, a weekend in Tunica, with a few bucks left over from the trade-in to stake you at the nickel slots."

"Well, if island hopping is out of the question, you might as well just take me home."

"Oh, well, if it's an *island* you want, I can take you to Jamaica."

"Now, *that's* a great pickup line."

"Good to know I didn't lose all my best lines in the divorce."

The information startled her and she opened her eyes. "You were married?"

"For about seven years."

"How long have you been divorced?"

"Mmm, let me think." He quietly enumerated the months, going backward. ". . . March . . . February . . ." Openly happy he remembered the date, he pronounced, "January. I've been divorced since January. I remember because I was on an assignment in Arkansas and Stacy had to fax the settlement papers for me to sign. She said that seemed appropriate since we'd basically had a long-distance marriage anyway."

"I take it you traveled a lot during the marriage."

"About ninety percent of my job is field work. But Stace knew that going in." He glanced over. "She thought I'd change. I've decided that's what all women do. They marry a man and then set about changing him into someone else."

"Nothing like a broad generalization. It's like saying a man only gets married to have someone to cook and clean for him. Although that one may actually be true."

He laughed. "Providing it's someone who will also have sex with him on a regular basis."

"Oh, yes, the fine print on the marriage license. Mitch liked to tease me and say he'd read it thoroughly before he signed and I should have done the same."

"But you were a starry-eyed bride and couldn't see anything except what you wanted to see. Am I right?"

"No. Not exactly. Did I go into marriage with some idealistic expectations? Sure. But I don't think that necessarily means I went into it believing Mitch needed to change to please me." But was that true? Really? She'd married Mitch because he was nothing like Jeff . . . and then felt disappointed—perhaps even a little betrayed—that he wasn't.

"I was wrong for Stacy from the get-go, and I knew it. But she helped me through a really rough time in my life, and I wasn't sure I could manage without her. We were good friends. Really good friends. I should have left it at that."

"How sad to lose a marriage and a friendship in one blow."

Reaching up, he took his sunglasses from a hook on the visor and slid them on. "I've lost things that are much sadder, believe me. And here we are at Wade House."

Abby pulled her purse straps up onto her shoulder. "Thank you, Noah. I owe you for this."

"No, you don't." He paused, grinned. "Unless you feel compelled to take me up on that Jamaica offer."

She laughed and was grateful to him for that, too. "I'll take a rain check. Are you coming in for lunch?"

"No, I'm heading up river this afternoon with my trusty sample kit. You want to come along? It's not what I'd call tropical, but I'll be happy to serve as your cabana boy."

"Tempting, but I've already fed the mosquitoes today. And I have to do something about my car. But thanks for the invitation. And the ride home."

"Always happy to be the hero," he said. "See you later. How about tomorrow morning? I've missed you on my morning run. Without you to set the pace, I'm working my way up to a five-minute mile."

"That's not good for you."

"I know. That's why I need you out there at sunrise in the morning."

"I'll try, but I'm not completely in my working mother routine yet."

"Okay, but if you hear anything about a streaker, I'll expect you to feel at least a little guilty."

She smiled as she stepped out of his Jeep, and waved as he backed out of the driveway. Thinking no further than a cool shower and a change of clothes, she walked around the house on her way to the garage apartment. She was halfway to the stairs when she saw her mother.

Wade House had a nice, big laundry room just off of the kitchen, added not so many years ago to lessen the amount of time Mae spent doing laundry. Yet, here she was, in the heat of the day, hanging freshly washed linens on the clothesline. Just as she'd been doing for as long as Abby could recall. Dropping her purse at the base of the garage steps, she went over to help.

"What are you doing, Mother?"

"I'm hanging sheets on the clothesline."

"It's a hundred degrees in the shade today. Just this once, couldn't you use the clothes dryer?"

"I like sheets dried in the sun. They smell clean and that makes for better sleeping. You know that."

Abby didn't think a good night's sleep was as simple as drying sheets in the sun, but she knew from past experience that argument was futile. Grabbing one of the hemmed edges, she folded it over the clothesline and held it in place while Mae clipped it with a wooden clothespin. They moved down the line together, working in tandem and in silence, the way they had many times before. As a little girl, Abby had loved these moments with her mother. Although now she didn't remember exactly why. Maybe it was the smell of wet cotton, the damp feel of the cloth in her hands, the warmth of the sun on her face, the steady snap of the clothespins in Mae's practiced fingers. Maybe it was the everyday grace her mother brought to this most menial of chores, the honor she accorded any labor, however tedious or trying. The memories lined up in Abby's mind, representing the qualities she admired in her mother. Mae approached life, good times and bad, with her chin up and her mind on the task at hand, doing whatever had to be done the best she knew how. She never flinched or faltered or stopped. She might be wrong, but she was never uncertain, and once set on a path, she didn't veer from it. Mae wasn't an easy person to live with or to love, but right now, at the clothesline, Abby thought her mother the finest woman she'd ever known.

"The Blazer died." The bad news welled up unexpectedly and spilled out. "It's the transmission."

Mae sighed. "Call John Ferguson. He sold his repair shop, but he's always working on somebody or other's car in his garage at home. I helped take care of Clydella when she broke her hip, and he's always tellin' me that if there's ever anything he can do for me, I should just ask. He'll take care of it, Abby, and keep the cost as low as he can. I'll get you the number when I go inside."

"Thank you." What else could she say? The Blazer had to be fixed, and if Mr. Ferguson would do it, Abby would accept the offer and be grateful for it. But the admiration she'd felt for her mother's take-charge style melted into a grainy blend of resentment and guilt. She could have—*would have*—handled the situation on her own, without her mother's help. And yet now she was in Mae's debt simply by stating what had happened. It would be churlish, stupid even, to refuse, but she'd managed problems like this before and she hadn't needed anyone telling her how to do it. But how did she say that to her mother without sounding ungrateful and critical?

"Denny had another accident last night," Mae said matter-of-factly, and Abby stopped worrying about cars and a mother who always knew best.

"He didn't say anything about it to me this morning."

"Sometimes I think he'd rather tell a complete stranger that he wet the bed than his own mother."

"What's that supposed to mean?"

Mae looked at her over the clothesline. "It means he worries more about his momma than any little boy ought to. That's what it means."

"I know he worries, Mother. I just don't have the magic words to make him . . ." *Normal.* The word stalled and wouldn't come out. ". . . like other little boys," she finished.

"He's never gonna be like Kyle, you know."

Abby didn't know how that was relevant. Of course, Denny would never be like his brother. He was a sweet, sensitive child with his own set of problems. "Maybe I should look for a therapist here. In Tulsa, I mean."

"Hmm," was Mae's noncommital reply. "If it was me, I'd leave Denny be for awhile and spend my worrying on Kyle."

Great. What had he done this time to put his grandmother in a snit? "I'm not going to make him get out of bed before I leave for work, Mom. Teenagers sleep a lot. They need sleep. There've been studies done about it. It's normal."

Mae took the extra clothespin she'd been holding with her teeth and clipped it on the line. "I don't think it's normal for a boy his age to tell his granny to mind her own business when she asks him where he's going."

Abby's heart stopped for a beat. "Kyle went somewhere? This morning?" The image of the big, black truck sprang readily to mind, and she was overrun with a maternal mix of emotion—abject fear and a fearsome anger. "Did he offer you any explanation at all?"

"Once I've been told to mind my own business, I do."

"You didn't even try to stop him?"

Mae clamped the last clothespin on the line with an audible *snap* and bent to pick up the empty basket. "He wasn't gonna be stopped, Abby, no matter what. You might've been able to do it, I don't know, but you weren't here. So he went."

Abby couldn't recall the last time she'd been so furious. At the moment, it was evenly split between Kyle and her mother, although logically she knew he deserved it all. "By himself?"

"He went with Billy Morris's boy, Cody, and Liddy Hilbert's boy. There were a couple of others in the truck I couldn't see too well, but it was Cody who was drivin'."

"A black truck with flames painted on the hood and down the sides." Abby clenched and unclenched her hands. "They passed me on Rawson Road. Did he give you any idea where they were going?"

"No, but if I was guessing, I'd say they're at the Burger Barn or the Dairy Queen. There aren't many places for kids to hang out in Sweetwater, you know."

There was the river, but Abby didn't want to think about that. "Can I borrow your car?"

Mae's lips tightened as she brought the basket up and held it against her. "Don't go after him, Abby. Chew his ear to a nub when he gets back, ground him for the rest of his life if you want, but if you go get him and embarrass him in front of these boys, you're only gonna push him into doing somethin' worse."

"There's something worse than telling his grandmother to mind her own business and going off with boys he barely knows without asking permission?"

"You know there is."

She did, and she knew going to get him would humiliate him beyond repair. He barely had two words to say to her now. Much as she'd like to do something about his behavior right this instant, she could only imagine the escalation of his hostility if she were to follow him to town and order him out of Cody's truck and into her mother's serviceable old Buick. If he flatly refused to come with her, she'd have left herself with no recourse. She couldn't match him physically, which meant if he didn't want to get out of that truck, she'd be left with nothing but threats. Hauling him out by force would be ridiculously melodramatic and, more than likely, highly embarrassing for them both. So she either had to stay here and wait for him to show up whenever he damn well felt like it or go on about her business and deal with him tonight. She was a working woman again. A working mother. Her absence was no excuse for Kyle to decide he had carte blanche to do anything he pleased, but neither was it a reason to allow his actions to ruin her day. She'd take a shower, change clothes, and go back to the office. Expending her energy on her job was, at the moment, more productive than allowing anger to control her. She would deal with Kyle this evening when she was calmer and her anger had cooled to a slow burn.

"Do you mind if I borrow your car?" she repeated.

"Of course not, but Abby—"

"Thank you," she said, cutting off any more unsolicited advice. "I'll phone Mr. Ferguson about the Blazer before I go back to the office."

"You're not going after Kyle?"

"I'm going to take a shower and change clothes." She answered and picked up her purse on her way up the garage stairs. "Then I'm going back to work."

"I think that's the wisest course," Mae said.

Abby didn't pause to answer, not really caring if her mother thought it was wise or not, but it seemed the best of the options Kyle had left open to her.

She did, however, have one punishment already in mind. Before she came home this evening, she intended to have a cell phone.

For her use only.

From now on, if Kyle wanted to go somewhere, he'd have no excuse for not calling to get permission first.

Chapter 16

"*Bzzzam!* Take that, T. rex! *Bzzzam! Bzzzam!*" The Black Hawk helicopter fired its laser beam rockets at the tyrannosaur until he toppled backward off the cliff and fell to his death far below where the pterodactyls and raptors attacked and stripped away the T. rex's scaly, dinosaur skin. "*Rrrourrr. Rrrourrr. Glomp! Glomp! Rrrourrr!*"

Meanwhile, the helicopter landed safely on the cliff. "Good work, men," Denny said in the deep voice of his favorite army man, Captain Rowdy. The captain hobbled over to the small band of soldiers who waited for his orders. "We killed the T. rex, men, but another, bigger one could come along any minute. We have to fix the time machine or we'll die when the asteroid hits. Hurry, men, there's no time to lose." The men saluted. They were dirty and wounded, but they were still brave. "Okay, Captain Rowdy," one of the soldiers said. "But it's gonna take two hours to put the velocity fluctuator on the time machine and the asteroid is only forty-two minutes from impact. What should we do, Captain Rowdy?"

"Don't worry, men. I'll use the robotic—"

Hearing the sighs of the house as the kitchen door opened and closed downstairs, Denny stopped his play, listening for sounds that might mean someone was approaching his hideout. Usually no one came down the second floor hallway as far as the attic door, but he was always very careful not to be too loud. This was the best hideout he'd ever had, and he didn't want anyone else to know about it. Well, lots of people *knew* about it. But they thought it was just a closet with blankets and pillows and stuff like that stored in it. Nobody but him knew about the secret room—the L-shaped section of the closet that angled back under the attic stairs. Someone had put shelves across the front, and he had to crawl under the bottom one to get to his hideout. But once in there, no one would ever find him. Unless he got too loud and they came looking for him. He could play with his army men in his hideout or read or work on his knots and no one came along to tell him he ought to go outside and do something else.

Listening hard, he could hear the rumble of voices from the kitchen below. Grandma's rough tones, his mom's softer voice. He quickly stuffed his army men into their shoe box and the dinosaurs into the plastic bag they'd come in from the store. Then he pushed both as far back under the stairwell as he could reach before crawling under the shelf and into the front part of the closet. At the door, he listened again, making sure he didn't hear anyone nearby. He opened the door a crack until he could see the hallway was vacant, then he stepped out and dusted off his knees. He could hear his mom's voice clearer now and she sounded mad. His heart pumped hard in his chest. He'd told Kyle not to go with those boys. He'd warned him Mom would find out. But Kyle never listened to him. Called him a twerp and told him to stop being a total dweeb. Kyle was always mad at him. *Ever since Dad died, Kyle had been mad at everybody.*

Pulling his rope from his hip pocket, Denny walked quietly to the end of the hall and edged toward the bannister. "Thank you, Mr. Ferguson," he heard his mom say. "I really appreciate it." Denny edged closer, working at the knots in his rope, thinking he could maybe lean over and see her, see if she was really upset or just sounded that way because she was tired. When she came home from her old job, she sometimes sounded upset, and Denny worried she was mad at him for something, but she always told him she wasn't mad or upset, only tired. She never said sad, but he thought maybe she was that, too. Although now he could hear her talking to his grandma again and she didn't sound worried. Or mad. Which made him feel better. Maybe he'd go downstairs and ask her how she liked her new job. But if she asked him about Kyle, he'd have to lie. And he didn't want to lie. Maybe he'd just go back to his hideout and play some more.

A door opened with a jerk behind him and Denny jumped, guilty all the way to his toes. "You there," a gruff voice rattled. "You, young man, come here. I need your assistance."

Grandpa Grumpy. That's what Lexie called him. And Denny thought it was funny, although it didn't seem very funny right now. "I-I'll get somebody t-to help you," he stammered as he inched along the bannister rail toward the stairs.

"I didn't ask you to get help for me. I said, I need *your* assistance. Is something wrong with your hearing?"

"N-no, sir." Denny felt stupid. And scared. Lexie's grandpa scared him and that made him feel stupid. Kyle was right. He was a dweeb. But at his grandma's house, if one of the boarders asked for help, he was supposed to help. And he liked to help . . . when it was Joe or Miz Violet or Miz Effie or Miz Rose. He liked Lowell and Archie, too. He wasn't scared of them. But his grandma wouldn't like it if he didn't help Mr. Garrett just because he was a grumpy old grandpa. And he couldn't tell his grandma he was scared, either. That would be worse.

He drew slowly away from the bannister and took a

hesitant step forward. "What k-kind of help do you need?" he asked, his voice rising to a squeak, his hand clutched around the knotted rope.

"If you will pick up your feet and walk in here, I will show you." Mr. Garrett stepped back and held the door open, a scowl in every wrinkle on his ugly, old face.

Denny picked up his feet and walked. He didn't want to, but he did.

"Now . . ." Mr. Garrett closed the door, put his hand on Denny's shoulder, and urged him further into the room. It was bigger than the room he and Kyle had to share in the garage apartment. And neater, too. There was a big television in one corner and a big stuffy looking chair over by the window. A small wood table next to the chair was piled high with books. Denny began to feel a little less scared.

"My magnifying glass fell on the floor and I accidentally kicked it under the bed when I came out of the bathroom. Will you see if you can retrieve it for me?"

"You want me to . . . to crawl under your bed?"

"Isn't that what I just said?" The gruffness returned to the old man's voice. "Are you this much trouble in school?"

"No." Denny couldn't figure out what school had to do with crawling under the bed. "No, sir. I'm good in school."

"Good at making your teachers want to pull their hair from their heads, I imagine." He ran his hand along the top of the footboard until he reached the polished wood knob at the end. Then he stopped and gestured vaguely to the floor on that side of the bed. "Somewhere under here."

Denny didn't wait for another stern order. He tucked his rope into his hip pocket, dropped on all fours, and looked under the bed. "I see it!" Flat on his belly, he squeezed under the bedstead and wiggled forward across the carpet until his fingers touched the silver handle. Pulling it into his grasp, he reversed his wiggle and moved out from under the bed. "Here." He laid it on the mattress and hopped to his feet. "I got it for you."

Mr. Garrett held out his hand, as if he expected the glass to be placed there, even though he could have just reached out and picked it up off the bed for himself. Old people were weird sometimes. But Denny picked up the magnifier, spent a half second wishing he could play with it, and then laid it in Grandpa Grumpy's outstretched hand.

"Thank you, young man." Mr. Garrett's gnarled fingers closed on the handle. "What's your name?"

"Denny."

"Denny, huh? No doubt named after the original Dennis the Menace."

He'd been called Dennis the Menace before. He hadn't liked it then and he didn't like it now. "I'm not Dennis," he said. "I'm Patrick Denton Ryan. Denton is after my dad. His name was Mitchell Denton Ryan, but everybody called him Mitch. And everybody calls me Denny."

The old man shuffled unsteadily from the bed to the chair, his hand out feeling his way, almost like he was too tired to watch where he was going. "I had a son named Alexander. Everybody called him Alex." Mr. Garrett sank heavily into the chair, laying the magnifying glass on his lap.

"I know," Denny said, not so scared anymore. "He died. Lexie told me."

The old man's shoulders sagged. "Yes, he died. Would you like to see a picture of him?"

Curiosity got the better of him. "Okay."

Lexie's grandpa pulled an album from beneath the stack of books and ran his rough, old hand over the front of it. It looked like he'd done that a lot because the blue cover was scratched and faded and all four corners were scuffed. Denny moved nearer, not wanting to get too close, but only close enough to see. When the album lay open, though, he sidled up next to Mr. Garrett's chair so that he could get a really good look at the pictures. "Which one is him?"

"Which one is *he*." Mr. Garrett put his finger on a fat baby with a big smile and no teeth. Or hair, either. "This is Alex at six months," he said.

"These are all the same picture," Denny pointed out after scanning the whole page of photographs.

"No, they were taken at the same time so they look similar, but each one is different. See this one?" His stubby finger pointed to a picture of the same fat baby at the bottom of the page. "He's not smiling. So it's similar, but not the same."

Denny couldn't tell much difference, but decided not to say so. "Are there any when he's my age?"

"I'm sure there must be. How old are you, Denny?"

"Eight. I'll be nine in February."

"February is a long time from now." Mr. Garrett flipped over several pages. "This should be about right."

Staring down at a boy about his size, Denny frowned. "Didn't he ever grow any hair?"

"What?" The old man squinted at the page, lowering his head and finally pulling the magnifying glass out and holding it above the picture. Then he chuckled, which startled Denny almost more than his gruff way of speaking. "Oh, he had hair. It was shaved for the summer."

"Shaved?" Denny didn't think he'd like to be shaved. For summer or any time. "You mean he had hair but he shaved it off?"

"Well, he didn't do it, himself. I took him to Terry Baxter at the barber shop."

"My mom cuts my hair sometimes, but she doesn't shave it all off."

"Alex did more sweating than a racehorse. Even as a baby he'd perspire if I put anything heavier than a sheet over him. When he was your age, it was more practical to keep his head shaved in the summertime."

"I don't like to sweat," Denny said. "My big brother doesn't mind so much. He likes playing soccer and basketball and games like that, but nobody ever shaved his head. Not that I know of."

"You don't like to play sports?"

Denny shook his head. "I like reading."

"Reading, huh? You're, what? Third grade?"

"I'll be in third when school starts."

Lexie's grandpa nodded. "What do third grade students read nowadays, Denny? It's been a long time since I knew what was being taught in our public schools."

"I don't know what third graders read," Denny said, leaning against the arm of the chair and scuffing his feet back and forth on the carpet. "In second grade, my teacher had us read boring, easy books and write one-page reports. And she wouldn't let me do reports on other books even when my mom told her I could read harder stuff."

"Above your grade level, you mean?"

Denny nodded. "The teachers never believe me when I tell them I've read *Huckleberry Finn* and *Tom Sawyer* and bigger books than that even."

"Have you really?" Grumpy Grandpa sounded like maybe he didn't believe it either. "So, tell me, Denton, did you like *Huckleberry Finn?*"

"Yeah. I've read it three times."

"The word is *yes*. Not yeah."

"Yes," Denny repeated. "I've read it three times."

"Good for you. I taught far too many high school students who were incapable of reading Twain. You must be very advanced for your age."

"I like to read." Denny lifted his shoulder in a shrug. "Did your little boy like to read?"

"Alex? No. He wasn't the student Jeff was, but he got by. I pressed him to do better with his academics, but he could never buckle down to it." His hand smoothed the crumpled corner of the album page, and then he turned pages until he came to pictures of a football player. "Alex the athlete, that's what I used to call him. Jeff was good, but Alex had the gift."

It didn't feel like Mr. Garrett was talking to him anymore, so Denny leaned over to look at the pictures better. "Can I use the magnifying glass?" he asked and felt good when it was laid in his hand. The magnifier blew the picture up huge. Denny turned it all different ways, put it close to the photo, and pulled back until everything was blurry. He concentrated on the football helmet, then on the black streaks under the boy's eyes, then on the number on the front of his football jersey. Eleven. If Denny put the glass right on top of the eleven and slowly pulled it away, the number curved and bent and wiggled on the background of white shirt. "Wow. This is pretty cool. How come you have this magnifier?"

"I need it to read."

"You should get glasses."

"I have glasses. They don't work very well for reading anymore."

Denny was still entranced with the lens. "I wish I had one of these."

"Do you? Enough to work for it?"

He looked at Lexie's grandpa, eyes wide. "I'm a good worker," he said. "Grandma tells me that all the time. Do you want me to crawl under your bed again?"

"No. I'd like for you to visit me everyday after lunch and read to me for one hour. Would you be willing to do that?"

This sounded way too easy. "Yeah," Denny answered.

"Yes," the old man corrected.

"Yes," Denny repeated. "Do you want me to bring a book? I have a bunch of them. What do you want me to read to ya?"

"I'll have to think about it. Do you have any suggestions?"

Denny thought hard. What would someone as old as his grandma like? "I gave my grandma the first *Harry Potter* book for Christmas last year, but I don't think she read it. She doesn't have a lot of time to read."

"A pity. I have the time and the desire, but am losing the ability. Do you think I would like this Potter book?"

Denny nodded, then afraid maybe Mr. Garrett couldn't see him too well, either, he said, "Uh-huh. *Everybody* likes *Harry Potter.*"

"Is that so? All right then. That's what I'd like for you to read."

This was way, way too easy. "You want me to go get it right now?"

Mr. Garrett smiled. "You remind me of my son."

"Alex the athlete?"

"No, my son Jeff. Lexie's dad." The wrinkles on his hand shook a little as he closed the album with a thud. "So, Denny, what are you waiting for? The Fourth of July? Go and get your book."

Denny didn't need more encouragement than that. A chance to read. And a magnifying glass as payment. He just might start to like living at his grandma's house.

Chapter 17

"You're not supposed to start taking long lunch hours until you've been here at least a week," Millie said when Abby walked into the office at a quarter after one. Then she spoiled the admonition with a wide grin. "Good thing the boss is playing hooky again today, huh?"

"Good thing," Abby agreed. "I'd hate to be late *and* have to tell him I didn't get the Sports World ad."

"Don't worry, you'll get it. Those big specialty stores excel at hiring kids who are still wet behind the ears and labeling them "Manager." Trust me, he's afraid to visit the little boys' room without first checking to make sure it's okay with headquarters. He'll call."

"I hope you're right. He asked to see Mark. In person."

"The jackass. Mark's not going to waste his time going out there. Tomorrow's his last day, and he will not spend it making a sales call. Mr. Sports World will have to learn to make a few decisions on his own. My guess is you scared the peewaddle out of him, and he tried to save his pimply face by saying he needed to see Mark."

"I scared him," Abby repeated with a laugh. "Right, Millie. I'm *so* intimidating."

"You're an attractive woman," Millie responded

promptly. "You know more about sex than he'll ever learn. Why wouldn't he be intimidated?"

One of the phone lines buzzed and Millie paused to answer. Abby pushed past the swinging gate, thinking there was never any telling what would come out of Millie's mouth. She had a good heart. And an ear to the pulse of the whole town. Nothing escaped her. And she loved to talk. But some of the things she said. . . .

As Abby closed the short gate behind her, Millie rolled her chair backward and caught her again with a slyly curious, "So, Abby, tell me about your lunch today."

"My lunch?"

"Don't be bashful. You can tell me anything." Millie laid her arms on the counter that formed the U-shape of the reception desk and leaned forward, inviting confidence.

"Okay," Abby said. "I had half a chicken salad sandwich and a peanut butter cookie."

Millie flatly refuted this truth with a roll of her eyes. "My friend, Cathy, saw you riding around town in a black Jeep. Which I know just happens to belong to that environmentalist guy, Noah, who's boarding out there at your mom's place. So if you were in his vehicle at lunch time, you must have had a lunch date and didn't tell me."

Ah, the joy of living in a fishbowl. "I was in his vehicle at lunch time," she admitted.

"I knew it. Now, spill your guts."

"Sorry to burst your bubble, Mil, but I had car trouble this morning and hitched a ride home with Noah. He left as soon as I got out of the Jeep, and I spent my lunch hour making phone calls to find someone who would tow the Blazer off the highway and take it over to John Ferguson's house. He's going to fix the transmission for me."

"Transmission went out, huh?"

"Well, that's my diagnosis, anyway."

"And that's the whole story?"

"The whole sorry story," she confirmed, starting toward her desk, stopping halfway there. "Hey, Millie, is there someplace in town where I can buy a cell phone?"

"What happened to your cell phone?"

"I don't have one and I was thinking I might get one."

"You don't have a cell phone?" Millie asked, incredulous.

"I don't have a cell phone."

"Everybody has a cell phone."

"So I've been told."

"Hmm, well. . . ." Millie rolled forward to answer another call, holding up her index finger to indicate she'd be back. In less than a minute, she returned. "There's a Cricket kiosk inside Dr. Hammond's office."

"Dr. Hammond?"

Millie nodded. "The dentist. You know him."

"Of course, I know him. But what does he do? Sell cell phones in between performing root canals and checking for cavities?"

"No, goose. He leases the space to Bernadine, who sells the phones in between filing insurance claims and scheduling appointments. An unorthodox arrangement, maybe, but pretty convenient for a lot of people in town."

"I'm all for convenience," Abby said. "Later this afternoon, I'll go by Dr. Hammond's office and get a phone."

"You don't need to, unless you're getting it for your kids," Millie informed her. "I'll take care of getting one for you. Cell phones are pretty much a necessity around here since everyone's in and out of the office, and the Trib has a corporate account with a place in Tulsa. If the rep has the right phone in stock, he'll probably deliver it this afternoon."

"But I want one for personal use."

"You'll see your statement at the end of the month and pay the paper back for any personal calls. Even with four kids, mine's never been more than thirty dollars."

"That's a nice perk."

"One of many we enjoy here at the *Sweetwater Tribune*. You'll get mileage, too. There should be some expense reports in your desk drawer. Mark will show you how to fill one out."

"I do believe this day's starting to improve." Abby again turned toward her desk and, again, Millie stopped her.

"One more thing," she said, motioning for Abby to wait while rolling to the front to answer another call, her tone switching into professional mode without a hitch. "No, R.J., he still isn't here. I know that's not like Jeff, but I swear I'll give him your message the minute he comes in." Her chin lifted, her tone got the slightest bit sharp. "Well, that's the best I can do because I'm not giving you his cell phone number. If he wanted you to have it, he'd have given it to you himself." Back she came, twirling the chair to face Abby, leaning across the counter, asking in a secretive whisper, "Have you heard the rumors?"

Abby hadn't heard. On purpose. It had taken considerable effort and some quick thinking to avoid the gossip about Jeff's separation from Melanie, about his abrupt filing for divorce. The news staff buzzed with speculation when Jeff was out of the office . . . and he'd been out more than in during the last four days. At Wade House, the boarders had no compunction about discussing over dinner what few facts they knew and what fiction they invented. The town had gone on point like Farmer John's bird dog, keeping a watchful eye on the situation, forecasting scandal and who-knew-what-all interesting happenings. Rumors passed from one resident to another like a basket of hot bread at the supper table.

And Abby prided herself on her abstention, on the way she'd flown under the radar, stayed above the fray. She'd met with customers, sat working in the middle of the office, changed the topic of conversation at dinner, and never once confided to anyone that Jeff had told her what he meant to do. She wished he hadn't. But maybe it was best she'd known before the gossip began. This way, nothing had caught her off guard. She'd maintained her own counsel and minded her own business. And that's the way she meant to continue. "No, Millie, actually I haven't, and that's . . ."

The door opened, Jeff walked in, and Millie rolled forward with a cheery and perfectly innocent greeting. "Hey, Boss. Want your messages?"

Jeff glanced from Millie to Abby with the look of someone who suspects he's the topic of discussion and isn't interested in confirming the suspicion. "Later, Millie, thanks. How are you doing, Abby? Mark got you up to speed, yet?"

"I'm learning," she said. "He sent me out on my first solo mission this morning."

"And she met up with her first balky client," Millie informed him. "The new Sports World manager."

A smile briefly lifted the corners of his lips. "That happens. Don't let it get to you. He'll most likely call you with the go-ahead once he's checked with the main office."

"There. Didn't I tell you?" Millie turned to answer another call and then another.

Jeff stood on one side of the gate, Abby on the other. A moment in which the unspoken hovered like a butterfly on a branch, waiting for a breeze to take it in one direction or the other. "When's Lexie get home from camp?" she asked, choosing distance over connection, asking not to establish parental small talk, but because she intended to police Kyle's activities much more closely from now on. "I believe she and Kyle have talked a couple of times since she left, but the only reason I know that is because he stretched the phone cord halfway down the outside stairs so no one could eavesdrop on the conversation."

"She gets back day after tomorrow." His eyes glinted gold with anticipation, the first sign of happiness they'd held since he walked through the door. "I can't wait to see her. It seems like she's been gone a month instead of only a week." He followed as Abby made her way to the desk that would be hers alone next Monday morning. She set her purse on the floor, aware Jeff had paused, that he seemed to want to say something else, but then he walked on and she heard the soft click of his office door as it closed.

One after the other, her co-workers sauntered through the door, back from lunch, ready for the afternoon's work, and slowly the office came up to full steam and a cacophony of newsy babel. Mark came in with Sam and they parted company like a precision drill team, Sam going left, Mark to the right. "How'd you do this morning?" Mark asked. "Run into any trouble?"

Abby told him about her morning, including the trouble with her car, and they spent the rest of the afternoon going over her newly acquired knowledge of the software package the Trib used for pasteup. She'd never done anything like this before and took copious notes, although Mark—being a nice guy—said she was more proficient after four days of instruction than he'd been after four weeks. He also assured her he'd be available by phone anytime she had a question Jeff couldn't answer, which wasn't likely since he'd taught Mark how to use the program. Still, knowing she could call him gave her a boost of confidence. She received another boost when, true to Millie's prediction, Brian from Sports World phoned with his decision to run the Fourth of July advertising. Exactly as she'd presented it that morning.

Throughout the afternoon, every time the phone on her desk rang, she thought it might be Kyle, calling to test the waters, but the only messages she received all day were about ads. Size. Cost. Positioning. Deadline. A flurry of last minute changes, deletions, and additions to the special advertising supplement. After next week, Mark assured her, it would be less hectic, back to normal. At least, until the summer sales hit their peak in mid-July. Then the back-to-school sales would begin and before she knew it, she'd be working to put together the advertising supplement for the Summer Daze wrap-up and Labor Day specials.

At five-thirty, Abby walked out of the office with Mark and Millie, feeling rather pleasantly overwhelmed.

"Sounds to me like Jeff's really going through with it," Mark said to Millie, leaning around Abby as the three of them walked together along the sidewalk. "Sam said he's put in an offer on the Fincannon place up on McKinley Hill."

"Well, Sheila Goodman over at Applegate Realty told me the owners accepted Jeff's offer for the house day before yesterday," Millie said, her voice low as if she were passing out secrets. "I won't be surprised if they close in a couple of weeks, either. He's going to want to get moved in as soon as possible would be my guess."

"Where's he staying now?"

"He's got a room over at the Comfort Lodge from what I hear, but I think he's spending most nights in his office."

Abby dug in her purse for her keys, tuning out the gossip as best she could since discouraging it didn't seem to have any effect. Hard as she'd tried, she couldn't completely escape the hushed exchanges, the whispers of divorce. She knew there wasn't a consensus on when, exactly, Jeff had moved out of the house he'd built for Melanie soon after they married. And she knew it was common knowledge that he'd been to see Rayburn Swann and subsequently filed for divorce. She knew, too, just from the excited air of those doing most of the talking, that the townsfolk expected hostilities to break out at any moment. Except for a handful of people who considered Melanie a friend, no one in town seemed to be wondering why Jeff had left. The only question, apparently, in the collective curiosity of Sweetwater residents was why he'd waited so long.

"If he buys a house, I don't see how any judge could give Melanie custody," Millie, who had no trouble at all walking and gossiping at the same time, said. "Lexie's old enough to choose and she'll go with Jeff in a heartbeat. Why would she stay with that woman, even if she is her mother?"

Already Abby had figured out that Melanie Garrett had burned more than her share of bridges with the *Tribune* staff. There was no love lost and no affection to be found, and if Jeff had ever let his wife get a foothold on his business, he'd have had a mutiny on his hands.

"She's a beautiful woman, but she must be dumb as a rock." Mark, on his way to another job in another town, had no reason to withhold any nuggets of potential, however hypothetical, truth. "I've seen her with that environmentalist guy in her Cadillac, the two of them driving around like two teenagers cruising the streets for a little action. You'd think she'd be smart enough not to get a new man before the divorce is granted."

"She's not dumb," Millie corrected his misconception. "She just believes she can get away with anything. If she's picked up a lover, you can bet she's got a plan to turn him to her advantage."

"How could she do that?"

"Who knows? But I'd put money on the table right

now that she's figured out a way to do it." Millie sighed. "Too bad, too, since I sorta hoped he might interest you, Abby."

"Not interested," she said firmly. And that went for the entire conversation.

Mark pulled his keys from his pocket as they turned onto the side street where their individual cars were parked. First his Camry, then Millie's Ram, and finally Mae's big Buick on the end. "What I'd like to know," he said, pointing his remote at the Toyota, "is why Jeff didn't leave her years ago."

"Lexie." Millie answered without hesitation. Because that, at least, was the gospel truth. And everyone knew it. "Melanie would have fought like a mud wrestler to keep her away from him. I've known Jeff a long time. He'd never take the chance he might lose his daughter."

Mark stepped off the curb by his sedan. "So what's changed?"

The pause probably didn't last a full second. Millie moved on to her monster truck, her quick glance brushing by Abby like a breath. "I don't have a clue," she said. "Not a clue. See you two tomorrow."

"My last day at the newspaper," Mark reminded. "Free lunch for everyone."

"Well, everyone but Jeff." Millie laughed. "Night, Abby."

"Good night." Abby veered toward her mother's Buick, her knuckles white where they folded around the leather purse strap.

So, it had begun.

The thing she'd dreaded. The one bit of gossip she'd hoped wouldn't make the cut. The one rumor she absolutely didn't want circulating on the grapevine. But she'd caught Millie's slight hesitation, the way her eyes had slid to Abby for that tiny instant, and she knew what people were already saying . . . that Jeff had left his marriage because Abby had finally come home.

Chapter 18

Cargo shorts and short-sleeved shirt baring his arms and legs to the noonday sun, Jeff leaned against his truck while exchanging pleasantries with a few of the mothers who were at the high school waiting, as he was, to pick up their daughters. The activity bus hadn't shown as yet, but it was only a few minutes late, and he and the other parents were a little early. He'd actually been the first parent to arrive. He often was. He liked waiting for Lexie. When she was three and wanted to be a ballerina, he'd driven her back and forth to Tulsa and waited while she pirouetted through her weekly lesson. At five, she started playing soccer, and he waited for her through the biweekly practice sessions, and then, on game days, he joined the throng of dutiful parents on the sidelines to cheer for the Sweetwater Babes, waiting to congratulate or console when the final whistle blew. At eight, she picked up a tomboyish love for horses, so he'd taken her out to Lindy Chappel's forty acres and waited while Lindy taught her to ride. In seventh grade, Lexie tried out for the cheerleading squad and headed off to camp for ten days every summer since. And every summer, as certain as sunrise he waited, with more or less the same group of parents, for the activity bus to bring her home.

He liked the camaraderie, enjoyed the simple conversation of adults who were listening hard for that first, distant hum of a big engine. There was a bond of kinship in discussing the mundane while waiting for the return of the important. It was, he'd always thought, one of those lovely anomalies of parenting that the delight in sending his child off to camp transformed over the course of a few days' separation into an eager impatience to welcome her back.

When the bus lumbered into sight on the crest of the hill, a palpable relief wound through the group of parents, the unspoken fear of accident or tragedy vanquished by the deep-throated rumble of the engine, the creaky shift of gears. Once more, the waiting was over and Lexie had come home. Jeff pushed away from the SUV, straightening as the bus pulled into the high school parking lot and stopped with a hissing sigh. Moving forward, he met the bus driver by the baggage compartment and helped him drag the duffles and suitcases from the interior of the bus. A piece at a time, the luggage disappeared, carried or dragged away by girls who called good-byes to friends, the coach, the adult sponsors and who, one by one, were gathered in and taken away home.

Jeff pulled another bag from the compartment, waiting for a first glimpse of Lexie's blond hair or the first sweet sound of her voice. He knew what he had to tell her would be difficult and dreaded the moment when the words must be said. For most of her life, he and Lexie had been allies, unwilling soldiers in Melanie's war with unhappiness, but he wasn't naive enough to believe his daughter would take the news of divorce with a shrug. She was fifteen and vulnerable, and he hated like hell to cause her pain. But he was responsible for force feeding her the lie his life had turned out to be. It seemed only fitting that he offer up the truth and bear the brunt of her emotions. He'd tried phoning Melanie earlier, hoping they could talk about how to explain the separation to Lexie. But Melanie didn't answer his call. Not today. Not at any time since he'd left. She wouldn't talk to his attorney. The last words they'd exchanged had been over a week ago, on the morning she'd shown up at the café with Noah Walker, determined to harass and intimidate someone.

Jeff had long since become inured to her veiled threats and fierce warnings, but he'd known he was merely her secondary target. She'd come for Abby that morning. Abby, her nemesis, the quarry Melanie could never quite corner. She hated Abby almost as much as she hated him, and Jeff hoped Abby had understood the warning he'd tried to give her. His decision to leave Melanie had nothing to do with Abby's return and yet everything to do with her presence. She'd been the other woman in his marriage since day one. Melanie had made her the crux of every argument, the reason for every rift. And he wouldn't deny that seeing Abby again, realizing she wasn't the girl he remembered, but a woman with regrets of her own, had forced him to face his own unpleasant truths, perhaps given him, finally, the courage to do what he had to do. However it might appear to an observer, the end of his marriage had happened a long time ago. This was just the messy residue that had to be officially cleared away.

But Melanie wouldn't rest until she had drawn Abby into the mess, marked her as the other woman, labeled her an adulteress and humiliated her in whatever way possible. He'd warned Abby. That was all he knew to do. Melanie would do what she would, and he knew it would be worse even than he could imagine.

"That's it." The bus driver closed the compartment and dusted his hands down the sides of his uniform. "Thanks."

"You're welcome," Jeff said, looking around for Lexie. His heart skipped a beat with a first, faint premonition when he didn't see her anywhere. Glancing back at the three pieces of luggage left, he realized not one of them looked familiar. She could still be on the bus, but even without checking, he knew she wasn't.

He knew.

Goddamn it, he knew.

"Julie?" He strode toward the cheerleading coach, a tall thin brunette bending over the open trunk of her car, trying to make room for a bevy of pom-poms and megaphones.

She turned her head at his approach. "Jeff. Hi. What are you doing here?"

"I thought I was here to pick up Lexie."

"Her mom picked her up at the dorm this morning. Didn't you know?"

Jeff forced a casual shrug. "Guess I got my wires crossed."

"I thought Lexie seemed pretty surprised, if you want to know the truth."

"Her mother likes to plan little surprises for us."

"Does she?" Julie made a few adjustments, then closed the trunk. "Well, she succeeded this morning, although I can't say it was a pleasant surprise for Lexie. She wanted to come home on the bus with her teammates, not go off somewhere with her mother. Of course, the girls worked super hard this year, so maybe her protests had more to do with being tired than not wanting to go."

"Maybe so," he said. "Well, thanks, Julie. And I appreciate the extra effort you give the squad. Lexie rates you right up there with her favorite rock star . . . although if you've listened to any of the music she favors, you might not consider that the compliment it is."

"I consider it high praise," she said with a laugh. "You know how much I love coaching this group of girls. They're all special to me, but Lexie has really won a place in my heart. She's the soul of this team. Everyone looks to her for support and encouragement . . . and she always comes through. I've never heard her say a negative word to anyone. She's a beautiful young woman. You should be very proud of her."

"I am." The words came out thick with pride and edgy with emotion. He needed to know where she was, that she was okay, that Melanie hadn't already abused her tender heart with a rash of ugly lies. "I'm very proud of her."

Julie's smile made her look about the same age as the girls she coached. "I'd better get this equipment put away, so I can get home and see how my husband and son managed without me."

Jeff told her good-bye, watched her pull out of the parking lot, and made it to the Mercedes and into the driver's seat before the emotion hijacked him, raising his pulse, tightening the muscles across his shoulders, along his jaw, twisting him into a knot of tension that quickly turned into a blistering rage directed more at himself than at Melanie. Sixteen years of placating her had made him shortsighted, always watching for the minutes of peace, never the hours. He spent so much of his energy protecting Lexie from the mood of the moment that he gave no thought to the life lesson his actions were teaching her. And all the while, Melanie hid behind migraines and discontent, coming out only to exploit his love for Lexie and keep him bound by the promise he'd made.

He should have expected Melanie to make a sneak attack on his most vulnerable point. He should have seen this coming, should have known she wouldn't hesitate to kidnap his daughter to prove her point.

But he hadn't.

And that, more than anything else, was what scared him.

* * *

"Hi, Daddy."

Her voice was music, settling his nerves with its first pure note. "Lexie." Jeff sank back in his chair, letting the familiar squeaks soothe him, gripping the phone like a lifeline as he stared blankly out his office window. "Hi, sweetheart. Are you okay? I've been trying to call your cell phone, but it wouldn't even ring through to your voice mail."

"The phone died."

"As in you couldn't charge the battery?"

"As in Mom dropped it and then ran over it with the car." A breath, quick and guarded. "She didn't mean to. It was sort of a freak accident."

Good going, Melanie. Cut off the line of communication and make it look like an accident.

"She bought me a new one already, but it has to charge for twenty-four hours before I can use it. Plus I lost all the numbers I had programmed into my old phone." She gave him the new number with an exaggerated sigh. "So how are things at home?"

"Terrible," he said. "You know how I hate having to eat a whole pizza by myself."

"Try ordering a medium instead of a large next time. Guess what I had for dinner?"

"A spinach salad." As a matter of principle, Melanie seldom ate real food in front of Lexie. She preferred to project a health-conscious image. If it wasn't green and leafy, it didn't get past her lips. Not when Lexie was around, anyway. "With some fancy no-fat dressing on the side."

"House salad, and fat-free poppyseed dressing on the side."

"Except you made an excuse to leave the table, caught the waiter, and ordered real dressing, fat grams and all, in place of the healthier variety. Then you swore him to secrecy and returned to your mother."

"Hey, you've been spying on me," she accused. "No fair."

"How can I spy on you when I don't even know where you are?"

"We're staying at the Galleria."

"In Dallas?"

"Yes, Dad." Out came the patient tone she sometimes used when she thought he wasn't paying close enough attention. "The Galleria is still in Dallas."

"Is your mother there with you?"

"No, she dropped me off with the credit card and told me to have a great time." Lexie laughed, teasing him. "Of course, she's here. It wouldn't be much of a mother–daughter trip otherwise, would it?"

"A mother–daughter trip," Jeff repeated, wondering if that sounded as strange to Lexie as it did to him. "That sounds like . . . fun."

"Umm. Not so much. Not yet, anyway." Her voice dropped to a whisper. "Can't you think of an emergency so we have to come home?"

As if Melanie would budge one second before it suited her purpose. "No hint of a migraine?"

"For me or her?" Lexie sighed into the phone and he could hear the rustle of her restlessness as she nested deeper into whatever spot she'd chosen. Even as a baby, she'd been a nester, foraging for warmth and comfort wherever she could find it. Her voice surged with a sudden buoyancy. "Mom said we're going to shop till we drop, didn't you, Mom?"

"We're going to shop until the credit card catches fire," Melanie said from the background, raising her pitch so he'd be sure to hear the triumph in her voice. "We're getting you all new school clothes. And a few new things for me."

"How long is this shopping trip going to last?" Jeff asked.

"Good question. Mom? When did you say we'd be home?"

Melanie's laughter trickled faintly through the phone line. "I *said* we aren't going home until we're good and ready."

"Did you hear that? When we're good and ready." Lexie came back to him cheerfully, then wedged in an urgent whisper. "Emergency, Dad. Think emergency."

"Think positive, Lex," he said. "Maybe you'll have a good time."

"Mmm, right, Dad. I'll try to keep that in mind."

He hated taking pleasure in the fact that Lexie didn't like being with her mother, and, yet, at the same time, he felt a certain satisfaction in her desire to come home. "It could happen," he said, although he knew as well as she did that the possibility was unlikely. "She's never taken you on a mother–daughter trip before."

"She said she got the idea from reading an article in *Better Homes and Gardens*. Something about a mother and daughter shopping for antiques." Doubt wove like a glittery thread through her voice, normal again, so apparently Melanie had left the room. "There's something shady about this trip, Dad," Lexie continued. "And I don't believe you told her you thought it was a brilliant idea. Brilliant being *your* word, not hers."

Melanie didn't usually get caught by something as simple as a word choice. The slip could have been a mistake, created by the adrenaline rush of success. He was more inclined, however, to think she'd purposefully used a word he wouldn't to let Lexie know there was something odd about the trip. Keeping everyone unsettled was Melanie's forte. She wouldn't have told Lexie he'd filed for divorce. Not yet. She'd want to hold that information back as long as possible. It was too powerful a weapon to use this early in the campaign.

"Your grampa says hello," he said, deciding it was time for a change of topic. "He said he hopes you'll have a wonderful time spending my hard-earned cash."

"He said that?"

Jeff smiled. "Well, he would have if he were talking to me."

The laughter returned to her voice, along with a casual, curious, upbeat, "So, you've been to see Grampa?"

"Just yesterday," he answered. "He wasn't in the mood for Sunday company."

"Imagine that. Don't worry, Dad. I'm sure he'll come around eventually. You probably didn't stay long, huh?"

"I stayed for awhile. Talked to Joe and Archie, said hello to Denny."

"How's Denny?"

"Still tying knots in his rope. He had a book under his arm, too. Quite a reader, that boy."

"Kyle says he never goes anywhere without that rope and a book. Did you, uh, happen to see Kyle?"

Jeff suspected she'd been working her way around to this question from the start. "No, but then earlier in the week, I did overhear his mother tell Millie he's grounded."

"Oh." There was relief in her tone, a sigh of easy understanding. "He hasn't called for a few days. That's probably why."

"Probably." Jeff paused, wanting to ask how often Kyle phoned her, how often she phoned him, if their friendship was shifting toward something more, if the shift had already happened. But this wasn't the time for that question. Not when he wasn't prepared to hear the answer. Not with this situation with Melanie hanging over them like an incoming storm. "Let me talk to your mother for a minute, Lex. Hey, and take it easy on my credit card, okay?"

"I won't break the bank. It's Mom you need to put on a budget. And remember, think emergency. E-mer-gen-cy." Her voice winged away from him. "Mom. Dad wants to talk to you."

Jeff had plenty of time to form the words he wanted to say, he'd been having this conversation in his head since he'd discovered Lexie wasn't on the bus. But Melanie's voice brought his anger to an instant boil.

"Now, Jeff, dear, don't be mad," she said without preamble. "Sometimes girls need a little vacation. Lexie and I are having a wonderful time, but then I'm sure she told you."

"How long, Melanie?"

"I don't know." She was playing him. The way she'd done a thousand times before. "A week. Maybe two. Does it really matter?"

"How long do you plan to keep her away from me?"

She laughed, a child's trill of amusement. "As long as it takes, Jeff. Just as long as it takes."

And she hung up before he could say another word, leaving him holding the phone and wondering what kind of emergency it would take to get Lexie home.

Chapter 19

"Hey, Twerp." Kyle's voice scraped like sandpaper against the gray dark. "You can stop pretending. I know you're not asleep."

Denny lay perfectly still, barely breathing, hoping Kyle would change his mind and go back to bed. He heard the whisper-soft sound as his brother tied his shoe laces and then the *swoosh* of the covers as he pulled the sheets over the pillows and plumped the result into a rumpled tangle. If their mother came in to check on them—which she wouldn't as late as it was—she'd see a lump the size of Kyle in his bed, and, in the dark, it wouldn't occur to her there were only pillows under the covers.

Denny hated these nights. He didn't like being alone in the bedroom. He didn't like thinking about where Kyle had gone, and if he'd make it back okay before morning. He didn't like lying in his bed, hearing every noise, tense with worry, while Kyle was out with his friends having fun. But more than any of that, the part Denny hated most was knowing that in a minute, Kyle would make him get up and hold the window. He'd hold it while Kyle slipped out, swung over, grabbed the old metal downspout, and shimmied to the ground. He'd hold it open until his brother was nothing more than a shadow, skimming the darkness on his way to places Denny couldn't even imagine. Then, like always, he'd lower the window carefully, silently easing it down to the sill where a small block from his Lincoln Logs set would keep it from closing completely. An inch of air was all Kyle needed to get back in. A space no bigger than his fingers. A crack between window and sill that couldn't be readily seen from below, a wedge hardly noticeable from anywhere inside the bedroom.

Trouble was, Denny knew it was there. Night noises were louder, and the air conditioner couldn't mask the wild night scent of outdoors. He couldn't sleep with the window open and Kyle gone. He felt exposed and frightened, listening, listening, straining through a haze of sleep to hear the faint creak of the downspout, a sound that brought him springing upright in bed, heart pounding, gasping for breath. He'd sit like that, still as a mouse, for a long, long time, waiting for Kyle to reach the window or for the intruder he feared would come instead.

Nights when Kyle left, Denny wet the bed. He didn't mean to, of course. But he was scared and wakeful and so tired when he finally got to sleep, he couldn't wake up. Not in time, anyway. Then he had to pretend he'd had a good night when his mom asked. He had to lie because he knew she worried if he didn't. And he always made his bed before he ever left his room in the morning. So she wouldn't know. So she wouldn't worry.

Grandma helped him change the sheets, although he could do it himself. But he didn't want Kyle to know, either. It was bad enough that Kyle made him an accomplice in these escapes, Denny didn't want to be called a pee-pot—or worse—on top of it.

"Come on, Dweeby." The covers were jerked back, and Denny shivered as the cool air sliced across his bare legs. "I'm meeting the guys in ten minutes." Kyle moved silently to the window, opened it carefully, slowly, pausing at the slightest creak of sound.

Denny sighed as he swung his legs over the side of

the bed and slid to the floor. He wanted to ask Kyle not to go, but he knew it wouldn't make any difference, and Kyle would only tease him for being a scaredy-cat. Or he'd get really mad. Denny didn't know which was worse.

Planting his hands on the underside of the window, he braced his feet to hold himself steady as his brother put one leg across the sill and then the other. For a minute Kyle sat, half in the room, half out the window, then he slid through the opening as quietly as a snake in the grass and held onto the sill until he could swing across and grasp the downspout. Denny listened to the scrape of body against the old metal and then the *umph* of landing. He watched as Kyle moved around the back of the garage, like a wraith, visible one minute, gone the next.

Then Denny lowered the window, pausing occasionally to listen for the pad of his mother's feet out in the hall or any noise that would mean she was up and out of bed. He didn't know what he'd do if she ever caught him. He'd be just as guilty as Kyle. He could have told her. He could walk into her room right now and tell her Kyle had gone out the window. But then his brother would hate him and his mother would be upset and angry. And Denny would be a tattletale for the rest of his life. And he wanted Kyle to like him. He wanted to be a good brother. Even if it meant he had to keep the secret. Even if it meant he wet the bed.

As he crawled back under the sheets, Denny thought about all the secrets he had to keep. He didn't know people could have so many secrets. Maybe that's what happened when a person grew up. Their secrets got bigger, too. His mom had secrets, even though she liked to pretend she didn't. His dad had had secrets, too. Places he hid bottles. Places he went and didn't tell anyone. Things he did. Even

Grandma had things she wouldn't talk about. She told Denny he was too young to hear an old woman's secrets. Kyle wasn't old, but he already had secrets. He went places at night. Sometimes with Lexie, although Lexie had been gone at camp for a long time now. Kyle was mad about that, but he wouldn't talk about it when Denny asked. *None of your freakin' business,* he'd said. But Denny knew Lexie hadn't called. And he knew she didn't answer when Kyle tried calling her. Lexie probably had secrets, too.

The only person who talked about secrets was Lexie's grandpa. After they stopped reading for the day, he told Denny secrets. About his son. About how he drowned in the river. About the 500-year flood that came on Labor Day weekend and washed his body someplace where no one could find it. Denny thought that was a terrible secret . . . and he wondered if that's what Kyle and his friends did in the middle of the night. If they went to the river and searched for the body that had never been found. He wondered if, maybe, they'd already found it. It would be a skeleton by now. Nothing but a skull and some bones. He'd like to see that, although he'd be scared. But he could do it. Maybe one night, he'd go with Kyle. Maybe one night, Kyle would say, *"Hey, Den, are you brave enough to see something really scary?"*

"Yes," he'd say. *"I'm brave enough."*

Hugging the covers around him, Denny huddled against the night to wait for whatever came, determined to keep the secrets he knew.

Chapter 20

"That looks like a good spot." Noah pointed out an area of the park midway between where they'd left the van and the stage where the pre-fireworks show would be held. "Close to the john, too. A bonus, considering the average age of our group is somewhere around eighty."

"Good thinking, Noah." Abby smiled to herself and kept walking, the lawn chairs she carried bumping against her legs. "That would be an excellent place to be during the fireworks, but we'll be sitting right . . . here." She plopped down one of the chairs, flipping it open with a flick of her wrist. Gesturing with her free hand, she claimed the section of grassy slope in front of the large gazebo and the freestanding stage. "This is where the Wade House flock sits every year. The boarders like to be close to the entertainment." She opened the other lawn chair and positioned it next to the first. "It's tradition."

He glanced at the expanse of unclaimed territory all around them. "Just like it's tradition to send scouts out early so no one else can stake out this exact spot?"

"Just like that." Abby began straightening the chairs Noah set up. "And you did volunteer."

"Only after I found out you were the designated scout."

Abby's stomach clenched. She didn't know how she

felt about the hints Noah had begun to drop into their conversations. Hints leading toward a turn in the tentative friendship they'd developed. Hints that he wanted something more. Hints that made her distinctly uncomfortable. Because she believed that where there was smoke, there was usually fire. She believed he'd been spending time with another man's wife. With Melanie. "I haven't been in Sweetwater for a Fourth of July celebration in years," she said, skipping past his implication. "So it's my turn to make sure this area by the stage is secure from interlopers. Usually the boys get the job, but I felt it was only fair for me to do it this year."

He straightened, hands on hips, studying the red, white, and blue bunting that draped the stage and gazebo in patriotism. "So what kind of entertainment can I expect when the show starts? Fire batons? Pig calling contest? The town's great uncle playing 'Stars and Stripes Forever' on his harmonica?"

"Now, now, City Boy." Abby scolded him with a *tsk, tsk.* "Sweetwater is big time compared to what you just described. Today, Mr. Walker, among other things, you'll hear a variety of patriotic music performed by the Sweetwater Tunes and the Community Chorus, an inspirational reading of the Declaration of Independence by our resident World War II hero, Orville Keener, and—if we're lucky—the Burton girls will sing 'America, the Beautiful.'"

A frown furrowed his brow. "I thought you hadn't been to this extravaganza in years."

"I haven't."

"Then how do you know the program won't be completely different from the last time you were here?"

"You could say I have special insight."

He rolled his eyes and dropped down to sit on the summer grass. "I know, I know. Tradition's a big deal in a small town, so the Fourth of July program never changes."

"Well, probably not since this week's *Tribune* went to press."

Noah looked up, caught her slow smile and returned it. "You wrote up the program for the newspaper."

"No, but I read it. And, except for a few new faces, the program is almost exactly like it was the last time I was here for the fireworks." *Her last Fourth of July in Sweetwater. The last time she remembered being unhesitatingly happy, secure in Jeff's love and life, unaware of the forces already at work, busily destroying the foundation of her dreams.* She sank to the grass, too, and wove her fingers through the slick blades. Dry, but not brittle. Not yet. They needed rain, but that wasn't likely until the fall, far too late to keep the grass from baking brown under the July sun.

Placing his hands behind his head, Noah reclined in the shadow of the belvedere. "What kept you away so long, Abby?"

She shrugged as if she didn't know. "School, marriage, kids, work. The usual stuff."

"So it had nothing to do with the accident?"

That caught her off guard. Not so much because he'd heard about the accident . . . but because he connected her absence to it. "I was already enrolled at Kansas State," she said. "Staying wouldn't have done anyone any good. Least of all me."

"Staying after the accident isn't quite the same as staying away for sixteen years, though, is it?"

Discomfort plopped down between them like a toddler, distracting and demanding and impossible to ignore. "I've been back a few times."

"Overnight trips to drop off the boys or pick them up again. Lora says this summer is the first time

you've spent more than twenty-four hours in Sweetwater since you left for college."

"I had other obligations. There's nothing mysterious about it."

"I heard Alex Garrett's death broke your heart and
you stayed away all these years to avoid seeing the person who killed him."

Abby could all but hear Melanie's voice saying those
exact words exactly that way. If she'd needed further
confirmation that the rumors were true, that Noah was
spending a great deal of time with Melanie, there it was.
Only Melanie would have cobbled together the truth in
such a deliberate manner, knowing that when it
reached Abby—as it inevitably had—she would feel the
pangs of guilt and regret, as well as the warning the
words carried. "Where did you hear that?" she asked
anyway.

This time, he shrugged. "Is it true?"

She hadn't talked about the accident in sixteen years,
and, for a heartbeat, she actually thought about telling
him her shameful part in Alex's death. There was something about Noah that sought the past and brought it
to the surface. Some pain inside him that echoed inside
her. But going into that pain, sharing it, well . . . she
wasn't prepared to do that. "It happened a long time
ago, Noah. Some things are best left in the past."

"You lose a friend you knew just about all your life
in an accident that could have been prevented, and
you can just leave it in the past, forgotten like yesterday's meatloaf?"

His tone startled her, its implicit reproach stung
like a slap in the face. "I didn't say I'd forgotten. I said
it was best left in the past, which is a polite way of saying I don't want to discuss it." Pushing up from the
ground, she brushed her hands across the back of her
shorts and started walking toward the parking lot and
the van Mae borrowed on special occasions from

Dewey Sloan, who owned the Chevy dealership out on Highway 75.

"Abby, wait."

She kept walking, wanting a few more minutes to gather her thoughts, settle her feelings.

He caught up with her easily. "Listen, I'm sorry. I guess I was out of line back there. It's just that I'm interested in finding out what happened to Alex Garrett that night."

"He died, Noah. The events leading up to the accident aren't important anymore, and I'm not going to talk about them to satisfy anyone's curiosity. Now, let's get the rest of the chairs so you can take the van back to the house. The boarders won't all be ready to leave at the same time, so plan on making three or four trips back and forth."

"It isn't just idle curiosity, Abby," he said. "I have my reasons. Good reasons, I believe."

A water analyst, fascinated by rivers and river towns, would naturally be interested in a flood theorists predicted could occur only once in 500 years. He'd want to understand the human cost of such an event and how best to prevent that loss in the future. But that didn't mean she had to help him. "Please, Noah." She paused with her hand on the back of the van. "Ask someone else."

"Melanie told me I should ask you," he persisted.

Abby wanted badly to inform him that he should be suspicious of anything Melanie said, but she'd learned the hard way that offering a warning was pointless. Alex hadn't listened to her. Neither had Jeff. They'd both been drawn into Melanie's orbit like planets seeking a sun. Noah would be no different, was in fact already as good as blinded by the brilliance of her fire. Abby lifted the latch and the van's back panel lifted slowly out and up. "Ask someone else," she repeated and pulled another pair of lawn chairs from the van. "Are you sure you want to be the Wade House chauffeur this evening? I'll trade if you'd rather stay here and guard our spot."

"Are you kidding?" he replied, accepting the change of topic with a forced lightness. "It's hotter than a firecracker out here. You'd have to arm wrestle me to get me to trade chores with you now, and there's no way I'd let you win."

"It's good to know chivalry is still alive."

"Hey, women fought hard for equal rights and today, especially, I applaud you for it."

She made a face as she passed him two more lawn chairs and watched him take off with them, heading back toward the belvedere. Then she dragged the last four chairs out of the van and stacked them against the bumper. So Noah had questions about the flood and the special tragedy it had brought to the town. Questions Melanie wouldn't answer directly, but had colored with her own questionable palette of truths. Then she'd pointed toward Abby, insinuating that there Noah could uncover the real story. It was characteristic of Melanie to create doubt and suspicion, to wrap the facts in mystery, and then send in an innocent party to do the dirty work and take the heat. Noah's questions had aroused painful memories for Abby, twisted the knife in wounds that could never heal . . . exactly as Melanie had intended. And Abby had no recourse. Directing her anger at Noah was pointless. He merely wanted to know about the flood.

Abby could have told him that all up and down the Arkansas River communities had been devastated by the disaster. The flood and the aberrant August rainfalls that preceded it had incurred millions of dollars of damage and washed away homes and the accumulations of many a lifetime. Destruction followed the flood's wide path all the way to the Mississippi River, swiping one tragedy from the headlines and replacing it with another almost as fast as the river had overflowed its banks. Lives had been lost in other towns, too, and although Sweetwater's losses were particularly grievous, they rated no more than a sidebar in the history of the river, a footnote about the deaths of four young people in a horrific accident pitting nature against machine. The flooding river had won an easy victory, carrying the flame red Firebird and its cargo miles downstream before the rescue crews could arrive. When the torrential rains finally stopped long enough to allow the vehicle to be pulled out of the water, it was battered, beaten, and bent into a shape barely recognizable as a car. The three bodies still inside were in even worse condition.

Or so it had been said. Dave Madison and John King, who'd lifted the teenagers from the wreckage that night, quit the Civil Defense team soon after the accident and both had eventually moved away from the area.

The flood left its high-water mark on the heart of Sweetwater as surely as it left a mark on the surrounding countryside. Hardly visible, but there still if one knew where to look. It hadn't been forgotten. But it wasn't the kind of thing people wanted to remember, either.

Going up on tiptoe, Abby strained to reach the upraised door. Her fingers brushed the edge and dropped as a hand came over her head and grasped the panel, pulling it down and closed. "Need some help with those chairs?" Jeff asked, even as he lifted them . . . two in each hand . . . and moved around the side of the van. "The usual spot?"

"Where else?" She followed him, grateful for the unexpected balm of his presence. Regardless of what had come after the accident, she and Jeff would always be bound by the terrible events of that night. He knew what she knew, shared the heavy sorrow of guilt and the helpless horror of an eyewitness. That night had torn them apart, but left them stranded together in memory's twilight, unwilling to remember, unable to forget. "I thought you were going to bring your dad tonight."

"That was my original intention." Jeff glanced back over his shoulder at her and shortened his stride so she could catch up. "But he doesn't want to see any fireworks. Unless they're aimed at me."

She fell into step beside him. "He's a stubborn man."

"And getting more so by the minute. I don't know why I bothered to move him up here."

"You did it because he's your father, stubborn or not, and you've always been a better son to him than he deserved."

"But never the son he wanted."

"That isn't your fault, Jeff."

"Hmm. Try convincing him of that, would you?"

"I did try, remember?"

He shot her a sudden grin as familiar as the scent of summer air. "Oh, yeah, that's right. I'd almost forgotten. I don't believe he had any idea you possessed such a fiery vocabulary. You were so furious, I think you very nearly gave him a heart attack."

"Him? I was so scared I threw up for an hour after I told him off. I thought at the very least I'd flunk his class and lose my scholarship. But he was always fair to everyone . . . except you."

"Thanks, Abby. You were my champion, and I hope you know how much I appreciated having you in my corner."

She shrugged, aware of how easily and unintentionally she'd reverted to the old pattern of their camaraderie.

"Something wrong with Noah?" Jeff nodded to the row of chairs and the man sitting at the row's end, his head in his hands, his palms massaging hard circles around his eyes. "Too much sun, maybe?"

"Maybe," Abby agreed, although she suspected it was another headache. She'd seen him with too many of such obvious discomfort for her to believe they were entirely allergy related. Migraines would be her professional guess, especially because he seemed reluctant to admit to them. In her experience, men were often reticent to admit they suffered from headaches at all, much less a debilitating sort. Mitch would never own up to having even the most innocuous headache, as if the acknowledgment would somehow cancel out his macho image. But then, Mitch never could face failure. To the end, he denied that alcohol—or any of his other addictions—posed a problem. For him or anyone else.

Jeff began a second row, setting down a chair and centering it behind two chairs in the first row, so that no one's view would be blocked, which was very important when dealing with the sometimes fussy boarders, something he knew from years past. He had the next chair in place when Noah stood and turned to help, his smile negating any sign of illness. "Here," he said as Jeff moved along the second row, bringing each chair into correlation with the ones in front of it. "I'll help you with that."

"That's okay. I'll do it," Jeff said. "You look a little . . . under the weather."

"I feel on top of the world." Noah began adjusting chairs, too.

"Heatstroke is nothing to fool around with, you know."

"I'm fine."

"You should sit down and drink some water."

"If I feel I need to, I will."

"It's the humidity that gets you, you know. Makes it

feel like a hundred and twenty degrees instead of just a hundred and five."

"I'm accustomed to heat and humidity."

"I've lived in Sweetwater all my life and I've never gotten used to the heat or the humidity. It must be worse where you come from."

"It is," Noah said with finality. "Memphis is a lot worse."

It struck Abby that their exchange was competitive, as was the careful way they each moved the chairs, being excessively precise in the positioning, even to the point of squaring a chair already set by the other. Understandable, she supposed, given that Jeff had to have heard the rumors about his wife and Noah. And however innocent Noah might consider the time he spent with Melanie, he had to feel a little uncomfortable around her husband. It would be odd only if the subtle animosity and sense of one-upmanship were missing, which didn't stop Abby from comparing their behavior to that of her own sons when they were intent upon aggravating the other.

"I don't want to rush you, Noah," she said, attempting to nip the possible rivalry before it escalated, "but you really should get back to the house. I want you to have plenty of time to get my Pepsi iced down."

"Oh, sure. Okay." He backed away from the chairs, relieved, Abby believed, to have an acceptable excuse to go. "You want to come with me? Jeff can save our spot."

"Can't do it, sorry." Jeff wasted not a second in claiming other commitments. "I have to scout out some photo ops for the next edition of the Trib. But I'd certainly appreciate an iced drink, too. When you come back. If you don't mind."

"An iced drink. Sure thing."

Now they reminded Abby of the way Jeff and Alex

used to goad each other with their *if you don't mind,
goon-head* and *sure thing, Jethro*. "Pepsi," she said, breaking up the act. "Very, very, *very* cold."

"Gotcha." Noah strode away, shoulders back, arms
swinging, familiar in the way his movements conveyed
that virile, "you can't touch this" machismo.

"Doesn't look much like he has a headache now,"
Jeff commented.

"No," Abby agreed. "I think deciding the humidity
is much worse in Memphis is probably what cured
him."

Jeff caught her wry smile and returned it. "It really
isn't, you know," he said. "Worse in Memphis."

"I never believed it for a minute." She settled into
one of the lawn chairs and stretched her bare legs out
to the sun.

"What was Chicago like, Abby?"

It had always felt like a foreign place to her, big and
blustery and busy, confusing in its mass of commuters
and its constant activity, and after living away from the
city for only a month, she actually had to stop and think
before she could recall what the weather had been like.
"Well, it's called the Windy City for good reason. Summers are fairly mild, although August can get pretty
hot, and the winters are often bitterly cold with the
most biting wind that can sting exposed skin like a bad
sunburn."

"Did you enjoy living there?"

"Some parts of it, yes."

"But?"

That was both the problem and the ease of talking
to Jeff. He sensed her every hesitation, heard what
she didn't put into words. "You can take the girl out
of the small town, but you can't, necessarily, take the
small town out of the girl," she admitted with a light-
hearted shrug. "Like any large metropolitan area,
Chicago is energy and motion, fast-paced, something

happening every minute. There were times I thought seriously about getting in the car and driving away from the incessant hum of it, times when I wanted desperately to come home."

"Yet you never did. Until now."

Jeff phrased it differently, made it a statement, but it was essentially the same question Noah had posed to her. *What kept you away?* But, of course, Jeff knew the answer as well as she did. "Coming home wouldn't have solved anything," she said. "My mother's still here, you know."

"And aren't you glad for that."

"Yes," she said, appreciating the shift of perspective. "Yes, I am."

"I'll trade parents with you any day you say."

His words brought up a dozen memories. Predictions they'd made about the kind of in-laws their parents would make. The type of grandparent. Memories she hadn't recalled in years . . . until now.

Professional. She wanted to keep everything strictly professional.

Yet the lines blurred, the past bled into the present, and the comfortable ways of their conversation returned like a long-lost pet, mysteriously, instinctively finding the path home. Jeff had betrayed her, but lately when she tried to call up the old pain, the animosity and outrage, it roused lazily, reluctant to offer her refuge.

So she beat a hasty retreat now to the safety net of work. "I got a lead on a new advertiser," she said. "Bill Applegate told me he's got a commitment for a lease on the old tea room space at Third and Broadway. Some sort of fitness and exercise gym. I can't imagine how they'll have enough floor space, but the owners will want to advertise, don't you think? I mean, they'll pretty much have to, if they want anyone to know they're there."

"Sounds like a good lead. When you make your call,

be sure to let them know we'll do a feature article about the opening."

"Great." Abby paused, then plunged on. "Maybe I could even write the article?"

Hands leveraged into the hip pockets of his jean shorts, Jeff stared up at the purple martin houses around the perimeter of the park. The city provided the birdhouses and maintenance and the swallows reciprocated summer after summer by helping deplete the mosquito population. A fair trade from everyone's standpoint.

"Or not," she said when he didn't answer.

"Huh? Oh, sure, if you want."

But she could tell by his voice his attention had drifted, that memories had distracted him, too. "I've been trying to work up my nerve to ask you about doing a little writing. Nothing major, of course, just an article here or there." She hesitated, giving him time to respond. He didn't. "I've always had a secret desire to have a byline, you know." Still no response. "But maybe that isn't such a good idea. I mean, I really should learn one job well before attempting to branch out into another. I don't know what makes me think I'm a journalist. I've never written anything other than college papers and that was a long time ago. And, after all, it is your newspaper, and I'm sure if you wanted me to do an article, you'd assign me to write it. You are the boss."

He made an effort to smile, but seemed to have lost the energy to push it through to completion. "Would you mind if we don't talk about work, Abby? It's a holiday. One you used to enjoy. Could we just talk like friends? Discuss the weather, the fireworks, politics, our kids?"

It was a bridge she didn't mean to rebuild, but the look in his eyes wouldn't allow her to refuse such a simple and earnest request. "I'm not sure discussing our kids is such a great idea," she offered. "My son is very upset that your daughter won't be here tonight."

"That makes two of us. Three, if I know my daughter." He sank into a chair two over from where she sat, close enough to be friendly, distant enough to be unobjectionable. "My guess is that Lexie is making her mother as miserable as possible at the moment."

"I thought that was a teenager's job . . . to make mothers miserable." She threw Jeff a warning glance. "And if you say Lexie never causes you a minute's worry, I may have to hurt you."

He smiled. "I've worried a bit more about her since your son arrived, but as for making me miserable, no, Lexie has always been a joy. She's a great kid."

"And, of course, as you and I know from personal experience, *great* kids never sneak out to the river at night or go joyriding or take long walks after midnight, while their parents believe they're tucked snugly in bed."

His eyes held a frown as they cut to her. "It's not nice to rip off a father's rose-colored glasses like that."

"You might as well share the worry. Lord knows, I have plenty to spare."

"Do you think Kyle sneaks out at night?"

"No, not yet. At least, I'm pretty sure he doesn't. He's always there in bed if I get up in the night and peek in. And I have Denny, who worries about everything Kyle does, and he wouldn't keep a secret like that from me if he knew." She weighed the possibility again, as she did at least several times everyday. "I figure I have until school starts before I have to worry about Kyle doing any of the things we used to do. But I don't know. Maybe I'm just kidding myself."

"You know," Jeff said thoughtfully. "I think I would rather talk about the weather."

Abby laughed, realizing how relaxing it felt to voice her concern, to share the perpetually apprehensive state of parenthood with someone who understood the difficulties of parenting a teenager. "One winter," she said, "we were snowed in for a week without electricity. We moved our beds into the den and used the fireplace for heat. We played board games by firelight and I-Spy and silly word games we made up just for entertainment. For meals, we set frozen dinners just inside the firebox and waited for them to thaw out and heat up. And we ate Goldfish crackers, Fruit Loops, and Captain Crunch right out of the box. We drew straws for the snack cakes or gave them as prizes, although it was against the rules to hoard them. The boys still claim that was the best winter storm ever."

"Hmm," Jeff mused. "How to top that? Let's see, a few years ago we had an ice storm. Shut down everything for almost a week. Very pretty, but bad news for the electric company. Great news for the kids, though. Lexie and I slid our way out to Chandler Park and sledded down the hill on inner tubes and plastic mats. Most fun I've ever had on ice."

She came back with a story of the windiest day on record in Illinois, which he countered with an account of the December tornadoes. From there, the conversation flowed from one thing to another, touched on people they'd known, college experiences, community events, everything and nothing, brushed close enough to the personal to satisfy a normal curiosity about each other's lives, but never breeched the intimate details of their separate pasts. She hadn't thought she'd ever talk with Jeff this way again, yet it felt perfectly natural, as comfortable as her favorite cotton shirt, as uncomplicated as the shift of the day into dusk. And when Noah appeared with Miz Rose on one arm and Lowell on the other, Abby could hardly believe the time had gone so fast. Already the sun edged toward the horizon and the park had filled with families, noisily awaiting the fun and fireworks.

"I should help get the other boarders." Jeff was on his feet, leaving their dialogue in mid-topic, as if it could be picked up again at any point, as if time and distance hadn't altered the connection between them no matter how profoundly it might have altered them.

"Mr. McAfee prefers to be on my right." Miz Violet fidgeted with the lawn chair, smoothing out the webbing of the seat, resettling the aluminum legs on the grass, eyeing the chair in which her sister had already settled. Jeff kept his hand on her elbow, doing his best to keep her from tipping headfirst into the webbed seat. A task that would have been simpler if she allowed someone else to hold the box containing her husband's ashes. But she insisted on having it with her at all times, toting it around as if it were as precious and volatile as an oxygen tank. "He is always on my right during the fireworks. He can see better from there. You know that, Rose."

"Oh, for Heaven's sake! Sit down, Vi," Rose snapped. "And put that ridiculous box under your chair. Or sit on it for all I care. Dexter McAfee couldn't see that well when he was alive, and his vision certainly hasn't improved in the twenty years he's been dead."

"I'm going to tell him you said that." Miz Violet huffed as she turned—with Jeff's hand sustaining her balance—and dropped into the seat, positioning Mr. McAfee's box just so in her lap. He wore his dress blues this evening—Air Force blue wrapping paper with a dignified silver ribbon and his Bronze Star taped in place on the left side. "I don't know why you have to be so hateful, Rose. I just asked you to switch chairs so my husband could sit next to me."

"Honestly, Vi, you're getting plumb senile. Hand over that box."

"You'll give him your seat?"

"Both cheeks."

Miz Violet gasped. "Rose!"

"I've just had a great idea." Jeff interrupted what promised to turn into a serious sibling squabble. "I'm going to take a picture of you two beautiful ladies—and Mr. McAfee, of course—and put it on the front page of the *Tribune*. Now, you stay right here while I go and get my camera."

Like magic, they forgot their fuss and began scolding Jeff for shamelessly trying to butter up two former schoolteachers, who had known him before he could spell baloney. And under no circumstances did they wish to see their wrinkled faces on any page of his newspaper.

Jeff teased them a little more. "It's you or Orville Keener, and he's made the front page so often he thinks he deserves a salary."

Miz Rose *tsk-tsk*ed. "You're a ring-tailed tooter, Jefferson Garrett, and don't you go arguing about it, either."

He would have continued the distracting chatter but he sensed the purposefulness of Abby's approach even before he heard her voice, low and confiding, behind him.

"Don't look now, but your dad seems to have changed his mind."

"What?" He bent his ear toward her, sure he must have misheard.

"Your dad. He arrived just now with Lora and Denny in the station wagon. They're tonight's hot dog and lemonade brigade." She shifted closer, and he felt not only her breath across his cheek, but the warmth of her body so near his that if he'd leaned only slightly he would have felt the soft, remembered curves of her against him. "What do you bet Lora convinced him he'd get no supper at all unless he came to the picnic."

"More likely, he's hoping to see me ride a Roman candle into the wild, blue yonder." Jeff looked over the bluish white hair of Miz Violet and Miz Rose to see Gideon settling into a chair at the end of the second row. Next to him, Denny Ryan pointed out the stage, the gazebo, and the distant point at which the fireworks display was set up and ready to go. "That stubborn old billy goat," he muttered. "He told me he wasn't setting foot outside Wade House tonight, that he'd rather stare at the ceiling than spend his evening listening to idiots ooh and ah over a few bottle rockets."

"Well, obviously, someone changed his mind for him." Abby moved back and away, withdrawing, leaving him absurdly lonesome for the momentary closeness they'd shared. "I'm going to help Lora get the food passed out. I just thought you might need a heads up."

"Much appreciated, thank you. Excuse me, Miz Violet, Miz Rose. Y'all enjoy the fireworks." Turning on his heels, he made his way around the reserved seating of Wade House residents and came up behind Gideon in time to hear him explain to Denny some of the historical significance of fireworks. How was it, he wondered, that a man could go fifteen years making hardly any effort to converse with his own grandchild and yet suddenly find his voice and enough interest to pass along some of his considerable knowledge to a little boy who was no relation to him at all. But then, Gideon had always played favorites . . . and had never been bothered by the consequences of his bias. "Hi, Dad," he said as pleasantly as he could. "I see you decided to join the celebration, after all."

"Hmmph." The growl frayed like worn velvet as it

rumbled from Gideon's throat. A listless *bah, humbug!* of a response.

"I talked him into it," Denny said proudly. "Nobody should miss the fireworks."

Jeff balanced genuine annoyance with his father against the pleasurable tug of Denny's little boy excitement. "How'd you manage it?" he asked the boy. "I tried every trick I knew to get him here."

"First, Lora told him to get off his duff and get ready to go." Denny's blue eyes were uncommonly serious. "And then I told him I wouldn't read to him anymore if he didn't come. He really likes *Harry Potter.*"

Jeff lifted his eyebrows and looked at his father.

"Don't be a smart aleck," was Gideon's only response. "How long before the show starts?"

"The singing and stuff'll start pretty soon," Denny explained. "Then, after Mr. Keener reads the Declaration of Independence, the fireworks start."

"Keener still does the reading?" Gideon snorted his disapproval. "Anybody ever convince that ignorant old geezer that 'assume' isn't pronounced 'ass-ume'?"

"Mr. Keener fought in World War II." Denny went readily on the defense. "He lost one of his legs and got a Purple Heart. Grandma says he earned the right to pronounce words any way he wants."

"Bah." Gideon pushed forward in his chair. "I'm going to the bathroom."

"You want me to show you where it is?" Jeff put a hand on his dad's arm and had it immediately, abruptly shaken off.

"I've never needed your help to get anywhere I wanted to go. Now, get out of my way."

Jeff stepped back, stung again by his father's caustic tongue. He watched Gideon push up from his chair with the graceless diligence of an aging man who clung fiercely to what was left of his dignity. He wavered a moment, a little unsteady on his feet, but he regained his equilibrium and walked off. Slowly, but with shoulders squared and head up, despite the shuffle of uncertainty in his steps. He was too young—only in his early seventies—to be such an old man. But then, Gideon had given up on living a meaningful life the day Alex died. A sigh pushed past the knot in Jeff's throat. A frustrated, angry, and painful sigh. It was such a waste. Such an awful waste.

The brush of a small hand against his dispelled the moment and brought his attention down to the little boy at his side.

Denny looked up at him with Abby's eyes. Blue instead of brown, thick sandy lashes instead of smudgy dark ones. But the shape, the gold flecks of understanding, the intelligence, the concern—those were Abby's. And in the time it took for his heart to beat twice, he allowed his imagination to flirt with the idea of what his and Abby's children would have been like. "Thanks, Denny," he said, "for convincing Dad to come to the fireworks. He'll pretend he doesn't, but he will enjoy it."

"I know. He pretends a lot of the time." Denny bit at his lip and twisted the knotted rope in his hands, pondering who knew what dilemma. "He misses his son," he finally blurted out, as if it were a huge secret. "They never found the body in the river and so he's stuck back there missing him."

Quite an insight for a child, Jeff thought. Apparently, Gideon had been doing as much talking as listening during the reading of *Harry Potter.* It was time to return Abby's heads up with the hint that Gideon probably wasn't the best companion for her impressionable son. Or anyone else, for that matter. "He's been stuck back there a long time, Denny. Longer than anyone should stay in the same place."

"One time I tried to stay in the same place in a

book," Denny said. "But I had to find out how the story ended even though I didn't want to."

Jeff smiled at Abby's son, a child studying hard on how to be a grown-up, and he wished the world could be a simpler, safer place for its children.

"Denny!" Mae's voice called just as the microphone squawked.

Mayor Raleigh Osborn tapped the amplifier. "Testing. Testing," he said. "One, two, three. Can you hear me in the back there?"

Mae motioned to her grandson. "Come sit with me. It won't be long before the fireworks start."

The boy slipped away as quickly as the last visible arc of sun, back into the innocence of childhood, the expectation of excitement, the thrill of noise and fire in the night. Jeff looked for Gideon, but he was lost in the dimming light, already a shadow in the crowd. Retrieving his camera, Jeff knew he'd be lucky to get more than a couple of good shots now. He'd catch Orville Keener on stage and maybe another photo op or two with the flash, and he usually managed to capture two or three explosions of color against the night sky, but darkness would limit his choices. Not that it mattered. The Trib's next edition would look very much like all its Independence Day predecessors . . . local faces, familiar captions, one or two shots of the fireworks display. That was one thing he liked about living in a small town . . . the constancy, the knowledge that change came at a leisurely, almost imperceptible pace, the comfortable knowing that he fit in with this tiny time-warped corner of the universe.

But that comfortable sameness felt suddenly stifling and constricted, as if he'd tried to stay on the same page of a book for too long.

The time had come to find out how the story that had begun on the day Alex died would end.

Before he became an old man, like Gideon, who had wasted his opportunities to live in the present by staying forever mired in the past.

Abby closed the lid of the cooler and pushed it farther back into the station wagon, glad to be finished with the Fourth of July picnic. She insisted Lora stay put and did all the clean up herself, and now she was looking forward to the Pepsi she'd promised herself once everything had been put away. Closing the car door, she picked up the soda can, its icy wetness welcome and refreshing against her palm. On stage, Teri and Tami Howard were clogging to a jaunty, Irish melody, the taps of their shoes broadcast, along with the music, through the portable PA system rigged up around the park.

Abby took her time walking across the parking lot, enjoying the cold carbonation as the first swallow of fizzy soda slid down her throat. Noah had never returned with the drink she'd requested earlier. In fact, she hadn't seen him since he'd left her with Jeff. He was probably around someplace . . . all the residents were here, and she knew by their remarks he'd delivered them. He might have stayed in the van, waiting to take them back to Wade House, still afflicted by the migraine. It was possible that, on reflection, he might feel a little embarrassed at the way he'd pressed her for information about Alex and the accident. But whatever his reasons, Noah had chosen not to join the merry band of Wade House residents for the pre-fireworks show, and she hadn't seen him on any of her trips back and forth to the station wagon.

The clogging ended and Mayor Osborn stepped up to the mike to thank the Howard twins for their performance and announce that the fireworks would begin right after the Burton sisters sang and Mr.

Keener did his yearly presentation of the Declaration of Independence.

Abby wandered out to the outer perimeter of the crowd, taking her time, looking for a glimpse of Kyle, who she'd allowed to come with his friends. She hoped she'd done the right thing, although she knew if she'd told him no, it would have been an unholy fight with her on the losing end. Kyle was growing up, and fearful as she was of granting him too much freedom too soon, she knew he deserved a chance to prove that he could be trusted. He was supposed to meet her at the van no later than thirty minutes after the fireworks finale, and she fervently hoped he wouldn't try to test her resolve by being late. Or not showing up at all. With Kyle, she never knew where or when the next confrontation would develop. She only knew it *would* develop.

As she walked, she couldn't help but recall the miscellaneous mischief she, Jeff, and Alex had managed to get into in summers long past. How different it felt to view those escapades from a parent's point of view. How clearly she saw now what could so easily have gone wrong. What, eventually, had gone wrong. The question for Abby had always been whether a few less secrets might have prevented the accident from happening at all. Would Mae have stepped in if she'd known the malicious game Melanie was playing? Was there any reason to believe the involvement of an adult would have changed the outcome? Abby didn't like to think about that, didn't like the sense of guilt such thoughts evoked. But now, as a parent, she could see the other side . . . and everything looked diametrically different.

Catching the hum of a sudden commotion, she turned toward the sound and saw a group of people clustered on the grassy slope not too far from the parking area behind her. Her pulse kicked up with a

practiced knowing. She recognized the hypnotic curiosity that caught people when they saw someone
hurt or in pain, the first moments of unreality, the stir
of hoping someone took action. Any action. She
began to run, apprehension riding the high of adren-
alin, her years of training enforcing a steely,
purposeful calm as she pushed through the crowd.
"I'm a nurse," she said. "What happened?"

"He fell."

"Grabbed at his chest. Like he was havin' a heart attack or something."

". . . saw him standing there, with his mouth moving, like he was trying to say something."

"He was staring off over there and then he just
keeled over."

The explanations came in an overlapping wave,
confused, curious, and relieved as the group parted
to make way for her. Her heart clutched when she realized it was Gideon Garrett lying on the grass, but she
quickly checked to see if he was breathing, ruled out
the idea that he might be choking, and located his
pulse even as she called over her shoulder. "Find out
if the ambulance is here, and if it isn't on the park
grounds, get the First Responder paramedics with the
fire trucks over here. Someone should get Jeff Garrett, too." She gave Gideon a slight shake to grab his
attention. "Mr. Garrett? Are you hurting? Can you tell
me what happened?"

Gideon blinked, opened his eyes, and, in a glance,
she noted that although his right pupil appeared normal, his left pupil was dilated and static, indicating the
possibility of a stroke or an intracranial bleed. He had
a strong pulse, a little fast, but not as erratic as it
would be if he were having a heart attack. "Do you
know what day it is?"

He blinked again, disoriented and distracted. "I . . .
saw . . . her." The words came on the heels of a grimace

as he sucked in a sharp breath, and were all but lost in the effort. "Sarah. I . . . saw her."

"Are you in pain?" Abby persisted. "Talk to me, Mr. Garrett. Tell me about Sarah. Where did you see her?" She wanted to keep him talking, glean what information she could to help the EMS paramedics correctly assess his condition, and if believing he'd seen his dead wife furthered that end, then that was fine with Abby. "Do you know where you are?"

His lips moved but released no sound.

She tucked two fingers against each of his palms. "Squeeze my hands, Mr. Garrett. Can you do that?"

He responded by weakly folding his hands around her fingers. Not enough pressure for her to tell much about his injury.

"Squeeze my hands, Mr. Garrett," she said more firmly.

"Not . . . Sarah. . . ." The rest of the words wisped away, if indeed, they were words at all.

"That's right, I'm not Sarah. I'm Abby. Now squeeze my hands as hard as you can."

This time he made no effort at all.

Abby leaned in, checking his pulse again, wondering why it was taking the emergency team so long, knowing what felt to her like hours had only been minutes. Seconds, even. The fire department was on the scene, as they always were when fireworks and a crowd commingled, and, with any luck, there'd be an ambulance on site as well.

"Mr. Garrett." She patted his cheeks, hard enough for him to draw his brows together in a frown, although his eyes remained closed.

"Dad?" Jeff, suddenly, knelt opposite her, bent over his father, his face lined with concern and worry. He pulled Gideon's' left hand into his own, clasped it tightly. "Hang in there, Dad."

"The paramedics should be here any minute," Abby told him.

"Dad," Jeff said, his tone sharper, demanding the old man live. "Come on, Dad. Open your eyes."

The faded brown eyes opened, then blinked. "Alex."

Jeff's eyes connected briefly with Abby's, and his pain charged her with an electric current of emotion, sharing an instant's understanding that no matter what he did or had ever done, he could never be the son Gideon wanted. Even when he was the only son Gideon had left. It wasn't fair. Or right. The favoritism had ruined Alex as thoroughly as it had wounded Jeff. And Abby hated the old man for his crime of choosing one child over the other.

"No, Dad. It's Jeff. Jeff. Not Alex."

"No!" Gideon said in a gruff whisper, displaying a moment of lucidity. "Alex. I saw . . . Sarah."

He seemed aware that his speech slurred and wasn't clear and he tried again, but wound up making only unintelligible sighs.

A siren gave a singular blat and—thank God!—the red and blue lights of the ambulance spun against the darkness. The crowd parted and the paramedics were there, making the same checks Abby had made, assessing the patient, already reporting to the emergency room doctor on call.

Abby stood and moved back, allowing them room to work, trusting them to do what she couldn't. It took only moments for them to have Gideon on oxygen and hooked up to a monitor and only slightly longer to have him in the ambulance and ready for transport. He'd have an IV going before they were out of the parking lot, and before they reached the highway, the doctor would have decided if he could make the trip into Tulsa via ambulance or if helicopter transport was indicated. Jeff never left his side, getting into the ambulance, a good son to a father who'd never given him an ounce of approval. Even had Alex lived, it would still have been Jeff with his father now. Jeff, who dutifully carried the responsibility. Jeff, who did what needed to be done. And Gideon would still want Alex.

Abby watched until the ambulance had disappeared from sight and the siren grew too distant to hear above Orville Keener's creaky voice on the sound system. Arms tucked tightly beneath her breasts, shaken by the emergency, Abby stood while the group of people around her dispersed. The majority of the revelers were unaware of what had happened, too far removed from the area, too caught up in anticipating the fireworks to realize that for Jeff and Gideon this Fourth of July night had taken a sudden, unexpected turn.

Not yet calm enough to deal with the questions her mother and the boarders would have, Abby turned and walked toward the van, thinking she'd watch the fireworks from there. Perhaps by the time the show ended, she'd be able to get an update on Gideon's condition to pass along. A few people had chosen to watch from their vehicles, but for the most part, the cars she passed were empty and dark. She was at the passenger door of the van before she remembered Noah had the key, so she moved forward to lean against the right fender and wait for the fireworks to begin.

"What happened?" Noah's voice came out of the darkness, startling her, jerking her heart into a frenzied rhythm.

"God, you scared the life out of me," she said.

"Sorry." His voice sounded strained and strange, issuing as it did from the shadows on the opposite side of the van. "What happened to the old man?"

"A stroke, I think." She took a deep breath, held it

a second, then released it in a long sigh. "I doubt we'll know much until tomorrow sometime."

"I saw him fall. He kind of folded in on himself as he went down, as if all the resistance seeped out of him first, and then his body just followed it to the ground. It was . . . odd."

"Yes," she agreed, as the sky lit up with a spray of red, white, and blue streamers and the Sweetwater Tunes orchestra filled the air with music.

More fireworks burst and scattered overhead, but Abby's thoughts circled back to Gideon. And stayed there with Jeff.

Chapter 21

Jeff awoke with a start, his neck and shoulders stiff, his thoughts dully considering how he'd managed to doze off in the uncomfortable chair next to Gideon's hospital bed. It took a moment to locate the sound that had roused him, but a soft footfall brought his attention to the door . . . and his daughter. Lexie had her back to him, attempting to draw the heavy interior door closed behind her, making a face at the *huff* of air it uttered as it sealed the private room off from the outer cubicle, which in turn sealed it from the hospital corridor outside.

"Lexie," he said, rising.

She spun around, apologized with a glance. "I'm sorry. I tried to be super quiet. It looked like you were asleep."

"Just resting my eyes."

She smiled. So did he. And they stepped forward at the same moment, father and daughter, meeting in the middle for a welcome back hug. A good hug. A strong happy-to-be-home hug. A hug he held onto for a heartbeat too long, conveying to her, despite his better intention, that he'd missed her, that he worried about her and the time she'd spent alone with her mother. "When did you get here?"

Her glance skittered away from him and then returned. A nothing of a reaction. But he knew the meaning of a hundred throw away gestures she made and he recognized the overly blithe innocence in her expression. "To the hospital, you mean?" she answered brightly. "Oh, just long enough to find the room. Mom dropped me off out front. She'll be up once she's parked the car." Lexie turned on the heels of a pair of strappy new sandals and moved closer to the still figure of her grandfather in the bed. "How's Grampa?"

"Pretty good, considering he had a stroke day before yesterday." Jeff let her redirect his focus, knowing if she harbored guilt over something, she'd confess sooner or later. Keeping secrets from him had never been her strong suit. "He's having trouble with his speech and there's some slight weakness on his left side, but the doctor said after a few weeks in rehab, he should be back to normal. Personally, I was hoping he might come out of this with a sweeter disposition, but so far I haven't seen any improvement. I'm pretty sure the nurses draw straws to see who has to come in here."

Lexie smiled softly. "He's in better shape than I expected if he's already terrorizing the nurses. Will he have to stay in the hospital for a long time?"

"No. The doctor wants him transferred to the rehab clinic in a few days, probably by the first of next week. Depending on how well he cooperates with the therapists, he could be there anywhere from two to six weeks."

"Do you think he will? Cooperate, I mean?"

Jeff shrugged. "I don't know. We'll just have to wait and see."

Gideon, his face bleached an unhealthy gray by the stark hospital-white sheets and vivid blue blanket, snored in his sleep, a great rattling blast of noise.

"Wow," Lexie whispered, stepping quickly backward from the bedside. "I didn't think he'd be able to make any sound at all."

"He can talk, but his voice slurs, and it's difficult to understand what he's trying to say." Except Jeff didn't have any trouble deciphering the blurry syllables. *Alex. Alex. Who else had Gideon ever asked for? Who else had he ever wanted?* "So, sweetheart, how was your trip? I can see you got some new clothes." He eyed the low-rise waist and tight fit of her summer slacks, the wide slash of belt riding her hips, the skimpy amount of fabric that covered her upper body, the quarter-inch of skin revealed between the bottom of one and the top of the other. And he felt proud of himself for managing a nonjudgmental, "Not exactly your usual style."

"You just haven't been paying attention," she said airily. "I've been wearing stuff like this all year."

"Oh, come on, Lexie. I'm not *that* unobservant."

A tinge of self-consciousness brought up her chin. Melanie's chin. Beautifully proportioned and suddenly as perversely stubborn as her mother's. Her long hair swayed with the movement, and he noticed the subtleties of a new cut and variegated streaks of blond—from caramel to fairy white—not put there by nature or exposure to the sun. She had on make-up, too, he realized. A whole palette of new make-up, artfully applied to give her the look of a grown woman and make her appear older and more mature than she was. He didn't know why teenage girls were encouraged to believe an alluring look was what counted, but he harbored no doubt as to who had encouraged his daughter to take the bait.

Melanie took tremendous pleasure in Lexie's striking resemblance, in being able to observe her own bewildering beauty as it was reborn in her daughter. There had been a time—Lexie had been barely three, just past the toddler stage and transforming into a fey, angelically pretty child—when Melanie dressed the two of them in matching mother/daughter outfits daily and paraded around town, showing off her little clone. Jeff had put his foot down, insistent that Lexie be allowed to make her own choices, develop her individuality, spend time socializing with other children instead of having to be her mother's playmate. Within days, he'd enrolled her in a preschool program and dance classes, and from then on kept her involved in enough outside activities to dilute Melanie's influence.

Melanie hated him all the more for it. Her headaches turned into migraines, her outward compliance evolved into subterfuge and deceit, and she began perfecting the sly art of nurturing her secrets into weapons.

"I like the haircut," he said, and Lexie's hand flew to her hair, touching it in a way that let him know she liked it, too, however uncertain she felt about this new, more grown-up image.

"I'm not sure about the streaking." She ran her fingers through the strands, trying to see the blend of colors in a sidelong look. "That was Mom's idea."

"Why doesn't that surprise me?" But he offered the comment with a wry smile. "I like it, Lex. It's very pretty."

She relaxed with the compliment, settled now that he wasn't disappointed in her or upset about the changes in her appearance. "It took forever! One whole afternoon at this froufrou spa the concierge recommended to Mom. I got the whole treatment, head to toe."

"Even a pedicure?" Since babyhood, Lexie hadn't liked anyone messing with her feet. Jeff had put it down to ticklishness and avoided all toe touching, except what cleanliness necessitated. Melanie, on the other hand, wanted her little Barbie doll to have painted nails, fingers *and* toes, matching each other and her own meticulous manicures. Lexie threw screaming fits until her mother finally gave up and settled for the occasional fingernail polish she would sometimes allow.

"Well, no. But don't tell Mom. She thinks it's silly for me to be so particular about my feet."

He glanced down at her coral-tipped toes and asked the question with a lift of his eyebrows.

"I did them myself," she explained, "while I waited for her to come back and get me." The skittery guilt came and went in her expression again, replaced too quickly by a diversion. She extended one foot and examined the polish. "I wanted to paint them purple, but the only shade I could find was an ungodly ugly puce so I got this color instead. Do you like it?"

"Your mother didn't get a head-to-toe treatment at this—what'd you call it?—froufrou spa?"

"You don't like it." She turned her ankle from side to side, frowning. "You're probably right, the color's way too orange for this outfit."

"I like the color. Where was your mother while you were at the spa?"

Lexie continued to concentrate on her coral toes. "Oh, she had some errands to do."

"Somehow, I can't picture her passing up an afternoon of pampering to run errands in Dallas traffic," he said. "Where did she go, Lex?"

Her sigh stretched long, but carried a breath of relief with it. "The library."

"The what?"

She put her foot back on the floor and tugged self-consciously at the short hem of her knit top. "The library. She went to the library."

"She told you she was going to the *library*?"

Lexie's brown eyes flicked to his with defensive speed. "I know what you're thinking, Dad, but she really did go to the library. She brought back a folder of photocopies and notes and articles and things. She showed a couple of them to me . . . information about becoming an interior designer."

Just by the tone of her voice, he knew she considered this a positive step and didn't want him to make fun of her mother for pursuing it.

"I think she really wants to do this, Dad. She spent a bunch of hours in the hotel's computer lab looking up information and sending out queries about schools and training and she got very excited when someone called the hotel room in answer to one of her e-mails."

Every alarm in Jeff's body went off like a fire bell. Nothing in Lexie's account sounded remotely like something Melanie would do. Not a trip to the library. Or hours spent searching the Net. Not the idea that she would seriously pursue a career. Or that she'd received a phone call in response to an e-mail about schooling. "Hmm," he said, trying to come up with some plausible correlation between what Lexie believed her mother had done and what Melanie had actually been up to. Years of experience with her underhanded methods told him one had nothing to do with the other. "Hmm."

Up came Lexie's chin. "Give her some credit, Dad. At least she's trying to improve herself. And she was in a great mood the whole trip. Didn't have a single headache. I know you probably think I'm not telling the truth about this, but the trip was actually kind of fun and I had a good time. It turned out way better than I expected."

The defensive stance in her voice and in the set of her hands on her slender hips convinced Jeff to back off the conversation. She'd been alone for several days with Melanie, who was, after all, her mother, and a wizard at spinning the ugliest of truths into the loveliest of lies. "I'm glad you had a good time," he said, choosing diplomacy. "But I certainly missed you. Several people asked where you were on the Fourth."

"Oh." Interest kindled in her expression. "Anyone in particular?"

"Anyone in particular you're thinking might have asked?"

"No," she said with a roll of her eyes. "No one in particular."

"Then, no, no one in particular asked." He chucked her under the chin and returned to his chair. "So tell me what else you got for going on this little shopping trip? Besides the new duds and a day at the spa?"

The guilty look flitted across her face like a shadow as she tucked one leg beneath her and sank onto the corner of Gideon's bed. "Oh, not that much, really. Not on the shopping trip. Just clothes, mainly. One early birthday present. And some other stuff. A few things Mom thought I needed."

"Your birthday's not until April. This is only July."

"I know. I said it was an early present." Lexie popped up off the bed, smoothed the blanket at Gideon's feet, and resettled in the other uncomfortable chair. "Do you think Grampa's going to be okay? Really okay?"

"I think he's going to be as cranky as ever. Really. So what is it?"

Her eyebrows drew down in a perfectly innocent look of confusion. "What is what?"

"The early birthday present. What did she think you had to have now that couldn't wait nine months until your birthday?"

The variegated blond streaks swung forward as she dipped her chin and muttered something that sounded oddly like, "A car."

"You want to say that one more time? A little clearer."

Lexie sighed, obviously tired of keeping secrets. "A car," she repeated. "She bought me a car."

"A *car*?"

"Yes. Before we came to the hospital, she drove to a car dealership and told me to pick out whatever I wanted."

"A new car? But you don't even have your license, yet."

"It's not like I *asked* her to do it, Dad."

"That isn't the point, Lexie. Why would she do such a thing without talking to me about it? It'll be next year before you can drive it."

"Mom said, under the circumstances, she thought I should apply for a hardship license so I can drive to school this fall."

"What circumstances?" Although he knew. This was about the divorce. A way for Melanie to yank his chain . . . a chain she'd managed to also wrap neatly around Lexie's neck so she would feel the pain, too . . . and he would suffer all the more.

"I don't know, Dad. I'm only telling you what she said."

"Don't get attached to the idea of having your own car, Lexie. It's going back."

"But, Dad. . . ."

Which was the moment Melanie pushed open the door and walked in, chilling the air around Jeff with nothing more than a cool smile. "Hello, Jeff."

"Melanie."

She walked to Gideon's bedside and looked down at him with a curious indifference, before turning her attention to Jeff. "So? Did you tell her?"

"Tell her what? That she can't have the car you should have known better than to buy for her in the first place? That under no circumstances does she need to get a special license so she can drive before she's sixteen?"

"No, Jeff." Satisfaction burned in the blue of her eyes, lingered like thick cream on what remained of her smile. "Did you tell her you've moved out of our home, that you're divorcing us?"

The freeze hit him. This was a game to her, a strategy,

a method of getting even with him. She didn't care that Lexie got hurt in the crossfire.

"Divorce?" Lexie's voice picked up a note of panic as she looked from one parent to the other. "You're getting _divorced?_"

Melanie gave a sad, impatient sigh. "You told me you wanted to tell her, Jeff, so I gave you the opportunity. I should have known you'd turn coward, and I'd be forced to deal with an unfortunate scene like this."

"If you hadn't stolen off to Dallas with her, Melanie, I would have been able to tell her as I planned and there wouldn't _be_ an unfortunate scene like this to deal with."

"I'm sorry, Jeff, but I can't cover for you this time. You have to take responsibility for what you've done. It isn't fair to expect me to continue keeping your secrets."

"_My_ secrets? Maybe you should explain to her about _your_ secrets, Melanie. Maybe you should—"

"Stop it!" Lexie hissed. "Just tell me. Are you getting a divorce?"

With all the warmth of a rattlesnake, Melanie walked over and cupped an arm around Lexie's shoulders. "I'm sorry, Alexis. He moved out of the house the day you left for cheerleading camp. I hoped he'd have changed his mind by the time we got back, but I see now that isn't going to happen." She hugged Lexie close. "I know how much this hurts you and I'm so very sorry for your sake. This wasn't my idea and I never wanted him to divorce us, but we'll survive, sweetness. You and I. Don't you worry. We'll manage just fine without him."

Lexie's eyes, wide and wounded, met Jeff's. "Daddy?"

In that one word, she asked for denial, to be told the life she knew wasn't collapsing around her. She asked for reassurance that he still loved her, that he wasn't leaving her. Yet, Melanie's words already were seeping deep into Lexie's heart, branding him as the traitor, and Jeff knew by the look in her eyes that he'd miscalculated. He'd told himself she'd be glad to escape the tensions of home, relieved to finally be free of her mother's moods. But in that moment he saw his error. However manipulative and selfish, however undependable and distant, Melanie was her mother. However necessary and right his leaving, Jeff was the betrayer. It was he who had left, he who had decided the myth that was their family should end. He'd done it as much for her as for himself, but Lexie took the news as a child, deprived suddenly, inexplicably of the only foundation she knew. One mother, one father, one family. He'd broken the commitment, the unstated promises she depended on, and no amount of logic or explanation could make this moment less traumatic for her. Jeff hadn't understood that before, and although he couldn't return, wouldn't go back to the marriage for any reason, his soul ached with the pain his choice now caused his daughter.

"Lexie." Extending his hand, he took a step toward her, holding her gaze and the connection between them, willing her to see he was still the father who loved her more than life.

The connection might have held, might have salvaged the moment, if a nurse hadn't walked in, clipboard in hand, making the usual rounds each shift change seemed to necessitate. Oblivious to the drama she'd innocently interrupted, she shed her smile equally on everyone in the room. "So, how's our patient, today?" Moving to the bed, she took Gideon's temperature and pulse, checked his blood pressure, and asked him questions to which he merely snuffled in reply.

Jeff didn't take his eyes off of Lexie. "Let's go to dinner. We'll talk about this."

"I don't want to talk," she said, her sweet voice uneven and tightly emotional. "I want to go home."

"Of course, you do." Melanie leaned her head against Lexie's, their hair blending into one serene halo of sunlit color, as alike in appearance as they were different in personality. But suddenly melded into one entity against which he could find no leverage. "Come on, Sweetness, I'll take you home."

But Lexie shrugged free of Melanie's arm, flung a hateful look at both parents, and bolted from the room. Anger rippled in her wake and merged with the river of fury flooding through Jeff's blood.

"I've seen you do some despicable things, Melanie," he said in a voice trembling with rage. "But that was a new low, even for you."

Serene as a starry night, Melanie hit him with the full benefit of her beauty and the stunning power of her Mona Lisa smile. "I warned you to stay away from Abby," she said softly. "You should have listened to me. But now . . . well, the time's finally come to pay the piper."

Leaving that threat to haunt him, she turned and followed Lexie out.

"Okay then." The nurse made a last notation on her chart, absorbed in her work, either ignoring or still unaware of the scene going on behind her. She rattled the water pitcher and made another note. "I'll ask the orderly to bring in some more water, Mr. Garrett. You let me know if you need anything else, all right?"

Gideon shuffled beneath the starchy sheets, roused, but not fully awakened by the nurse's voice and movements. "Alex," he whispered in a blurry garble of sound. "Alex."

"Don't worry." The nurse smiled reassuringly at Jeff

as she pulled open the door to leave. "You'll be able to understand what he's saying soon enough. It may take a little extra effort, but you'll get there."

Effort. As if any amount of effort could transform him into the favored son. As if effort could ever change the fact that he had killed his brother.

"Alex," Gideon whispered hoarsely, unintelligibly.

Jeff sank into the discomfort of the chair, down into the thorny nest of his frantic, angry thoughts and, putting his head in his hands, whispered, "Lexie."

Chapter 22

The night and the river conversed like two old men playing gin rummy and repeating stories they'd told a hundred times before and would tell a hundred times more, stories no one else cared to hear. The trees stirred restlessly, rooted and unable to escape, like fidgety children yearning to run free but listening politely to their elders as they'd been charged to do. Certainly the conversation held no interest for any of the youth gathered at the sandbar. They ignored everything except their own interests, exulted in being together, in congregating where they were forbidden to go and experimenting with what they were forbidden to touch. At their age, it was the sweetest of freedoms . . . indulging the thirst for independence while parents slept, unaware of any transgression.

The number of teens fluctuated as some left and others arrived, slipping in and out by circuitous routes through the trees and around the river road barriers. They parked in shadowed turnoffs and walked as far as necessary to keep their rendezvous point private. And, should they be caught, they could easily scatter, increasing the odds for all, or most, to escape.

Kyle liked the river and being a part of the group that gathered there after the town closed down for the night. In a little more than a month, he'd come to feel accepted in this hicksville of a town . . . and he'd never in a million years expected to like a single thing about the place. Well, except for Lexie. If it hadn't been for her, he'd probably still be holed up in his room, e-mailing his Chicago friends and making plans to get away from here and go back there. Lexie had introduced him to her friends, invited him into the river gang, as she called them, and expected that he would be accepted as one of them. And so he was. Even in her absence, while she'd been at camp and then in Dallas with her mother, the guys came by to get him. He'd been a little surprised by that, but grateful and eager to prove he belonged.

On the nights they could slip out, they'd search the back streets of Sweetwater until they met up with an old guy everyone called Calvin the Cadillac Man. Calvin did business from the front seat of a rusted-out, black Cadillac that served as his home on wheels. He was happy to take whatever cash they'd managed to collect and buy them whatever liquor they requested. For the price of a few bottles of Mad Dog—Calvin's fee for services rendered—the underage youth of Sweetwater could order up all the alcoholic beverages they could afford.

"Get me another drink?" Lexie asked in a sultry whisper.

Kyle took the empty Pepsi can out of her hand, folded her fingers in on her palm, and held them there as he leaned in to kiss her. Sweet. God, she was sweet. The taste of cherry clung to her lips, the warmth of vodka loosened her inhibitions, and she swayed against him, pliant, trusting, aware, but unconscious of the fire she fueled inside him. "Don't move," he whispered, "I'll be back before you can miss me."

"I miss you already." Her lips, soft as a sigh, seduced by the alcohol, pressed into his again, and he would have done anything for her, fought for her, died for her.

She pulled back from the kiss, only to lay her head

on his shoulder and breathe desire in a moist heated lick of her tongue across his neck. His hand slid beneath her blouse and upward across her satin skin to her breast, its budding fullness falling like ripe fruit into the heated cup of his palm. Sex surged in his blood, flooded his senses, merged past and future into this one moment of the present, which was worth everything. Everything.

Seeking her mouth with his, he thrust his tongue inside, and the flames of first love burned beneath his skin, scorched the breath they exchanged, brought her body bumping, pushing against his.

"Hey, Ryan! Sell tickets, why don't you?" Hoots and catcalls broke the haze of lust, and Kyle struggled to pull himself out of the grip of his impatient libido. But Lexie held onto the embrace, her kisses begged him to taste her, counseled him to pay no attention to their audience. He searched blindly through a mind melting with images of Lexie. Her breasts in his hands, her body naked under his. . . .

Baseball. He should think about baseball. The Cardinals. The best game he'd ever seen them play. Name the players. He could do that. No, he couldn't. His brain produced seductive pictures faster than he could recall what a baseball looked like. Dragging in a deep breath, he set Lexie away from him, regretting the lost opportunity, but certain, too, that if he stayed this close to her another minute, he'd embarrass himself royally in front of her and everyone else. A guy could only take so much encouragement before . . . well, before something had to happen. "You're dangerous, Lexie Garrett," he murmured. "A dangerous, dangerous woman."

Her inebriated giggle vibrated like a little girl's. "Me?" Hair turned silver by the moonlight moved like buttery silk with the slight shake of her head. "It's the river that's dangerous. Didn't I warn you?"

His free hand stroked across her face in farewell and, reluctantly, he left her to wind his way through the brush, past other couples lingering in the shadows, past a pride of swaggering boys and a huddle of coquettish girls, each group separate and apart from the other, but connected by possibility. Kyle made it to the cooler and dipped his hand into the icy slush that cooled a seemingly endless supply of soda. Elbow deep in cold, he retrieved two cans of cola and brought them out, shaking off the excess moisture, too pleasantly buzzed from the alcohol to care if the contents spewed when he snapped open the lid. He intended to pour half of the Pepsi into the rich river soil, anyway. The rest he'd mix with enough syrupy cherry vodka to fuel this midnight rebellion.

He briefly considered not spiking his Pepsi this go-around. But he felt good. Not drunk. Not as drunk as Lexie was, for sure. He'd never seen her so charged before, so uninhibited and free. She glowed tonight with a radical fire, a *dare me* attitude. She'd already consumed more alcohol than she normally drank in a whole week of trips to the river. Getting high wasn't normally Lexie's aim in sneaking out at night and coming here. She scorned the drugs that occasionally showed up and the few kids who took them. She refused offers of cigarettes, a drag of weed, and usually mixed her own drink so no one could slip something into it. She stayed close to the group, friendly with everyone, flirtatious and free, but careful—always careful—that no one interpreted her coquetry as invitation or enticed her to stray beyond the parameters of her own principles.

But tonight. . . .

Tonight she encouraged familiarity, intimacy. Her body shouted invitation to his. Her wildness caught him by surprise, scared him, rattled his control. He'd touched her breast, kissed her like a man kisses a woman—all things she'd never allowed to happen before. He thought maybe she *expected* him to press for even more. His groin pulsed with the ache of wanting, hormonal urges overrode his thoughts, blazing like neon lights in his brain.

Sex.

It called to him like an echo of splendid pleasure, claimed every nerve in his body, ruled him with the clarity of a covenant, and beckoned him to make his move. Now. While temptation and opportunity converged. Before the moment for action slipped away with the dawn.

This was new to him. All new. Scary as hell, and exciting. He'd never gotten this close before, never thought Lexie, the girl he'd secretly longed for since three summers before, might be the one. That she would fall for him, too. Love him back. Want him.

God. It could happen. Tonight.

He was pretty sure she'd never had sex before either. She was probably scared, too. So that was good. They'd be scared together. And he figured he knew more than she did anyway. So even if he made a mistake, she might not notice, might think it was just the way sex was supposed to be.

Kyle poured out half of the Pepsi, added cherry vodka to top it off again, and started back to her, anticipating what she would say, how he could suggest they find a place to be alone. He said a quick word to Cody and Tyler in passing and noticed two silhouettes on the cusp of the darkness, coupling with the night and the steady sounds of the slow-flowing river. He paid attention to the direction they took. Stumbling on another pair of lovers seeking privacy among the shadows might spoil the mood, and he didn't want to take any chances.

"Kyle. . . ." Lexie's voice called him back to longing, to her, and he kissed her again as he slid the cold, mixed soda into her hand.

But she pulled away, more interested in drinking than kissing. "You're my hero, Ryan."

He didn't like her calling him by his last name. Not like that. Like he was anybody. Like he was no one special. Like she hadn't been eagerly kissing him just a few minutes ago. Like she hadn't been pressing her body against his. Like he was a hero only because he'd carried back more vodka for her to drink. He didn't like the way she raised the soda can either. Or the way she tipped back her head, swaying as she sucked down more alcohol.

"Hey, slow down." Reaching for the can, he tried to pull it away from her lips, tried to move into that private space again, those intimate moments of before where only the two of them existed, where she kissed him with real desire, real love, where she let him touch her, wanted him to touch her. But his hand collided with hers, and the syrupy drink splashed out and onto her face and hair, splattering down the front of her blouse.

"You made me spill my drink," she said in a slur of syllables, wiping at the drops of dark, sticky cola on her face, pulling at the stains that clung in wet splotches to the fabric of her blouse. "Now look what you did. My mother just bought this outfit for me and you ruined it."

Kyle plucked at the shirt, too, tugging the wetness away from her skin. A button popped off, revealing her smooth stomach and the topaz stud that breached her navel. The jewel winked at him in the darkness, mesmerized him with a seductive glint. His hand was on her stomach before he quite realized he meant to touch her . . . and just as quickly she slapped it away.

"Don't touch me."

The rejection hit him like a bullet, exploding inside, leaving a gaping hole of wounded pride and humiliating betrayal. "That's not what you said a few minutes ago."

"Well, that's what I say now." She tossed her head, defiant, inexplicably angry. With him. And when she raised the can to down even more of the alcohol, he couldn't stand it.

Grabbing the soda can, sticky with a syrupy residue, Kyle threw it as hard as he could toward the river, satisfied when he heard it splash into the dark water. Then he slid his hand into the pocket of her shorts, going for the keys to the Honda her mother had bought her. "Come on, Lexie. Let's go."

She tried to snag the keys from his hold. "No. The only place I'm going is to get another drink."

"You've had enough."

An edge of frost cut the haze of intoxication in her eyes. "You're not the boss of me, Kyle Ryan," she said.

"Somebody needs to be."

"Screw you." She brushed by him with the careless haste of someone past the point of reasonable discourse.

He caught her arm again, held on, and tried to sound persuasive. "Don't be stupid, Lexie. I just want us to go somewhere we can be alone."

"And I want to stay here." Jerking free, she stumbled but righted herself and moved on. "Hey, Trev? Be my hero and fix me a drink."

Trevor Wardley separated from a group of jocks, smiling lazily as Lexie walked unsteadily toward him . . . and Kyle felt the threat of competition ball up inside his gut like a time bomb. Trev and Lexie had dated last year, and although she swore he was nothing but hot air in a jock strap, he was the one she sashayed up to now.

"What's in it for me, Beautiful?"

She giggled, openly flirting, openly excluding Kyle, showing him she could choose any boy she wanted and have any one she chose. "That depends," she said. "If I like the way you do it, I might let you take me home."

The other jocks grinned, whistled softly, and began teasing Trevor with raunchy innuendoes.

"I've never had any complaints about how I do it," he said. "Especially not from you." He tugged her toward the cooler, toward the outer fringes of the darkness.

Kyle started after her. Had she done it with Trevor? Had she lied about her relationship with him? Didn't it matter to her that Wardley was a brainless dick? That he'd trumpet his conquest all over town and back? Kyle couldn't bear that, couldn't stand the thought of his girl with such a dickwad. He wanted to punch Trevor Wardley in the face and kick him in the balls. He wanted to pick Lexie up, toss her over his shoulder, and carry her out of this place.

But he wasn't brave enough to face public rejection. And he wasn't drunk enough to believe he could pound Wardley into a pulp and still walk off with the girl. She'd only hate him more for resorting to a fistfight.

He had her keys. He'd go to the car and wait for her. Lexie wouldn't let Trevor take her home. She wouldn't let Trevor kiss her like Kyle had. Or touch her. Or . . . or anything else. She wouldn't do it. She just wouldn't.

And if she did? . . .

Well, to hell with her.

To hell with her.

He stalked off, trailing the anger of rejection, walking straight into the humiliating shadows of regret.

Chapter 23

The hospital elevator moved upward, its passengers avoiding eye contact with one another by watching the numbers above the door blink on and off. Each floor passed in unremarked silence, broken only by the occasional throat clearing or sniffle. When the elevator stopped, Abby stepped back, drawing Denny with her, to allow a man and woman to move past them and get out at the fourth floor. A Mylar balloon—IT'S A GIRL!—bobbed in their wake, floating from a curly pink ribbon that secured it to the flower arrangement of daisies and pink roses they carried. The scent of fresh flowers lingered even after the doors closed and the elevator resumed its journey, the self-concerned hush returning as the hypnotic blink of the numbers—five, six, seven—began again.

Denny's bony shoulders pressed back against Abby, his head butted up under her heart, and she looked down at the delicate whorl of hair crowning his still baby-blond head, a sight as beautiful to her as anything she ever expected to see in a whole lifetime. His pressure increased slightly, just enough of a touch to reassure him of her nearness, to remind her he was with her and didn't want to be left behind or forgotten. As if.

Abby nudged him and he looked up, startled and unsure of her motive, worried perhaps he'd done something wrong until he saw her smile. He ducked his head then, bashful at having been caught seeking reassurance, and returned her smile with a reticent charm.

A smile.

A rush of love for her boy seized her, carried on the wings of an immense gratitude for the slow, but certain change in him. He still carried the length of rope, still tied knots in it, still kept his nose in a book more hours than not, still worried about a world that seemed too brash and big to be a safe place for him. He still looked at Kyle as if, at any moment, his looked-up-to and admired older brother might go off like a rocket, as if Denny, somehow, would be to blame when it happened. He still retreated into himself and vanished to whatever hideout he'd found for himself if voices grew loud, if he sensed an argument about to inhabit the air he breathed, or if he thought he might have done something wrong.

Denny was still a long way from *normal*, Abby knew.

But he'd begun to smile. Not often. Not with the careless ease of childhood. Or with the impish delight of contentment. But he smiled.

And for now, that was enough. More, really, than she'd expected. More, actually, than she deserved.

Nine.

The elevator doors slid open and, taking Denny's hand, Abby led him onto the floor. Checking the numbers, she started down the hallway looking for Room 921. Gideon Garrett's room. Denny had asked her to bring him here on her day off, Saturday, insisting that Mr. Garrett would expect him to visit, would expect Denny to read to him. That was their bargain. Every day. Denny read. At the end of summer, when school started, Mr. Garrett would give him a big magnifying glass as payment. But because of the hospital, Denny had missed six whole days. He had to go today. Tomorrow wouldn't work, tomorrow would make it a whole week since he'd upheld his end of the deal. Denny had wheedled, routing every excuse Abby made, pleading when she still balked at his request. "I know Mr. Garrett is sick, Mom, but he's old and he can't see to read good anymore. He needs me. He'll feel better when he knows what happens to Harry Potter in the Forbidden Forest. I know he will, Mom. You just have to drive me. You don't have to stay. I know he'll be real happy you brought me. He always says he's glad I come to read to him. He always says that. I can make him feel better, Mom. Honest. I wouldn't kid you about something like that."

He'd never kidded her in his life. About anything. He'd never thought he could make anyone feel better, either. Certainly not by doing something he loved so much. So how could she refuse such a petition? As difficult as it was to imagine, and however reluctant she might be to admit it, Gideon Garrett had initiated this change in her shy, backward son simply by sharing his own love for books, by allowing Denny to share his love of reading in return. It was an odd bargain, a hybrid deal struck by mutual need between two loners. She didn't have to like the man for it, didn't need to forgive his past transgressions to appreciate the self-esteem he'd somehow nurtured in her son.

And so, here they were. Denny with a thick book tucked protectively under his arm, his length of knotted rope stuffed out of sight and out of mind in his pocket, his little boy face lit up with eagerness. She with more than a few degrees of reluctance and half a hope that the familiar sights and smells and sounds of the hospital would remind her of her true calling and convince her to return to nursing. Regardless of how far she had to drive.

Within a few steps down the hall, though, she knew she didn't miss the caregiving she'd trained to do. Not the idea of trying to give care to more patients than she had time for. Not the endless paperwork, or the petty rules of an overly zealous administration bent on cost-cutting, or the hierarchy of doctors and their many and various subordinates. A hospital was a hotbed of political dos and don'ts, with a rule behind every rule, a system that could often seem as complex and unknowable as the tax code.

"This is it," Denny pointed to the number beside the big, thick door. Abby lent an unobtrusive helping hand, bearing some of the weight as he pushed the door open and they moved into the outer cubicle, which contained a storage area and a sink. Another door blocked the entrance to the private room itself, and a glass window offered a preview of the patient's activity. Denny, not quite tall enough to get a good look through the glass, glanced up at her, then held his finger to his lips. "Sshh," he whispered. "Mr. Garrett might be asleep."

She nodded and pressed a finger to her lips to show she understood. Through the window she could see Gideon was awake, sitting up at an angle. Jeff was with him, standing beside the bed, holding a glass for his father, helping him drink from a straw. Her heart tightened with a sudden, errant memory, a time when he had held a glass for her just that way, helped her drink from a straw while she recuperated from having her tonsils removed. She'd been fourteen, a little younger than Kyle and Lexie were now, and a string of throat infections had finally convinced Doctor Brown a tonsillectomy offered the best chance for a cure.

Her good buddy, Alex, promised faithfully to visit her, to make chicken soup for her, cut funny faces into her Jell-O, bring her milkshakes, and watch television with her. But he'd never showed; he sent his brother instead with a can of Campbell's soup and his excuses. Alex always had an excuse, but Jeff presented this one as if he believed it, as if whatever alibi he'd come to offer had merit. Abby might have suffered hurt feelings over the easy way Alex wiggled free of his promises—but she never expected he would keep his promise to begin with. She didn't honestly believe he'd sent Jeff in his place, either. Jeff had heard the same *I'm gonnas* she had and, as he often did, he tried to cover for Alex, make it appear that his brother cared how she felt and was concerned about her recovery.

Alex was fun, always ready to party, ever eager to sacrifice good behavior for tomfoolery. He'd been that way as far back as third grade when Mrs. Newsom had seated students alphabetically by first name and Abby, whose name in roll call came directly before Alex's, took the desk in front of his. He pulled her hair, stole her pencils, copied from her papers, threw paper clips at her back, and generally made a nuisance of himself. For whatever reason, she'd taken his harassment as the compliment he intended, and from then on they were buds. Not friends. Never exactly that. But pals.

Maybe they remained pals because Abby never asked him to make promises, didn't expect him to keep them if he did, and mostly accepted his *I'm gonnas* as good intentions. She liked him enough to find him entertaining and to enjoy short doses of his company, but not enough to let his irresponsible ways bother her. And when Jeff came to visit her after her tonsillectomy, she thanked her lucky stars that sickness made Alex uncomfortable, that he didn't feel any compulsion to keep his word, and that his good intentions had produced this unexpected result. She was too young to date, of course, too innocent to understand the cost of giving her whole heart to the first love of her life. But Jefferson Garrett was older, roughly handsome, and everything that a small-town girl saw as perfection. He had a great smile and all of Alex's charm, but none of his blarney. He had a plan and a purpose for his future and he kept his promises, no matter what.

Abby found the plans fascinating, the purpose inspiring, and his sense of responsibility admirable. But she loved him in that first heartbeat because of the way he held the straw to her lips so she could get a drink.

And in ways she had only begun to remember, she had loved him with every heartbeat since.

"Mom?" Denny frowned at her and gave her hand a sharp tug. "You don't have to be scared. Mr. Garrett will be happy to see you, too. He's not always in a bad mood."

She didn't think she'd ever seen Gideon Garrett in anything but a bad mood, but it was too late to hustle Denny out of here now. He'd already pushed open the inside door and stepped into the room, bringing her with him.

"Hi, Mr. Garrett. It's me. Denny. I came to read to ya. Aren't you glad?"

Jeff set down the glass and turned. "Abby," he said. "Denny. What a nice surprise. Look who's here, Dad."

Gideon lifted one side of his mouth in a grimace or a smile, hard to tell which, and said, "Denton."

At least that's what Abby thought he said. It was hard to tell about that, too, his voice—that roar of a voice that had terrified new students for years—had turned mushy and hushed, a caricature of itself, a wisp of what it had been only a week ago.

"I brought *Harry Potter.*" Denny held up the book to prove it as he approached the bed. "You got a nice room here," he said conversationally. "Where do you want me to sit?"

Jeff took hold of a chair arm and pulled it over to the bed, setting it toward the foot and slanting it so that Denny could see Gideon and Gideon could see Denny. "This side's probably best," he confided in an aside. "Dad's having a little trouble with his speech since the stroke so you might not be able to understand what he says."

"It's okay. He can just listen. Sometimes all a person needs is just to listen." Denny plopped an extra pillow in the chair and then plunked his minute self on top of it, settling in, the book still clutched close in his hands. As excited as if he were about to see the circus. Brimming with a mystical sort of self-confidence. Eager to get started. He opened the book, tucked the bookmark between the last two pages, and looked at the old man he'd come all this way to see. "Remember where we left off?" he asked.

And Gideon, marshaling his effort, pinched out a whispery, "Forest."

"Yep." Denny cleared his throat. Then editing his own grammar, continued "I mean, yes, that's correct." His finger already marked the spot when he glanced up at Abby. "You can go now, Mom," he said. "You've already read this book. You don't want to hear it again."

Abby blinked, thinking that somewhere between the outer and inner doors of this room, the shy boy who'd ridden up with her in the elevator had been switched for this take-charge little mister. A mister who obviously didn't want or need his mother hanging around. "I don't mind listening," she said, "if you'd like for me to stay."

Denny pressed his lips tight together, the quandary of how to avoid hurting her feelings and still get her to leave written right into his expression. "I think you ought to go," he said finally, seriously. "Mr. Garrett doesn't like too much company. He's still kind of sick, you know, and if you stay, you'll talk."

Well.

"I could use a cup of coffee." Jeff sized up the situation and offered a solution. "And as it happens, I've also read *Harry Potter.*"

Abby looked at him, helplessly pleased by Denny's new streak of independence. "And if you stay, you might talk."

"No doubt about it," Jeff agreed with a shrug. "Come on, I'll buy you a cup of coffee."

"You like coffee, Mom," Denny rushed to remind her.

"Yes, I do. So how about if Jeff and I go get some coffee while you read to Mr. Garrett?"

And there . . . there was the smile again. "That's a good plan, Mom."

"I think so, too." And she smiled back. "We'll be back in a few minutes. Call the nurse if . . . well, if Mr. Garrett should suddenly need anything."

Denny rolled his eyes. "I know what to do, Mom. Just go, okay?"

"Okay." She punctuated their agreement with a solid nod and walked out. Jeff reached over her head to hold first one door for her and then the other. He touched the small of her back as they turned and started down the hospital corridor to the bank of elevators. It was nothing, a supportive impulse, a guide to the direction they needed to go, the kind of gesture men made with unconscious courtesy, the kind of gesture women barely noticed, if they noticed at all. It was a mere brush of human interaction.

Only the fact that she noticed and felt somehow nostalgic for the time when he had protected and loved her, made it something more.

And she very consciously moved away from him.

"We have a couple of choices here," he said. "If you like your coffee hot, fresh and flavored with condiments, we should head downstairs to the grill. If, on the other hand, you prefer a more challenging brew, I can slip past the nurses' station and swipe a cup from their private stash."

"I'm surprised at you, Jeff. Stealing caffeine from the poor nurses who are trying to take care of your ailing father?"

"Guilty," he said without remorse. "Although in my defense, they told me I could. So name your poison, Abby."

"No contest. I've had enough coffee from the nurses' station to last a lifetime. Let's try the grill."

"Good choice." He punched the button and, like magic, an elevator reached their floor on its way down.

A few minutes later, Abby faced him across a worn tabletop, the steam off the coffee in their Styrofoam cups rising in wisps between them, dissipating like idle thoughts in a comfortable silence.

"So," Jeff said. "Do you miss it?"

She smiled a little, then raised her cup and blew before taking a sip, knowing without asking what he referred to, understanding without effort the layering in his question, the bottom line he wanted to know. The years had changed them, made them different people, but the connection, the way their thoughts followed similar tracks, remained unbroken. It hadn't even turned rusty from disuse.

"No," she answered truthfully. "I'm not sure I'll ever miss it. I got into nursing by default. My college advisor encouraged me to try it because my science scores were strong. Mitch encouraged me because he was talking about applying to med school and the idea of playing doctor and nurse appealed to him. And you know how my mother values security. She encouraged me because she knew—even if God didn't—that there'd always be a need for nurses and I would never have to worry about getting a job." Abby set down her cup and offered up a wry smile. "Little did she know."

"I'd be willing to bet your mother still believes nursing was the right choice, though, and that working at the newspaper is a waste of your talent."

"A waste of my education, for certain. And for my mother that's a much more aggravating error."

"Are you sorry?"

"That she's aggravated? Or that I asked you for the job?"

He didn't answer. He didn't have to.

"I like the newspaper," she said. "I like the atmosphere. I like the flexibility. I like the people. I like that if there's a mistake in this week's edition, there can be a correction printed next week and that takes care of it. I like what I'm doing and Mom will get over being disappointed with my choices. Or not."

He nodded, no stranger to disappointing a parent. "Do you think our kids will get over being disappointed in us?"

"I doubt our kids give us enough thought to *be* disappointed." She paused, hesitant to venture into his personal affairs, yet feeling his current difficulty should at least be acknowledged. "Millie told me Lexie isn't taking the divorce well. Not that any child would. It's a tough adjustment."

He turned the Styrofoam cup in a circle on the tabletop. "She's still not talking to me."

"She's a teenager, Jeff. Not talking is one of their specialties."

"I guess I always assumed that when I finally left Melanie, Lexie would be ready. That she'd be relieved. Instead, now that it's happened, she's really angry. With me."

"Kyle's been angry with me for years. It's only since Mitch died I've been able to admit he has some justification."

"Does he blame you for what happened to his father?"

She shrugged. "At times, I'm sure he does. And maybe he's right in thinking I should have—and could have—done something to keep Mitch from self-destructing. At the very least, I should have gotten the boys out of the situation before it imploded. It was my responsibility to protect them . . . and I didn't. Kyle has a right to be angry with me."

"Regret is not an option," Jeff said, invoking the either/or game they'd once played as both challenge and entertainment, as a channel to explore deeper issues and feelings too fragile for conversation, as a way to lessen tension or give it a bump in the opposite direction. A game she hadn't thought about in years. "Would you rather be nearsighted or farsighted?"

"Nearsighted," she answered quickly. "Because then I'd be able to see what's right in front of my nose."

"And I'd rather be farsighted, so I could see trouble coming. Plus you can pick up cheap reading glasses practically anywhere without a prescription." He checked his watch, then asked another. "Okay, how about this: would you rather be a rock star or a renowned ballerina?"

"Are you kidding? Rock star, all the way."

He grinned. "Me, too."

"Too easy for you. Rock star or famous novelist?"

"Still has to be rock star. I don't think novelists have groupies, do they?"

"Probably not the kind you're thinking of, anyway. But what about this: would you rather be the lead singer in a knockout band or be a solo singer sensation?"

"Lead singer, definitely. I like having backup."

"Me, too."

And that's the way it had always been with them. Two no-doubt-about-it agreements for every one different perspective. Abby had nearly forgotten how much fun they'd once had, the privilege of easy conversation, the ability to say whatever came to mind, the feeling of safety when saying it. The honesty of it. The trust.

Which he'd broken and betrayed.

When they weren't a whole lot older than Lexie and Kyle are now.

And there it was.

A shadow, still, without substance or form. But she recognized its essence, knew it as the one thing she'd vowed she would never give him.

Forgiveness.

"I should probably get back upstairs," she said, retreating. "Before Denny wears your father out with the adventures of Harry Potter."

Jeff pushed back his chair immediately, aware—as she was—that becoming too comfortable with each other wasn't a good option, that it could too easily lead them to places they didn't mean to go. "It's more likely Dad's snoring so loudly Denny can't hear himself read. He'll probably be ecstatic to see you."

"I doubt it. He insisted on coming today," she said, reiterating the obvious, wanting to be sure Jeff understood this hadn't been her idea. "Wouldn't take no for an answer."

"It made for a nice break in the day. For me, as well as Dad. And for my part, at least, thanks for bringing him."

She'd done it for her son. Not for Jeff. Or Gideon. But there was no reason to say anything except a polite, "I'm glad it worked out so he could come."

"So," Jeff asked as they waited for the elevator again. "Are Lexie and Kyle still scorching up the computers, or have they progressed to long phone conversations after bedtime?"

Abby hoped the telephone was as far as they'd progressed, but she wouldn't take any bets on it. "Actually, Kyle's been in a particularly foul mood the past couple of days, and my motherly instincts tell me it has something to do with your daughter."

"You think they're fighting?"

The implications feathered his words, giving support to her own concerns. Teenagers were all about sex. Even years later, she remembered clearly that the only real fights she'd ever had with Jeff were about sex. Having it. Not having it. Wanting it. Toying with it. Backing away from it. Coming close. So close. In one form or another, adolescents were constantly stretching toward or away from the subject. Like a game of tetherball, their hormones kept them focused on the goal. No matter which way or how many times the ball got knocked around, it never veered far from its tether.

"I think something's not the way it was," she ventured. "But that's only a guess."

"And since Lexie's not talking to me at the moment. . . ."

"And since Kyle would rather eat roofing nails than discuss anything of a personal nature with me. . . ."

"We may never know what happened."

"*If* anything happened at all." Abby hoped it was that, hoped Kyle's mood reflected ordinary fifteen-year-old angst and not . . . well, not something else.

The elevator stopped for them, and Jeff's fingertips brushed her back once again as she stepped in ahead of him. And out of nowhere, her body remembered his touch, his kiss, the raw craving for more. More.

Okay, so sex wasn't that far from her consciousness, either.

Which was a normal reaction for a healthy young woman who hadn't had sex in a long time. A very, very long time. It would be more troubling if she never experienced the occasional yearning at all.

Especially in connection with the man she'd once believed would be her first and only lover. A man with whom she'd laid bare her soul, but never her body.

Regret is not an option.

"Would you rather be a bag of M&Ms or a box of Godiva chocolates?"

Jeff smiled, but only just. "M&Ms," he said. "Hands down."

"Me, too."

But she didn't smile at all.

Chapter 24

If he'd thought long and hard about it, Jeff probably wouldn't have bought the house. At least not without looking at several others first. But he wanted to establish stability, a permanence and presence he could offer his daughter as proof that he hadn't left her. He wanted bricks and mortar, a solid place for her to know as home, a place she could live in and leave from, a place of shelter and security, a place she could consider a soft spot to fall. From that angle, most any house would have done just as well.

But Jeff had always liked the old Fincannon place, liked the way it sat on the slope of McKinley Hill, liked the stately angles of its roofline and the graceful dignity of its fall into neglect. No question the house needed attention . . . it had been rented for the past four years to a couple with three dogs, two cats, and four children. They'd left it dirty, disheveled, and worn out. From attic to basement, it needed work. Little wonder it had sat vacant for the last several months. But on his first walk-through, Jeff had a sense that he and the house were kindred spirits, both in need of ventilation and a different perspective.

It was empty, offered the possibility of quick occupancy, and was underpriced for its location. So he'd made an offer right then, on the spur of the moment, within thirty-six hours of walking out of the house he still owned with Melanie. Forty-eight hours after that, the out-of-state owners had accepted the contract. And now, a month later, the deal had gone through, closing without a hitch, and he was the proud owner of a house that qualified as a true Handyman's Special.

The thought of that made him smile. He'd paid only superficial attention to building the other house. He'd hired workmen, paid contractors, and walked into the completed house with only the vaguest sense of ownership. It was Melanie's domain. His was the Trib. But now, suddenly, he got excited over the idea of taking out the half-wall between the dining room and den, of painting the master bedroom gold, of putting pegboard up in the two-car garage, and of putting ceramic tile down in the kitchen. He planned to strip and sand every piece of woodwork in the place and install new lighting throughout. New windows, too, if his budget stretched that far. Definitely, he'd replace the chipped Formica on the kitchen counters, because it gave him pleasure to think about tossing his keys there, wherever they fell, and leaving them until he went out again. He'd already picked out new appliances and, as soon as they arrived, he was going to stock the refrigerator as if a famine were coming. And the trash . . . well, he planned to consider it disposable.

No doubt about it, the divorce would be expensive.

And worth every penny.

He'd never felt right about using the part of his grandparents' trust that would have gone to Alex, so that was Lexie's. It would put her through college and still leave her with a nest egg for her future. That, at least, Melanie couldn't touch. The rest . . . well, she could have the house and everything in it. All he wanted was the newspaper and his daughter . . . and if he were forced to choose between them, he'd take

Lexie. No contest. Rayburn said custody shouldn't be an issue in the eyes of the court. Lexie was fifteen now, old enough and mature enough in the eyes of the legal system to have a legitimate say in her own future. The judge would ask Lexie where she wanted to go and that would be the decision. Barring any allegations of abuse or parental neglect from either party—and Rayburn assured Jeff not to worry, that even should Melanie be stupid enough to bring up such nonsense, it could easily be disproved—the custody issue was basically a nonstarter.

But it wasn't the legal issue that kept Jeff awake at night. He'd always known that he had a legal claim. His name, after all, appeared on her birth certificate. It was knowing what Melanie was capable of doing, would undoubtedly do, that had kept him from leaving all these years. And now, it was not knowing how to go about regaining custody of his daughter's trust that kept him from a sound sleep. Lexie had refused to have a meaningful conversation with him since her return from Dallas. It took no great leap of imagination to figure out that Melanie had been busy adjusting his daughter's view of him.

She'd always said she could make Lexie hate him and he believed her, always known that if he left the marriage, there'd be no question of fairness, no thought of what was best for Lexie. It would be war. An ugly, dirty, back-alley fight to the death. Wrapped in a slick disguise of civility. Melanie would couch every innuendo so that Lexie couldn't quite discount it. Each small lie would be backed up with a point of fact, or maybe more, and there would always be just enough possibility to create doubt in his daughter's mind. Instilling bias didn't require real communication, only a plausible link to the facts and the subtlety of insinuation. And if that failed, then there was the truth of what he'd done—the biggest weapon in Melanie's arsenal.

Unless he got the chance to defuse it first.

Lexie was talking to him now, but only just. She answered her phone if he called and seemed pleased enough to hear from him. She hadn't initiated any phone calls to him, but she had e-mailed him at the office, forwarding whatever comic relief came across her computer. He took her to lunch as often as she agreed to go—once so far—and he made a point of inviting her along each time he went to visit Gideon at the rehabilitation clinic. She had yet to accept, although he knew Melanie had taken her to see her grandfather at least once. Every attempt he'd made so far to draw Lexie out of her mother's web met with rejection. She was wounded, angry, and afraid. And at the moment, she saw him as the bad guy, the instigator of this change that had rocked her world. So she'd locked him out, shut down like a carnival ride suddenly unplugged from its power source.

She wasn't talking, and she sure as hell wasn't listening.

Not to him, anyway.

Jeff accepted the blame for that. He'd mishandled Melanie from the beginning, preserved peace at an awful cost. It was too late now to ride in like a knight on a white horse and simply sweep his daughter away to safety. He'd taught her to live within the parameters of Melanie's manipulations for too long to think he could undo the damage in a single conversation. It was going to take more than the mere offer of another place to live, a new bedroom, and a well-stocked refrigerator to change fifteen years of parental failure. It would take effort to recover the ease of their relationship, hard work to reestablish the bonds of trust, and some emotional pain to neutralize the lies Melanie had told and the lies he'd allowed Lexie to believe.

Jeff wasn't counting on anything at this point. But he could make himself readily available to his daughter. He could maintain contact. He could call her, leave messages, offer to drive her places when she needed a ride. And he knew she often did. The nonsense about getting a hardship license seemed to be on the back burner . . . if not completely off Melanie's agenda. The little Honda sat in pristine isolation in the driveway, gathering dust and waiting for Lexie's sixteenth birthday. He didn't mention the car during their brief conversations and neither did Lexie. Jeff doubted she even asked to drive it. After all, that would require Melanie to be the designated licensed driver, and she wouldn't give up the driver's seat of her Cadillac for that.

This was the one positive note he could find in the situation. Melanie was still as self-centered and selfish as ever. She hadn't—and wouldn't—change.

Lexie was a savvy young woman . . . and in the midst of the most self-centered years of her own life.

The two of them together, without him to act as buffer, were a combustible combination. It couldn't last.

She might feel pressured now to support and defend her mother, might need to consider the facts as Melanie presented them, but he knew that soon enough he'd get the chance to present his side of the story.

And once she gave him the slightest opening, he intended to tell her everything—the mistakes he'd made, the regrets he would always carry, the joy and purpose she had brought to his life. He'd tell it all, as he knew it. Asking for nothing. Not understanding. Not forgiveness. But offering his daughter the only thing he had worth giving.

Truth.

* * *

At the first hesitant tap on his door, Jeff looked up from his cluttered desk and realized Abby awaited his attention.

"Got a minute to look at these proof sheets?" she asked.

"Sure." He pulled himself together, came out of his lost thoughts, and smiled at her. "What have you got?"

"The new fitness center," she said, a glimmer of pride in her expression when she laid the proof sheets in front of him. "I persuaded the new owner, Candace Kove—a really lovely woman—to run a few promotional ads before the opening. A series of 'Guess what's coming to town?' teasers."

"Good thinking, Abby. I'm impressed."

"Thanks. I impressed myself on this one. But I'm not entirely happy with the proofs and I want them to be really great before I show them to Candace."

He looked at the ads, made a couple of changes in the text, and handed the sheets back. "Flop the graphics and the text side to side on the first ad, then swop them again, top to bottom, on the second. See if you like that look better."

"You're a genius," she said. "And I'll bet I'm the first person to tell you that today."

"Now that you mention it, you're the first person to tell me that all month. What's wrong with the rest of the staff? It must be time I threatened to fire somebody."

"Mmhmm, you're such a tough guy." She turned to go.

"Good job, Abby. Have you started work on the feature article yet?"

She turned back. "The feature article? You mean, for the Grand Opening at the fitness center?"

"That would be the one."

"You want me to write it? Really?"

"You've already sold the client on the Trib. Now give her a chance to sell you and all of our readers on the benefits of joining the fitness center. Write something up and I'll take a look at it."

Her smile was worth a thousand words. "Thanks, Jeff. I'll get started on it right away."

He watched the spring in her step as she walked out, moving through the doorway with the stride he remembered. Long, leisurely, lovely. Just watching her walk provided a better view than many men saw in a week of workdays, and Jeff accepted it for the simple pleasure it was and thought about how she was a breath of fresh air in a day that had seemed stuffy and stale until just this minute. Hard to believe he'd actually thought working with her would be difficult, that he'd spend his days pretending he barely knew she was there, constantly reminded of his regrets, of the choices he'd made and could not change.

Quite the contrary.

She'd established herself in the camaraderie of the office within the first week, found her niche in the mostly male newsroom, and wasn't intimidated or distracted by the often boisterous discourse going on around her. By the end of the second week, she'd taken up Mark's responsibilities in a nearly seamless transition. By the end of the third, she'd begun to interact with Jeff in the same way his other employees did . . . easily, honestly, and with an openness he certainly hadn't expected from her. And now almost a month since she'd come to work at the Trib, he'd become accustomed to seeing her every day.

And liking it.

The bottom line? Abby in the office made him happy. Just her nearness reminded him of the man he'd meant to become. Had him thinking maybe it wasn't too late to be the man he might have been.

Oh, he had no illusions that Abby would ever forgive him for his betrayal, or that her future had a significant spot for him in it. He didn't expect that, but then he hadn't expected this either, hadn't imagined the possibility they could form a new friendship. One based not on who they'd once been, but who they now were. And even if all he ever had of her was this professional, amiable interaction—for however long it lasted—then he would consider himself a lucky man.

Jeff's office seemed small to begin with, but when Sheriff Ray walked in and settled in one of the chairs, it shrank like cotton in hot water, felt a little tight, a tad snug all around. Built like an Olympic weightlifter, the sheriff took up maximum space with minimum comfort and always appeared to be considering the question of whether he'd be less conspicuous sitting or standing. In truth of fact, Billy Don Ray didn't care much how he looked, or thought much about if he was comfortable. What he did care about was Sweetwater and the people who lived there. What he did think about was keeping it a nice, safe place. "It's that time of year," he said without preamble. "Kids are sneaking out to the river and you know what that means."

Jeff did know. He'd once been one of those kids. As had the sheriff. They knew the dangers and the trouble that could happen. They knew the infallible, foolish courage of youth and the ultimate futility of advising against it. They knew the limitations of policing the river road. And they knew they'd been lucky for the past few years. No shootings. No drug busts. No accidents, injuries, or deaths among the rebellious area teens. Which didn't mean no laws had been broken, just that no one had gotten caught breaking them.

"I've got Calvin and his Cadillac in my sights," the sheriff went on. "And we'll catch him passing hootch to the kids one of these nights soon. But there's always another Calvin waiting to take up the slack. We do what we can, you know. Shut down one point and the kids pop up in another. I'm here to ask if you'll run the usual story, print up a picture or two of the sandbar, warn parents it's only a matter of time until somebody gets hurt out there."

"Sure thing, Billy Don." Jeff leaned back in his chair, refusing to think about Lexie and the very real possibility she could be one of the kids the sheriff was talking about. He didn't think so. He didn't want to think so. He'd made it very clear to her that sneaking out wouldn't be tolerated under any circumstances and that sneaking out to the river elevated the offense to a serious rift between father and daughter. But he wasn't completely convinced she believed him. He'd certainly never paid the slightest heed to his father's warnings. "I'll go out there this afternoon with the camera. We'll run the story, front page, next week."

"I appreciate it." Sheriff Ray pushed to his sizable feet and reached across the desk to shake Jeff's hand. Jeff's chair rolled out from under him as he stood to take the handshake, the wheels delivering a sharp *smack* to the wood floor as they slid off the plastic floor protector. "Thing is, Jeff, we can't be sure if taking up space in your newspaper does any real good. But it's a tool, ya know? It'd be better all around if parents enforced their own curfews or helped us enforce the local one, but it's summer and so many of 'em aren't payin' attention. And there're those who don't care to begin with. So we do what we can. We just do the best we can."

"You do a good job, Billy Don."

"I've got a good team." The sheriff deflected the praise to his under deputies without a hint of false modesty. "They're stretched too thin, but they do a damn good job." He moved to the doorway and stopped, turning his hat in his hands. "So you'll go out this afternoon, then? Take a few pictures?"

Jeff confirmed it with a nod. "This afternoon. Probably in the next couple of hours."

"Good. Good. We've noticed some signs of activity around the two-mile mark, but they could be congregating anywhere along the river. Thing about kids is they don't stay in the same place, but I guess you know that about as well as I do."

"I'll let you know if I spot anything suspicious."

Sheriff Ray nodded again, too, his big head bobbing like a fishing lure at first nibble. "I know you will, Jefferson. I know you will."

Jeff slid the strap off his shoulder and swung the camera bag onto the backseat of his SUV. He closed the rear door and reached for the front door latch just as Abby walked around the corner, briefcase in one hand, a Sonic Route 66 cup in the other. Probably returning from an early afternoon sales call. Maybe coming back from a late lunch. He watched her for a minute, caught himself in the enjoyment of it, and abruptly turned away to open the car door.

"Slipping out early?" she asked, catching him as he got in the car. "I just came from the café and Ginger sent you a message."

"Which is?"

"Stuffed peppers."

He grinned, one of many that seemed to sneak up on him lately. "Maybe that means I've been taking a few too many meals at their place."

"More likely it means you're in cahoots with Ginger to fool Mary Jo with another sheriff and his cinnamon buns mystery."

"Me? Nah." His grin merely deepened. "She didn't

happen to mention what desserts she's putting on the menu tonight, did she?"

Abby arched an eyebrow. "Maybe you should head over there now and ask her yourself."

"Can't do it. I've got to go out to the river."

Her easy smile faded. "Has something happened?"

Stupid not to have realized she'd always associate the river with trouble and crisis. "No. The sheriff thinks it's time to run the usual safety warnings, start up the Keep Our Kids Safe campaign again. So I'm going out to take some pictures, see if I happen onto any evidence of trespassing."

"Can I go with you?"

"Do you want to?"

"Yes. No." She stopped, considered, then looked at him with troubled eyes. "Yes. I think I do."

"Then hop in."

He expected her to think better of it, change her mind, but she didn't.

All the way to the bridge, she sipped at her soda, occasionally jabbing the straw into the ice several times in quick and fierce succession before pulling it out and sucking the crushed ice into her mouth. He remembered the habit, remembered telling her how annoying it was, remembered the saucy way she told him he should get used to it. He wasn't really surprised when she glanced over at him now and said, "Sonic has the best ice, you know. I've missed it."

"What? You couldn't find crushed ice in Chicago?"

She stabbed the straw into the ice again. "Not like this. No cherry limeades nearly as good as this, either. It's funny, the little pleasures you miss about a place."

"And what little pleasures do you miss about Chicago?"

"Nothing yet, but I could get a desperate desire for a real Chicago-style hot dog tomorrow. You never know."

He let her crunch the ice in pleasurable silence, as aware of the direction of her thoughts as he was of his own, knowing before they reached the river road, one or the other of them would put those thoughts into words. It could only be a matter of time before he, or she, named the worry that sat like a sullen teenager between them. Taking the on-ramp and accelerating into the highway traffic, he wondered if there was any good way to tactfully ask what he wanted to know, if there was an answer that would satisfy his nagging unease. They made it all the way to the turnoff onto the river road before the question arose spontaneously, and they each spoke at once with the same level of parental concern, with almost the exact same words.

"Do you think he's? . . ."

"Do you think she's? . . ."

They stopped. Jeff looked at her. Abby looked back. "You first," she said. "Do you think Lexie's going out there?"

"No," he responded promptly, positively, stating what he wanted to be true. "No, I don't think Lexie's sneaking out to the river at night."

"Me, either," she agreed. "I mean, I don't think Kyle is, either."

"Good." Jeff managed a clear, confident tone. "That's good. It means we can be objective, conduct an unbiased investigation as a community service."

"Right. Objective reporting. That's all we're doing." Then the breath rushed out of her on a sigh. "Wrong. I think he might be," she admitted. "Slipping out, I mean. He sleeps so late. And he looks so tired. And he's so secretive. More than usual even. I don't think he's sneaking out at night, but I have this horrible feeling he might be. And before I talk to him about it, I want to see what's out here for myself. Try to recall, if I can, what it was like, why I found it so appealing."

"I thought it was me you found appealing, and the

river just happened to be the place we went to be to-gether."

She jabbed more ice up into the straw. Absently, as if hardly conscious of what she did. And when she answered his half-teasing comment, she did it in solemn tones. "At the time, Jeff, I'm sure I thought that was true. But I tend to see it from a different angle now. A mother's angle. And from here, it seems to me we must have come out to the river looking for the trouble we eventually found."

He pulled the SUV onto the shoulder of the road, near the first of the barriers, put the gear in park, and turned off the ignition. For a long moment, he sat there, wondering if she was right, if choosing the place had, in essence, chosen the outcome. But that was a question for another day. Not now. He reached for his door handle. "Then let's see if we can figure out what trouble looks like through our kids' eyes. What d'ya say?"

For a moment, she sat still as a stone, then she set the cup of ice aside. "Okay," she said.

But rebellion—or any pertinent sign of it—wasn't that easy to locate. They traipsed through the tangle of vines and bushes that grew thickly in places and sparsely in others, across the sandy shale of one sandbar and the thick moist sand of another. By the time they'd spent nearly an hour in the humidity, Abby had stripped down to her scoop-necked tank top, tying the matching linen shirt around her waist, and Jeff had rolled his shirt sleeves up well above his elbows. She'd picked up a slight limp. He'd shed the idea that they were going to find anything other than a few empty booze bottles, some cigarette stubs, and the occasional discarded soda can. When they finally reached a section that showed some wear and tear, bore the scuff of footprints, sported fragments of glass from a broken bottle or two, and looked, in general, as if a very small herd of delinquents might recently have made camp there, he was ready to call it quits and dropped down onto a sun-baked rock to rest.

"I'm going to take a couple of shots right here and then we're getting the heck out of this place."

She sat down beside him, pulled off a shoe that hadn't been made for walking, much less tramping through the underbrush, and began rubbing her foot. "Are you sure we used to think this was fun?"

"Yeah," he said. "We were so stupid."

She laughed and kept rubbing her foot. "And so sure we were smarter than our parents. Sometimes I wonder if the main reason I came out here was to thumb my nose in my mother's face." Pausing, she looked out at the slow-going current of the river, the red-brown molasses of its waters. "Do you think my mother knew? I mean, don't you think she *had* to know? She set my curfew at ten-thirty. Ten-thirty! With daylight savings time, that's barely past dark. Did she really think I just went upstairs and went to bed?"

"Remember, we're talking about your mother, Abby."

"You're right," she said on a sigh. "My no-shades-of-gray, everything-is-black-or-white mother. It probably never once occurred to her that it might occur to *me* to sneak out at night."

"She'd have barred the windows *and* sat up all night beside your bed if she'd had an inkling of what you were doing."

Abby pursed her lips, considering what Jeff had said. "And she'd have killed me if she knew I was drinking."

"Since you're still alive, I'd say, no, she didn't know. Unlike my dad, who knew and couldn't have cared less."

"Well, you were older and should have known better." She flashed a half-teasing smile. "Why did you come out here, anyway, Jeff? You were already in college. Two years ahead of the rest of the river rat gang. And even though you weren't living on campus, it couldn't have been that much fun for you to hang out with a bunch of high school kids. Most of whom were your brother's pals."

"I came out here because here is where you wanted to come and, since I wanted to be with you. . . ." He debated adding the rest of it, but what the hell. It had all happened such a long time ago. "And I came to make sure nothing bad happened to you, Abby."

"That was noble," she said drily.

He grinned. "Okay, so maybe I wanted to make sure nothing bad happened to me, either, and that meant I had to be here to keep some dumb new high school graduate from putting the moves on my girl."

"I never knew you felt so possessive."

"I hid it well. Plus, I preferred to consider myself noble in those days. It was easier than thinking my kid brother would have cut me out of your affections with a filet knife if he'd gotten half a chance."

Abby went still as a bird on a limb. Then she smoothed her sock and prepared to put her shoe back on her foot. "How long did you know?"

"That he was in love with you?" Jeff thought about it, tried to pinpoint a moment when he'd seen the yearning in Alex's eyes and known it was for Abby. "It's kind of hard to remember. Alex was never easy to read, and he did a good job of covering up his feelings with that who-gives-a-shit act. Or maybe it wasn't an act. I don't know. But I realized a month or so after you and I started dating that Alex wasn't happy about it. And the first time the three of us went to the Summer Daze carnival together, I knew for sure. The competition for your attention got to be front burner with him after that. He talked louder than I did, talked more than I did, talked about me if that's the only way he could get you to interact with him. By that final summer, it seemed so obvious, I thought you must know."

She brought the other leg up and slipped off the shoe, so she could massage her right foot the way she'd massaged the left. "We see what we want to see, I suppose. I honestly didn't know until the night of the accident. He came to the house an hour or so before you got there, and we stood out on the lawn talking for quite a while, and then he said he loved me. He wanted me to go to OU with him instead of to Kansas with you. I think he'd actually planned it all out in his head. Where we'd live, what we'd do, how it would be so perfect. Alex, who never planned anything in his life except how to play football, thought I'd chuck my scholarship, *and* you, to go with him."

She pushed hard into her instep . . . Jeff saw her thumb turn red with the effort, her nail go white under the pressure. "I hurt him that night. He caught me off guard, and he'd already been drinking and . . . I laughed. I laughed at him, because it was so ridiculous, so like him to blurt out such a bizarre idea. I thought it was one of his dumb jokes, a way to stir up the last lazy days before summer's end. It never crossed my mind until too late that he might be serious." She released a soft regret. "I really hurt him, Jeff. That's when he got defensive and told me you'd been seeing Melanie behind our backs, been having sex with her for months, that you'd gotten her pregnant. He said he was going to beat you to a pulp for treating me that way."

Her glance slid toward him. Then back to her foot. Then out to the river again. "I told him he was an idiot to think you'd treat *him* that way, much less me."

Jeff hadn't thought he could feel worse about what he'd done. Until this minute. He'd never wanted Melanie, although he'd known she wanted him. Her hints were subtle, but unmistakable. And, hell, he was flattered. He was young, she was beautiful, and sex radiated from her like music, overpowering men, young and old, with the possibility of having her. She was a wet dream waiting to happen the night she nailed him, showing up with Alex at a bachelor party for one of Jeff's college friends, persuading Jeff to take her home when his brother wouldn't. Jeff had been drunk on the night's excesses already—bar hopping, tequila shots, a stripper, and all the other crazy-stupid things young men do when one of them is about to be married. None of which supplied any excuse for what he'd done. He barely even remembered getting in her car, never thought until much, much later how odd it was that she and Alex had come to the party in separate vehicles. The only pure memory he recalled from the whole night was a slow, dreamlike awakening in her car, in the dark, with his pants down around his ankles, her clothes decorating the dashboard, her lips all over him, his hand on her breast. Her bare breast. And the smell of her sex on his fingers. The taste of it in his mouth.

And he remembered—with amazing clarity—how he had stumbled out of the car, jerked up his pants, and puked his guts out in the parking lot behind the high school field house.

He'd never told anyone the story, still felt sick when the thought of it caught up with him. Now was no exception. "I can't believe I did it," he said, offering no excuses. "You were the best thing that ever happened to me, Abby. I never meant to screw that up."

She didn't comment, but then comment was hardly necessary. They both knew how badly he'd screwed up. His life. Hers. Everything.

When she did speak, Abby's voice was soft, low, as if it were struggling to fight its way back from a far-away place. "That's the thing, you know, Jeff. I didn't believe it. If you hadn't admitted to having sex with her,

I'd never have given her story a second thought." She stopped rubbing her foot, then cupped the shoe back into place. "That's how much I trusted you."

The pain of that was hardly new. He'd lived with the knowledge a long time. In one stupid, un-thinking act he'd betrayed Abby. He'd betrayed them all. And if he'd only denied it, said it never happened, then maybe all the bad things that came after wouldn't have happened, either. Maybe Alex would still be alive. Maybe Gideon would have in-sisted, finally, that Alex take responsibility for his own actions. Maybe Alex would have married Melanie despite his vehement statements that he wouldn't. Maybe Jeff could have had Abby and still have had Lexie in his life, too.

But there the foundation cracked. An uncle instead of a father? Melanie and Alex as Lexie's parents? The only worse thing Jeff could imagine was Melanie rais-ing Alex's daughter alone. "That night," he said, the words coming unexpectedly, one on top of the other, like a confession too long held in reserve. "The night of the accident, Melanie came to me in tears. She said she was pregnant, that Alex was the father, that he wouldn't even talk to her, that she didn't know what to do. That sounded exactly like Alex. No conse-quences Alex. The whole summer he'd gibed at me, made plays for you, then laughed when I called him on them, said he was only kidding around. But I knew better and I was primed for a fight. So I went out look-ing for him that night. I told Melanie she didn't have anything to worry about, that I'd make sure Alex took responsibility for what he'd done. I swore she wouldn't have to raise the child alone. I promised her that no matter what I had to do to make it happen, my brother's child was going to have the father she deserved." Jeff stroked his fingers across his jaw, grit-ted his teeth at the irony of that. "I was so stupid. It didn't once occur to me Melanie had told Alex a different story, that she'd told him I was the one who'd fathered her baby and that I'd played him for a fool all along. He was ready for me, too, when I found him at your place. And we went at it like sworn enemies. He hated me for having you, and I hated him for having Dad. And there wasn't ever going to be an end to it."

Abby rose, sort of bouncing to her feet as if she couldn't bear to sit still another second. She walked to the river's edge, stood there with her hands on her hips—exactly where hip pockets would be if her slacks had pockets—looking at the muddy Arkansas River. Just as Jeff remembered her. Yet not as he remembered her at all. "I feel guilty, too, Jeff. I laughed in his face when he said he loved me. I stepped into the middle of your fight and broke it up before it was finished. I sent Alex off, knowing he'd head first for the Cadillac man and then for the river. And I didn't stop you from going after him."

"You weren't the one who let him goad you into a drag race on the river road, Abby. And you sure as hell weren't the one who rammed his car and sent him into the river."

Murder. The word hung there over his head. A coronet of guilt he would wear to his grave. *I'll tell Lexie you murdered your brother.* Melanie's ultimate threat. *I'll tell her he's her real father and that you murdered him so you could marry me.* A lie he couldn't disprove, because he had married her, had taken his brother's child to raise as his own, had agreed to assume the responsibility that rightfully belonged to Alex, had claimed the daughter there was only one chance in thousands he had fathered. And he'd done it because in his heart he believed his brother and three innocent people would still be alive if not for his own unyielding anger that night. He'd done it because he knew he deserved to suffer. He'd done it because it was the only penance he could pay. He'd done it because none of it would have happened if he hadn't betrayed Abby in the first place.

"I killed him," he said now. "I killed them all." A fact, simply stated, irrevocable.

"If that were true, Jeff, you'd have spent the last sixteen years in prison."

"What makes you think I haven't?" He shoved to his feet, opened the camera bag, and snapped a lens on the camera. He aimed and shot, snapping off frames in rapid succession, working off the emotion this impossible admission had provoked. He'd lived with the reality of what he'd done every day for sixteen years and never once indulged in the luxury of confession. He hated that he'd done so now, hated that Abby had been the one to hear it. It was his burden. His alone. He'd made the choice, and she had no reason and no right to share in the consequences of it.

But then she was beside him, stopping him in mid-click of the shutter with the merest touch of her hand on his arm. "You tried to stop him, Jeff. It was raining like crazy. The road was slick. He was drunk."

"And I wasn't. I knew better than to play that cat and mouse game with him. I'm responsible for what happened."

"It was an accident. You tapped his fender to try to slow him down. If anyone was responsible, it was Alex. And Melanie. Don't forget her part in this. She maneuvered us all into place that night. She played you against Alex, Alex against you. She used you both to get at me and she put us all out there on the river road and waited to see what would happen."

She had waited for Jeff to bring a chastened Alex home, had waited to see which brother would be responsible for the innocent child she carried, waited to find out the results of what she had set in motion.

"Melanie has a lot to answer for," Jeff conceded. "But not the accident. That was my fault. Mine. Four people are dead because of me. Now, I'll take a couple more shots and then we can get out of this place."

But when he went to raise the camera again, she kept her hand on his arm, brought up her chin, and forced him to stare down the truth she held in her eyes. "You deserved a better father than you got, Jeff. You've been a better father to Lexie than Alex ever could or would have been. You've more than paid for the mistakes you made. And you didn't kill anyone. Not Alex. Not Amy or Kelly or Brian. I was there. In the car with you. You did not cause the accident. Let go of it and go on."

Unexpectedly then and with startling assurance, she put her hands on either side of his face, rose up on her tiptoes, and kissed him full on the lips. His heart stopped, literally skipped over one beat, he was so shocked. But then the shock mellowed into surprise, and the surprise swelled into pleasure, and the camera slid to the end of its strap, pulling taut across his arm, dangling heavily at his side as his hands spanned her waist and he held on and forgot to breathe as the kiss blossomed and her mouth opened under his. He took what she offered, without hesitation, greedily, not caring if it came out of pity or remorse or grief. He took it and used it and decided this was one moment he would not live to regret.

Abby kissed him.

With passion and all the unfulfilled desire of their youth.

Jeff kissed her back.

The same way.

He forced in some air when the kiss ended, when she stepped back out of his reach. Her chest rose and fell in rapid imitation of his. Her lips were plump and rouged from the pressure. Her eyelids she kept closed. His, he kept open, drinking in the sight of her, thinking she looked like a woman savoring her lover's touch, choosing to believe, for that one moment, that the kiss meant more than it did, that there would be another kiss. And another. And another. And more than kisses, too. And what had happened wouldn't matter. And life would pick him up again where it had left him. And he would let go and go on from here. With Abby. He wanted to reach for her again, bury the past in her arms, bury himself in her. But he didn't.

He didn't.

A low hum slid past her lips like a whisper, and then her eyelashes flicked up and he was staring into brown eyes rimmed with hazel green and flecked with points of gold, eyes as familiar to him as his own. "I probably shouldn't have done that," she said, holding his gaze with honesty and apology. "But I wanted to remember what it was like. I wanted to remember you."

He drug the camera strap up onto his shoulder again, felt the weight of the camera resettle against him, felt it ground him again in what was, not what for a breath he'd imagined might be. "I think we've found what trouble looks like. I'm just not sure what we want to do about it."

"Well, I'm going to talk to Kyle about this tonight." She segued from personal to parental without a blink, as if they hadn't just uprooted the past and planted it squarely in the present. "I don't know yet what I'll say, but I want him to know I'm paying attention."

Jeff retrieved the camera bag and together they walked back to the car, across the wooded stretch of ground that lay between the river and the old river road.

It wasn't a long way at all.

It only seemed that way.

Chapter 25

ryank432:	hey.
lexiegarr:	hey.
ryank432:	i saw you were online.
lexiegarr:	yeah. just chatting with some girls from cheerleading camp.
ryank432:	oh. you going to the river tonight?
lexiegarr:	maybe. haven't thought about it. why? you going?
ryank432:	nah. got better things to do.
lexiegarr:	like what?
ryank432:	what do you care? wardley not keeping you busy enough?
lexiegarr:	he'd keep me plenty busy if i wanted him to.
ryank432:	seemed pretty clear to me that is what you wanted.
lexiegarr:	that why you haven't called?
ryank432:	you haven't called either.
lexiegarr:	my mom. she's like a shadow. listening at the door and stuff. reading my email. stifling.
ryank432:	i figured you were back with wardley.
lexiegarr:	no. look, that night, it had nothing to do with you, okay?

ryank432:   no skin off my ass. worked out better for me anyway. i got to drive your car.

lexiegarr: that's a mean thing to say.

ryank432:   it was a mean thing to do. what if sheriff caught me drivin' your car without you in it?

lexiegarr: i didn't remember i had a car. i was sick as a lab rat after.

ryank432:   what'd your mom say?

lexiegarr: that i shouldn't eat junk food. then she blamed my dad.

ryank432:   because you had a hangover? man, i wish my mom would be that stupid.

lexiegarr: she's not stupid. she just blames my dad for everything.

ryank432:   yeah? like what?

lexiegarr: like getting her pregnant.

ryank432:   disgusting, but not a big 411.

lexiegarr: like that's why they had to get married. like he wanted her to abort, but she wouldn't.

ryank432:   oh. shit.

lexiegarr: yeah. and now they're getting divorced.

ryank432:   you want them to stay together?

lexiegarr: as if. i just don't know how bad it'll get.

ryank432:   when my dad got killed, it was bad. but not so bad as i thought it'd be. he was kind of a disruption, ya know?

lexiegarr: disruption. yeah. i know. let's go to the river.

ryank432:   tonight?

lexiegarr: yeah. don't you want to?

ryank432:   my mom suspects. she had to talk to me about it. big yawner.

lexiegarr: i don't care if i get caught. i'm going.

ryank432: what about the shadow?

lexiegarr: out with the mysterious stranger. he gives me the jeebies.

ryank432: so, how soon do we go?

lexiegarr: that's why i like u, ryank432. no rules.

ryank432: one rule. nobody else can drive you home.

lexiegarr: okay.

ryank432: that's it? okay? we're back?

lexiegarr: i can play hard to get if you want.

ryank432: nah, i like you just the way you are.

lexiegarr: CU in 10.

ryank432: be there in 7.

Chapter 26

"Stacy. Hi, it's me."

The pause at the other end of the phone line stretched awkwardly across the hundreds of miles and thousands of regrets that separated them. "Hello, Noah."

Her voice wove a familiar comfort through him, grounded him in the life he remembered. He could imagine her dressed in her scrubs, blue, because everyone in the clinic wore their blue scrubs on Tuesdays, and because she seldom changed out of them in the evening unless she was going out. She'd have her hair pulled back in a clip if she'd gotten ready at her normal hurry-scurry pace that morning. Or—if she'd gotten out of bed early enough to fix and fiddle with it before work—it might be brushed out and flipped up at the ends, its seal brown sleekness ending in a stylish chin-length bounce around her face.

Stacy spent less time on her appearance than any woman he knew and looked all the better for it. Not that she cared one way or the other. She was healthy and fit, a bundle of barely restrained energy and controlled motion. Physical fitness mattered more to her than what anyone might think about how she looked or what she wore. She'd been the therapy technician who worked with him—as an outpatient—after his accident. She'd bullied him into recovery, talked him into believing he would get better, and somehow convinced him it was okay—even the right thing to do—to trust her.

And he'd repaid her with a miserable marriage, with unfaithfulness and disrespect.

But now, when he desperately needed someone to talk to, she was the only friend he had. Maybe the only real friend he'd ever known. "Did I catch you at a bad time?"

"No." A pause, in which he figured she debated her curiosity, weighed the reason he'd called against the odds that the conversation would end with hurt feelings. Hers. Never his. He wasn't sure he'd ever trusted anyone . . . not even her . . . quite that much.

"Why are you calling, Noah?"

"I need to talk to someone and . . ."

"And I'm the first someone you thought of."

He imagined her smile, the wry, wistful smile. Not the wide, welcoming smile that first had drawn him into her optimistic view of the world. But the disheartened smile. The one he'd taught her. The one he'd come to know best during the last few years. "You're the only one I thought of, Stace," he said truthfully.

"I don't find that so flattering anymore, Noah. When we were married, I was the last person you wanted to talk to."

"I—things have changed. Something's happened."

"Something's happened." With the repetition of the words, her voice sprouted hope and happiness like summer dandelions. A compassion he'd never earned and didn't deserve. "What have you found?"

"I don't know. Nothing concrete. It's only a feeling. Well, a little more than that. There's something here, Stacy. In this town. Something . . . I don't know. It just feels . . . possible, you know. For the first time, it feels really possible."

"Where are you?"

"Oklahoma. A little town on the Arkansas River. Sweetwater. I've been here six weeks."

"You never stay anywhere six weeks. What does Burdon labs have to say about that?"

"I'm using vacation time." Which he shouldn't have mentioned, considering how she'd begged him to take time off so they could have a vacation, some real time together. But he'd had to keep working, searching for that one clue that would lead him back where he'd begun. "And I can travel up or down river using this as a base. I figure even if I have to take sick leave, I can manage to stay here until September without jeopardizing the job. I can't not pursue this, Stacy. See, the thing is there's a woman here. . . ."

Instantly a freeze came through the phone line and he grappled to regain the connection.

"No," he said quickly, a little desperately. "Not like that. It's not like that, Stace."

"It's always like that with you, Nick."

It was. And this was like that, too. Melanie wasn't the first married woman he'd been involved with, not by a long shot. But that played only a small part in the attraction. She had something to offer him, some intangible knowledge he could almost, *almost*, grab hold of, something she kept just out of his reach, hinted at, but never confirmed. She might know something. She might not. But he couldn't take the chance it was nothing. And his connection with Melanie flirted with his memory, teased him with the trace of things he couldn't quite recall, left him hovering, uncertain where to land. That was why he'd called Stacy. Talking to her grounded him, helped him get that one step of perspective he needed in order to see with some clarity. No one knew him better or loved him more. *Had* loved him. There was that. But his need for her insight and understanding outweighed every other consideration. "There's no one else I can talk to about this, Stacy. Please. I need your help."

The silence poised there between them, long and considering, and then she said. "I'm listening."

Which was all the encouragement he needed.

More than he had a right to expect.

He told her about the accident that had killed Alex Garrett, the timing of it, the five-hundred year flood. "They never found his body, Stace. They never found him."

"Oklahoma's a long way from Memphis. How could a body go into the river there and come out alive a whole state away? I know you want this to be the answer, Noah. But I just don't see how it could be." She hesitated, waited carefully before asking, "Unless . . . are you starting to remember?"

He wanted to tell her yes if only because he knew she wanted that for him. Because he wanted it for himself. Sixteen years ago, he had awakened in a world of strangers, and strangeness was no fit punishment for any man, no matter what he'd done. Noah felt he must have done something terrible to bring on the loss of his past, the amnesia that plucked him from nothingness and put him on a collision course with a pickup on the outskirts of Memphis.

He'd been born full-grown that rainy night, broken, bloody, and lost. Awakened while standing on the shoulder of a busy highway with no memory before that moment, no clue as to who he'd been or how he'd come to be there. Later—a week, two, maybe three . . . it was all a fog in his head—a trucker had called the hospital after seeing a news story in *The Commercial Appeal* about the man the doctors had dubbed "Noah," claiming he'd picked up a hitchhiker in Little Rock, a young man who looked like he'd been in one hell of a fight but who didn't want medical attention, who'd acted skittish and frightened when it was mentioned. The trucker figured him for a runaway or in trouble with the law and on the lam. When they reached Memphis, the kid wanted out and that's where the trucker had dropped him, bruised and battered, his face messed up and swollen even before the pickup skimmed by, breaking his leg in one place, his arm in two, and fracturing his jaw. Or maybe his jaw had been fractured earlier. Maybe his arm had, too. The doctors weren't sure and couldn't say with certainty exactly when or how he'd incurred any one particular injury. The trucker's theory seemed as likely as any, especially when a month passed and then another and still no one came to claim him.

Stacy told him he'd had five surgeries total—which was three more than he remembered—before she met him. He'd had plastic surgery after their marriage to repair a couple of slight malformations on his mid-facial bones, injuries that had gone undiagnosed and untreated in the flurry of fixing the broken rest of him. And to this day, he had no idea if the new and reconditioned face he saw in the mirror bore any resemblance to the old one. He had no pictures, no driver's license, no wallet, no ID of any kind, and no memory to corroborate an identity other than this one.

Noah Walker.

A young man walking in the rain.

"I don't remember, Stace. Not real things, anyway. It feels familiar here, though, and I seem to know how to find places, seem to have an idea of where one location is in relation to another. But real memory . . . no. Close, maybe, a couple of times, but no big breakthrough, nothing I can claim as true."

"Dr. Gossman told you it could take a long time. Years." Her voice gentled him like a soothing hand, diminishing the frustration and helplessness he felt . . .

even though what the doc had actually said when pushed to the wall, was that he had a better chance of winning the lottery than of recovering his forgotten past. But optimistic, rosy-outlook Stacy hoped. And he hoped with her. "If this really seems possible to you, Noah, then you're doing the right thing by staying there."

And that was the reason he'd called her.

"I've been to the library, checked out the high school yearbooks," he said. "Alex Garrett graduated in June and died the following Labor Day weekend, a week before I showed up in Memphis. So the timing, at least, fits."

"What about pictures? Do you look like him?"

"Yeah. Maybe. The coloring's a match. Brown hair. Brown eyes. And facial structure . . . there's something of a resemblance. It's hard to say for sure." When he opened the yearbook for the first time, Noah's hands trembled like an old man's because he knew—he just knew—he'd recognize the face as his own the minute he saw it. But like so many expectations before, that hadn't happened. Alex Garrett looked like a boy on the cutting edge of manhood. A youthful package of possibilities. He had a strong jawline . . . like Noah. His forehead was right, too. His eyebrows, also similar if not exactly the same. His eyes, his nose, his smile . . . those were harder to analyze. Noah had taken some hard knocks on all those features and even if he hadn't, life could change the way a man looked as he got older. It did seem possible to him. Not likely, perhaps. Or even probable. But still possible. If only he could remember some detail, some incontrovertible fact to tie the man he was today to this boy he might have been. "He was just a kid, you know, barely eighteen, when he disappeared. He'd look different today."

"And you had those surgeries," she pointed out,

helpfully, attempting to support his wobbly hypothesis. "It's possible that could be you, Noah, and you wouldn't look much like him at all."

"He was a football player. A running back."

"You love football. You always say you're sure you played football in a former life." For Stacy, that was enough. A common interest. A link. It felt good to know she still wanted this for him as much as he wanted it for himself. "Have you asked around? Maybe there's someone who will recognize you. Someone who'll snap his fingers and say, 'Hey, I thought you looked familiar.'"

And that was why he'd left her. Her simplicity. The uncomplicated way she shifted what might be possible into what she wanted to believe was true. "I haven't asked around," he said. "But no one has come up and said, 'Hey, aren't you Alex Garrett?'"

"Well, they wouldn't, though, would they? They all believe he's dead."

Gideon Garrett believed his son was dead, and yet he'd come face to face with Noah in the Fourth of July crowd, stared as if he'd seen a ghost and whispered, *Sarah. Sarah.* Then he'd fallen, sinking down like a heavy sigh. The moment had shaken Noah, stirred up fear and hope in unequal measures. He hadn't been able to forget it, although common sense told him the old man hadn't been looking at him at all, but at someone lost in memory.

"He probably is dead, Stacy." Already her hope plucked at his, fraying it into a tattered strand, making what he'd thought possible when he dialed her number seem ludicrous, a pipe dream based on circumstantial evidence and silly conjecture. "I know rivers. I know people drown in them. I know the odds are long against a man coming out alive even a mile downstream. How could I think I might have survived that kind of flood and wound up three hundred miles away?"

"It's possible, Noah. You could have hitchhiked for days before you got to Little Rock. You could have walked for miles before that. You could have found a hole someplace and slept for a week. How it happened isn't that important. You didn't just arrive on the planet sixteen years ago. You came from somewhere. You had a life before. Parents. Friends. Teachers. And if they all believed you died, that there's no possible way you could have survived, then it makes sense that they never went looking for you."

"It makes more sense that they didn't care what happened to me."

"No, it doesn't. You know it doesn't. Look, we've gone over a hundred scenarios just as problematic as this one, and the thing is, Noah, one of them has to be true. This one isn't any more unlikely or any less possible than the others. Right?"

He sighed heavily. "Maybe. I don't know."

She sighed, too. Stacy could handle only so much melancholy. He could handle only so much optimism. Another reason their marriage had been doomed from the outset. That and his penchant for pursuing other women. "So," she said after a moment. "What does this . . . this woman say about it?"

Melanie. It had been her sideways comments, her verbal musings that stirred this crazy idea in him. She'd plied him with questions from the start, studied him like a science experiment, and compared him to the boy she'd known. Intimately. Noah couldn't say exactly how she'd planted the idea that he was Alex and then cultivated it from a pleasant fantasy into a possible reality. But over the length of their affair, she'd nurtured and honed it until she'd convinced him it was the only explanation. He couldn't be certain if everything Melanie said was true, but he had no cause to doubt her, either. "Melanie says I'm Alex, but that the family situation is complicated and there are reasons I need to keep quiet, take it slowly, and let her lay the groundwork."

"And that's okay with you?"

"Well, yeah. Why wouldn't it be? She's married to his brother. *My* brother, maybe. She knows the family situation better than I do."

"That is so like you, Noah."

"What does that mean?"

"It means you're having an affair with your brother's wife and you believe she's helping you lay the groundwork to take your rightful place in the family. Didn't it occur to you she might have an ulterior motive?"

"Of course," he said, although he hadn't actually thought about it in that light. "Do you think I'm an idiot?"

"Yes. And I think you're more afraid of finding out who you might have been than of living the rest of your life not knowing."

The second reason he'd had to leave her. She could bull's-eye his fear without half trying. "Well, you're wrong."

"Am I? Then take a DNA test and be done with it. Stop playing games and find out what is fact and what isn't."

"It's not that easy, Stace."

"You want easy answers, call someone else. I can't do this anymore, Noah. We're divorced. I need to let go of the past. I need to let go of you. Please, don't call me anymore."

He knew by the tone of her voice, but he asked anyway. "You've met someone, haven't you? There's a man in your life."

"Yes. About time, don't you think? You had a new

woman in your life every other week for six out of the seven years we were married."

That stung. Because it was true. Because he'd been the worst kind of bastard. Because calling her like this meant he hadn't changed. "I hope he knows where he came from," Noah said, offering her the best, most hopeful compliment he could. Whether she knew it or not.

"I find it more comforting that he knows where he wants to go." A pause, no bigger than a teardrop. "Don't call me again."

She hung up then. Without a good-bye. Without expressing hope that he'd find what he kept searching for.

He closed his cell phone, clipped it to his belt, and turned to do battle with his fear. Alone, as he'd always been.

As, perhaps, he'd always meant to be.

Chapter 27

The wind whipped around the side of the house and blustered its way across the porch, kicking up wisps of dirt as silky as smoke, peeking under Miz Effie's skirt before spinning off over the yard to roll a pop can across the street. "Storm's comin'." Joe pushed up out of the rocking chair and moved toward the door. "Let's go inside and play gin rummy, Lowell. What d'ya say?"

"I'll get the braille deck." Lowell tapped his cane across the porch and followed Joe into the house. Miz Effie—one hand holding down the front of her skirt, while the other hand crimped all the play out of the back—wasn't far behind them.

The wind danced back, grabbing hold of the *Tribune's* Wednesday edition and tugging Mae into a fight for control of the front pages. "Well, I'm not putting up with this." She crunched the newspaper firmly in her hand as she, too, pushed up off the rocker and retired to the house.

The wind skipped off in the opposite direction, provoked a few more dust devils, and returned to tease Miz Rose, catching one of her embroidery silks and whisking it away. "I don't like this wind," she said in the same way she might have told her fifth graders she did not like the way they performed on the math quiz. And she, too, headed for the calm indoors.

"Mr. McAfee says this'll be a bad one." Miz Violet

got up to carry her late husband's ashes in out of the wind. In deference to his weather prediction, his box was wrapped in rain slicker yellow with a rubber duck wearing a purple hat in place of a bow. "Y'all better not sit out here too much longer," she warned Abby and Denny, who remained where they were on the porch steps. "You'll get soaked to the skin."

The wind caught the screen door as it closed behind the women, flipped it back on its hinges, and slammed it shut again. A minute later, Mae came to the door. "I'm latching this screen," she said. "When you're ready to come in, come through the side door." Then she stood there a minute looking at the storm roiling in the distance. "Nasty looking clouds," she said. "I think I'll turn on the television. Check the storm warnings."

"It's gonna be a bad one. Mr. McAfee never misses on storms." Archie gave up holding down his rocking chair, picked up his sweaty glass of iced tea, and walked past Mae and into the house before she latched the door. "He's better than the National Weather Service and the television weathermen combined."

Abby leaned into Denny, nudging him with her arm and thigh, elbow and knee. "Think we ought to wait inside?" she asked.

He shook his head and stayed put, with his chin propped on his hands, elbows propped on his skinny knees. The wind whirled back, ruffling his summer blond hair, teasing Abby's dark hair, lifting up one strand and then another and fanning them across her face.

"You can watch out the window," she offered, pushing the hair back behind her ears, where the wind instantly tugged it free again.

He shook his head, continued to watch the road with the eagerness of an orphan awaiting the arrival of prospective parents. When he caught the sound of a car turning onto their street, he sat up expectantly and craned his neck to see who was driving in. His shoulders drooped a little when Noah's Jeep pulled alongside the curb and parked in front of the house.

Noah got out and walked across the yard, stopping once to look at the bank of dark purple clouds in the west, a bruise rising off the horizon, puffed and bulging like a black eye on a perfectly good summer sky. "Looks like we're going to get a storm," he said. "That looks ugly."

"Mr. McAfee predicts it'll be a—" Abby looked over at Denny. "What did Miz Violet call it?" she asked.

"A rip-snorter," Denny replied, taking a moment from his vigil to check the fast-moving clouds. "She said Mr. McAfee said we were gettin' a rip-snorter of a storm."

"Is that anything like a frog-strangler?" Noah came up the steps and settled next to Abby. "Storms make me nervous," he said. "I've never known why."

Abby felt a frisson of fear, too, when she looked at the threatening sky, saw the way lightning shaded the clouds. Too many tornadoes swept through Oklahoma every year not to be leery of a sky darkening as fast as this one. "Summer storms aren't my favorite, either. But there's something mesmerizing about watching one coming at you."

"Sixteen years ago, the Midwest got more rain from April to July than any preceding year since rainfall was recorded." Noah kept his eye on the clouds and spoke with a sing-song kind of flatness, as if he were quoting from a starchy government report or reading from an almanac. "The excessive precipitation that summer resulted in the largest flood any of us is ever likely to see."

Denny's head swiveled toward Noah. "A five hundred—year flood," he said. "Mr. Garrett told me."

Noah nodded, his brow drawn tight. "That's right.

A flood that statistically would only occur once in five hundred years. Mr. Garrett lost a son in that flood, you know."

"I know," Denny said importantly. "He told me. He showed me pictures of him, too. His name was Alex."

"What kind of pictures?"

"Old ones. They never found his body. It's still out there somewhere."

Abby's elbow connected with her son's, advising him gently that some information wasn't appropriate.

"And Mr. Garrett is sorry he couldn't bury the body." Denny finished with a *what's-wrong-with-that?* look. Some trace of rebellion in the set of his chin, in the way he hadn't ducked his head and complied, made Abby think that her eight-year-old was going on nine and growing up, that another moody adolescent lurked around the next corner of her life. She'd do a better job with Denny. She would. She'd lurch onward with Kyle, getting two things wrong for every one she got right, believing that, somehow, by some miracle, they'd come out okay on the other side. But with Denny, she'd do better. She'd do things differently. And she'd definitely do them better.

"A person couldn't survive long in a river at flood stage and a body . . . there's no telling where a body might have wound up."

Abby glanced at Noah, frowned, thought how odd he'd been the last couple of weeks. Always looking as if he were on the verge of a revelation, as if he were sitting on a secret like a chicken trying to nest an ostrich egg. "We're waiting for Mr. Garrett to arrive," she explained, switching the track of the conversation. "He's coming home from the rehab today."

"He's all better from the stroke," Denny said proudly, as if he'd coached the old man from death's door to restored vigor.

"That's good." Noah rubbed his hands together,

palm to palm. A nervous gesture. "I hope he gets here before the storm breaks."

"Storms bother you that much?" Abby asked.

"I get headaches."

She arched her brows. "Atmospheric pressure?"

"Memories."

And that was the strangest answer she'd ever heard anyone give.

A horn beeped a quicksilver dance of notes, and a moment later, a shiny silver Honda pulled into the drive, backed out again, and parked on the opposite side of the street with a slight bump of tires against the curb.

Behind Abby, the screen door smacked open and closed and, in between, Kyle walked out onto the porch. "You can latch it back behind me, Grandma," he called over his shoulder into the house, obviously ignoring instructions to leave the screen door latched and go out the side door. She looked up at her son, at the size and man's shape of him, and saw his attention was elsewhere. Out there. On the car across the street. On the girl stepping out from behind the wheel.

Kyle leaped off the porch like a young gazelle, his foot clearing Denny's head by no more than an inch, still a kid in so many ways, already a man in so many others. He met Lexie as she reached the end of the driveway and they conversed there for a minute, her looking up at him, him looking down at her, their blond heads bent toward each other, their body language suggesting tender topics a mother didn't want to know about.

"She's not old enough to drive," Noah said. "She's only fifteen."

Abby's opinion exactly. If Jeff knew his daughter had driven over here by herself, he'd have a fit. If Kyle made a move to get in that car with her, it would be Abby who had fit enough for the both of them.

"Hi, Lexie." Denny's face lit up as Lexie and Kyle reached the foot of the steps, his voice all covered in shy admiration. "Your grampa's on his way home from the clinic," he said.

"I know. That's why I'm here."

"Do you have a license to drive that car?" Noah asked abruptly, and she turned her gorgeous eyes on him with a haughtiness that would have made her mother proud.

"Yes," she answered, her tone appending a silent, *"not that it's any of your business,"* as she turned a radiant smile on Denny, who was already well and truly dazzled by her anyway. "Once Grandpa's settled in his room, Dad said he'd ride shotgun so I could drive us all down to the Dairy Queen for ice cream. You want to come with us, Denny?"

Denny glanced first at Kyle to seek permission, received no overt objection, and then turned to ask Abby. "Can I, Mom? Is it okay if I go?"

In a million years, she'd couldn't have said no. Not to that happy little face. Not when, for once, Kyle didn't seem to feel the need to stomp Denny's enthusiasm like it was a crunchy june bug. "As long as there's a licensed driver in the car, I think that would be fine."

"Okay." Denny gave his agreement to Lexie with a nod and eyes like shooting stars of excitement. "I'll go."

Jeff's SUV pulled into the driveway and drew up level with the side porch. In the backseat, Gideon looked out from the window, appearing chastened, somehow, by his time away from Wade House, changed perhaps by the recognition of his mortality, or by the chemistry of the stroke itself. Jeff came around the rear of the vehicle, opened the back, and glanced at the gathering on the stairs. He greeted them all with a cheerful, "We made it." Then he seemed to connect the Honda on the street with his daughter. "Lexie? Did you drive over here by yourself?"

Lexie brought up her chin, defiance flaring like sunspots, sudden, intense, and totally unlike her. What Abby knew about her, anyway. "Mom was supposed to bring me, but she didn't show. You wanted me to be here when you got back with Grampa, so here I am. And it's not like I had to drive on the highway. I took the back streets."

"Next time, wait for your mother. Or take a cab." He turned his attention to unloading Gideon's walker, unfolding it into its U-shaped design, and setting it upright on the grass while he pulled down the hatch and closed the back of the car. "Looks like we're in for a storm," he said to the group at large. "Weather service says rain and hail, possible tornadoes."

"A rip-snorter," Noah said, looking ungodly pale in the dimming light. "That's Mr. McAfee's prediction. Need some help with Da . . . with your dad?"

"That'd be good once he gets himself to the steps. The therapist was firm about that. He's got to do his own walking, however long it takes him." Jeff picked up the walker. "I just don't know which steps would be easier for him."

Noah stood, assessed the broad stair under his feet. "These," he suggested. "They're a little wider than the ones on the side. Getting him upstairs to his room will be the hard part."

"Miz Mae and I have already worked that out. She's putting him in the room off the kitchen for the time being. It's not as nice, but the doorways are wider and there's less chance of him falling." Jeff carried the walker to the side of the car and opened the door for his father.

Gideon started to turn in his seat, slowly, with all the grumbling and mutterings of a weary old man, just as Melanie's Cadillac swung into the driveway behind the SUV. Parked at an angle, one tire on the grass, the Caddie's engine shut down with a shudder, like a horse worked fast and hard. The door opened and the chime began its tuneless warning that the key was still in the ignition. Melanie stepped out, as perfect a picture as always, dressed in virginal blush all the way to her sandals and the French manicure on her toes. She didn't pause for effect this time, didn't allow opportunity for those present to appreciate her entrance. She simply tapped the door to close it and shut up the monotonous chime. Then she walked across the lawn, approaching Noah with a mysterious smile on her lips and a long envelope in her hands. "It's here," she said to him, acknowledging no one else, not even the wind that tossed her champagne hair like a rowdy lover. "The results are here."

Beside Abby, Noah went stiff as a blank canvas. "And?" he asked.

Melanie nodded, satisfaction thick as clotted cream in her voice and her gestures. "Yes. I was right all along. You are Alex Garrett."

The wind whipped through the trees and dived down to lash Abby's hair, to fill her ears with its hollow whistle. But that didn't stop the funhouse echo inside her head, which stretched unbearably, like the moment in a horror movie when the orchestration drops out and the suspense gets under the skin and into the heartbeat and there's no air to breath and no escape. Abby poised in that split second between knowing something was coming and realizing it had arrived.

She saw Jeff turn, saw the blood drain from his face. She felt Denny's stillness beside her, Kyle's and Lexie's instant alertness. She heard Lowell, inside the house, call out, "Gin!" And then Gideon's scratchy voice fell into the lull like a feather. "What? What did she say about Alex?"

Melanie carried the envelope with her and walked closer to the SUV. "I said, Gideon, that Noah Walker is your son. Alex didn't die. He came out of the river with no memory and he hitchhiked all the way to Memphis. He's been there all these years. Noah is Alex. Alex is Noah. I have the medical proof right here in my hand."

Jeff looked as if he'd like to stuff the proof down her throat, but his hand settled on Gideon's, calming and calm. "It's okay, Dad. Just sit there in the car for a minute. Let me talk to Melanie. In private."

"Don't be silly, Jeff." She took another step closer, smiling in at her father-in-law. "The prodigal son has returned to us. You can't talk about that in *private*. This is a celebration. Alex was dead and now he's alive. He's come home. Gideon has waited a long time for this. As have I."

One minute, Jeff stood beside his father, the next he towered over Melanie, blocking Gideon's view. "I don't know what the hell you think you're doing," he said in a taut whisper that the wind carried clearly to the small circle of listeners on the stairs. "But Dad isn't up for this kind of drama. Do you want to give him another stroke?"

"I want to give him back the son he lost. The son he wants. The *only* son he wants."

"Get in your car and go, Melanie. You're not a part of this family any longer, and I won't let you play your malicious games with me or with my father or with Lexie. Not anymore."

"Games?" The word slithered from her throat like an asp, smooth and sleekly dangerous. "You think I'm playing *games*?"

Abby stood then, her shoulder bumping against Noah, who hadn't moved a muscle since the astounding announcement. Except, she realized, he didn't seem to be astounded. Or even surprised. "Noah?" She looked at him, trying to figure out the mix of fear and expectancy in his expression. "What is this about?"

"It's the memories," he said, his eyes fixed on Melanie, whose fingers were now sliding beneath the clasp of the envelope. The ominous envelope. "Sometimes in a storm, I can almost touch them and then . . ." his fingers fluttered, "then, they're gone, and I don't know if I remembered them at all. But Melanie knew. I told her about the memories . . . and she knew."

"Mom?"

It was Denny's hand at the hem of her blouse that drew Abby's eyes first to him and then to Lexie. The girl's long hair blew about her face, up, down, across, and back, its color bleached to moon silver in the steadily darkening twilight. Her skin, too, had lost its healthy glow, turned as white as ghostweed. Kyle's arm circled her shoulders, his body cupped hers in a gentle, protective support, yet she stood stiffly, uncertainly, probably unaware he was even there. Whatever else was coming was bad. Abby felt it as surely as she felt the heavy, storm-filled air. The clouds rumbled, no longer distant, but quickly overtaking the sky, and the lightning came more often, with the thunder. Somehow, she had enough forethought, enough clarity, to lean down to Denny, whisper in his ear, ask him to go inside. *Now. Stay with your grandmother.* No matter what. And she was relieved when he slipped away from her, off the porch, to the side of the house, without protest.

"I thought it would all come back to me in a whole piece," Noah said to no one. "I thought I'd *know,* that the questions would stop. I thought when the test came back, I'd remember." He rubbed the pad of his hand hard across his forehead, as if he thought that could erase his confusion. "I want to remember."

"Are you Alex?" Abby looked hard at him then and tried to see the face of the boy she'd known inside the features of this man. It could be. Around the eyes, the mouth. She'd noticed a familiarity there before. And his actions, the way he moved. Yes. Maybe. But it might not be, either. It had been a long time. People change. And Alex was dead. She'd watched his car disappear into the river. How could he suddenly be alive and standing next to her?

A faint noise, like a car door closing, was all but lost in a clap of thunder, all but unnoticed in the high drama playing out on the front lawn. But it was enough to turn Abby's attention from Noah and settle it again on Melanie and Jeff.

"Lexie, Sweetness." Melanie had opened the envelope now and she pulled out the contents, smiling gently, persuasively. The pages, crisp and white, flapped in her hand, but she held them tightly against the wind as she turned to her daughter, positioning herself in such a way that Jeff could see them both. "Your father has something to tell you."

Lexie swallowed hard, glanced nervously to Jeff. "Dad?"

"No, Sweetheart," Melanie said. "Not Jeff. Alex." She nodded to indicate Noah. "Your real father."

A gunshot couldn't have have done a better job of blowing a hole through a child's heart, and Abby bled for Lexie and the pain Melanie had so intentionally inflicted. She moved down a step, intending to help, to comfort. Somehow. But Jeff's voice caught her and held her in place.

"Goddamn it." Jeff grabbed Melanie and spun her around to face him. "Stop this, Melanie. Stop it now."

"It's too late, Jeff. It's done." And there was triumph in her voice. Pure, honeyed victory in her eyes as she glanced back at Lexie. "Remember, Sweetness, when Dr. Brown drew the blood and I told you it was just a routine test? Well, that was a tiny little fib. I needed a blood sample for a paternity test." The paper fluttered in her hand. "A test to prove that Noah Walker is really Alex Garrett who really *is* your daddy. He's come back to you. Isn't that wonderful?"

Jeff snatched the papers from her, then quickly scanned the facts in his hand. "I don't know how you did this, Melanie, but it doesn't prove anything except how low you're willing to sink to get your way."

"My way? This is what you forced me to do, Jeff. I told you before. Abby ruins everything. But you couldn't stay away from her. You wouldn't stop loving her. Did you think I wouldn't know? Did you think I was that stupid? Well, now, I'll finally have everything *I* want. Everything. The house. Your newspaper. Lexie. And I'll have Alex, too. And for the rest of your life you can have your precious Abby and know that you lost everything you ever cared about because of her."

"You're taking nothing from me, Melanie. I was a fool to believe you ever could."

"I will take my daughter, Jeff. You have no claim on her. You never did."

"We'll let Lexie decide that."

Melanie smiled, an ugly, awful smile. "Lexie?" she called, not even bothering to look around at her daughter, just reaching her hand behind her, gesturing for the girl to come to her, focusing her hatred singly on the man who stood his ground in front of her. "This man murdered your father so he could marry me. What do you think of your *daddy* now?"

Lightning ripped the sky and thunder crushed the remains of the daylight. Mae came to the door. "Y'all need to get Gideon inside," she said. "None of you need to be out in this."

Abby glanced back over her shoulder at her

mother. "Just keep Denny inside," she said. "Don't let him come back out here."

"Denny?" Mae questioned. "Denny's not in here with me."

Swinging back around, Abby scanned the yard, the street, and suddenly knew where he was. The sound of a car door closing. Denny, invited for the first time to go with his brother and his brother's girl. He'd been afraid they might forget him. So he hadn't gone inside. He'd slipped out to Lexie's Honda.

And, mesmerized by the drama, the adults had been slow to turn to the children and, in a flash of inattention, all three were gone. Almost the same instant that Abby realized Lexie and Kyle were no longer standing where they'd been, the Honda's ignition clicked over and its engine purred to sleepy life. Lexie gunned the motor and Kyle slammed the passenger door and with a sudden jerking start, the car fired to life and burst off the curb, racing away like the hounds of hell were giving chase.

Jeff reacted first and, in a split second, Abby's thoughts tracked his from his parked SUV with Gideon inside to Melanie's sprawling Cadillac behind it to Noah's Jeep. In a heartbeat, he'd made the decision and raced to the Cadillac.

"Help Gideon," Abby called to her mother, then she ran, too, diving into the passenger seat of Melanie's Cadillac a moment before Jeff threw the gearshift into reverse. As the car swerved crookedly backward into the street, Noah's black Jeep shot past, Melanie a pale blur behind the wheel, Noah a ghostly image beside her.

"What the hell are they doing?" Jeff asked, although it was clear he didn't require an answer. He rammed the gearstick into drive, and the Cadillac took off like a thoroughbred.

"Denny's in the car." Abby fought down a mounting panic.

Jeff glanced at her. "What?"

"Denny. He's in the car with Lexie and Kyle. In the backseat."

His jaw clenched, Jeff kicked the speedometer up to forty-five, then pushed it higher. "Lexie damn sure better have made sure he put on a seatbelt."

"I just hope she realizes he's there." The fear claimed Abby then. It would be just like Denny to ignore all her admonitions about safety and crouch behind the seats, afraid if Kyle discovered him it would be worse than not knowing he was there at all. Her hands trembled, and she clenched the fingers tight into her palms. Both of her boys were in that car. Both of them. With an inexperienced driver. Heading into a threatening storm. "Give me your phone," she said.

"What?"

"Your cell phone. Let me have it."

He unclipped it from its cradle on his belt and handed it over.

"What's Lexie's number?"

"It's programmed in. Hit one."

She did and waited while the phone rang. And rang. And clicked over to voice mail. *"Hi! This is Lexie! Leave a message!"* Each phrase ending on a happier, higher note than the last. Abby closed the phone and dropped it into her lap. "No answer. Where do you think they're going?"

"Not to the Dairy Queen." He tapped the brakes at a stop sign, hastily looking right and left, before rolling through and picking up the speed they'd lost. "I think she'll stay off the highway," he said. "And there are only so many back streets in Sweetwater."

Several of which led, crookedly or straight, to the river road. But there was no need to point that out. Jeff knew it as well as Abby did. "We've got to find them before Melanie does," Abby said, although that was an unnecessary point to make, too. "I could kill her for what she just did to Lexie."

Jeff's knuckles turned white on the steering wheel, and Abby wondered how many other hurtful, horrible crimes Melanie had committed against her daughter. How many had he been able to prevent and how many had he deflected and how many had he taken for Lexie, full in the heart. Pain was in every nuance of his determination now. He had to find his daughter. Letting Melanie get to her first was not an option.

"I don't see any sign of the Jeep," she said. "Melanie must have taken the highway."

"If only she'd take it out of town and never come back."

They both knew that wouldn't happen. Melanie would never leave Sweetwater. Not as long as Jeff was there. And if he left, she would follow him. She'd forever be a disruptive presence in his life and in Lexie's. Nothing would ever make her happy except his unhappiness. And nothing would ever stop her.

Abby watched the road ahead, prayed hard that her sons would remain safe, tried not to think about where a wounded, angry young girl would take them, where one of them, at least, might urge her to go. "I wish Lexie's car were a different color," she said, hardly aware she had voiced her random thoughts. "Red or green or blue. Anything would be easier to see in this dusk than the silver." Any color but the pale gray that blended like a chameleon into this unnatural twilight.

"She has no business having a car, no matter what color it is." He glanced down a side street, moved on. "Melanie's idea, of course."

"I figured."

"I don't know what she's after with this Alex business."

"What did that report say?"

"That there's a ninety-six point nine probability Noah Walker is the biological father of the minor child, Lexie Garrett."

"But . . . how?" She caught a glimpse of taillights ahead and pointed. "There?"

Jeff looked. "A pickup," he said. "Not them."

"I don't understand," she said. "How can Noah be Alex?"

"I don't know, but with Melanie, even the most impossible lie can seem like the truth. At least until she moves on to the next lie."

"But . . . what if the story's really true? What if somehow Alex survived? Noah kept saying he doesn't remember. Maybe he is Alex."

"And maybe Melanie's invented the whole ridiculous story for God knows what purpose of her own. I've never filed for divorce before. In the past, I always let her reel me back in because I knew what she'd do to Lexie if I didn't. But this time's different and she knows it. She's desperate."

"Millie says she's having an affair with him."

"That's one way to get a man to tell you anything you want to know. Or get him to believe whatever you want to tell him." Jeff leaned forward, intent on whatever he'd seen in the distance. Suddenly, he floored the gas pedal and the Cadillac bumped up its speed, coming up fast on the smaller vehicle, which just as suddenly made a quick turn and took off. "They're going to the river," he stated, his tone agitated and angry and scared. "Damn it to hell. They're turning onto the river road."

At that instant, thunder cracked like a whip, the heavens opened, and the rain flooded down.

Abby's heart pounded, punching her ribs with the fury of a fist. Again and again and again. She could see the red taillights now as the Honda scooted around the first bend and onto the river road, fish-tailing a little on the gravel before it vanished into the fast-pouring rain. "Slow down, Lexie," Jeff muttered. "Slow it down. Remember what you learned in driver's ed. Remember what I taught you. Slow down."

But there was no sign of the silver car as the Cadillac swooped around the first bend and gained purchase on the wet pavement. It was a good half-mile, maybe a little more, before Abby caught sight of the Honda again. Up ahead. Slicing into the sheets of silver rain, barely visible except when the lightning rent the sky with gold, revealing the road ahead for a bare moment in time.

"Why doesn't she stop?" Abby wondered aloud. "She knows we're behind her. Why doesn't she stop?"

"We're in Melanie's car," Jeff answered tautly, as if that, too, had only just occurred to him. "She thinks it's Melanie who's behind her."

The fear rose in her throat now, a ball of tension lodged in her windpipe, and Abby jumped when the thunder boomed out across the night. "Then we have to stop, Jeff. Stop. We have to stop."

His foot lifted off the accelerator, but before it reached the brake, a horn blasted through the steady pelting of the rain and headlights ripped from the back of the Cadillac to the front as a black beast roared up behind them and swept past as if they were standing still.

Jeff caught a glimpse of the Jeep on its way by, saw the face in the passenger window staring down and back at him, distorted by the rain, but clearly . . . so clearly . . . his brother. Fear clawed its way out of his gut and mangled itself into a consuming anger. "No," he whispered, then louder. "No!"

Gripping the wheel, he put his foot back on the gas pedal and went after the Jeep. He motioned at the cell phone still in Abby's lap. "Call Billy Don," he told her. "Tell him to get an ambulance out here."

"An *ambulance*?" Her voice shook on the word and she stiffened beside him, but she dialed and repeated the message. "No," he heard her say. "No. Not yet."

Not yet. No one was hurt. Yet. But Jeff knew it would happen. He'd been here before. He'd experienced firsthand the dangerous combination of the river road and rain and he knew Melanie didn't have the sense to back off. She'd run Lexie off the road to stop her. And she meant to stop her. She meant to force Lexie to accept the truth as she intended for it to be. She meant to force Jeff out of Lexie's life and force Noah—or Alex—in. She was desperate now, and she would do anything, however perilous, to get her way.

Well, he was desperate, too. Desperate to take his daughter home this night. Desperate to free her from the parody of a mother Melanie had become. Desperate to return Abby's sons to her, safe and sound. There were three innocent children on the river road tonight and Jeff meant to protect them. All of them. No matter what it cost.

"I'm going to try to get between the Jeep and the Honda," he told Abby. "And then I'm going to slow down and force Melanie to do the same."

He felt the weight of Abby's gaze, knew that she understood what he was saying. Melanie wouldn't stop and he couldn't force her to slow. He could only put the Cadillac in her path as a barrier, put his and Abby's lives between Melanie and the children. And if she didn't stop, well, that was a risk he had to take. For his daughter. And for Abby's sons.

"You're driving, Jeff. Do anything you have to do to keep them safe."

Her trust buoyed him, made him more intent on the safety of all as he hit the accelerator and the Cadillac shot around the next curve to overtake the Jeep. He came up fast on their left, but Melanie cut him off, and he pulled back and came up on the right. The

Jeep swerved into him then, striking the front fender and veering crazily toward the limestone bluffs before rocking and righting itself on the pavement and roaring forward again with renewed velocity. Jeff fought the wheel, slowed enough to regain the momentary control the bump on the fender had cost him, and then tried again, gaining enough ground in one surge of speed to draw even. The cars raced neck and neck for the next curve, the sharpest bend in the five-mile stretch, and Jeff heard Abby gasp in alarm as they came around it, going way too fast. Up ahead, he saw Lexie's car, nothing but two pinpoints of red in the thickening storm, and he knew they would overtake her in a minute or less. It was now or never.

But even as he gauged the distance, calculated the most likely projectories of both vehicles once he bumped the Jeep, the cold hand of memory clamped onto the mindless determination that drove him. He'd done this before, tried to stop disaster with action, thought he was doing the right thing, the only thing that would save his brother. He'd forced Alex off the river road to save him. And he'd killed him, instead. This time it was Lexie and how could he take that chance?

Yet how could he not?

If she would only slow down, pull over, stop, Melanie would fly by without hitting her. But if she kept going, trying to outrun them all. . . .

And then he knew. No matter how great his fear, no matter how real the danger, he owed his daughter the opportunity he hadn't allowed Alex.

Choice.

He had to trust Lexie to choose the best way to save herself.

He hit the brakes hard and the anti-locks clicked, held, even as the tires slid on the wet road before coming to a shuddering stop. The Jeep shot on ahead, coming up on the Honda just as lightning split the sky, striking a tree not fifty feet from the road. Abby's hand took cover within his, and in that moment, that single breath of a moment, while they hovered on the edge of tragedy or salvation, she forgave him. For whatever came next. For all that had gone before. Her forgiveness washed over him like pure, sweet water. And it meant everything. And it meant nothing, as they stared into the dusky light, praying in tense, tandem silence that God would reach down and pluck their children from danger.

Then, in an instant, the brake lights of the Honda flashed once and then flared steadily, brightly, as the car skidded, slowed, and came to a stop in the middle of the river road. Another bolt of lightning followed quickly after the first, and Jeff caught a glimpse of the struggle going on inside the Jeep. He didn't need a sunlit view to know Noah had made a grab for the steering wheel, had jerked their direction away from the Honda, that Melanie was fighting him for control, and that the resulting skid turned the vehicle sideways, slanting it toward the river and sending it hydroplaning forward. It missed the Honda by a hairsbreadth and struck the first concrete barrier at an angle that sent the Jeep nose downward and flipped the rear end up and over, taking the car across the barrier and crashing it, end over end, down the slope to the river.

It stopped there, finally, the momentum carrying it several inches into the muddy sandbar before it settled, wheels spinning, whining in the pouring rain.

Jeff threw open the car door at the same moment Abby flung open hers. The Honda doors flew open, too, and they met their children somewhere on the road between the two cars. Rain battered them fiercely as Jeff pulled a sobbing Lexie into his arms and held her, smoothing her wet hair, calming her in

the midst of the storm. Next to them, Abby hugged
her sons, squeezing the life out of them and then
breathing it back in with a loving, shaky sigh. Thunder rumbled overhead and when it died the sound
of sirens replaced it, coming closer. Closer.

Setting Lexie aside, Jeff moved to the shoulder,
skirted the broken barriers, and half-walked, half-slid
down to where the Jeep rested.

Up on the road, the ambulance arrived. Sheriff Ray
pulled in right behind it. And in the sweep of the
combined lights, Jeff could tell the damage to the
Jeep was extensive. He didn't see how anyone could
have survived the crash, but he called out anyway.
"Melanie? Alex?"

But no one answered.

Chapter 28

It took six months for the county to send out a crew to replace the damaged barrier on the river road. Summer ended, then autumn. Another school year began and a semester passed. Denny's birthday came and went. Halloween, Thanksgiving, and Christmas, too, slid one into the other and were gone. Jeff buried Melanie in a private ceremony and then took Lexie away for awhile. An extended tour of places neither of them had ever been. Just the two of them. A father and his motherless child. To heal. Or maybe just to begin figuring out what had to be mended in order for them to go on.

Abby stayed at the newspaper, enrolling in a couple of journalism classes at the University of Tulsa that fall and taking another in the spring. Which meant she put off getting a house of her own until the following summer. But the apartment over Mae's garage was comfortable enough, and Abby had begun to like the feeling of having family around her . . . the boarders, Lora, Mae. It felt good to have a foundation again, even if she and her mother would never see eye to eye on the structure of what made a home, a home. The boys disliked sharing a room, but they seemed to have made the adjustment, and although they hadn't turned into the best of friends, Abby saw signs of new affection between big brother and little one.

Denny had lost his knotted rope, but not his smile, and he read to all the boarders now. Well, all except Archie and Joe, who'd rather talk than listen any day, and Mr. McAfee, who never listened at all. Kyle pined for Lexie during her absence. But once school began, Abby noted the frequent mention of a girl named Darcy. And when Lexie returned in mid-October, she seemed caught up in catching up, in cheerleading and school activities, and she visited Wade House less frequently than before. Maybe their brush with disaster had changed the course of first love. Or, perhaps, love was merely on hiatus and would return in a month or two or three. Stronger and more resilient than before. Or it might be that Kyle and Lexie would choose just to be friends. Or not really friends at all. They were only on the cusp of life, with everything ahead of them, and the future beckoned without limits.

As it should.

Like a cat with nine lives, Noah came out of the wreck with only minor injuries, but no more memory than he'd had before, no bright explosion of remembrances, no better sense of who he was or where he belonged. He left Sweetwater soon after the accident, promising he'd return again, saying he wanted to get to know his family, reestablish his roots. But months went by without word from him, and by spring, Gideon began to take more interest in Lora's vegetable garden than in his scrapbooks. Whatever Lexie and Jeff had decided in relation to this man who was father, uncle, brother, and stranger was private and no whispers of it made their way onto the town grapevine. Not even Millie, who had her ear to Sweetwater's lips, or Alice Bearpaw, who usually knew something about everything, would talk about Alex's resurrection. It was simple. Sweetwater protected its own, and Noah Walker, whatever the DNA results might say, didn't make the cut. Jeff and Lexie did.

After Jeff returned to work at the *Tribune*, Abby maintained the professional distance she'd already established, but allowed their friendship to grow unchecked beneath it, like grass sprouting through a chink in the sidewalk to find the sun. Timing was everything and, for now, he had Lexie to tend to and Gideon. She had Kyle, Denny, and Mae and a new outlook on her future. A future that, although still at least a year from looking round and rosy, held the promise of happiness and a fulfillment she'd thought she might never find.

Jeff finished work on the house in early April, and Millie insisted he have a housewarming, which conveniently or not, she planned on the same day as Lexie's sixteenth birthday. It was a blustery day for a party, but the warmth of friendship and laughter baptized the old Fincannon place and re-christened it the Garrett home. From noon until night, well-wishers came and went, bringing little gifts of food or fancy, leaving with foil-wrapped treats from the surplus refreshments Millie had on hand. Lexie, who'd taken her driver's test first thing that morning and passed, couldn't wait to get behind the wheel and, as it happened, Kyle was the first person she invited to go with her.

Abby had been admiring the refinished wood of Jeff's dining room table—his grandmother's table, if she remembered correctly—when she heard Lexie's invitation and Kyle's quick acceptance. From an inside window, she watched them go, her beautiful blond son with Jeff's beautiful blond daughter, talking together, laughing as they crossed the lawn.

"Where are they off to?" Jeff said, coming up to watch with her.

"Around the block is what they told me," Abby

replied. "But I'm betting the block includes the Dairy Queen."

"All this food in the house and they're headed for the Dairy Queen?"

The kids split up when they reached the Honda, Kyle going to the left, Lexie to the right. Abby continued watching them until they were both in the car and driving away. They'd always, she realized, be driving away. And that was the way it was supposed to be. Letting go and going on. "It's the journey that matters," she told Jeff. "Not the destination."

"And not," he added softly, "how long the road that leads you home."

For a moment then, no longer than it took for a hummingbird to alight on a branch and move on, they looked at each other and pledged to continue the journey they'd begun before their hearts were fully grown, before they'd lived and lost and survived and remembered their way home again.

They were meant to be together.

And they meant to be together.

Not today. Or perhaps tomorrow. But soon.

Soon.